THE MARTIAN

BY

GEORGE DU MAURIER

AUTHOR OF "TRILBY" "PETER IBBETSON"

WITH ILLUSTRATIONS BY THE AUTHOR

"Aprés le plaisir vient la peine;
*Après la peine, la vertu"—*ANON

Fredonia Books
Amsterdam, The Netherlands

The Martian

by
George Du Maurier

ISBN: 1-4101-0053-7

Copyright © 2003 by Fredonia Books

Reprinted from the 1897 edition

Fredonia Books
Amsterdam, The Netherlands
http://www.fredoniabooks.com

All rights reserved, including the right to reproduce
this book, or portions thereof, in any form.

In order to make original editions of historical works
available to scholars at an economical price, this
facsimile of the original edition of 1897 is
reproduced from the best available copy and has
been digitally enhanced to improve legibility, but the
text remains unaltered to retain historical
authenticity.

LIST OF ILLUSTRATIONS

	PAGE
PORTRAIT OF GEORGE DU MAURIER	*Frontispiece*
INSTITUTION F. BROSSARD	7
THE NEW BOY	11
A LITTLE PEACE-MAKER	17
LORD RUNSWICK AND ANTOINETTE JOSSELIN	29
"'QUEL AMOUR D'ENFANT!'"	33
"AMIS, LA MATINÉE EST BELLE"	51
"TOO MUCH 'MONTE CRISTO,' I'M AFRAID"	55
LE PÈRE POLYPHÈME	71
FANFARONNADE	79
MÉROVÉE RINGS THE BELL	85
"WEEL MAY THE KEEL ROW"	107
A TERTRE-JOUAN TO THE RESCUE!	113
MADEMOISELLE MARCELINE	115
"'IF HE ONLY KNEW!'"	117
"'MAURICE AU PIQUET!'"	121
"QUAND ON PERD, PAR TRISTE OCCURRENCE," ETC	127
THREE LITTLE MAIDS FROM SCHOOL (1853)	139
SOLITUDE	149
"'PILE OU FACE—HEADS OR TAILS?'"	153
"A LITTLE WHITE POINT OF INTERROGATION"	159
"'BONJOUR, MONSIEUR BONZIG'"	171
"'DEMI-TASSE—VOILÀ, M'SIEUR'"	179
PETER THE HERMIT AU PIQUET	187
"THE CARNIVAL OF VENICE"	197
"'À VOUS, MONSIEUR DE LA GARDE!'"	207
"'I AM A VERY ALTERED PERSON!'"	213
"THE MOONLIGHT SONATA"	227
ENTER MR. SCATCHERD	237
BARTY GIVES HIMSELF AWAY	243

iv   LIST OF ILLUSTRATIONS

PAGE

SO NEAR AND YET SO FAR 245

" ' HÉLAS ! MON JEUNE AMI . . .' " 251

" ' YOU ASK ME WHY I LOOK SO PALE ?' ". 277

" ' YOU DON'T MEAN TO SAY YOU'RE GOING TO PAINT FOR
    HIRE!' " 281

" ' HE MIGHT HAVE THROWN THE HANDKERCHIEF AS HE
    PLEASED ' " 287

DR. HASENCLEVER AND MRS. BLETCHLEY 305

" ' MARTIA, I HAVE DONE MY BEST ' " 311

AM RHEIN. 315

" ' DOES SHE *KNOW* YOU'RE VERY FOND OF HER ?' " 319

" LEAH WAS SUMMONED FROM BELOW " 333

" BETWEEN TWO WELL KNOWN EARLS " 341

" LE DERNIER DES ABENCERRAGES " 345

" SARDONYX ". 355

" ' RATAPLAN, RATAPLAN ' " 359

" ' HE PRESENTS ME FIRST TO MADAME JOSSELIN ' " 387

" ' I DON'T THINK I EVER HEARD HIM MENTION YOUR NAME ' " 401

" ' I'M A PHILISTINE, AND AM NOT ASHAMED ' " 411

" ' ZE BRINCESS VOULD BE SO JARMT ' " 431

MARTY 453

THE MARTIAN

THE MARTIAN

"BARTY JOSSELIN IS NO MORE. . . ."

WHEN so great a man dies, it is generally found that a tangled growth of more or less contentious literature has already gathered round his name during his lifetime. He has been so written about, so talked about, so riddled with praise or blame, that, to those who have never seen him in the flesh, he has become almost a tradition, a myth — and one runs the risk of losing all clew to his real personality.

This is especially the case with the subject of this biography—one is in danger of forgetting what manner of man he was who has so taught and touched and charmed and amused us, and so happily changed for us the current of our lives.

He has been idealized as an angel, a saint, and a demigod ; he has been caricatured as a self-indulgent sensualist, a vulgar Lothario, a buffoon, a joker of practical jokes.

He was in reality the simplest, the most affectionate, and most good-natured of men, the very soul of honor, the best of husbands and fathers and friends, the most fascinating companion that ever lived, and one who kept to the last the freshness and joyous spirits of a schoolboy and the heart of a child ; one who never said or did an unkind thing ; probably never even thought one.

Generous and open-handed to a fault, slow to condemn, quick to forgive, and gifted with a power of immediately inspiring affection and keeping it forever after, such as I have never known in any one else, he grew to be (for all his quick-tempered impulsiveness) one of the gentlest and meekest and most humble-minded of men !

On me, a mere prosperous tradesman, and busy politician and man of the world, devolves the delicate and responsible task of being the first to write the life of the greatest literary genius this century has produced, *and of revealing the strange secret of that genius,* which has lighted up the darkness of these latter times as with a pillar of fire by night.

This extraordinary secret has never been revealed before to any living soul but his wife and myself. And that is *one* of my qualifications for this great labor of love.

Another is that for fifty years I have known him as never a man can quite have known his fellow-man before —that for all that time he has been more constantly and devotedly loved by me than any man can ever quite have been loved by father, son, brother, or bosom friend.

Good heavens ! Barty, man and boy, Barty's wife, their children, their grandchildren, and all that ever concerned them or concerns them still—all this has been the world to me, and ever will be.

He wished me to tell the *absolute truth* about him, just as I know it ; and I look upon the fulfilment of this wish of his as a sacred trust, and would sooner die any shameful death or brave any other dishonor than fail in fulfilling it to the letter.

The responsibility before the world is appalling ; and also the difficulty, to a man of such training as mine. I feel already conscious that I am trying to be literary myself, to seek for turns of phrase that I should never have dared to use in talking to Barty, or even in writing to him; that I am not at my ease, in short—not *me*—but straining every nerve to be on my best behavior; and that's about the worst behavior there is.

Oh! may some kindly light, born of a life's devotion and the happy memories of half a century, lead me to mere naturalness and the use of simple homely words, even my own native telegraphese! that I may haply blunder at length into some fit form of expression which Barty himself might have approved.

One would think that any sincere person who has learnt how to spell his own language should at least be equal to such a modest achievement as this; and yet it is one of the most difficult things in the world!

My life is so full of Barty Josselin that I can hardly be said to have ever had an existence apart from his; and I can think of no easier or better way to tell Barty's history than just telling my own—from the days I first knew him—and in my own way; that is, in the best telegraphese I can manage — picking each precious word with care, just as though I were going to cable it, as soon as written, to Boston or New York, where the love of Barty Josselin shines with even a brighter and warmer glow than here, or even in France; and where the hate of him, the hideous, odious odium theologicum— the *sæva indignatio* of the Church—that once burned at so white a heat, has burnt itself out at last, and is now as though it had never been, and never could be again.

P. S.—(an after-thought):

And here, in case misfortune should happen to me before this book comes out as a volume, I wish to record my thanks to my old friend Mr. du Maurier for the readiness with which he has promised to undertake, and the conscientiousness with which he will have performed, his share of the work as editor and illustrator.

I also wish to state that it is to my beloved god-daughter, Roberta Beatrix Hay (née Josselin), that I dedicate this attempt at a biographical sketch of her illustrious father.

ROBERT MAURICE.

Part First

" De Paris à Versailles, lon, là,
De Paris à Versailles—
Il y a de belles allées,
Vive le Roi de France !
Il y a de belles allées,
Vivent les écoliers !"

ONE sultry Saturday afternoon in the summer of 1847 I sat at my desk in the junior school-room, or *salle d'études des petits*, of the Institution F. Brossard, Rond-point de l'Avenue de St.-Cloud ; or, as it is called now, Avenue du Bois de Boulogne—or, as it was called during the Second Empire, Avenue du Prince Impérial, or else de l'Impératrice ; I'm not sure.

There is not much stability in such French names, I fancy ; but their sound is charming, and always gives me the nostalgia of Paris—Royal Paris, Imperial Paris, Republican Paris ! . . . whatever they may call it ten or twelve years hence. Paris is always Paris, and always will be, in spite of the immortal Haussmann, both for those who love it and for those who don't.

All the four windows were open. Two of them, freely and frankly, on to the now deserted play-ground, admitting the fragrance of lime and syringa and lilac, and other odors of a mixed quality.

Two other windows, defended by an elaborate network of iron wire and a formidable array of spiked iron rails beyond, opened on to the Rond-point, or meeting of the cross-roads—one of which led northeast to Paris through the Are de Triomphe; the other three through woods and fields and country lanes to such quarters of the globe as still remain. The world is wide.

In the middle of this open space a stone fountain sent up a jet of water three feet high, which fell back with a feeble splash into the basin beneath. There was comfort in the sound on such a hot day, and one listened for it half unconsciously; and tried not to hear, instead, Weber's "Invitation à la Valse," which came rippling in intermittent waves from the open window of the distant *parloir*, where Chardonnet was practising the piano.

> "Tum-te-dum-tum-tum . . .
> Tum-te-dum-di, diddle-iddle um !"

e da capo, again and again. Chardonnet was no heaven-born musician.

Monsieur Bonzig—or "le Grand Bonzig," as he was called behind his back—sat at his table on the estrade, correcting the exercises of the eighth class (huitième), which he coached in Latin and French. It was the lowest class in the school; yet one learnt much in it that was of consequence; not, indeed, that Balbus built a wall—as I'm told we learn over here (a small matter to make such a fuss about, after so many years)—but that the Lord made heaven and earth in six days, and rested on the seventh.

He (Monsieur Bonzig) seemed hot and weary, as well he might, and sighed, and looked up every now and then to mop his brow and think. And as he gazed into the green and azure depths beyond the north window, his dark brown eyes quivered and vibrated from side to side through his spectacles with a queer quick tremolo, such as I have never seen in any eyes but his.

About five-and-twenty boys sat at their desks; boys

INSTITUTION F. BROSSARD

of all ages between seven and fourteen—many with closely cropped hair, "à la malcontent," like nice little innocent convicts; and nearly all in blouses, mostly blue; some with their garments loosely flowing; others confined at the waist by a tricolored ceinture de gymnastique, so deep and stiff it almost amounted to stays.

As for the boys themselves, some were energetic and industrious—some listless and lazy and lolling, and quite languid with the heat—some fidgety and restless, on the lookout for excitement of any kind: a cab or carriage raising the dust on its way to the Bois—a water-cart laying it (there were no hydrants then); a courier bearing royal despatches, or a mounted orderly; the Passy omnibus, to or fro every ten or twelve minutes; the marchand de coco with his bell; a regiment of the line with its band; a chorus of peripatetic Orphéonistes—a swallow, a butterfly, a humblebee; a far-off balloon, oh, joy!—any sight or sound to relieve the tedium of those two mortal school-hours that dragged their weary lengths from half past one till half past three—every day but Sunday and Thursday.

(Even now I find the early afternoon a little trying to wear through without a nap, say from two to four.)

At 3.30 there would come a half-hour's interval of play, and then the class of French literature from four till dinner-time at six—a class that was more than endurable on account of the liveliness and charm of Monsieur Durosier, who journeyed all the way from the Collége de France every Saturday afternoon in June and July to tell us boys of the quatrième all about Villon and Ronsard, and Marot and Charles d'Orléans (*exceptis excipiendis*, of course), and other pleasant people who didn't deal in Greek or Latin or mathematics. and knew better

than to trouble themselves overmuch about formal French
grammar and niggling French prosody.

Besides, everything was pleasant on a Saturday afternoon on account of the nearness of the day of days—

> "And that's the day that comes between
> The Saturday and Monday ". . . .

in France.

I had just finished translating my twenty lines of
Virgil—

> "Infandum, regina, jubes renovare," etc.

Oh, crimini, but it *was* hot ! and how I disliked the
pious Æneas ! I couldn't have hated him worse if I'd
been poor Dido's favorite younger brother (not mentioned
by Publius Vergilius Maro, if I remember).

Palaiseau, who sat next to me, had a cold in his head,
and kept sniffing in a manner that got on my nerves.

" Mouche-toi donc, animal !" I whispered ; "tu me
dégoûtes, à la fin !"

Palaiseau always sniffed, whether he had a cold or not.

"Taisez-vous, Maurice—ou je vous donne cent vers à
copier !" said M. Bonzig, and his eyes quiveringly glit-
tered through his glasses as he fixed me.

Palaiseau, in his brief triumph, sniffed louder.

" Palaiseau," said Monsieur Bonzig, " si vous vous ser-
viez de votre mouchoir—hein ? Je crois que cela ne
gênerait personne !" (If you were to use your pocket-
handkerchief—eh ? I don't think it would inconvenience anybody !)

At this there was a general titter all round, which was
immediately suppressed, as in a court of law ; and Palaiseau reluctantly and noisily did as he was told.

In front of me that dishonest little sneak Rapaud, with

a tall parapet of books before him to serve as a screen, one hand shading his eyes, and an inkless pen in the other, was scratching his copy-book with noisy earnestness, as if time were too short for all he had to write about the pious Æneas's recitative, while he surreptitiously read the *Comte de Monte Cristo*, which lay open in his lap—just at the part where the body, sewn up in a sack, was going to be hurled into the Mediterranean. I knew the page well. There was a splash of red ink on it.

It made my blood boil with virtuous indignation to watch him, and I coughed and hemmed again and again to attract his attention, for his back was nearly towards me. He heard me perfectly, but took no notice whatever, the deceitful little beast. He was to have given up *Monte Cristo* to me at half-past two, and here it was twenty minutes to three! Besides which, it was *my Monte Cristo*, bought with my own small savings, and smuggled into school by me at great risk to myself.

"Maurice!" said M. Bonzig.

"Oui, m'sieur!" said I. I will translate :

"You shall conjugate and copy out for me forty times the compound verb, 'I cough without necessity to distract the attention of my comrade Rapaud from his Latin exercise !'"

"Moi, m'sieur ?" I ask, innocently.

"Oui, vous !"

"Bien, m'sieur !"

Just then there was a clatter by the fountain, and the shrill small pipe of D'Aurigny, the youngest boy in the school, exclaimed :

"Hé! Hé! Oh là là! Le Roi qui passe !"

And we all jumped up, and stood on forms, and craned our necks to see Louis Philippe I. and his Queen drive quickly by in their big blue carriage and four, with their

THE NEW BOY

two blue-and-silver liveried outriders trotting in front, on their way from St.-Cloud to the Tuileries.

"Sponde! Sélancy! fermez les fenêtres, ou je vous mets tous au pain sec pour un mois!" thundered M. Bonzig, who did not approve of kings and queens—an appalling threat which appalled nobody, for when he forgot to forget he always relented; for instance, he quite forgot to insist on that formidable compound verb of mine.

Suddenly the door of the school-room flew open, and the tall, portly figure of Monsieur Brossard appeared, leading by the wrist a very fair-haired boy of thirteen or so, dressed in an Eton jacket and light blue trousers, with a white chimney-pot silk hat, which he carried in his hand—an English boy, evidently; but of an aspect so singularly agreeable one didn't need to be English one's self to warm towards him at once.

"Monsieur Bonzig, and gentlemen!" said the head master (in French, of course). "Here is the new boy; he calls himself Bartholomiou Josselin. He is English, but he knows French as well as you. I hope you will find in him a good comrade, honorable and frank and brave, and that he will find the same in you.—Maurice!" (that was me).

"Oui, m'sieur!"

"I specially recommend Josselin to you."

"Moi, m'sieur?"

"Yes, *you;* he is of your age, and one of your compatriots. Don't forget."

"Bien, m'sieur."

"And now, Josselin, take that vacant desk, which will be yours henceforth. You will find the necessary books and copy-books inside; you will be in the fifth class, under Monsieur Dumollard. You will occupy yourself with the study of Cornelius Nepos, the commentaries of Cæsar, and Xenophon's retreat of the ten thousand. Soyez diligent et attentif, mon ami ; à plus tard !"

He gave the boy a friendly pat on the cheek and left the room.

Josselin walked to his desk and sat down, between d'Adhémar and Laferté, both of whom were *en cinquième.* He pulled a Cæsar out of his desk and tried to read it. He became an object of passionate interest to the whole school-room, till M. Bonzig said,

"The first who lifts his eyes from his desk to stare at '*le nouveau*' shall be *au piquet* for half an hour !" (To be *au piquet* is to stand with your back to a tree for part of the following play-time ; and the play-time which was to follow would last just thirty minutes.)

Presently I looked up, in spite of piquet, and caught the new boy's eye, which was large and blue and soft, and very sad and sentimental, and looked as if he were thinking of his mammy, as I did constantly of mine during my first week at Brossard's, three years before.

Soon, however, that sad eye slowly winked at me, with an expression so droll that I all but laughed aloud.

Then its owner felt in the inner breast pocket of his Eton jacket with great care, and delicately drew forth by the tail a very fat white mouse, that seemed quite tame, and ran up his arm to his wide shirt collar, and tried to burrow there ; and the boys began to interest themselves breathlessly in this engaging little quadruped.

M. Bonzig looked up again, furious ; but his spectacles had grown misty from the heat and he couldn't see, and he wiped them ; and meanwhile the mouse was quickly smuggled back to its former nest.

Josselin drew a large clean pocket-handkerchief from his trousers and buried his head in his desk, and there was silence.

"La !—ré, fa !—la !—ré"—

So strummed, over and over again, poor Chardonnet in his remote parlor—he was getting tired.

I have heard "L'Invitation a la Valse" many hundreds of times since then, and in many countries, but never that bar without thinking of Josselin and his little white mouse.

"Fermez votre pupitre, Josselin," said M. Bonzig, after a few minutes.

Josselin shut his desk and beamed genially at the usher.

"What book have you got there, Josselin—Cæsar or Cornelius Nepos ?"

Josselin held the book with its title-page open for M. Bonzig to read.

"Are you dumb, Josselin ? Can't you speak ?"

Josselin tried to speak, but uttered no sound.

"Josselin, come here—opposite me."

Josselin came and stood opposite M. Bonzig and made a nice little bow.

"What have you got in your mouth, Josselin—chocolate ?—barley-sugar ?—caoutchouc ?—or an India-rubber ball ?"

Josselin shrugged his shoulders and looked pensive, but spoke never a word.

"Open quick the mouth, Josselin !"

And Monsieur Bonzig, leaning over the table, deftly put his thumb and forefinger between the boy's lips, and drew forth slowly a large white pocket-handkerchief, which seemed never to end, and threw it on the floor with solemn dignity.

The whole school-room was convulsed with laughter.

"Josselin—leave the room—you will be severely punished, as you deserve—you are a vulgar buffoon—a jo-

crisse—a paltoquet, a mountebank! Go, petit polisson
—go!"

The polisson picked up his pocket-handkerchief and
went—quite quietly, with simple manly grace; and that's
the first I ever saw of Barty Josselin—and it was some
fifty years ago.

At 3.30 the bell sounded for the half-hour's recreation, and the boys came out to play.

Josselin was sitting alone on a bench, thoughtful,
with his hand in the inner breast pocket of his Eton
jacket.

M. Bonzig went straight to him, buttoned up and severe—his eyes dancing, and glancing from right to left
through his spectacles; and Josselin stood up very politely.

"Sit down!" said M. Bonzig; and sat beside him,
and talked to him with grim austerity for ten minutes
or more, and the boy seemed very penitent and sorry.

Presently he drew forth from his pocket his white
mouse, and showed it to the long usher, who looked at
it with great seeming interest for a long time, and finally took it into the palm of his own hand—where it stood
on its hind legs—and stroked it with his little finger.

Soon Josselin produced a small box of chocolate drops,
which he opened and offered to M. Bonzig, who took
one and put it in his mouth, and seemed to like it.
Then they got up and walked to and fro together, and
the usher put his arm round the boy's shoulder, and
there was peace and good-will between them; and before
they parted Josselin had intrusted his white mouse to
"le grand Bonzig"—who intrusted it to Mlle. Marceline, the head lingère, a very kind and handsome person, who found for it a comfortable home in an old bon-

bon-box lined with blue satin, where it had a large family and fed on the best, and lived happily ever after.

But things did not go smoothly for Josselin all that Saturday afternoon. When Bonzig left, the boys gathered round "le nouveau," large and small, and asked questions. And just before the bell sounded for French literature, I saw him defending himself with his two British fists against Dugit, a big boy with whiskers, who had him by the collar and was kicking him to rights. It seems that Dugit had called him, in would-be English, "Pretty voman," and this had so offended him that he had hit the whiskered one straight in the eye.

Then French literature for the *quatrième* till six; then dinner for all—soup, boiled beef (not salt), lentils; and Gruyère cheese, quite two ounces each; then French rounders till half past seven; then lesson preparation (with *Monte Cristos* in one's lap, or *Mysteries of Paris*, or *Wandering Jews*) till nine.

Then, ding-dang-dong, and, at the sleepy usher's nod, a sleepy boy would rise and recite the perfunctory evening prayer in a dull singsong voice—beginning, "Notre Père, qui êtes aux cieux, vous dont le regard scrutateur pénêtre jusque dans les replis les plus profonds de nos cœurs," etc., etc., and ending, "au nom du Père, du Fils, et du St. Esprit, ainsi soit-il!"

And then, bed—Josselin in my dormitory, but a long way off, between d'Adhémar and Laferté; while Palaiseau snorted and sniffed himself to sleep in the bed next mine, and Rapaud still tried to read the immortal works of the elder Dumas by the light of a little oil-lamp six yards off, suspended from a nail in the blank wall over the chimney-piece.

The Institution F. Brossard was a very expensive pri-

A LITTLE PEACE-MAKER

vate school, just twice as expensive as the most expensive of the Parisian public schools—Ste.-Barbe, François Premier, Louis-le-Grand, etc.

These great colleges, which were good enough for the sons of Louis Philippe, were not thought good enough for me by my dear mother, who was Irish, and whose only brother had been at Eton, and was now captain in an English cavalry regiment—so she had aristocratic notions. It used to be rather an Irish failing in those days.

My father, James Maurice, also English (and a little Scotch), and by no means an aristocrat, was junior partner in the great firm of Vougeot-Conti et Cie., wine merchants, Dijon. And at Dijon I had spent much of my childhood, and been to a day school there, and led a very happy life indeed.

Then I was sent to Brossard's school, in the Avenue de St.-Cloud, Paris, where I was again very happy, and fond of (nearly) everybody, from the splendid head master and his handsome son, Monsieur Mérovée, down to Antoine and Francisque, the men-servants, and Père Jaurion, the concierge, and his wife, who sold croquets and pains d'épices and "blom-boudingues," and sucre-d'orge and nougat and pâte de guimauve ; also pralines, dragées, and gray sandy cakes of chocolate a penny apiece ; and gave one unlimited credit ; and never dunned one, unless bribed to do so by parents, so as to impress on us small boys a proper horror of debt.

Whatever principles I have held through life on this important subject I set down to a private interview my mother had with le père et la mère Jaurion, to whom I had run in debt five francs during the horrible winter of '47–8. They made my life a hideous burden to me for a whole summer term, and I have never owed any one a penny since.

The Institution consisted of four separate buildings, or "corps de logis."

In the middle, dominating the situation, was a Greco-Roman pavilion, with a handsome Doric portico elevated ten or twelve feet above the ground, on a large, handsome terrace paved with asphalt and shaded by horse-chestnut trees. Under this noble esplanade, and ventilating themselves into it, were the kitchen and offices and pantry, and also the refectory—a long room, furnished with two parallel tables, covered at the top by a greenish oil-cloth spotted all over with small black disks; and alongside of these tables were wooden forms for the boys to sit together at meat—"la table des grands," "la table des petits," each big enough for thirty boys and three or four masters. M. Brossard and his family breakfasted and dined apart, in their own private dining-room, close by.

In this big refectory, three times daily, at 7.30 in the morning, at noon, and at 6 P.M., boys and masters took their quotidian sustenance quite informally, without any laying of cloths or saying of grace either before or after ; one ate there to live—one did not live merely to eat, at the Pension Brossard.

Breakfast consisted of a thick soup, rich in dark-hued garden produce, and a large hunk of bread—except on Thursdays, when a pat of butter was served out to each boy instead of that Spartan broth—that "brouet noir des Lacédémoniens," as we called it.

Everybody who has lived in France knows how good French butter can often be—and French bread. We triturated each our pat with rock-salt and made a round ball of it, and dug a hole in our hunk to put it in, and ate it in the play-ground with clasp-knives, making it last as long as we could.

This, and the half-holiday in the afternoon, made Thursday a day to be marked with a white stone. When you are up at five in summer, at half past five in the winter, and have had an hour and a half or two hours' preparation before your first meal at 7.30, French bread-and-butter is not a bad thing to break your fast with.

Then, from eight till twelve, class — Latin, Greek, French, English, German—and mathematics and geometry—history, geography, chemistry, physics—everything that you must get to know before you can hope to obtain your degree of Bachelor of Letters or Sciences, or be admitted to the Polytechnic School, or the Normal, or the Central, or that of Mines, or that of Roads and Bridges, or the Military School of St. Cyr, or the Naval School of the Borda. All this was fifty years ago ; of course names of schools may have changed, and even the sciences themselves.

Then, at twelve, the second breakfast, meat (or salt fish on Fridays), a dish of vegetables, lentils, red or white beans, salad, potatoes, etc.; a dessert, which consisted of fruit or cheese, or a French pudding. This banquet over, a master would stand up in his place and call for silence, and read out loud the list of boys who were to be kept in during the play-hour that followed :

"*À la retenue*, Messieurs Maurice, Rapaud, de Villars, Jolivet, Sponde," etc. Then play till 1.30 ; and very good play, too ; rounders, which are better and far more complicated in France than in England ; "barres"; "barres traversières," as rough a game as football; fly the garter, or "la raie," etc., etc., according to the season. And then afternoon study, at the summons of that dreadful bell whose music was so sweet when it rang the hour for meals or recreation or sleep—so hideously discordant at 5.30 on a foggy December Monday morning.

Altogether eleven hours work daily and four hours play, and sleep from nine till five or half past; I find this leaves half an hour unaccounted for, so I must have made a mistake somewhere. But it all happened fifty years ago, so it's not of much consequence now.

Probably they have changed all that in France by this time, and made school life a little easier there, especially for nice little English boys—and nice little French boys too. I hope so, very much; for French boys can be as nice as any, especially at such institutions as F. Brossard's, if there are any left.

Most of my comrades, aged from seven to nineteen or twenty, were the sons of well-to-do fathers—soldiers, sailors, rentiers, owners of land, public officials, in professions or business or trade. A dozen or so were of aristocratic descent—three or four very great swells indeed; for instance, two marquises (one of whom spoke English, having an English mother); a count bearing a string of beautiful names a thousand years old, and even more— for they were constantly turning up in the Classe d'Histoire de France au moyen âge; a Belgian viscount of immense wealth and immense good-nature; and several very rich Jews, who were neither very clever nor very stupid, but, as a rule, rather popular.

Then we had a few of humble station—the son of the woman who washed for us; Jules, the natural son of a brave old caporal in the trente-septième légère (a countryman of M. Brossard's), who was not well off—so I suspect his son was taught and fed for nothing—the Brossards were very liberal; Filosel, the only child of a small retail hosier in the Rue St.-Denis (who thought no sacrifice too great to keep his son at such a first-rate private school), and others.

During the seven years I spent at Brossard's I never

once heard paternal wealth (or the want of it) or paternal rank or position alluded to by master, pupil, or servant—especially never a word or an allusion that could have given a moment's umbrage to the most sensitive little only son of a well-to-do West End cheese-monger that ever got smuggled into a private suburban boarding-school kept "for the sons of gentlemen only," and was so chaffed and bullied there that his father had to take him away, and send him to Eton instead, where the "sons of gentlemen" have better manners, it seems; or even to France, where "the sons of gentlemen" have the best manners of all—or used to have before a certain 2d of December—as distinctly I remember; nous avons changé tout cela!

The head master was a famous republican, and after February, '48, was elected a "representant du peuple" for the Dauphiné, and sat in the Chamber of Deputies —for a very short time, alas!

So I fancy that the titled and particled boys—"les nobles"—were of families that had drifted away from the lily and white flag of their loyal ancestors—from Rome and the Pope and the past.

Anyhow, none of our young nobles, when at home, seemed to live in the noble Faubourg across the river, and there were no clericals or ultramontanes among us, high or low—we were all red, white, and blue in equal and impartial combination. All this *par parenthèse*.

On the asphalt terrace also, but separated from the head master's classic habitation by a small square space, was the *lingerie*, managed by Mlle. Marceline and her two subordinates, Constance and Félicité; and beneath this, le père et la mère Jaurion sold their cheap goodies, and jealously guarded the gates that secluded us from the wicked world outside—where women are. and merchants

of tobacco, and cafés where you can sip the opalescent
absinthe, and libraries where you can buy books more
diverting than the *Adventures of Telemachus!*

On the opposite, or western, side was the gymnastic
ground, enclosed in a wire fence, but free of access at
all times—a place of paramount importance in all French
schools, public and private.

From the doors of the refectory the general play-
ground sloped gently down northwards to the Rond-point,
where it was bounded by double gates of wood and iron
that were always shut ; and on each hither side of these
rose an oblong dwelling of red brick, two stories high,
and capable of accommodating thirty boys, sleeping or
waking, at work or rest or play ; for in bad weather we
played indoors, or tried to, chess, draughts, backgammon, and the like—even blind-man's-buff (*Colin Mail-
lard*)—even puss in the corner (*aux quatre coins!*).

All the class-rooms and school-rooms were on the
ground - floor ; above, the dormitories and masters'
rooms.

These two buildings were symmetrical ; one held the
boys over fourteen, from the third class up to the first ;
the other (into the " salle d'études " of which the reader
has already been admitted), the boys from the fourth
down to the eighth, or lowest, form of all—just the reverse of an English school.

On either side of the play-ground were narrow strips
of garden cultivated by boys whose tastes lay that way,
and small arbors overgrown with convolvulus and other
creepers—snug little verdant retreats, where one fed the
mind on literature not sanctioned by the authorities, and
smoked cigarettes of caporal, and even colored pipes, and
was sick without fear of detection (*piquait son renard
sans crainte d'être collé*).

Finally, behind Père Brossard's Ciceronian Villa, on the south, was a handsome garden (we called it Tusculum); a green flowery pleasaunce reserved for the head master's married daughter (Madame Germain) and her family—good people with whom we had nothing to do.

Would I could subjoin a ground-plan of the Institution F. Brossard, where Barty Josselin spent four such happy years, and was so universally and singularly popular!

Why should I take such pains about all this, and dwell so laboriously on all these minute details ?

Firstly, because it all concerns Josselin and the story of his life—and I am so proud and happy to be the biographer of such a man, at his own often expressed desire, that I hardly know where to leave off and what to leave out. Also, this is quite a new trade for me, who have only dealt hitherto in foreign wines, and British party politics, and bimetallism—and can only write in telegraphese!

Secondly, because I find it such a keen personal joy to evoke and follow out, and realize to myself by means of pen and pencil, all these personal reminiscences ; and with such a capital excuse for prolixity!

At the top of every page I have to pull myself together to remind myself that it is not of the Right Honorable Sir Robert Maurice, Bart., M.P., that I am telling the tale—any one can do that—but of a certain Englishman who wrote *Sardonyx*, to the everlasting joy and pride of the land of his *fathers*—and of a certain Frenchman who wrote *Berthe aux grands pieds*," and moved his *mother*-country to such delight of tears and tender laughter as it had never known before.

Dear me ! the boys who lived and learnt at Brossard's school fifty years ago, and the masters who taught there (peace to their ashes!), are far more to my taste than the actual human beings among whom my dull existence of business and politics and society is mostly spent in these days. The school must have broken up somewhere about the early fifties. The stuccoed Doric dwelling was long since replaced by an important stone mansion, in a very different style of architecture — the abode of a wealthy banker—and this again, later, by a palace many stories high. The two school-houses in red brick are no more; the play-ground grew into a luxuriant garden, where a dozen very tall trees overtopped the rest; from their evident age and their position in regard to each other they must have been old friends of mine grown out of all knowledge.

I saw them only twenty years ago, from the top of a Passy omnibus, and recognized every one of them. I went from the Arc de Triomphe to Passy and back quite a dozen times, on purpose — once for each tree! It touched me to think how often the author of *Sardonyx* has stood leaning his back against one of those giants—*au piquet!*

They are now no more; and Passy omnibuses no longer ply up and down the Allée du Bois de Boulogne, which is now an avenue of palaces.

An umbrageous lane that led from the Rond-point to Chaillot (that very forgettable, and by me quite forgotten, quarter) separated the Institution F. Brossard from the Pensionnat Mélanie Jalabert — a beautiful pseudo-Gothic castle which was tenanted for a while by Prince de Carabas-Chenonceaux after Mlle. Jalabert had broken up her ladies' school in 1849.

My mother boarded and lodged there, with my little sister, in the summer of 1847. There were one or two other English lady boarders, half-pupils—much younger than my mother—indeed, they may be alive now. If they are, and this should happen to meet their eye, may I ask them to remember kindly the Irish wife of the Scotch merchant of French wines who supplied them with the innocent vintage of Mâcon (ah! who knows that innocence better than I?), and his pretty little daughter who played the piano so nicely; may I beg them also not to think it necessary to communicate with me on the subject, or, if they do, not to expect an answer?

One night Mlle. Jalabert gave a small dance, and Mérovée Brossard was invited, and also half a dozen of his favorite pupils, and a fair-haired English boy of thirteen danced with the beautiful Miss ——.

They came to grief and fell together in a heap on the slippery floor; but no bones were broken, and there was much good-natured laughter at their expense. If Miss —— (that was) is still among the quick, and remembers, it may interest her to know that that fair-haired English boy's name was no less than Bartholomew Josselin; and that another English boy, somewhat thick-set and stumpy, and not much to look at, held her in deep love, admiration, and awe—and has not forgotten!

If I happen to mention this, it is not with a view of tempting her into any correspondence about this little episode of bygone years, should this ever meet her eye.

The Sunday morning that followed Barty's début at Brossard's the boys went to church in the Rue de l'Église, Passy—and he with them, for he had been brought up a Roman Catholic. And I went round to Mlle. Jalabert's to see my mother and sister.

I told them all about the new boy, and they were much interested. Suddenly my mother exclaimed:

"Bartholomew Josselin? why, dear me! that must be

Lord Runswick's son — Lord Runswick, who was the eldest son of the present Marquis of Whitby. He was in the 17th lancers with your uncle Charles, who was very fond of him. He left the army twenty years ago, and married Lady Selina Jobhouse—and his wife went mad. Then he fell in love with the famous Antoinette Josselin at the 'Bouffes,' and wanted so much to marry her that he tried to get a divorce; it was tried in the House of Lords, I believe ; but he didn't succeed—so they—a— well — they contracted a — a *morganatic* marriage, you know ; and your friend was born. And poor Lord Runswick was killed in a duel about a dog, when his son was two years old ; and his mother left the stage, and,—"

Just here the beautiful Miss —— came in with her sister, and there was no more of Josselin's family history ; and I forgot all about it for the day. For I passionately loved the beautiful Miss —— ; I was just thirteen !

But next morning I said to him at breakfast, in English,

"Wasn't your father killed in a duel ?"

"Yes," said Barty, looking grave.

"Wasn't he called Lord Runswick ?"

"Yes," said Barty, looking graver still.

"Then why are you called Josselin ?"

"Ask no questions and you'll get no lies," said Barty, looking very grave indeed—and I dropped the subject.

And here I may as well rapidly go through the well-known story of his birth and early childhood.

His father, Lord Runswick, fell desperately in love with the beautiful Antoinette Josselin after his own wife had gone hopelessly mad. He failed to obtain a divorce, naturally ; Antoinette was as much in love with him, and they lived together as man and wife, and Barty was born. They were said to be the handsomest couple in Paris, and immensely popular among all who knew them, though of course society did not open its doors to la belle Madame de Ronsvic, as she was called.

She was the daughter of poor fisher-folk in Le Pollet, Dieppe. I, with Barty for a guide, have seen the lowly dwelling where her infancy and childhood were spent, and which Barty remembered well, and also such of her kin as was still alive in 1870, and felt it was good to come of such a race, humble as they were. They were physically splendid people, almost as splendid as Barty himself; and, as I was told by many who knew them well, as good to know and live with as they were good to look at—all that was easy to see—and their manners were delightful.

When Antoinette was twelve, she went to stay in Paris with her uncle and aunt, who were concierges to Prince Scorchakoff in the Rue du Faubourg St.-Honoré; next door, or next door but one, to the Élysée Bourbon, as it was called then. And there the Princess took a fancy to her, and had her carefully educated, especially in music; for the child had a charming voice and a great musical talent, besides being beautiful to the eye—gifts which her son inherited.

Then she became for three or four years a pupil at the Conservatoire, and finally went on the stage, and was soon one of the most brilliant stars of the Parisian theatre at its most brilliant period.

Then she met the handsome English lord, who was forty, and they fell in love with each other, and all happened as I have told.

In the spring of 1837 Lord Runswick was killed in a duel by Lieutenant Rondelis, of the deuxième Spahis. Antoinette's dog had jumped up to play with the lieu-

LORD RUNSWICK AND ANTOINETTE JOSSELIN

tenant, who struck it with his cane (for he was "*en pé-kin*," it appears—in mufti) ; and Lord Runswick laid his own cane across the Frenchman's back ; and next morning they fought with swords, by the Mare aux Biches, in the Bois de Boulogne — a little secluded, sedgy pool, hardly more than six inches deep and six yards across. Barty and I have often skated there as boys.

The Englishman was run through at the first lunge, and fell dead on the spot.

A few years ago Barty met the son of the man who killed Lord Runswick—it was at the French Embassy in Albert Gate. They were introduced to each other, and M. Rondelis told Barty how his own father's life had been poisoned by sorrow and remorse at having had " la main si malheureuse " on that fatal morning by the Mare aux Biches.

Poor Antoinette, mad with grief, left the stage, and went with her little boy to live in the Pollet, near her parents. Three years later she died there, of typhus, and Barty was left an orphan and penniless ; for Lord Runswick had been poor, and lived beyond his means, and died in debt.

Lord Archibald Rohan, a favorite younger brother of Runswick's (not the heir), came to Dieppe from Dover (where he was quartered with his regiment, the 7th Royal Fusileers) to see the boy, and took a fancy to him, and brought him back to Dover to show his wife, who was also French — a daughter of the old Gascon family of Lonlay-Savignac, who had gone into trade (chocolate) and become immensely rich. They (the Rohans) had been married eight years, and had as yet no children of their own. Lady Archibald was delighted with the child, who was quite beautiful. She fell in love with the little creature at the first sight of him—and fed him, on the

evening of his arrival, with crumpets and buttered toast.
And in return he danced "La Dieppoise" for her, and
sang her a little ungrammatical ditty in praise of wine
and women. It began :

> " Beuvons, beuvons, beuvons donc
> De ce vin le meilleur du monde . . .
> Beuvons, beuvons, beuvons donc
> De ce vin, car il est très-bon !
> Si je n'en beuvions pas,
> J'aurions la pépi-e !
> Ce qui me. . . ."

I have forgotten the rest—indeed, I am not quite sure
that it is fit for the drawing-room !

"Ah, mon Dieu ! quel amour d'enfant ! Oh ! gardons-
le !" cried my lady, and they kept him.

I can imagine the scene. Indeed, Lady Archibald has
described it to me, and Barty remembered it well. It
was his earliest English recollection, and he has loved
buttered toast and crumpets ever since—as well as wom-
en and wine. And thus he was adopted by the Archibald Rohans. They got him an English governess and
a pony; and in two years he went to a day school in
Dover, kept by a Miss Stone, who is actually alive at
present and remembers him well; and so he became
quite a little English boy, but kept up his French
through Lady Archibald, who was passionately devoted
to him, although by this time she had a little daughter
of her own, whom Barty always looked upon as his sister, and who is now dead. (She became Lord Frognal's
wife—he died in 1870—and she afterwards married Mr.
Justice Robertson.)

Barty's French grandfather and grandmother came
over from Dieppe once a year to see him, and were well
pleased with the happy condition of his new life ; and

the more Lord and Lady Archibald saw of these grandparents of his, the more pleased they were that he had become the child of their adoption. For they were first-rate people to descend from, these simple toilers of the sea ; better, perhaps, *cæteris paribus*, than even the Rohans themselves.

All this early phase of little Josselin's life seems to have been singularly happy. Every year at Christmas he went with the Rohans to Castle Rohan in Yorkshire, where his English grandfather lived, the Marquis of Whitby—and where he was petted and made much of by all the members, young and old (especially female), of that very ancient family, which had originally come from Brittany in France, as the name shows ; but were not millionaires, and never had been.

Often, too, they went to Paris—and in 1847 Colonel Lord Archibald sold out, and they elected to go and live there, in the Rue du Bac ; and Barty was sent to the Institution F. Brossard, where he was soon destined to become the most popular boy, with boys and masters alike, that had ever been in the school (in any school, I should think), in spite of conduct that was too often the reverse of exemplary.

Indeed, even from his early boyhood he was the most extraordinarily gifted creature I have ever known, or even heard of ; a kind of spontaneous humorous Crichton, to whom all things came easily—and life itself as an uncommonly good joke. During that summer term of 1847 I did not see very much of him. He was in the class below mine, and took up with Laferté and little Bussy-Rabutin, who were first-rate boys, and laughed at everything he said, and worshipped him. So did everybody else, sooner or later ; indeed, it soon became evident that he was a most exceptional little person.

"''QUEL AMOUR D'ENFANT!'"

In the first place, his beauty was absolutely angelic, as will be readily believed by all who have known him since. The mere sight of him as a boy made people pity his father and mother for being dead!

Then he had a charming gift of singing little French and English ditties, comic or touching, with his delightful fresh young pipe, and accompanying himself quite nicely on either piano or guitar without really knowing a note of music. Then he could draw caricatures that we boys thought inimitable, much funnier than Cham's or Bertall's or Gavarni's, and collected and treasured up. I have dozens of them now—they make me laugh still, and bring back memories of which the charm is indescribable; and their pathos, to me!

And then how funny he was himself, without effort, and with a fun that never failed! He was a born buffoon of the graceful kind — more whelp or kitten than monkey — ever playing the fool, in and out of season, but somehow always *à propos;* and French boys love a boy for that more than anything else; or did, in those days.

Such very simple buffooneries as they were, too—that gave him (and us) such stupendous delight!

For instance—he is sitting at evening study between Bussy-Rabutin and Laferté; M. Bonzig is usher for the evening.

At 8.30 Bussy-Rabutin gives way; in a whisper he informs Barty that he means to take a nap (*"piquer un chien"*), with his Gradus opened before him, and his hand supporting his weary brow as though in deep study. "But," says he—

"If Bonzig finds me out (si Bonzig me colle), give me a gentle nudge!"

"All right!" says Barty—and off goes Bussy-Rabutin into his snooze.

8.45.—Poor fat little **Laferté** falls into a snooze too, after giving Barty just the same commission—to nudge him directly he's found out from the *chaire*.

8.55.—Intense silence ; everybody hard at work. Even Bonzig is satisfied with the deep stillness and studious *recueillement* that brood over the scene — steady pens going—quick turning over of leaves of the Gradus ad Parnassum. Suddenly Barty sticks out his elbows and nudges both his neighbors at once, and both jump up, exclaiming, in a loud voice :

"Non, m'sieur, je n'dors pas. J'travaille."

Sensation. Even Bonzig laughs—and Barty is happy for a week.

Or else, again — a new usher, Monsieur Goupillon (from Gascony) is on duty in the school - room during afternoon school. He has a peculiar way of saying "*oê, vô !*" instead of "*oui, vous !*" to any boy who says "moi, m'sieur ?" on being found fault with ; and perceiving this, Barty manages to be found fault with every five minutes, and always says "moi, m'sieur ?" so as to elicit the "*oê, vô !*" that gives him such delight.

At length M. Goupillon says,

"Josselin, if you force me to say '*oê, vô !*' to you once more, you shall be *à la retenue* for a week !"

"Moi, m'sieur ?" says Josselin, quite innocently.

"*Oê, vô !*" shouts M. Goupillon, glaring with all his might, but quite unconscious that Barty has earned the threatened punishment ! And again Barty is happy for a week. And so are we.

Such was Barty's humor, as a boy—mere drivel—but of such a kind that even his butts were fond of him. He would make M. Bonzig laugh in the middle of his severest penal sentences, and thus demoralize the whole school-room and set a shocking example, and be ordered *à la porte* of the salle d'études—an exile which was quite to his taste ; for he would go straight off to the lingerie and entertain Mlle. Marceline and Constance and Félicité (who all three adored him) with comic songs and break-downs of his own invention, and imitations of everybody in the school. He was a born histrion — a kind of French Arthur Roberts—but very beautiful to the female eye, and also always dear to the female heart —a most delightful gift of God !

Then he was constantly being sent for when boys' friends and parents came to see them, that he might sing and play the fool and show off his tricks, and so forth. It was one of M. Mérovée's greatest delights to put him through his paces. The message "on demande Monsieur Josselin au parloir" would be brought down once or twice a week, sometimes even in class or school room, and became quite a by-word in the school ; and many of the masters thought it a mistake and a pity. But Barty by no means disliked being made much of and showing off in this genial manner.

He could turn le père Brossard round his little finger, and Mérovée too. Whenever an extra holiday was to be begged for, or a favor obtained for any one, or the severity of a *pensum* mitigated, Barty was the messenger, and seldom failed.

His constitution, inherited from a long line of frugal seafaring Norman ancestors (not to mention another long line of well-fed, well-bred Yorkshire Squires), was magnificent. His spirits never failed. He could see the satellites of Jupiter with the naked eye ; this was often tested by M. Dumollard, maître de mathématiques (et de cosmographie), who had a telescope, which, with a little good-will on the gazer's part, made Jupiter look as big as the moon, and its moons like stars of the first magnitude.

37

His sense of hearing was also exceptionally keen. He could hear a watch tick in the next room, and perceive very high sounds to which ordinary human ears are deaf (this was found out later) ; and when we played blind-man's-buff on a rainy day, he could, blindfolded, tell every boy he caught hold of—not by feeling him all over like the rest of us, but by the mere smell of his hair, or his hands, or his blouse ! No wonder he was so much more alive than the rest of us ! According to the amiable, modest, polite, delicately humorous, and even tolerant and considerate Professor Max Nordau, this perfection of the olfactory sense proclaims poor Barty a degenerate ! I only wish there were a few more like him, and that I were a little more like him myself !

By-the-way, how proud young Germany must feel of its enlightened Max, and how fond of him, to be sure ! Mes compliments !

But the most astounding thing of all (it seems incredible, but all the world knows it by this time, and it will be accounted for later on) is that at certain times and seasons Barty knew by an infallible instinct *where the north was*, to a point. Most of my readers will remember his extraordinary evidence as a witness in the " Rangoon" trial, and how this power was tested in open court, and how important were the issues involved, and how he refused to give any explanation of a gift so extraordinary.

It was often tried at school by blindfolding him, and turning him round and round till he was giddy, and asking him to point out where the north pole was, or the north star, and seven or eight times out of ten the answer was unerringly right. When he failed, he knew beforehand that for the time being he had lost the power, but could never say why. Little Doctor Larcher could never get over his surprise at this strange phenomenon, nor explain it, and often brought some scientific friend from Paris to test it, who was equally nonplussed.

When cross-examined, Barty would merely say :

"Quelquefois je sais—quelquefois je ne sais pas—mais quand je sais, je sais, et il n'y a pas à s'y tromper !"

Indeed, on one occasion that I remember well, a very strange thing happened; he not only pointed out the north with absolute accuracy, as he stood carefully blindfolded in the gymnastic ground, after having been turned and twisted again and again — but, still blindfolded, he vaulted the wire fence and ran round to the refectory door which served as the home at rounders, all of us following; and there he danced a surprising dance of his own invention, that he called "La Paladine," the most humorously graceful and grotesque exhibition I ever saw ; and then, taking a ball out of his pocket, he shouted : "À l'amandier !" and threw the ball. Straight and swift it flew, and hit the almond-tree, which was quite twenty yards off ; and after this he ran round the yard from base to base, as at "la balle au camp," till he reached the camp again.

"If ever he goes blind," said the wondering M. Mérovée, "he'll never need a dog to lead him about."

"He must have some special friend above !" said Madame Germain (Mérovée's sister, who was looking on).

Prophetic words ! I have never forgotten them, nor the tear that glistened in each of her kind eyes as she spoke. She was a deeply religious and very emotional person, and loved Barty almost as if he were a child of her own.

Such women have strange intuitions.

Barty was often asked to repeat this astonishing performance before sceptical people—parents of boys, visit-

ors, etc.—who had been told of it, and who believed he
could not have been properly blindfolded ; but he could
never be induced to do so.

There was no mistake about the blindfolding—I helped
in it myself ; and he afterwards told me the whole thing
was "aussi simple que bonjour" if once he felt the north
—for then, with his back to the refectory door, he knew
exactly the position and distance of every tree from
where he was.

"It's all nonsense about my going blind and being able
to do without a dog"—he added ; "I should be just as
helpless as any other blind man, unless I was in a place I
knew as well as my own pocket—like this play-ground !
Besides, *I* sha'n't go blind ; nothing will ever happen to
my eyes—they're the strongest and best in the whole
school !"

He said this exultingly, dilating his nostrils and chest;
and looked proudly up and around, like Ajax defying the
lightning.

"But what *do* you feel when you feel the north, Barty
—a kind of tingling ?" I asked.

"Oh—I feel where it is—as if I'd got a mariner's compass trembling inside my stomach—and as if I wasn't
afraid of anybody or anything in the world—as if I could
go and have my head chopped off and not care a fig."

"Ah, well—I can't make it out—I give it up," I exclaimed.

"So do I," exclaims Barty.

"But tell me, Barty," I whispered, "*have* you—have
you *really* got a—a—*special friend above?*"

"Ask no questions and you'll get no lies," said Barty,
and winked at me one eye after the other — and went
about his business.   And I about mine.

Thus it is hardly to be wondered at that the spirit of

this extraordinary boy seemed to pervade the Pension F. Brossard, almost from the day he came to the day he left it—a slender stripling over six feet high, beautiful as Apollo but, alas ! without his degree, and not an incipient hair on his lip or chin !

Of course the boy had his faults. He had a tremendous appetite, and was rather greedy—so was I, for that matter—and we were good customers to la mère Jaurion; especially he, for he always had lots of pocket-money, and was fond of standing treat all round. Yet, strange to say, he had such a loathing of meat that soon by special favoritism a separate dish of eggs and milk and succulent vegetables was cooked expressly for him—a savory mess that made all our mouths water merely to see and smell it, and filled us with envy, it was so good. Aglaé the cook took care of that !

" C'était pour Monsieur Josselin !"

And of this he would eat as much as three ordinary boys could eat of anything in the world.

Then he was quick-tempered and impulsive, and in frequent fights—in which he generally came off second best ; for he was fond of fighting with bigger boys than himself. Victor or vanquished, he never bore malice—nor woke it in others, which is worse. But he would slap a face almost as soon as look at it, on rather slight provocation, I'm afraid—especially if it were an inch or two higher up than his own. And he was fond of showing off, and always wanted to throw farther and jump higher and run faster than any one else. Not, indeed, that he ever wished to *mentally* excel, or particularly admired those who did !

Also, he was apt to judge folk too much by their mere outward appearance and manner, and not very fond of dull, ugly, commonplace people—the very people, unfortunately, who were fondest of him ; he really detested them, almost as much as they detest each other, in spite of many sterling qualities of the heart and head they sometimes possess. And yet he was their victim through life—for he was very soft, and never had the heart to snub the deadliest bores he ever writhed under, even undeserving ones ! Like ——, or ——, or the Bishop of ——, or Lord Justice ——, or General ——, or Admiral ——, or the Duke of ——, etc., etc.

And he very unjustly disliked people of the bourgeois type—the respectable middle class, *quorum pars magna fui!* Especially if we were very well off and successful, and thought ourselves of some consequence (as we now very often are, I beg to say), and showed it (as, I'm afraid, we sometimes do). He preferred the commonest artisan to M. Jourdain, the bourgeois gentilhomme, who was a very decent fellow, after all, and at least clean in his habits, and didn't use bad language or beat his wife !

Poor dear Barty ! what would have become of all those priceless copyrights and royalties and what not if his old school-fellow hadn't been a man of business ? and where would Barty himself have been without his wife, who came from that very class ?

And his admiration for an extremely good - looking person, even of his own sex, even a scavenger or a dustman, was almost snobbish. It was like a well-bred, well-educated Englishman's frank fondness for a noble lord.

And next to physical beauty he admired great physical strength ; and I sometimes think that it is to my possession of this single gift I owe some of the warm friendship I feel sure he always bore me ; for though he was a strong man, and topped me by an inch or two, I was stronger still—as a cart-horse is stronger than a racer.

For his own personal appearance, of which he always took the greatest care, he had a naïve admiration that he did not disguise. His candor in this respect was comical; yet, strange to say, he was really without vanity.

When he was in the Guards he would tell you quite frankly he was " the handsomest chap in all the Household Brigade, bar three "—just as he would tell you he was twenty last birthday. And the fun of it was that the three exceptions he was good enough to make, splendid fellows as they were, seemed as satyrs to Hyperion when compared with Barty Josselin. One (F. Pepys) was three or four inches taller, it is true, being six foot seven or eight—a giant. The two others had immense whiskers, which Barty openly envied, but could not emulate—and the mustache with which he would have been quite decently endowed in time was not permitted in an infantry regiment.

To return to the Pension Brossard, and Barty the school-boy :

He adored Monsieur Mérovée because he was big and strong and handsome—not because he was one of the best fellows that ever lived. He disliked Monsieur Durosier, whom we were all so fond of, because he had a slight squint and a receding chin.

As for the Anglophobe, Monsieur Dumollard, who made no secret of his hatred and contempt for perfidious Albion . . .

" Dis donc, Josselin !" says Maurice, in English or French, as the case might be, "why don't you like Monsieur Dumollard ? Eh ? He always favors you more than any other chap in the school. I suppose you dislike him because he hates the English so, and always runs them down before you and me—and says they're all traitors and sneaks and hypocrites and bullies and cowards and liars and snobs; and we can't answer him, because he's the mathematical master!"

"Ma foi, non!" says Josselin—"c'est pas pour ça!"

"Pourquoi, alors?" says Maurice (that's me).

"C'est parce qu'il a le pied bourgeois et la jambe canaille!" says Barty. (It's because he's got common legs and vulgar feet.)

And that s about the lowest and meanest thing I ever heard him say in his life.

Also, he was not always very sympathetic, as a boy, when one was sick or sorry or out of sorts, for he had never been ill in his life, never known an ache or a pain —except once the mumps, which he seemed to thoroughly enjoy—and couldn't realize suffering of any kind, except such suffering as most school-boys all over the world are often fond of inflicting on dumb animals : this drove him frantic, and led to many a licking by bigger boys. I remember several such scenes—one especially.

One frosty morning in January, '48, just after breakfast, Jolivet trois (tertius) put a sparrow into his squirrel's cage, and the squirrel caught it in its claws, and cracked its skull like a nut and sucked its brain, while the poor bird still made a desperate struggle for life, and there was much laughter.

There was also, in consequence, a quick fight between Jolivet and Josselin ; in which Barty got the worst, as usual—his foe was two years older, and quite an inch taller.

Afterwards, as the licked one sat on the edge of a small stone tank full of water and dabbed his swollen eye with a wet pocket-handkerchief, M. Dumollard, the mathematical master, made cheap fun of Britannic sentimentality about animals, and told us how the English noblesse were privileged to beat their wives with sticks no thicker than their ankles, and sell them "*au rabais*" in the horse-market of Smissfeld ; and that they paid men to box each other to death on the stage of Drury Lane, and all that—deplorable things that we all know and are sorry for and ashamed, but cannot put a stop to.

The boys laughed, of course ; they always did when Dumollard tried to be funny, "and many a joke had he," although his wit never degenerated into mere humor.

But they were so fond of Barty that they forgave him his insular affectation ; some even helped him to dab his sore eye ; among them Jolivet trois himself, who was a very good-natured chap, and very good-looking into the bargain ; and he had received from Barty a sore eye too —*gallicè*, "un pochon"—*scholasticè*, "un œil au beurre noir !"

By-the-way, *I* fought with Jolivet once—about Æsop's fables ! He said that Æsop was a lame poet of Lacedæmon—I, that Æsop was a little hunchback Armenian Jew ; and I stuck to it. It was a Sunday afternoon, on the terrace by the lingerie.

He kicked as hard as he could, so I had to kick too. Mlle. Marceline ran out with Constance and Félicité and tried to separate us, and got kicked by both (unintentionally, of course). Then up came Père Jaurion and kicked *me!* And they all took Jolivet's part, and said I was in the wrong, because I was English ! What did *they* know about Æsop ! So we made it up, and went in Jaurion's loge and stood each other a blomboudingue on tick—and called Jaurion bad names.

"Comme c'est bête, de s'battre, hein ?" said Jolivet, and I agreed with him. I don't know which of us really got the worst of it, for we hadn't disfigured each other in the least—and that's the best of kicking. Anyhow he was two years older than I, and three or four inches taller ; so I'm glad, on the whole, that that small battle was interrupted.

It is really not for brag that I have lugged in this story—at least, I hope not. One never quite knows.

To go back to Barty : he was the most generous boy in the school. If I may paraphrase an old saying, he really didn't seem to know the difference betwixt tuum et meum. Everything he had, books clothes, pocket-money—even agate marbles, those priceless possessions to a French school-boy—seemed to be also everybody else's who chose. I came across a very characteristic letter of his the other day, written from the Pension Brossard to his favorite aunt, Lady Caroline Grey (one of the Rohans), who adored him. It begins :

" MY DEAR AUNT CAROLINE,—Thank you so much for the magnifying-glass, which is not only magnifying, but magnifique. Don't trouble to send any more gingerbread-nuts, as the boys are getting rather tired of them, especially Laferté and Bussy-Rabutin. I think we should all like some Scotch marmalade," etc., etc.

And though fond of romancing a little now and then, and embellishing a good story, he was absolutely truthful in important matters, and to be relied upon implicitly.

He seemed also to be quite without the sense of physical fear—a kind of callousness.

Such, roughly, was the boy who lived to write the *Motes in a Moonbeam* and *La quatrième Dimension* before he was thirty ; and such, roughly, he remained through life, except for one thing : he grew to be the very soul of passionate and compassionate sympathy, as who doesn't feel who has ever read a page of his work, or even had speech with him for half an hour ?

Whatever weaknesses he yielded to when he grew to man's estate are such as the world only too readily condones in many a famous man less tempted than Josselin was inevitably bound to be through life. Men of the Josselin type (there are not many — he stands pretty much alone) can scarcely be expected to journey from adolescence to middle age with that impeccable decorum which I—and no doubt many of my masculine readers— have found it so easy to achieve, and find it now so pleasant to remember and get credit for. Let us think of *The Footprints of Aurora*, or *Étoiles mortes*, or *Déjanire et Dalila*, or even *Les Trépassées de François Villon!*

Then let us look at Rajon's etching of Watts's portrait of him (the original is my own to look at whenever I like, and that is pretty often). And then let us not throw too many big stones, or too hard, at Barty Josselin.

Well, the summer term of 1847 wore smoothly to its close—a happy " trimestre " during which the Institution F. Brossard reached the high-water mark of its prosperity.

There were sixty boys to be taught, and six house-masters to teach them, besides a few highly paid outsiders for special classes—such as the lively M. Durosier for French literature, and M. le Professeur Martineau for the higher mathematics, and so forth ; and crammers and coachers for St.-Cyr, the Polytechnic School, the École des Ponts et Chaussées.

Also fencing - masters, gymnastic masters, a Dutch master who taught us German and Italian — an Irish master with a lovely brogue who taught us English. Shall I ever forget the blessed day when ten or twelve of us were presented with an *Ivanhoe* apiece as a class-book, or how Barty and I and Bonneville (who knew English) devoured the immortal story in less than a week—to the disgust of Rapaud, who refused to believe that we could possibly know such a beastly tongue as English well enough to read an English book for mere pleasure — on our desks in play-time, or on our laps in school, *en cachette!* "Quelle sacrée pose !"

He soon mislaid his own copy, did Rapaud ; just as he mislaid my *Monte Cristo* and Jolivet's illustrated *Wandering Jew*—and it was always :

"Dis donc, Maurice !—prête-moi ton *Ivanhoé!*" (with an accent on the e), whenever he had to construe his twenty lines of Valtère Scott—and what a hash he made of them !

Sometimes M. Brossard himself would come, smoking his big meerschaum, and help the English class during preparation, and put us up to a thing or two worth knowing.

"Rapaud, comment dit-on '*pouvoir*' en anglais ?"

"Sais pas, m'sieur !"

"Comment, petit crétin, tu ne sais pas !"

And Rapaud would receive a *pincée tordue*—a "twisted pinch"—on the back of his arm to quicken his memory.

"Oh, là, là!" he would howl—"je n' sais pas !"

"Et toi, Maurice ?"

"Ça se dit '*to be able*,' m'sieur !" I would say.

"Mais non, mon ami—tu oublies ta langue natale—ça se dit, '*to can*'! Maintenant, comment dirais-tu en anglais, '*je voudrais pouvoir*' ?"

"Je dirais, '*I would like to be able.*'"

"Comment, encore ! petit cancre ! allons—tu es Anglais—tu sais bien que tu dirais, '*I vould vill to can*'!"

Then M. Brossard turns to Barty : "A ton tour, Josselin !"

"Moi, m'sieur ?" says Barty.

" Oui, toi !—comment dirais-tu, '*je pourrais vouloir*'?"

" Je dirais '*I vould can to vill,*' " says Barty, quite unabashed.

" À la bonne heure ! au moins tu sais ta langue, toi !" says Père Brossard, and pats him on the cheek ; while Barty winks at me, the wink of successful time-serving hypocrisy, and Bonneville writhes with suppressed delight.

What lives most in my remembrance of that summer is the lovely weather we had, and the joy of the Passy swimming - bath every Thursday and Sunday from two till five or six ; it comes back to me even now in heavenly dreams by night. I swim with giant side-strokes all round the Île des Cygnes between Passy and Grenelle, where the École de Natation was moored for the summer months.

Round and round the isle I go, up stream and down, and dive and float and wallow with bliss there is no telling—till the waters all dry up and disappear, and I am left wading in weeds and mud and drift and drought and desolation, and wake up shivering—and such is life.

As for Barty, he was all but amphibious, and reminded me of the seal at the Jardin des Plantes. He really seemed to spend most of the afternoon under water, coming up to breathe now and then at unexpected moments, with a stone in his mouth that he had picked up from the slimy bottom ten or twelve feet below—or a weed—or a dead mussel.

Part Second

> "Laissons les regrets et les pleurs
> À la vieillesse ;
> Jeunes, il faut cueillir les fleurs
> De la jeunesse !"—BAÏF.

SOMETIMES we spent the Sunday morning in Paris, Barty and I—in picture-galleries and museums and wax-figure shows, churches and cemeteries, and the Hôtel Cluny and the Baths of Julian the Apostate—or the Jardin des Plantes, or the Morgue, or the knackers' yards at Montfaucon—or lovely slums. Then a swim at the Bains Deligny. Then lunch at some restaurant on the Quai Voltaire, or in the Quartier Latin. Then to some café on the Boulevards, drinking our demi-tasse and our chasse-café, and smoking our cigarettes like men, and picking our teeth like gentlemen of France.

Once after lunch at Vachette's with Berquin (who was seventeen) and Bonneville (the marquis who had got an English mother), we were sitting outside the Café des Variétés, in the midst of a crowd of consommateurs, and tasting to the full the joy of being alive, when a poor woman came up with a guitar, and tried to sing "Le petit mousse noir," a song Barty knew quite well—but she couldn't sing a bit, and nobody listened.

"Allons, Josselin, chante-nous ça !" said Berquin.

And Bonneville jumped up, and took the woman's guitar from her, and forced it into Josselin's hands, while the crowd became much interested and began to applaud.

Thus encouraged, Barty, who never in all his life knew what it is to be shy, stood up and piped away like a bird ; and when he had finished the story of the little black cabin-boy who sings in the maintop halliards, the applause was so tremendous that he had to stand up on a chair and sing another, and yet another.

"Écoute-moi bien, ma Fleurette !" and "Amis, la matinée est belle !" (from *La Muette de Portici*), while the pavement outside the Variétés was rendered quite impassable by the crowd that had gathered round to look and listen—and who all joined in the chorus :

> "Conduis ta barque avec prudence,
> Pêcheur ! parle bas !
> Jette tes filets en silence
> Pêcheur ! parle bas !
> Et le roi des mers ne nous échappera pas !" (*bis*).

and the applause was deafening.

Meanwhile Bonneville and Berquin went round with the hat and gathered quite a considerable sum, in which there seemed to be almost as much silver as copper—and actually *two five-franc pieces and an English half-sovereign!* The poor woman wept with gratitude at coming into such a fortune, and insisted on kissing Barty's hand. Indeed it was a quite wonderful ovation, considering how unmistakably British was Barty's appearance, and how unpopular we were in France just then !

He had his new shiny black silk chimney-pot hat on, and his Eton jacket, with the wide shirt collar. Berquin, in a tightly fitting double-breasted brown cloth swallow-tailed coat with brass buttons, yellow nankin bell-mouthed trousers strapped over varnished boots, butter-colored gloves, a blue satin stock, and a very tall hairy hat with a wide curly brim, looked such an out-

"AMIS, LA MATINÉE EST BELLE"

and-out young gentleman of France that we were all
proud of being seen in his company—especially young
de Bonneville, who was still in mourning for his father
and wore a crape band round his arm, and a common
cloth cap with a leather peak, and thick blucher boots;
though he was quite sixteen, and already had a little
black mustache like an eyebrow, and inhaled the smoke
of his cigarette without coughing and quite naturally,
and ordered the waiters about just as if he already
wore the uniform of the École St. - Cyr, for which he
destined himself (and was not disappointed. He should
be a marshal of France by now—perhaps he is).

Then we went to the Café Mulhouse on the Boulevard
des Italiens (on the "*Boul. des It.,*" as we called it, to be
in the fashion)—that we might gaze at Señor Joaquin
Eliezegui, the Spanish giant, who was eight feet high
and a trifle over (or under—I forget which) : he told
us himself. Barty had a passion for gazing at very tall
men; like Frederic the Great (or was it his Majesty's
royal father ?).

Then we went to the Boulevard Bonne-Nouvelle,
where, in a painted wooden shed, a most beautiful Cir-
cassian slave, miraculously rescued from some abomina-
ble seraglio in Constantinople, sold pen'orths of "galette
du gymnase." On her raven hair she wore a silk turban
all over sequins, silver and gold, with a yashmak that
fell down behind, leaving her adorable face exposed :
she had an amber vest of silk, embroidered with pearls
as big as walnuts, and Turkish pantalettes—what her
slippers were we couldn't see, but they must have been
lovely, like all the rest of her. Barty had a passion for
gazing at very beautiful female faces—like his father before him.

There was a regular queue of postulants to see this

heavenly Eastern houri and buy her confection, which is very like Scotch butter-cake, but not so digestible; and even more filling at the price. And three of us sat on a bench, while three times running Barty took his place in that procession—soldiers, sailors, workmen, chiffonniers, people of all sorts, women as many as men—all of them hungry for galette, but hungrier still for a good humanizing stare at a beautiful female face; and he made the slow and toilsome journey to the little wooden booth three times—and brought us each a pen'orth on each return journey; and the third time, Katidjah (such was her sweet Oriental name) leaned forward over her counter and kissed him on both cheeks, and whispered in his ear (in English—and with the accent of Stratford-atte-Bowe):

"You little *duck!* *your* name is *Brown, I* know!"

And he came away, his face pale with conflicting emotions, and told us!

How excited we were! Bonneville (who spoke English quite well) went for a pen'orth on his own account, and said: "My name's Brown too, Miss Katidjah!" But he didn't get a kiss.

(She soon after married a Mr.——, of ——, the well-known —— of ——shire, in ——land. She may be alive now.)

Then to the Palais Royal, to dine at the "Dîner Européen" with M. Berquin père, a famous engineer; and finally to stalls at the "Français" to see the two first acts of *Le Cid;* and this was rather an anticlimax—for we had too much "Cid" at the Institution F. Brossard already!

And then, at last, to the omnibus station in the Rue de Rivoli, whence the "Accélérées" (en correspondence avec les Constantines) started for Passy every ten minutes;

and thus, up the gas-lighted Champs-Élysées, and by the Arc de Triomphe, to the Rond-point de l'Avenue de St.-Cloud ; tired out, but happy—happy—happy *comme on ne l'est plus !*

Before the school broke up for the holidays there were very severe examinations—but no " distribution de prix"; we were above that kind of thing at Brossard's, just as we were above wearing a uniform or taking in day boarders.

Barty didn't come off very well in this competition ; but he came off anyhow much better than I, who had failed to be " diligent and attentive "—too much *Monte Cristo*, I'm afraid.

At all events Barty got five marks for English History, because he remembered a good deal about Richard Cœur de Lion, and John, and Friar Tuck, and Robin Hood, and especially one Cedric the Saxon, a historical personage of whom the examiner (a decorated gentleman from the Collège de France) had never even heard !

And then (to the tune of " Au clair de la lune "):

> " Vivent les vacances—
> *Denique tandèm ;*
> Et les pénitences—
> *Habebunt finèm!*
> Les pions intraitables,
> *Vultu Barbarò,*
> S'en iront aux diables,
> *Gaudio nostrò.*"

N.B.—The accent is always on the last syllable in French Latin—and *pion* means an usher.

Barty went to Yorkshire with the Rohans, and I spent most of my holidays with my mother and sister (and the beautiful Miss——) at Mademoiselle Jalabert's, next door —coming back to school for most of my meals, and at

"TOO MUCH 'MONTE CRISTO,' I'M AFRAID"

night to sleep, with a whole dormitory to myself, and no
dreadful bell at five in the morning; and so much time
to spare that I never found any leisure for my holiday
task, that skeleton at the feast; no more did Jules, the
sergeant's son; no more did Caillard, who spent his vacation at Brossard's because his parents lived in Russia,
and his "correspondant" in Paris was ill.

The only master who remained behind was Bonzig,
who passed his time painting ships and sailors, in oil-
colors; it was a passion with him: corvettes, brigan-
tines, British whalers, fishing-smacks, revenue-cutters,
feluccas, caïques, even Chinese junks—all was fish that
came to his net. He got them all from *La France
Maritime*, an illustrated periodical much in vogue at
Brossard's; and also his storms and his calms, his rocks
and piers and light-houses—for he had never seen
the sea he was so fond of. He took us every morning
to the Passy swimming-baths, and in the afternoon for
long walks in Paris, and all about and around, and especially to the Musée de Marine at the Louvre, that we
might gaze with him at the beautiful models of three-
deckers.

He evidently pitied our forlorn condition, and told us
delightful stories about seafaring life, like Mr. Clark
Russell's; and how he, some day, hoped to see the ocean
for himself before he died—and with his own eyes.

I really don't know how Jules and Caillard would have
got through the hideous *ennui* of that idle September
without him. Even I, with my mother and sister and
the beautiful Miss —— within such easy reach, found
time hang heavily at times. One can't be always reading,
even Alexandre Dumas; nor always loafing about, even
in Paris, by one's self (Jules and Caillard were not allowed outside the gates without Bonzig); and beautiful

English girls of eighteen, like Miss ——s, don't always want a small boy dangling after them, and show it sometimes ; which I thought very hard.

It was almost a relief when school began again in October, and the boys came back with their wonderful stories of the good time they had all had (especially some of the big boys, who were " en rhétorique et en philosophie ")—and all the game that had fallen to their guns—wild-boars, roebucks, cerfs-dix-cors, and what not ; of perilous swims in stormy seas—tremendous adventures in fishing-smacks on moonlight nights (it seemed that the moon had been at the full all through those wonderful six weeks); rides *ventre à terre* on mettlesome Arab steeds through gloomy wolf-haunted forests with charming female cousins ; flirtations and " good fortunes " with beautiful but not happily married women in old mediæval castle keeps. Toujours au clair de la lune ! They didn't believe each other in the least, these gay young romancers —nor expect to be believed themselves ; but it was very exciting all the same ; and they listened, and were listened to in turn, without a gesture of incredulity—nor even a smile ! And we small boys held our tongues in reverence and awe.

When Josselin came back he had wondrous things to tell too—but so preposterous that they disbelieved him quite openly, and told him so. How in London he had seen a poor woman so tipsy in the street that she had to be carried away by two policemen on a stretcher. How he had seen brewers' dray-horses nearly six feet high at the shoulder —and one or two of them with a heavy cavalry mustache drooping from its upper lip.

How he had been presented to the Lord Mayor of London, and even shaken hands with him, in Leadenhall Market, and that his Lordship was quite plainly dressed ;

and how English Lord Mayors were not necessarily "hommes du monde," nor always hand in glove with Queen Victoria !

Splendide mendax !

But they forgave him all his mendacity for the sake of a new accomplishment he had brought back with him, and which beat all his others. He could actually turn a somersault backwards with all the ease and finish of a professional ·acrobat. How he got to do this I don't know. It must have been natural to him and he never found it out before; he was always good at gymnastics— and all things that required grace and agility more than absolute strength.

Also he brought back with him (from Leadenhall Market, no doubt) a gigantic horned owl, fairly tame— and with eyes that reminded us of le grand Bonzig's.

School began, and with it the long evenings with an hour's play by lamp-light in the warm salle d'études ; and the cold lamp-lit ninety minutes' preparation on an empty stomach, after the short perfunctory morning prayer—which didn't differ much from the evening one.

Barty was still *en cinquième*, at the top ! and I at the tail of the class immediately above—so near and yet so far ! so I did not have many chances of improving my acquaintance with him that term ; for he still stuck to Laferté and Bussy-Rabutin—they were inseparable, those three.

At mid-day play-time the weather was too cold for anything but games, which were endless in their variety and excitement; it would take a chapter to describe them.

It is a mistake to think that French school-boys are (or were) worse off than ours in this. I will not say that any one French game is quite so good as cricket or football for a permanency. But I remember a great many that are very nearly so.

Indeed, French rounders (la balle au camp) seems to me the best game that ever was—on account of the quick rush and struggle of the fielders to get home when an inside boy is hit between the bases, lest he should pick the ball up in time to hit one of them with it before the camp is reached ; in which case there is a most exciting scrimmage for the ball, etc., etc.

Barty was good at all games, especially la balle au camp. I used to envy the graceful, easy way he threw the ball — so quick and straight it seemed to have no curve at all in its trajectory : and how it bounded off the boy it nearly always hit between the shoulders !

At evening, play in the school-room, besides draughts and chess and backgammon ; M. Bonzig, when *de service,* would tell us thrilling stories, with "la suite au prochain numéro" when the bell rang at 7.30 ; a long series that lasted through the winter of '47–'48. *Le Tueur de Daims, Le Lac Ontario, Le Dernier des Mohicans, Les Pionniers, La Prairie*—by one Fénimore Coupère ; all of which he had read in M. Defauconpret's admirable translations. I have read some of them in their native American since then, myself. I loved them always— but they seemed to lack some of the terror, the freshness, and the charm his fluent utterance and solemn nasal voice put into them as he sat and smoked his endless cigarettes with his back against the big stone stove, and his eyes dancing sideways through his glasses. Never did that "ding-dang-dong" sound more hateful than when le grand Bonzig was telling the tale of Bas-de-cuir's doings, from his innocent youth to his noble and pathetic death by sunset, with his ever-faithful and still-serviceable but no longer deadly rifle (the friend of sixty years)

lying across his knees. I quote from memory; what a
gun that was !

Then on Thursdays, long walks, two by two, in Paris,
with Bonzig or Dumollard ; or else in the Bois to play
rounders or prisoners' base in a clearing, or skate on
the Mare aux Biches, which was always so hard to find
in the dense thicket . . . poor Lord Runswick ! *He*
found it once too often !

La Mare d'Auteuil was too deep, and too popular with
"la flotte de Passy," as we called the Passy voyous, big
and small, who came there in their hundreds—to slide
and pick up quarrels with well-dressed and respectable
school-boys. Liberté—égalité—fraternité ! ou la mort!
Vive la république ! (This, by-the-way, applies to the
winter that came *next*.)

So time wore on with us gently ; through the short
vacation at New-year's day till the 23d or 24th of February, when the Revolution broke out, and Louis Philippe premier had to fly for his life. It was a very troublous time, and the school for a whole week was in a
state of quite heavenly demoralization ! Ten times a
day, or in the dead of night, the drum would beat *le
rappel* or *la générale*. A warm wet wind was blowing—
the most violent wind I can remember that was not an
absolute gale. It didn't rain, but the clouds hurried
across the sky all day long, and the tops of the trees
tried to bend themselves in two ; and their leafless
boughs and black broken twigs littered the deserted play-
ground—for we all sat on the parapet of the terrace by
the lingerie ; boys and servants, le père et la mère Jaurion, Mlle. Marceline and the rest, looking towards Paris
—all feeling bound to each other by a common danger,
like wild beasts in a flood. Dear me ! I'm out of breath
from sheer pleasure in the remembrance.

One night we had to sleep on the floor for fear of stray bullets ; and that was a fearful joy never to be forgotten—it almost kept us awake ! Peering out of the school-room windows at dusk, we saw great fires, three or four at a time. Suburban retreats of the over-wealthy, in full conflagration ; and all day the rattle of distant musketry and the boom of cannon a long way off, near Montmartre and Montfaucon, kept us alive.

Most of the boys went home, and some of them never came back—and from that day the school began to slowly decline. Père Brossard—an ancient "Brigand de la Loire," as the republicans of his youth were called—was elected a representative of his native town at the Chamber of Deputies ; and possibly that did the school more harm than good—ne sutor ultra crepidam ! as he was so fond of impressing on *us !*

However, we went on pretty much as usual through spring and summer—with occasional alarms (which we loved), and beatings of *le rappel*—till the July insurrection broke out.

My mother and sister had left Mlle. Jalabert's, and now lived with my father near the Boulevard Montmartre. And when the fighting was at its height they came to fetch me home, and invited Barty, for the Rohans were away from Paris. So home we walked, quite leisurely, on a lovely peaceful summer evening, while the muskets rattled and the cannons roared round us, but at a proper distance ; women picking linen for lint and chatting genially the while at shop doors and porter's lodge - gates ; and a piquet of soldiers at the corner of every street, who felt us all over for hidden cartridges before they let us through ; it was all entrancing ! The subtle scent of gunpowder was in the air—the most suggestive smell there can be. Even now, here in England, the night of the fifth of November never comes round but I am pleasantly reminded of the days when I was "en pleine révolution" in the streets of Paris with my father and mother, and Barty and my little sister—and genial *piou-pious* made such a conscientious examination of our garments. Nothing brings back the past like a sound or a smell—even those of a penny squib!

Every now and then a litter borne by soldiers came by, on which lay a dead or wounded officer. And then one's laugh died suddenly out, and one felt one's self face to face with the horrors that were going on.

Barty shared my bed, and we lay awake talking half the night; dreadful as it all was, one couldn't help being jolly! Every ten minutes the sentinel on duty in the court-yard below would sententiously intone :

"Sentinelles, prenez-garde à vous!" And other sentinels would repeat the cry till it died away in the distance, like an echo.

And all next day, or the day after—or else the day after that, when the long rattle of the musketry had left off—we heard at intervals the "feu de peloton" in a field behind the church of St.-Vincent de Paul, and knew that at every discharge a dozen poor devils of insurgents, caught red-handed, fell dead in a pool of blood!

I need hardly say that before three days were over the irrepressible Barty had made a complete conquest of my small family. My sister (I hasten to say this) has loved him as a brother ever since ; and as long as my parents lived, and wherever they made their home, that home has ever been his—and he has been their son—almost their eldest born, though he was younger than I by seven months.

Things have been reversed, however, for now thirty

years and more ; and his has ever been the home for me, and his people have been my people, and ever will be— and the God of his worship mine !

What children and grandchildren of my own could ever be to me as these of Barty Josselin's ?

"Ce sacré Josselin—il avait tous les talents !"

And the happiest of these gifts, and not the least important, was the gift he had of imparting to his offspring all that was most brilliant and amiable and attractive in himself, and leaving in them unimpaired all that was strongest and best in the woman I loved as well as he did, and have loved as long—and have grown to look upon as belonging to the highest female type that can be ; for doubtless the Creator, in His infinite wisdom, might have created a better and a nicer woman than Mrs. Barty Josselin that was to be, had He thought fit to do so ; but doubtless also He never did.

Alas ! the worst of us is that the best of us are those that want the longest knowing to find it out.

My kind-hearted but cold-mannered and undemonstrative Scotch father, evangelical, a total abstainer, with a horror of tobacco—surely the austerest dealer in French wines that ever was—a puritanical hater of bar sinisters, and profligacy, and Rome, and rank, and the army, and especially the stage—he always lumped them together more or less — a despiser of all things French, except their wines, which he never drank himself — remained devoted to Barty till the day of his death ; and so with my dear genial mother, whose heart yet always yearned towards serious boys who worked hard at school and college, and passed brilliant examinations, and got scholarships and fellowships in England, and state sinecures in France, and married early, and let their mothers choose their wives for them, and train up their children in the way they should go. She had lived so long in France that she was Frencher than the French themselves.

And they both loved good music—Mozart, Bach, Beethoven—and were almost priggish in their contempt for anything of a lighter kind; especially with a lightness English or French! It was only the musical lightness of Germany they could endure at all! But whether in Paris or London, enter Barty Josselin, idle schoolboy, or dandy dissipated guardsman, and fashionable man about town, or bohemian art student; and Bach, lebewohl! good-bye, Beethoven! bonsoir le bon Mozart! all was changed: and welcome, instead, the last comic song from the Château des Fleurs, or Evans's in Covent Garden; the latest patriotic or sentimental ditty by Loïsa Puget, or Frédéric Bérat, or Eliza Cook, or Mr. Henry Russell.

And then, what would Barty like for breakfast, dinner, supper after the play, and which of all those burgundies would do Barty good without giving him a headache next morning? and where was Barty to have his smoke?—in the library, of course. "Light the fire in the library, Mary; and Mr. Bob [that was me] can smoke there, too, instead of going outside," etc., etc., etc. It is small wonder that he grew a bit selfish at times.

Though I was a little joyous now and then, it is quite without a shadow of bitterness or envy that I write all this. I have lived for fifty years under the charm of that genial, unconscious, irresistible tyranny; and, unlike my dear parents, I have lived to read and know Barty Josselin, nor merely to see and hear and love him for himself alone.

Indeed, it was quite impossible to know Barty at all intimately and not do whatever he wanted you to do. Whatever he wanted, he wanted so intensely, and at once;

and he had such a droll and engaging way of expressing
that hurry and intensity, and especially of expressing his
gratitude and delight when what he wanted was what
he got—that you could not for the life of you hold your
own ! Tout vient à qui ne sait pas attendre !

Besides which, every now and then, if things didn't
go quite as he wished, he would fly into comic rages, and
become quite violent and intractable for at least five minutes, and for quite five minutes more he would silently
sulk. And then, just as suddenly, he would forget all
about it, and become once more the genial, affectionate,
and caressing creature he always was.

But this is going ahead too fast ! revenons. At the
examinations this year Barty was almost brilliant, and I
was hopeless as usual ; my only consolation being that
after the holidays we should at last be in the same class
together, *en quatrième,* and all through this hopelessness
of mine !

Laferté was told by his father that he might invite two
of his school-fellows to their country-house for the vacation, so he asked Josselin and Bussy-Rabutin. But Bus-
sy couldn't go—and, to my delight, I went instead.

That ride all through the sweet August night, the
three of us on the impériale of the five-horsed diligence,
just behind the conductor and the driver—and freedom,
and a full moon, or nearly so—and a tremendous saucisson de Lyon (à l'ail, bound in silver paper)—and petits
pains—and six bottles of bière de Mars—and cigarettes
ad libitum, which of course we made ourselves !

The Lafertés lived in the Department of La Sarthe, in
a delightful country-house, with a large garden sloping
down to a transparent stream, which had willows and
alders and poplars all along its both banks, and a beautiful country beyond.

Outside the grounds (where there were the old brick walls, all overgrown with peaches and pears and apricots, of some forgotten mediæval convent) was a large farm ; and close by, a water-mill that never stopped.

A road, with thick hedge-rows on either side, led to a small and very pretty town called La Tremblaye, three miles off. And hard by the garden gates began the big forest of that name : one heard the stags calling, and the owls hooting, and the fox giving tongue as it hunted the hares at night. There might have been wolves and wild-boars. I like to think so very much.

M. Laferté was a man of about fifty—entre les deux âges ; a retired maître de forges, or iron-master, or else the son of one : I forget which. He had a charming wife and two pretty little daughters, Jeanne et Marie, aged fourteen and twelve.

He seldom moved from his country home, which was called "Le Gué des Aulnes," except to go shooting in the forest ; for he was a great sportsman and cared for little else. He was of gigantic stature—six foot six or seven, and looked taller still, as he had a very small head and high shoulders. He was not an Adonis, and could only see out of one eye—the other (the left one, fortunately) was fixed as if it were made of glass—perhaps it was—and this gave him a stern and rather forbidding expression of face.

He had just been elected Mayor of La Tremblaye, beating the Comte de la Tremblaye by many votes. The Comte was a royalist and not popular. The republican M. Laferté (who was immensely charitable and very just) was very popular indeed, in spite of a morose and gloomy manner. He could even be violent at times, and then he was terrible to see and hear. Of course his wife and daughters were gentleness itself, and so was his son, and everybody who came into contact with him. *Si vis pacem, para bellum,* as Père Brossard used to impress upon us.

It was the strangest country household I have ever seen, in France or anywhere else. They were evidently very well off, yet they preferred to eat their mid-day meal in the kitchen, which was immense ; and so was the midday meal—and of a succulency ! . . .

An old wolf - hound always lay by the huge log fire ; often with two or three fidgety cats fighting for the soft places on him and making him growl ; five or six other dogs, non-sporting, were always about at meal-time.

The servants—three or four peasant women who waited on us—talked all the time; and were *tutoyées* by the family. Farm-laborers came in and discussed agricultural matters, manures, etc., quite informally, squeezing their bonnets de coton in their hands. The postman sat by the fire and drank a glass of cider and smoked his pipe up the chimney while the letters were read—most of them out loud—and were commented upon by everybody in the most friendly spirit. All this made the meal last a long time.

M. Laferté always wore his blouse—except in the evening, and then he wore a brown woollen vareuse, or jersey; unless there were guests, when he wore his Sunday morning best. He nearly always spoke like a peasant, although he was really a decently educated man—or should have been.

His old mother, who was of good family and eighty years of age, lived in a quite humble cottage in a small street in La Tremblaye, with two little peasant girls to wait on her ; and the La Tremblayes, with whom M. Laferté was not on speaking terms, were always coming into the village to see her and bring her fruit and flowers and game. She was a most accomplished old lady, and an excellent musician, and had known Monsieur de Lafayette.

We breakfasted with her when we alighted from the diligence at six in the morning ; and she took such a fancy to Barty that her own grandson was almost forgotten. He sang to her, and she sang to him, and showed him autograph letters of Lafayette, and a lock of her hair when she was seventeen, and old-fashioned miniatures of her father and mother, Monsieur and Madame de something I've quite forgotten.

M. Laferté kept a pack of bassets (a kind of bow-legged beagle), and went shooting with them every day in the forest, wet or dry ; sometimes we three boys with him. He lent us guns—an old single-barrelled flint-lock cavalry musket or carbine fell to my share ; and I knew happiness such as I had never known yet.

Barty was evidently not meant for a sportsman. On a very warm August morning, as he and I squatted "à l'affût" at the end of a long straight ditch outside a thicket which the bassets were hunting, we saw a hare running full tilt at us along the ditch, and we both fired together. The hare shrieked, and turned a big somersault and fell on its back and kicked convulsively—its legs still galloping—and its face and neck were covered with blood ; and, to my astonishment, Barty became quite hysterical with grief at what we had done. It's the only time I ever saw him cry.

"*Caïn! Caïn! qu'as-tu fait de ton frère?*" he shrieked again and again, in a high voice, like a small child's— like the hare's.

I calmed him down and promised I wouldn't tell, and he recovered himself and bagged the game—but he never came out shooting with us again ! So I inherited his gun, which was double-barrelled.

Barty's accomplishments soon became the principal recreation of the Laferté ladies; and even M. Laferté himself would start for the forest an hour or two later or come back an hour sooner to make Barty go through his bag of tricks. He would have an arm-chair brought out on the lawn after breakfast and light his short black pipe and settle the programme himself.

First, "*le saut périlleux*"—the somersault backwards —over and over again, at intervals of two or three minutes, so as to give himself time for thought and chuckles, while he smoked his pipe in silent stodgy jubilation.

Then, two or three songs—they would be stopped, if M. Laferté didn't like them, after the first verse, and another one started instead; and if it pleased him, it was encored two or three times.

Then, pen and ink and paper were brought, and a small table and a kitchen chair, and Barty had to draw caricatures, of which M. Laferté chose the subject.

"Maintenant, fais-moi le profil de mon vieil ami M. Bonzig, que j' n' connais pas, que j' n'ai jamais vu, mais q' j'aime beaucoup." (Now do me the side face of my old friend M. Bonzig, whom I don't know, but am very fond of.)

And so on for twenty minutes.

Then Barty had to be blindfolded and twisted round and round, and point out the north—when he felt up to it.

Then a pause for reflection.

Then : "Dis-moi qué'q' chose en anglais."

"How do you do very well hey diddle-diddle Chichester church in Chichester church-yard !" says Barty.

"Qué'q' çà veut dire ?"

"Il s'agit d'une église et d'un cimetière ?" says Barty —rather sadly, with a wink at me.

"C'est pas gai! Qué vilaine langue, hein? J' suis joliment content que j' sais pas l'anglais, moi!" (It's not lively! What a beastly language, eh? I'm precious glad *I* don't know English.)

Then: "Démontre-moi un problème de géométrie."

Barty would then do a simple problem out of Legendre (the French Euclid), and M. Laferté would look on with deep interest and admiration, but evidently no comprehension whatever. Then he would take the pen himself, and draw a shapeless figure, with A's and B's and C's and D's stuck all over it in impossible places, and quite at hazard, and say:

"Démontre-moi que A+B est plus grand que C+D." It was mere idiotic nonsense, and he didn't know better!

But Barty would manage to demonstrate it all the same, and M. Laferté would sigh deeply, and exclaim, "C'est joliment beau, la géométrie!"

Then: "Danse!"

And Barty danced "la Paladine," and did Scotch reels and Irish jigs and break - downs of his own invention, amidst roars of laughter from all the family.

Finally the gentlemen of the party went down to the river for a swim—and old Laferté would sit on the bank and smoke his brûle-gueule, and throw carefully selected stones for Barty to dive after—and feel he'd scored off Barty when the proper stone wasn't found, and roar in his triumph. After which he would go and pick the finest peach he could find, and peel it with his pocket-knife very neatly, and when Barty was dressed, present it to him with a kindly look in both eyes at once.

"Mange-moi ça—ça t' fera du bien!"

Then, suddenly: "Pourquoi q' tu n'aimes pas la chasse? t'as pas peur, j'espère!" (Why don't you like shooting? you're not afraid, I hope!)

LE PÈRE POLYPHÈME

"'Sais pas,'" said Josselin ; "don't like killing things, I suppose.'"

So Barty became quite indispensable to the happiness and comfort of Père Polyphème, as he called him, as well as of his amiable family.

On the 1st of September there was a grand breakfast in honor of the partridges (not in the kitchen this time), and many guests were invited ; and Barty had to sing and talk and play the fool all through breakfast ; and got very tipsy, and had to be put to bed for the rest of the day. It was no fault of his, and Madame Laferté declared that "ces messieurs" ought to be ashamed of themselves, and watched over Barty like a mother. He has often declared he was never quite the same after that debauch—and couldn't feel the north for a month.

The house was soon full of guests, and Barty and I slept in M. Laferté's bedroom—his wife in a room adjoining.

Every morning old Polyphemus would wake us up by roaring out :

"Hé ! ma femme !"

"Voilà, voilà, mon ami !" from the next room.

"Viens vite panser mon cautère !"

And in came Madame L. in her dressing-gown, and dressed a blister he wore on his big arm.

Then : "Café !"

And coffee came, and he drank it in bed.

Then : "Pipe !"

And his pipe was brought and filled, and he lit it.

Then : "Josselin !"

"Oui, M'sieur Laferté."

"Tire moi une gamme."

"Dorémifasollasido—Dosilasolfamirédo !" sang Josselin, up and down, in beautiful tune, with his fresh bird-like soprano.

"Ah! q' ça fait du bien!" says M. L.; then a pause, and puffs of smoke and grunts and sighs of satisfaction.

"Josselin?"

"Oui, M'sieur Laferté!"

"'La brune Thérèse!'"

And Josselin would sing about the dark-haired Thérèsa—three verses.

"Tu as changé la fin du second couplet—tu as dit '*des comtesses*' au lieu de dire '*des duchesses*'—recommence!" (You changed the end of the second verse—you said "countesses" instead of "duchesses"—begin again.)

And Barty would re-sing it, as desired, and bring in the duchesses.

"Maintenant, 'Colin, disait Lisette!'"

And Barty would sing that charming little song, most charmingly:

> "'Colin,' disait Lisette,
> 'Je voudrais passer l'eau!
> Mais je suis trop pauvrette
> Pour payer le bateau!'
> 'Entrez, entrez, ma belle!
> Entrez, entrez toujours!
> Et vogue la nacelle
> Qui porte mes amours!"

And old L. would smoke and listen with an air of heavenly beatitude almost pathetic.

"Elle était bien gentille, Lisette—n'est-ce pas, petiot? —recommence!" (She was very nice, Lisette; wasn't she, sonny?—being again!)

"Now both get up and wash and go to breakfast. Come here, Josselin—you see this little silver dagger" (producing it from under his pillow). "It's rather pointy, but not at all dangerous. My mother gave it me when I was just your age—to cut books with; it's for you. Allons, file! [cut along] no thanks!—but look here—are you coming with us à la chasse to-day?"

"Non, M. Laferté."

"Pourquoi?—t'as pas peur, j'espère!"

"Sais pas. J' n'aime pas les choses mortes—ça saigne —et ça n' sent pas bon—ça m' fait mal au cœur." (Don't know. I'm not fond of dead things. They bleed— and they don't smell nice—it makes me sick.)

And two or three times a day would Barty receive some costly token of this queer old giant's affection, till he got quite unhappy about it. He feared he was despoiling the House of Laferté of all its treasures in silver and gold; but he soothed his troubled conscience later on by giving them all away to favorite boys and masters at Brossard's — especially M. Bonzig, who had taken charge of his white mouse (and her family, now quite grown up — children and grandchildren and all) when Mlle. Marceline went for her fortnight's holiday. Indeed, he had made a beautiful cage for them out of wood and wire, with little pasteboard mangers (which they nibbled away).

Well, the men of the party and young Laferté and I would go off with the dogs and keepers into the forest— and Barty would pick filberts and fruit with Jeanne and Marie, and eat them with bread-and-butter and jam and *cernaux* (unripe walnuts mixed with salt and water and verjuice — quite the nicest thing in the world). Then he would find his way into the heart of the forest, which he loved—and where he had scraped up a warm friendship with some charcoal-burners, whose huts were near an old yellow-watered pond, very brackish and stagnant and deep, and full of leeches and water-spiders. It was in the densest part of the forest, where the trees were so tall and leafy that the sun never fell on it, even at noon. The charcoal-burners told him that in '93 a young de la Tremblaye was taken there at sunset to be hanged on a giant oak-tree—but he talked so agreeably and was so pleasant all round that they relented, and sent for bread and wine and cider and made a night of it, and didn't hang him till dawn next day; after which they tied a stone to his ankles and dropped him into the pond, which was called "the pond of the respite" ever since; and his young wife, Claire Élisabeth, drowned herself there the week after, and their bones lie at the bottom to this very day.

And, ghastly to relate, the ringleader in this horrible tragedy was a beautiful young woman, a daughter of the people, it seems—one Séraphine Doucet, whom the young viscount had betrayed before marriage—le droit du seigneur!—and but for whom he would have been let off after that festive night. Ten or fifteen years later, smitten with incurable remorse, she hanged herself on the very branch of thé very tree where they had strung up her noble lover; and still walks round the pond at night, wringing her hands and wailing. It's a sad story —let us hope it isn't true.

Barty Josselin evidently had this pond in his mind when he wrote in "Âmes en peine":

> Sous la berge hantée
> L'eau morne croupit—
> Sous la sombre futaie
> Le renard glapit,
> Et le cerf-dix-cors brame, et les daims viennent boire à l'Étang du Répit.
> "Lâchez-moi, Loupgaroux!"

Que sinistre est la mare
Quand tombe la nuit ;
La chouette s'effare—
Le blaireau s'enfuit !
L'on y sent que les morts se réveillent—qu'une ombre sans nom vous poursuit.
" Lâchez-moi, Loup-garoux !"

Forêt ! forêt ! what a magic there is in that little French dissyllable ! Morne forêt ! Is it the lost "s," and the heavy "^" that makes up for it, which lend such a mysterious and gloomy fascination ?

Forest ! that sounds rather tame — almost cheerful ! If *we* want a forest dream we have to go so far back for it, and dream of Robin Hood and his merrie men ! and even then Epping forces itself into our dream—and even Chingford, where there was never a were - wolf within the memory of man. Give us at least the *virgin* forest, in some far Guyana or Brazil — or even the forest primeval—

". . . where the murmuring pines and the hemlocks,
Bearded with moss and in garments green, indistinct in the twilight,
Stand like druids of eld, with voices sad and prophetic,
Stand like harpers hoar "—

that we may dream of scalp - hunting Mingoes, and grizzly-bears, and moose, and buffalo, and the beloved Bas-de-cuir with that magic rifle of his, that so seldom missed its mark and never got out of repair.

" Prom'nons-nous dans les bois
Pendant que le loup n'y est pas. . . ."

That's the first song I ever heard. Céline used to sing it, my nurse—who was very lovely, though she had a cast in her eye and wore a black cap, and cotton in her ears, and was pitted with the smallpox. It was in Burgundy, which was rich in forests, with plenty of wolves in them, and wild-boars too—and that was only a hundred years ago, when that I was a little tiny boy. It's just an old nursery rhyme to lull children to sleep with, or set them dancing—pas aut' chose—but there's a deal of Old France in it!

There I go again — digressing as usual and quoting poetry and trying to be literary and all that! C'est plus fort que moi. . . .

One beautiful evening after dinner we went, the whole lot of us, fishing for crayfish in the meadows beyond the home farm.

As we set about waiting for the crayfish to assemble round the bits of dead frog that served for bait and were tied to the wire scales (which were left in the water), a procession of cows came past us from the farm. One of them had a wound in her flank—a large tumor.

"It's the bull who did that," said Marie. "Il est très méchant!"

Presently the bull appeared, following the herd in sulky dignity. We all got up and crossed the stream on a narrow plank—all but Josselin, who remained sitting on a camp-stool.

"Josselin! Josselin! venez donc! il est très mauvais, le taureau!"

Barty didn't move.

The bull came by; and suddenly, seeing him, walked straight to within a yard of him—and stared at him for five minutes at least, lashing its tail. Barty didn't stir. Our hearts were in our mouths!

Then the big brindled brute turned quietly round with a friendly snort and went after the cows—and Barty got up and made it a courtly farewell salute, saying, " Bon voyage—au plaisir !"

After which he joined the rest of us across the stream, and came in for a good scolding and much passionate admiration from the ladies, and huggings and tears of relief from Madame Laferté.

" I knew well he wouldn't be afraid !" said M. Laferté ; " they are all like that, those English—le sang-froid du diable ! nom d'un Vellington ! It is we who were afraid —we are not so brave as the little Josselin ! plucky little Josselin ! But why did you not come with us ? Temerity is not valor, Josselin !"

" Because I wanted to show off [*faire le fanfaron*] !" said Barty, with extreme simplicity.

" Ah, diable ! Anyhow, it was brave of you to sit still when he came and looked at you in the white of the eyes ! it was just the right thing to do ; ces Anglais ! je n'en reviens pas ! à quatorze ans ! hein, ma femme ?"

" Pardi !" said Barty, " I was in such a blue funk [j'avais une venette si bleue] that I couldn't have moved a finger to save my life !"

At this, old Polyphemus went into a Homeric peal of laughter.

" Ces Anglais ! what originals—they tell you the real truth at any cost [ils vous disent la vraie vérité, coûte que coûte] !" and his affection for Barty seemed to increase, if possible, from that evening.

Now this was Barty all over — all through life. He always gave himself away with a liberality quite uncalled for—so he ought to have some allowances made for that reckless and impulsive indiscretion which caused him to be so popular in general society, but got him into so many awkward scrapes in after-life, and made him such

FANFARONNADE

mean enemies, and gave his friends so much anxiety and distress.

(And here I think it right to apologize for so much translating of such a well-known language as French ; I feel quite like another Ollendorf—who must have been a German, by-the-way—but M. Laferté's grammar and accent would sometimes have puzzled Ollendorf himself !)

. . . . . .

Towards the close of September, M. Laferté took it into his head to make a tour of provincial visits *en famille*. He had never done such a thing before, and I really believe it was all to show off Barty to his friends and relations.

It was the happiest time I ever had, and shines out by itself in that already so unforgettably delightful vacation.

We went in a large charabancs drawn by two stout horses, starting at six in the morning, and driving right through the Forest of la Tremblaye ; and just ahead of us, to show us the way, M. Laferté driving himself in an old cabriolet, with Josselin (from whom he refused to be parted) by his side, singing or talking, according to order, or cracking jokes ; we could hear the big laugh of Polyphemus !

We travelled very leisurely ; I forget whether we ever changed horses or not—but we got over a good deal of ground. We put up at the country houses of friends and relations of the Lafertés ; and visited old historical castles and mediæval ruins—Châteaudun and others—and fished in beautiful pellucid tributaries of the Loire—shot over " des chiens anglais "—danced half the night with charming people—wandered in lovely parks and woods, and beautiful old formal gardens with fishponds, terraces, statues, marble fountains; charmilles, pelouses, quinconces; and all the flowers and all the fruits of France! And the sun shone every day and all day long—and in one's dreams all night.

And the peasants in that happy country of the Loire spoke the most beautiful French, and had the most beautiful manners in the world. They're famous for it.

It all seems like a fairy tale.

If being made much of, and petted and patted and admired and wondered at, make up the sum of human bliss, Barty came in for as full a share of felicity during that festive week as should last an ordinary mortal for a twelvemonth. *Figaro quà, Figaro là,* from morning till night in three departments of France!

But he didn't seem to care very much about it all; he would have been far happier singing and tumbling and romancing away to his charbonniers by the pond in the Forest of la Tremblaye. He declared he was never quite himself unless he could feel the north for at least an hour or two every day, and all night long in his sleep —and that he should never feel the north again—that it was gone forever; that he had drunk it all away at that fatal breakfast — and it made him lonely to wake up in the middle of the night and not know which way he lay! "dépaysé," as he called it—"désorienté—perdu!"

And laughing, he would add, "Ayez pitié d'un pauvre orphelin!"

.   .   .   .   .   .

Then back to Le Gué des Aulnes. And one evening, after a good supper at Grandmaman Laferté's, the diligence de Paris came jingling and rumbling through the main street of La Tremblaye, flashing right and left its two big lamps, red and blue. And we three boys, after the most grateful and affectionate farewells, packed ourselves into the coupé, which had been retained for us, and rumbled back to Paris through the night.

There was quite a crowd to see us off. Not only Lafertés, but others—all sorts and conditions of men, women, and children—and among them three or four of Barty's charcoal-burning friends; one of whom, an old man with magnificent black eyes and an immense beard, that would have been white if he hadn't been a charcoal-burner, kissed Barty on both cheeks, and gave him a huge bag full of some kind of forest berry that is good to eat; also a young cuckoo (which Barty restored to liberty an hour later); also a dormouse and a large green lizard; also, in a little pasteboard box, a gigantic pale green caterpillar four inches long and thicker than your thumb, with a row of shiny blue stars in relief all along each side of its back—the most beautiful thing of the kind you ever saw.

"Pioche bien ta géométrie, mon bon petit Josselin ! c'est la plus belle science au monde, crois-moi !" said M. Laferté to Barty, and gave him the hug of a grizzly-bear; and to me he gave a terrific hand-squeeze, and a beautiful double-barrelled gun by Lefaucheux, for which I felt too supremely grateful to find suitable thanks. I have it now, but I have long given up killing things with it.

I had grown immensely fond of this colossal old "bourru bienfaisant," as he was called in La Tremblaye, and believe that all his moroseness and brutality were put on, to hide one of the warmest, simplest, and tenderest hearts in the world.

Before dawn Barty woke up with such a start that he woke me :

"Enfin ! ça y est ! quelle chance !" he exclaimed.

"Quoi, quoi, quoi?" said I, quacking like a duck.

"Le nord—c'est revenu—it's just ahead of us—a little to the left!"

We were nearing Paris.

And thus ended the proudest and happiest time I ever had in my life. Indeed I almost had an adventure on my own account—*une bonne fortune,* as it was called at Brossard's by boys hardly older than myself. I did not brag of it, however, when I got back to school.

It was at "Les Laiteries," or "Les Poteries," or "Les Crucheries," or some such place, the charming abode of Monsieur et Madame Pélisson — only their name wasn't Pélisson, or anything like it. At dinner I sat next to a Miss ——, who was very tall and wore blond side ringlets. I think she must have been the English governess.

We talked very much together, in English; and after dinner we walked in the garden together by starlight arm in arm, and she was so kind and genial to me in English that I felt quite chivalrous and romantic, and ready to do doughty deeds for her sake.

Then, at M. Pélisson's request, all the company assembled in a group for evening prayer, under a spreading chestnut-tree on the lawn : the prayer sounded very much like the morning or evening prayer at Brossard's, except that the Almighty was addressed as "toi" instead of "vous"; it began :

"Notre Père qui es aux cieux—toi dont le regard scrutateur pénètre jusque dans les replis les plus profonds de nos cœurs"—and ended, "Ainsi soit-il!"

The night was very dark, and I stood close to Miss ——, who stood as it seemed with her hands somewhere behind her back. I was so grateful to her for having talked to me so nicely, and so fond of her for being English, that the impulse seized me to steal my hand into hers — and her hand met mine with a gentle squeeze which I returned ; but soon the pressure of her hand increased, and by the time M. le Curé had got to "au nom du Père" the pressure of her hand had become an agony —a thing to make one shriek !

"Ainsi soit-il!" said M. le Curé, and the little group broke up, and Miss —— walked quietly indoors with her arm around Madame Pélisson's waist, and without even wishing me good-night—and my hand was being squeezed worse than ever.

"Ah ha ! Lequel de nous deux est volé, petit coquin ?" hissed an angry male voice in my ear—(which of us two is sold, you little rascal ?).

And I found my hand in that of Monsieur Pélisson, whose name was something else—and I couldn't make it out, nor why he was so angry. It has dawned upon me since that each of us took the other's hand by mistake for that of the English governess !

All this is beastly and cynical and French, and I apologize for it—but it's true.

October !

It was a black Monday for me when school began again after that ideal vacation. The skies they were ashen and sober and the leaves they were crisped and sere. But anyhow I was still *en quatrième,* and Barty was in it too—and we sat next to each other in "L'étude des grands."

There was only one étude now ; only half the boys came back, and the pavillon des petits was shut up, study, class-rooms, dormitories, and all—except that two masters slept there still.

Eight or ten small boys were put in a small school-

MÉROVÉE RINGS THE BELL

room in the same house as ours, and had a small dormitory to themselves, with M. Bonzig to superintend them.

I made up my mind that I would no longer be a *cancre* and a *crétin,* but work hard and do my little best, so that I might keep up with Barty and pass into the *troisième* with him, and then into *Rhétorique* (seconde), and then into *Philosophie* (première)—that we might do our humanities and take our degree together—our " *Bachot,*" which is short for *Baccalauréat-ès-lettres.* Most especially did I love Monsieur Durosier's class of French Literature—for which Mérovée always rang the bell himself.

My mother and sister were still at Ste.-Adresse, Hâvre, with my father ; so I spent my first Sunday that term at the Archibald Rohans', in the Rue du Bac.

I had often seen them at Brossard's, when they came to see Barty, but had never been at their house before.

They were very charming people.

Lord Archibald was dressing when we got there that Sunday morning, and we sat with him while he shaved —in an immense dressing-room where there were half a dozen towel-horses with about thirty pairs of newly ironed trousers on them instead of towels, and quite thirty pairs of shiny boots on trees were ranged along the wall. James, an impeccable English valet, waited on " his lordship," and never spoke unless spoken to.

" Hullo, Barty ! Who's your friend ?"

" Bob Maurice, Uncle Archie."

And Uncle Archie shook hands with me most cordially.

"And how's the north pole this morning ?"

" Nicely, thanks, Uncle Archie."

Lord Archibald was a very tall and handsome man,

about fifty—very droll and full of anecdote ; he had stories to tell about everything in the room.

For instance, how Major Welsh of the 10th Hussars had given him that pair of Wellingtons, which fitted him better than any boots Hoby ever made him to measure ; they were too tight for poor Welsh, who was a head shorter than himself.

How Kerlewis made him that frock-coat fifteen years ago, and it wasn't threadbare yet, and fitted him as well as ever—for he hadn't changed his weight for thirty years, etc.

How that pair of braces had been made by "my lady" out of a pair of garters she wore on the day they were married.

And then he told us how to keep trousers from bagging at the knees, and how cloth coats should be ironed, and how often—and how to fold an umbrella.

It suddenly occurs to me that perhaps these little anecdotes may not be so amusing to the general reader as they were to me when he told them, so I won't tell any more. Indeed, I have often noticed that things look sometimes rather dull in print that were so surprisingly witty when said in spontaneous talk a great many years ago !

Then we went to breakfast with my lady and Daphne, their charming little daughter — Barty's sister, as he called her—" m'amour "—and who spoke both French and English equally well.

But we didn't breakfast at once, ravenous as we boys were, for Lady Archibald took a sudden dislike to Lord A.'s cravat, which, it seems, he had never worn before. It was in brown satin, and Lady A. declared that Loulou (so she called him) never looked *" en beauté "* with a brown cravat ; and there was quite a little quarrel between husband and wife on the subject—so that he had to go back to his dressing-room and put on a blue one.

At breakfast he talked about French soldiers of the line, and their marching kit (as it would be called now), quite earnestly, and, as it seemed to me, very sensibly—though he went through little mimicries that made his wife scream with laughter, and me too ; and in the middle of breakfast Barty sang "Le Chant du Départ" as well as he could for laughing :

"La victoire en chantant nous ouvre la carrière !
La liberté-é gui-i-de nos pas" . . .

while Lord A. went through an expressive pantomime of an overladen foot-soldier up and down the room, in time to the music. The only person who didn't laugh was James—which I thought ungenial.

Then Lady A. had *her* innings, and sang "Rule Britannia, Britannia rule de vaves"—and declared it was far more ridiculous really than the "Chant du Départ," and she made it seem so, for she went through a pantomime too. She was a most delightful person, and spoke English quite well when she chose ; and seemed as fond of Barty as if he were her own and only son—and so did Lord Archibald. She would say :

"Quel dommage qu'on ne peut pas avoir des crompettes [crumpets]! Barty les aime tant ! n'est-ce pas, mon chou, tu aimes bien les crompettes ? voici venir du buttered toast—c'est toujours ça !"

And, "Mon Dieu, comme il a bonne mine, ce cher Barty —n'est-ce pas, mon amour, que tu as bonne mine ? regarde-toi dans la glace."

And, "Si nous allions à l'Hippodrôme cette après-midi voir la belle écuyère Madame Richard ? Barty adore les jolies femmes, comme son oncle ! n'est-ce pas, méchant

petit Barty, que tu adores les jolies femmes ? et tu n'as
jamais vu Madame Richard ? Tu m'en diras des nou-
velles ! et vous, mon ami [this to me], est-ce que vous
adorez aussi les jolies femmes ?"

"Ô oui," says Daphne, "allons voir M'ame Richard ;
it 'll be *such* fun ! oh, bully !"

So after breakfast we went for a walk, and to a café
on the Quai d'Orsay, and then to the Hippodrôme, and
saw the beautiful écuyère in graceful feats of la haute
école, and lost our hearts — especially Lord Archibald,
though him she knew; for she kissed her hand to him,
and he his to her.

Then we dined at the Palais Royal, and afterwards
went to the Café des Aveugles, an underground coffee-
house near the Café de la Rotonde, and where blind men
made instrumental music ; and we had a capital evening.

I have met in my time more intellectual people, perhaps, than the Archibald Rohans—but never people more
amiable, or with kinder, simpler manners, or who made
one feel more quickly and thoroughly at home—and the
more I got to know them, the more I grew to like them ;
and their fondness for each other and Daphne, and for
Barty too, was quite touching ; as was his for them. So
the winter sped happily till February, when a sad thing
happened.

I had spent Sunday with my mother and sister, who
now lived on the ground-floor of 108 Champs Élysées.

I slept there that Sunday night, and walked back to
school next morning. To my surprise, as I got to a
large field through which a diagonal footpath led to
Père Jaurion's loge, I saw five or six boys sitting on the
terrace parapet with their legs dangling outside. They
should have been in class, by rights. They watched me
cross the field, but made no sign.

"What on earth *can* be the matter?" thought I.

The cordon was pulled, and I came on a group of boys all stiff and silent.

"Qu'est-ce que vous avez donc, tous?" I asked.

"Le Père Brossard est mort!" said De Villars.

Poor M. Brossard had died of apoplexy on the previous afternoon. He had run to catch the Passy omnibus directly after lunch, and had fallen down in a fit and died immediately.

"Il est tombé du haut mal"—as they expressed it.

His son Mérovée and his daughter Madame Germain were distracted. The whole of that day was spent by the boys in a strange, unnatural state of *désœuvrement* and suppressed excitement for which no outlet was possible. The meals, especially, were all but unbearable. One was ashamed of having an appetite, and yet one had —almost keener than usual, if I may judge by myself— and for some undiscovered reason the food was better than on other Mondays!

Next morning we all went up in sorrowful procession to kiss our poor dear head-master's cold forehead as he lay dead in his bed, with sprigs of boxwood on his pillow, and above his head a jar of holy water with which we sprinkled him. He looked very serene and majestic, but it was a harrowing ceremony. Mérovée stood by with swollen eyes and deathly pale—incarnate grief.

On Wednesday afternoon M. Brossard was buried in the Cimetière de Passy, a tremendous crowd following the hearse; the boys and masters just behind Mérovée and M. Germain, the chief male mourners. The women walked in another separate procession behind.

Béranger and Alphonse Karr were present among the notabilities, and speeches were made over his open grave, for he was a very distinguished man.

And, tragical to relate, that evening in the study
Barty and I fell out, and it led to a stand-up fight next
day.

There was no preparation that evening; he and I sat
side by side reading out of a book by Châteaubriand—
either *Atala,* or *René* or *Les Natchez,* I forget which.   I
have never seen either since.

The study was hushed; M. Dumollard was *de service*
as *maître d'études,* although there was no attempt to do
anything but sadly read improving books.

If I remember aright, René, a very sentimental young
Frenchman, who had loved the wrong person not wisely,
but too well (a very wrong person indeed, in his case),
emigrated to North America, and there he met a beautiful Indian maiden, one Atala, of the Natchez tribe, who
had rosy heels and was charming, and whose entire skin
was probably a warm dark red, although this is not insisted upon.   She also had a brother, whose name was
Outogamiz.

Well, René loved Atala, Atala loved René, and they
were married; and Outogamiz went through some ceremony besides, which made him blood brother and bosom
friend to René—a bond which involved certain obligatory
rites and duties and self-sacrifices.

Atala died and was buried.   René died and was buried
also; and every day, as in duty bound, poor Outogamiz
went and pricked a vein and bled over René's tomb, till
he died himself of exhaustion before he was many weeks
older.   I quote entirely from memory.

This simple story was told in very touching and beautiful language, by no means telegraphese, and Barty and I
were deeply affected by it.

"I say, Bob!" Barty whispered to me, with a break in
his voice, "some day I'll marry your sister, and we'll all

go off to America together, and she'll die, and *I*'ll die, and you shall bleed yourself to death on my tomb !"

"No," said I, after a moment's thought. "No—look here ! *I*'ll marry *your* sister, and *I*'ll die, and *you* shall bleed over *my* tomb !"

Then, after a pause :

"I haven't got a sister, as you know quite well—and if I had she wouldn't be for *you !*" says Barty.

"Why not ?"

"Because you're not good-looking enough !" says Barty.

At this, just for fun, I gave him a nudge in the wind with my elbow—and he gave me a "twisted pinch" on the arm—and I kicked him on the ankle, but so much harder than I intended that it hurt him, and he gave me a tremendous box on the ear, and we set to fighting like a couple of wild-cats, without even getting up, to the scandal of the whole study and the indignant disgust of M. Dumollard, who separated us, and read us a pretty lecture :

"Voilà bien les Anglais !—rien n'est sacré pour eux, pas même la mort ! rien que les chiens et les chevaux." (Nothing, not even death, is sacred to Englishmen— nothing but dogs and horses.)

When we went up to bed the head-boy of the school— a first-rate boy called d'Orthez, and Berquin (another first-rate boy), who had each a bedroom to himself, came into the dormitory and took up the quarrel, and discussed what should be done. Both of us were English—ergo, both of us ought to box away the insult with our fists ; so "they set a combat us between, to fecht it in the dawing"—that is, just after breakfast, in the school-room.

I went to bed very unhappy, and so, I think, did Barty.

Next morning at six, just after the morning prayer,

M. Mérovée came into the school-room and made us a most straightforward, manly, and affecting speech ; in which he told us he meant to keep on the school, and thanked us, boys and masters, for our sympathy.

We were all moved to our very depths—and sat at our work solemn and sorrowful all through that lamp-lit hour and a half ; we hardly dared to cough, and never looked up from our desks.

Then 7.30—ding-dang-dong and breakfast. Thursday —bread-and-butter morning !

I felt hungry and greedy and very sad, and disinclined to fight. Barty and I had sat turned away from each other, and made no attempt at reconciliation.

We all went to the réfectoire : it was raining fast. I made my ball of salt and butter, and put it in a hole in my hunk of bread, and ran back to the study, where I locked these treasures in my desk.

The study soon filled with boys : no masters ever came there during that half-hour ; they generally smoked and read their newspapers in the gymnastic ground, or else in their own rooms when it was wet outside.

D'Orthez and Berquin moved one or two desks and forms out of the way so as make a ring—l'arène, as they called it—with comfortable seats all round. Small boys stood on forms and window-sills eating their bread-and-butter with a tremendous relish.

"Dites donc, vous autres," says Bonneville, the wit of the school, who was in very high spirits ; "it's like the Roman Empire during the decadence — *'panem et circenses !'* "

"What's that, *circenses ?* what does it mean ?" says Rapaud, with his mouth full.

"Why, *butter*, you idiot ! Didn't you know *that ?*" says Bonneville.

Barty and I stood opposite each other; at his sides as seconds were d'Orthez and Berquin ; at mine, Jolivet trois (the only Jolivet now left in the school) and big du Tertre-Jouan (the young marquis who wasn't Bonneville).

We began to spar at each other in as knowing and English a way as we knew how—keeping a very respectful distance indeed, and trying to bear ourselves as scientifically as we could, with a keen expression of the eye.

When I looked into Barty's face I felt that nothing on earth would ever make me hit such a face as that—whatever he might do to mine. My blood wasn't up ; besides, I was a coarse-grained, thick-set, bullet-headed little chap with no nerves to speak of, and didn't mind punishment the least bit. No more did Barty, for that matter, though he was the most highly wrought creature that ever lived.

At length they all got impatient, and d'Orthez said :

" Allez donc, godems — ce n'est pas un quadrille ! Nous n'sommes pas à La Salle Valentino !"

And Barty was pushed from behind so roughly that he came at me, all his science to the winds and slogging like a French boy ; and I, quite without meaning to, in the hurry, hit out just as he fell over me, and we both rolled together over Jolivet's foot—Barty on top (he was taller, though not heavier, than I); and I saw the blood flow from his nose down his lip and chin, and some of it fell on my blouse.

Says Barty to me, in English, as we lay struggling on the dusty floor :

" Look here, it's no good. I *can't* fight to-day ; poor Mérovée, you know. Let's make it up !"

" All right !" says I. So up we got and shook hands, Barty saying, with mock dignity :

"Messieurs, le sang a coulé ; l'honneur britannique est sauf ;" and the combat was over.

"Cristi ! J'ai joliment faim !" says Barty, mopping his nose with his handkerchief. "I left my crust on the bench outside the réfectoire. I wish one of you fellows would get it for me."

"Rapaud finished your crust [ta miche] while you were fighting," says Jolivet. "I saw him."

Says Rapaud : "Ah, Dame, it was getting prettily wet, your crust, and I was prettily hungry too ; and I thought you didn't want it, naturally."

I then produced *my* crust and cut it in two, butter and all, and gave Barty half, and we sat very happily side by side, and breakfasted together in peace and amity. I never felt happier or hungrier.

"Cristi, comme ils se sont bien battus," says little Vaissière to little Cormenu. "As-tu vu ? Josselin a saigné tout plein sur la blouse à Maurice." (How well they fought ! Josselin bled all over Maurice's blouse !)

Then says Josselin, in French, turning to me with that delightful jolly smile that always reminded one of the sun breaking through a mist :

"I would sooner bleed on your blouse than on your tomb." (J'aime mieux saigner sur ta blouse que sur ta tombe.)

So ended the only quarrel we ever had.

Part Third

"Que ne puis-je aller où s'en vont les roses,
Et n'attendre pas
Ces regrets navrants que la fin des choses
Nous garde ici-bas!"—ANON.

BARTY worked very hard, and so did I—for *me!* Horace — Homer — Æschylus — Plato — etc., etc., etc., etc., etc., and all there was to learn in that French schoolboy's encyclopædia—"Le Manuel du Baccalauréat"; a very thick book in very small print. And I came to the conclusion that it is good to work hard : it makes one enjoy food and play and sleep so keenly—and Thursday afternoons.

The school was all the pleasanter for having fewer boys ; we got more intimate with each other, and with the masters too. During the winter M. Bonzig told us capital stories—*Modeste Mignon,* by Balzac—*Le Chevalier de Maison-rouge,* by A. Dumas père—etc., etc..

In the summer the Passy swimming-bath was more delightful than ever. Both winter and summer we passionately fenced with a pupil (un prévôt) of the famous M. Bonnet, and did gymnastics with M. Louis, the gymnastic master of the Collège Charlemagne — the finest man I ever saw—a gigantic dwarf six feet high, all made up of lumps of sinew and muscles, like . . . . .

Also, we were taught equitation at the riding-school in the Rue Duphot.

On Saturday nights Barty would draw a lovely female

profile, with a beautiful big black eye, in pen and ink, and carefully shade it; especially the hair, which was always as the raven's wing! And on Sunday morning he and I used to walk together to 108 Champs Élysées and enter the rez-de-chaussée (where my mother and sister lived) by the window, before my mother was up. Then Barty took out his lovely female pen-and-ink profile to gaze at, and rolled himself a cigarette and lit it, and lay back on the sofa, and made my sister play her lightest music—"La pluie de Perles," by Osborne—and "Indiana," a beautiful valse by Marcailhou—and thus combine three or four perfect blisses in one happy quart d'heure.

Then my mother would appear, and we would have breakfast—after which Barty and I would depart by the window as we had come, and go and do our bit of Boulevard and Palais Royal. Then to the Rue du Bac for another breakfast with the Rohans; and then, *"au petit bonheur"*; that is, trusting to Providence for whatever turned up. The programme didn't vary very much : either I dined with him at the Rohans', or he with me at 108. Then, back to Brossard's at ten—tired and happy.

One Sunday I remember well we stayed in school, for old Josselin the fisherman came to see us there—Barty's grandfather, now a widower ; and M. Mérovée asked him to lunch with us, and go to the baths in the afternoon.

Imagine old Bonzig's delight in this *"vieux loup de mer,"* as he called him ! That was a happy day for the old fisherman also ; I shall never forget his surprise at M. Dumollard's telescope—and how clever he was on the subject.

He came to the baths, and admired and criticised the good swimming of the boys — especially Barty's, which was really remarkable. I don't believe he could swim a stroke himself.

Then we went and dined together at Lord Archibald's, in the Rue du Bac—"Mon Colonel," as the old fisherman always called him. He was a very humorous and intelligent person, this fisher, though nearer eighty than seventy ; very big, and of a singularly picturesque appearance—for he had not *endimanché* himself in the least ; and very clean. A splendid old man ; oddly enough, somewhat Semitic of aspect—as though he had just come from a miraculous draught of fishes in the Sea of Galilee, out of a cartoon by Raphael !

I recollect admiring how easily and pleasantly everything went during dinner, and all through the perfection of this ancient sea-toiler's breeding in all essentials.

Of course the poor all over the world are less nice in their habits than the rich, and less correct in their grammar and accent, and narrower in their views of life ; but in every other respect there seemed little to choose between Josselins and Rohans and Lonlay-Savignacs ; and indeed, according to Lord Archibald, the best manners were to be found at these two opposite poles—or even wider still. He would have it that Royalty and chimney-sweeps were the best - bred people all over the world—because there was no possible mistake about their social status.

I felt a little indignant—after all, Lady Archibald was built out of chocolate, for all her Lonlay and her Savignac ! just as I was built out of Beaune and Chambertin.

I'm afraid I shall be looked upon as a snob and a traitor to my class if I say that I have at last come to be of the same opinion myself. That is, if absolute simplicity, and the absence of all possible temptation to try and seem an inch higher up than we really are— . But there ! this is a very delicate question, about which I don't care a straw ; and there are such exceptions, and so many, to confirm any such rule !

Anyhow, I saw how Barty *couldn't help* having the manners we all so loved him for. After dinner Lady Archibald showed old Josselin some of Barty's lovely female profiles—a sight that affected him strangely. He would have it that they were all exact portraits of his beloved Antoinette, Barty's mother.

They were certainly singularly like each other, these little chefs-d'œuvre of Barty's, and singularly handsome —an ideal type of his own ; and the old grandfather was allowed his choice, and touchingly grateful at being presented with such treasures.

The scene made a great impression on me.

So spent itself that year—a happy year that had no history — except for one little incident that I will tell because it concerns Barty, and illustrates him.

One beautiful Sunday morning the yellow omnibus was waiting for some of us as we dawdled about in the school-room, titivating ; the masters nowhere, as usual on a Sunday morning; and some of the boys began to sing in chorus a not very edifying *chanson,* which they did not " Bowdlerize," about a holy Capuchin friar ; it began (if I remember rightly):

> " C'était un Capucin, oui bien, un père Capucin,
>   Qui confessait trois filles—
>   Itou, itou, itou, là là là !
>   Qui confessait trois filles
>   Au fond de son jardin—
>   Oui bien—
>   Au fond de son jardin !
>   Il dit à la plus jeune—

Itou, itou, itou, là là là !
Il dit à la plus jeune
. . 'Vous reviendrez demain !'"
Etc, etc., etc.

I have quite forgotten the rest.

Now this little song, which begins so innocently, like a sweet old idyl of mediæval France—*"un écho du temps passé"*—seems to have been a somewhat Rabelaisian ditty; by no means proper singing for a Sunday morning in a boys' school. But boys will be boys, even in France; and the famous "esprit Gaulois" was somewhat precocious in the forties, I suppose. Perhaps it is now, if it still exists (which I doubt—the dirt remains, but all the fun seems to have evaporated).

Suddenly M. Dumollard bursts into the room in his violent sneaky way, pale with rage, and says :

"Je vais gifler tous ceux qui ont chanté" (I'll box the ears of every boy who sang).

So he puts all in a row and begins :

"Rubinel, sur votre parole d'honneur, avez - vous chanté ?"

"Non, m'sieur !"

"Caillard, avez-vous chanté ?"

"Non, m'sieur !"

"Lipmann, avez-vous chanté ?"

"Non, m'sieur !"

"Maurice, avez-vous chanté ?"

"Non, m'sieur" (which, for a wonder, was true, for I happened not to know either the words or the tune).

"Josselin, avez-vous chanté ?"

"Oui, m'sieur !"

And down went Barty his full length on the floor, from a tremendous open-handed box on the ear. Dumol-

lard was a very Herculean person—though by no means
gigantic.

Barty got up and made Dumollard a polite little bow,
and walked out of the room.

"Vous êtes tous consignés !" says M. Dumollard—and
the omnibus went away empty, and we spent all that
Sunday morning as best we might.

In the afternoon we went out walking in the Bois.
Dumollard had recovered his serenity and came with us ;
for he was *de service* that day.

Says Lipmann to him :

"Josselin drapes himself in his English dignity—he
sulks like Achilles and walks by himself."

"Josselin is at least a *man*," says Dumollard. "He
tells the truth, and doesn't know fear—and I'm sorry
he's English !"

And later, at the Mare d'Auteuil, he put out his hand
to Barty and said :

"Let's make it up, Josselin—au moins vous avez du
cœur, vous. Promettez-moi que vous ne chanterez plus
cette sale histoire de Capucin !"

Josselin took the usher's hand, and smiled his open,
toothy smile, and said :

"Pas le dimanche matin toujours—quand c'est vous
qui serez de service, M. Dumollard !" (Anyhow not Sunday morning when *you're* on duty, Mr. D.)

And Mr. D. left off running down the English in pub-
lic after that—except to say that they *couldn't* be simple
and natural if they tried ; and that they affected a ridic-
ulous accent when they spoke French—not Josselin and
Maurice, but all the others he had ever met. As if plain
French, which had been good enough for William the
Conqueror, wasn't good enough for the subjects of her
Britannic Majesty to-day !

The only event of any importance in Barty's life that year was his first communion, which he took with several others of about his own age. An event that did not seem to make much impression on him—nothing seemed to make much impression on Barty Josselin when he was very young. He was just a lively, irresponsible, irrepressible human animal — always in perfect health and exuberant spirits, with an immense appetite for food and fun and frolic ; like a squirrel, a collie pup, or a kitten.

Père Bonamy, the priest who confirmed him, was fonder of the boy than of any one, boy or girl, that he had ever prepared for communion, and could hardly speak of him with decent gravity, on account of his extraordinary confessions—all of which were concocted in the depths of Barty's imagination for the sole purpose of making the kind old curé laugh ; and the kind old curé was just as fond of laughing as was Barty of playing the fool, in and out of season. I wonder if he always thought himself bound to respect the secrets of the confessional in Barty's case !

And Barty would sing to him—even in the confessional :

> "Stabat mater dolorosa
> Juxta crucem lachrymosa
> Dum pendebat filius " . . .

in a voice so sweet and innocent and pathetic that it would almost bring the tears to the good old curé's eyelash.

"Ah ! ma chère Mamzelle Marceline !" he would say— "au moins s'ils étaient tous comme ce petit Josselin ! çà irait comme sur des roulettes ! Il est innocent comme un jeune veau, ce mioche anglais ! Il a le bon Dieu dans le cœur !"

"Et une boussole dans l'estomac !" said Mlle. Marceline.

I don't think he was quite so *innocent* as all that, perhaps—but no young beast of the field was ever more *harmless*.

That year the examinations were good all round ; even *I* did not disgrace myself, and Barty was brilliant. But there were no delightful holidays for me to record. Barty went to Yorkshire, and I remained in Paris with my mother.

There is only one thing more worth mentioning that year.

My father had inherited from *his* father a system of shorthand, which he called *Blaze*—I don't know why ! *His* father had learnt it of a Dutch Jew.

It is, I think, the best kind of cipher ever invented (I have taken interest in these things and studied them). It is very difficult to learn, but I learnt it as a child— and it was of immense use to me at lectures we used to attend at the Sorbonne and Collège de France.

Barty was very anxious to know it, and after some trouble I obtained my father's permission to impart this calligraphic crypt to Barty, on condition he should swear on his honor never to reveal it : and this he did.

With his extraordinary quickness and the perseverance he always had when he wished a thing very much, he made himself a complete master of this occult science before he left school, two or three years later : it took *me* seven years—beginning when I was four ! It does equally well for French or English, and it played an important part in Barty's career. My sister knew it, but imperfectly ; my mother not at all—for all she tried so hard and was so persevering ; it must be learnt young. As far as I am aware, no one else knows it in England or

France—or even the world—although it is such a useful invention ; quite a marvel of simple ingenuity when one has mastered the symbols, which certainly take a long time and a deal of hard work.

Barty and I got to talk it on our fingers as rapidly as ordinary speech and with the slightest possible gestures : this was *his* improvement.

Barty came back from his holidays full of Whitby, and its sailors and whalers, and fishermen and cobles and cliffs—all of which had evidently had an immense attraction for him. He was always fond of that class ; possibly also some vague atavistic sympathy for the toilers of the sea lay dormant in his blood like an inherited memory.

And he brought back many tokens of these good people's regard—two formidable clasp-knives (for each of which he had to pay the giver one farthing in current coin of the realm); spirit-flasks, leather bottles, jet ornaments ; woollen jerseys and comforters knitted for him by their wives and daughters ; fossil ammonites and coprolites ; a couple of young sea-gulls to add to his menagerie ; and many old English marine ditties, which he had to sing to M. Bonzig with his now cracked voice, and then translate into French. Indeed, Bonzig and Barty became inseparable companions during the Thursday promenade, on the strength of their common interest in ships and the sea ; and Barty never wearied of describing the place he loved, nor Bonzig of listening and commenting.

" Ah ! mon cher ! ce que je donnerais, moi, pour voir le retour d'un baleinier à Ouittebé ! Quelle ' marine' ça ferait ! hein ? avec la grande falaise, et la bonne petite église en haut, près de la Vieille Abbaye—et les toits rouges qui fument, et les trois jetées en pierre, et le vieux pont-levis—et toute cette grouille de mariniers avec leurs femmes et leurs enfants—et ces braves filles qui attendent le retour du bien-aimé ! nom d'un nom ! dire que vous avez vu tout ça, vous—qui n'avez pas encore seize ans . . . quelle chance ! . . . dites—qu'est-ce que ça veut bien dire, ce

'Ouïle mé sekile rô !'

Chantez-moi ça encore une fois !"

And Barty, whose voice was breaking, would raucously sing him the good old ditty for the sixth time :

> "Weel may the keel row, the keel row, the keel row,
> Weel may the keel row
> That brings my laddie home !"

which he would find rather difficult to render literally into colloquial seafaring French !

He translated it thus :

> "Vogue la carène,
> Vogue la carène
> Qui me ramène
> Mon bien aimé !"

"Ah ! vous verrez," says Bonzig—"vous verrez, aux prochaines vacances de Pâques—je ferai un si joli tableau de tout ça ! avec la brume du soir qui tombe, vous savez —et le soleil qui disparait—et la marée qui monte et la lune qui se lève à l'horizon ! et les mouettes et les goëlands—et les bruyères lointaines — et le vieux manoir seigneurial de votre grand-père . . . c'est bien ça, n'est-ce pas ?"

"Oui, oui, M'sieur Bonzig—vous y êtes, en plein !"

And the good usher in his excitement would light himself a cigarette of caporal, and inhale the smoke as

if it were a sea-breeze, and exhale it like a regular sou'-
wester ! and sing :

" Ouïle—mé—sekile rô,
Tat brinn my laddé ôme !"

Barty also brought back with him the complete poetical works of Byron and Thomas Moore, the gift of his
noble grandfather, who adored these two bards to the
exclusion of all other bards that ever wrote in English.
And during that year we both got to know them, possibly as well as Lord Whitby himself. Especially " Don
Juan," in which we grew to be as word-perfect as in
Polyeucte, Le Misanthrope, Athalie, Philoctète, Le Lutrin,
the first six books of the Æneid and the Iliad, the *Ars
Poetica,* and the *Art Poétique* (Boileau).

Every line of these has gone out of my head—long
ago, alas ! But I could still stand a pretty severe examination in the now all-but-forgotten English epic—from
Dan to Beersheba—I mean from " I want a hero " to
" The phantom of her frolic grace, Fitz-Fulke !"

Barty, however, remembered everything — what he
ought to, and what he ought not ! He had the most
astounding memory : wax to receive and marble to retain ; also a wonderful facility for writing verse, mostly
comic, both in English and French. Greek and Latin
verse were not taught us at Brossard's, for good French
reasons, into which I will not enter now.

We also grew very fond of Lamartine and Victor Hugo,
quite openly—and of De Musset under the rose.

" C'était dans la nuit brune
Sur le clocher jauni,
La lune,
Comme un point sur son i !"

(not for the young person).

"WEEL MAY THE KEEL ROW"

I have a vague but pleasant impression of that year. Its weathers, its changing seasons, its severe frosts, with Sunday skatings on the dangerous canals, St.-Ouen and De l'Ourcq; its genial spring, all convolvulus and gobéas, and early almond blossom and later horse-chestnut spikes, and more lime and syringa than ever; its warm soft summer and the ever-delightful school of natation by the Isle of Swans.

This particular temptation led us into trouble. We would rise before dawn, Barty and Jolivet and I, and let ourselves over the wall and run the two miles, and get a heavenly swim and a promise of silence for a franc apiece; and run back again and jump into bed a few minutes before the five-o'clock bell rang the réveillé.

But we did this once too often—for M. Dumollard had been looking at Venus with his telescope (I *think* it was Venus) one morning before sunrise, and spied us out *en flagrant délit;* perhaps with that very telescope. Anyhow, he pounced on us when we came back. And our punishment would have been extremely harsh but for Barty, who turned it all into a joke.

After breakfast M. Mérovée pronounced a very severe sentence on us under the acacia. I forget what it was—but his manner was very short and dignified, and he walked away very stiffly towards the door of the étude. Barty ran after him without noise, and just touching his shoulders with the tips of his fingers, cleared him at a bound from behind, as one clears a post.

M. Mérovée, in a *real* rage this time, forgot his dignity, and pursued him all over the school—through open windows and back again—into his own garden (Tusculum)—over trellis railings—all along the top of a wall—and finally, quite blown out, sat down on the edge of the tank: the whole school was in fits by this time, even M. Dumollard—and at last Mérovée began to laugh too. So the thing had to be forgiven—but only that once !

Once also, that year, but in the winter, a great compliment was paid to la perfide Albion in the persons of MM. Josselin et Maurice, which I cannot help recording with a little complacency.

On a Thursday walk in the Bois de Boulogne a boy called out "À bas Dumollard !" in a falsetto squeak. Dumollard, who was on duty that walk, was furious, of course—but he couldn't identify the boy by the sound of his voice. He made his complaint to M. Mérovée—and next morning, after prayers, Mérovée came into the school-room, and told us he should go the round of the boys there and then, and ask each boy separately to own up if it were he who had uttered the seditious cry.

" And mind you !" he said—" you are all and each of you on your 'word of honor '—*l'étude entière !*"

So round he went, from boy to boy, deliberately fixing each boy with his eye, and severely asking—" Est-ce *toi ?*" " Est-ce *toi ?*" " Est-ce *toi ?*" etc., and waiting very deliberately indeed for the answer, and even asking for it again if it were not given in a firm and audible voice. And the answer was always, " Non, m'sieur, ce n'est pas moi !"

But when he came to each of *us* (Josselin and me) he just mumbled his " Est-ce toi ?" in a quite perfunctory voice, and didn't even wait for the answer !

When he got to the last boy of all, who said " Non, m'sieur," like all the rest, he left the room, saying, tragically (and, as I thought, rather theatrically for *him*):

" Je m'en vais le cœur navré—il y a un lâche parmi vous !" (My heart is harrowed—there's a coward among you.)

There was an awkward silence for a few moments.

Presently Rapaud got up and went out. We all knew that Rapaud was the delinquent—he had bragged about it so—overnight in the dormitory. He went straight to M. Mérovée and confessed, stating that he did not like to be put on his word of honor before the whole school. I forget whether he was punished or not, or how. He had to make his apologies to M. Dumollard, of course.

To put the whole school on its word of honor was thought a very severe measure, coming as it did from the head master in person. "La parole d'honneur" was held to be very sacred between boy and boy, and even between boy and head master. The boy who broke it was always "mis à la quarantaine" (sent to Coventry) by the rest of the school.

" I wonder why he let off Josselin and Maurice so easily ?" said Jolivet, at breakfast.

" Parce qu'il aime les Anglais, ma foi !" said M. Dumollard—" affaire de goût !"

" Ma foi, il n'a pas tort !" said M. Bonzig.

Dumollard looked askance at Bonzig (between whom and himself not much love was lost) and walked off, jauntily twirling his mustache, and whistling a few bars of a very ungainly melody, to which the words ran :

> "Non ! jamais en France,
> Jamais Anglais ne règnera !"

As if we wanted to, good heavens !

(By-the-way, I suddenly remember that both Berquin and d'Orthez were let off as easily as Josselin and I. But they were eighteen or nineteen, and "en Philosophie," the highest class in the school—and very first-rate boys indeed. It's only fair that I should add this.)

By-the-way, also, M. Dumollard took it into his head to persecute me because once I refused to fetch and carry for him and be his "moricaud," or black slave (as du Tertre-Jouan called it): a mean and petty persecution which lasted two years, and somewhat embitters my memory of those happy days. It was always "Maurice au piquet pour une heure !". . "Maurice à la retenue !" . . "Maurice privé de bain !". . "Maurice consigné dimanche prochain !" . . . for the slightest possible offence. But I forgive him freely.

First, because he is probably dead, and "de mortibus nil desperandum !" as Rapaud once said—and for saying which he received a "twisted pinch" from Mérovée Brossard himself.

Secondly, because he made chemistry, cosmography, and physics so pleasant—and even reconciled me at last to the differential and integral calculus (but never Barty!).

He could be rather snobbish at times, which was not a common French fault in the forties—we didn't even know what to call it.

For instance, he was fond of bragging to us boys about the golden splendors of his Sunday dissipation, and his grand acquaintances, even in class. He would even interrupt himself in the middle of an equation at the blackboard to do so.

"You mustn't imagine to yourselves, messieurs, that because I teach you boys science at the Pension Brossard, and take you out walking on Thursday afternoons, and all that, that I do not associate *avec des gens du monde!* Last night, for example, I was dining at the Café de Paris with a very intimate friend of mine—he's a marquis—and when the bill was brought, what do you think it came to ? you give it up ?" (vous donnez votre langue aux chats ?). "Well, it came to fifty - seven francs, fifty centimes ! We tossed up who should pay— et, ma foi, le sort a favorisé M. le Marquis !"

To this there was nothing to say; so none of us said anything, except du Tertre-Jouan, *our* marquis (No. 2), who said, in his sulky, insolent, peasantlike manner :

"Et comment q'ça s'appelle, vot' marquis ?" (What does it call itself, your marquis ?)

"Upon which M. Dumollard turns very red ("pique un soleil"), and says :

"Monsieur le Marquis Paul — François — Victor du Tertre-Jouan de Haultcastel de St.-Paterne, vous êtes un paltoquet et un rustre ! . . ."

And goes back to his equations.

Du Tertre-Jouan was nearly six feet high, and afraid of nobody—a kind of clodhopping young rustic Hercules, and had proved his mettle quite recently—when a brutal usher, whom I will call Monsieur Boulot (though his real name was Patachou), a Méridional with a horrible divergent squint, made poor Rapaud go down on his knees in the classe de géographie ancienne, and slapped him violently on the face twice running—a way he had with Rapaud.

It happened like this. It was a kind of penitential class for dunces during play-time. M. Boulot drew in clalk an outline of ancient Greece on the blackboard, and under it he wrote—

"Timeo Danaos, et dona ferentes !"

"Rapaud, translate me that line of Virgil !" says Boulot.

"J'estime les Danois et leurs dents de fer !" says poor Rapaud (I esteem the Danish and their iron teeth). And we all laughed. For which he underwent the brutal slapping.

The window was ajar, and outside I saw du Tertre-Jouan, Jolivet, and Berquin, listening and peeping through. Suddenly the window bursts wide open, and

A TERTRE-JOUAN TO THE RESCUE!

du Tertre-Jouan vaults the sill, gets between Boulot and his victim, and says:

"Le troisième coup fait feu, vous savez! touchez-y encore, à ce moutard, et j'vous assomme sur place!" (Touch him again, that kid, and I'll break your head where you stand!).

There was an awful row, of course — and du Tertre-Jouan had to make a public apology to M. Boulot, who disappeared from the school the very same day; and Tertre-Jouan would have been canonized by us all, but that he was so deplorably dull and narrow-minded, and suspected of being a royalist in disguise. He was an orphan and very rich, and didn't fash himself about examinations. He left school that year without taking any degree — and I don't know what became of him.

This year also Barty conceived a tender passion for Mlle. Marceline.

It was after the mumps, which we both had together in a double-bedded infirmerie next to the lingerie—a place where it was a pleasure to be ill; for she was in and out all day, and told us all that was going on, and gave us nice drinks and tisanes of her own making—and laughed at all Barty's jokes, and some of mine! and wore the most coquettish caps ever seen.

Besides, she was an uncommonly good-looking woman —a tall blonde with beautiful teeth, and wonderfully genial, good-humored, and lively—an ideal nurse, but a terrible postponer of cures! Lord Archibald quite fell in love with her.

"C'est moi qui voudrais bien avoir les oreillons ici!" he said to her. "Je retarderais ma convalescence autant que possible!"

"Comme il sait bien le français, votre oncle—et comme

MADEMOISELLE MARCELINE

il est poli !" said Marceline to the convalescent Barty, who was in no hurry to get well either !

When we did get well again, Barty would spend much of his play-time fetching and carrying for Mlle. Marceline—even getting Dumollard's socks for her to darn—and talking to her by the hour as he sat by her pleasant window, out of which one could see the Arch of Triumph, which so triumphantly dominated Paris and its suburbs, and does so still—no Eiffel Tower can kill that arch !

I, being less precocious, did not begin my passion for Mlle. Marceline till next year, just as Bonneville and Jolivet trois were getting over theirs. Nous avons tous passé par là !

What a fresh and kind and jolly woman she was, to be sure ! I wonder none of the masters married her. Perhaps they did ! Let us hope it wasn't M. Dumollard !

It is such a pleasure to recall every incident of this epoch of my life and Barty's that I should like to go through our joint lives day by day, hour by hour, microscopically—to describe every book we read, every game we played, every *pensum* (*i.e.*, imposition) we performed ; every lark we were punished for—every meal we ate. But space forbids this self-indulgence, and other considerations make it unadvisable—so I will resist the temptation.

La pension Brossard ! How often have we both talked of it, Barty and I, as middle-aged men ; in the billiard-room of the Marathoneum, let us say, sitting together on a comfortable couch, with tea and cigarettes—and always in French whispers ! we could only talk of Brossard's in French.

"Te rappelles-tu l'habit neuf de Berquin, et son chapeau haute-forme ?"

"IF HE ONLY KNEW!"

"Te souviens-tu de la vieille chatte angora du père Jaurion?" etc., etc., etc.

Idiotic reminiscences! as charming to revive as any old song with words of little meaning that meant so much when one was four—five—six years old! before one knew even how to spell them!

> "Paille à Dine—paille à Chine—
> Paille à Suzette et Martine—
> Bon lit à la Dumaine!"

Céline, my nurse, used to sing this—and I never knew what it meant; nor do I now! But it was charming indeed.

Even now I dream that I go back to school, to get coached by Dumollard in a little more algebra. I wander about the playground; but all the boys are new, and don't even know my name; and silent, sad, and ugly, every one! Again Dumollard persecutes me. And in the middle of it I reflect that, after all, he is a person of no importance whatever, and that I am a member of the British Parliament—a baronet—a millionaire—and one of her Majesty's Privy Councillors! and that M. Dumollard must be singularly "out of it," even for a Frenchman, not to be aware of this.

"If he only knew!" says I to myself, says I—in my dream.

Besides, can't the man see with his own eyes that I'm grown up, and big enough to tuck him under my left arm, and spank him just as if he were a little naughty boy—confound the brute!

Then, suddenly:

"Maurice, au piquet pour une heure!"

"Moi, m'sieur?"

"Oui. vous!"

"Pourquoi, m'sieur!"

"Parce que ça me plaît!"

And I wake—and could almost weep to find how old I am!

And Barty Josselin is no more—oh! my God! . . . . and his dear wife survived him just twenty-four hours!

Behold us both "en Philosophie!"

And Barty the head boy of the school, though not the oldest—and the brilliant show-boy of the class.

Just before Easter (1851) he and I and Rapaud and Laferté and Jolivet trois (who was nineteen) and Palaiseau and Bussy-Rabutin went up for our "bachot" at the Sorbonne.

We sat in a kind of big musty school-room with about thirty other boys from other schools and colleges. There we sat side by side from ten till twelve at long desks, and had a long piece of Latin dictated to us, with the punctuation in French : "un point—point et virgule—deux points—point d'exclamation—guillemets—ouvrez la parenthèse," etc., etc.—monotonous details that enervate one at such a moment!

Then we set to work with our dictionaries and wrote out a translation according to our lights—a *pion* walking about and watching us narrowly for cribs, in case we should happen to have one for this particular extract, which was most unlikely.

Barty's nose bled, I remember—and this made him nervous.

Then we went and lunched at the Café de l'Odéon, on the best omelet we had ever tasted.

"Te rappelles-tu cette omelette?" said poor Barty to me only last Christmas as ever was!

Then we went back with our hearts in our mouths to

find if we had qualified ourselves by our "version écrite" for the oral examination that comes after, and which is so easy to pass—the examiners having lunched themselves into good-nature.

There we stood panting, some fifty boys and masters, in a small, whitewashed room like a prison. An official comes in and puts the list of candidates in a frame on the wall, and we crane our necks over each other's shoulders.

And, lo! Barty is plucked—*collé!* and *I* have passed, and actually Rapaud—and no one else from Brossard's!

An old man—a parent or grandparent probably of some unsuccessful candidate—bursts into tears and exclaims,

"Oh! qué malheur—qué malheur!"

A shabby, tall, pallid youth, in the uniform of the Collège Ste.-Barbe, rushes down the stone stairs shrieking,

"Ça pue l'injustice, ici!"

One hears him all over the place : terrible heartburns and tragic disappointments in the beginning of life resulted from failure in this first step—a failure which disqualified one for all the little government appointments so dear to the heart of the frugal French parent. "Mille francs par an! c'est le Pactole!"

Barty took his defeat pretty easily—he put it all down to his nose bleeding—and seemed so pleased at my success, and my dear mother's delight in it, that he was soon quite consoled ; he was always like that.

To M. Mérovée, Barty's failure was as great a disappointment as it was a painful surprise.

"Try again, Josselin! Don't leave here till you have passed. If you are content to fail in this, at the very

"'MAURICE AU PIQUET!'"

outset of your career, you will never succeed in anything through life ! Stay with us as my guest till you can go up again, and again if necessary. *Do*, my dear child— it will make me so happy ! I shall feel it as a proof that you reciprocate in some degree the warm friendship I have always borne you—in common with everybody in the school ! Je t'en prie, mon garçon !"

Then he went to the Rohans and tried to persuade them. But Lord Archibald didn't care much about Bachots, nor his wife either. They were going back to live in England, besides ; and Barty was going into the Guards.

I left school also—with a mixture of hope and elation, and yet the most poignant regret.

I can hardly find words to express the gratitude and affection I felt for Mérovée Brossard when I bade him farewell.

Except his father before him, he was the best and finest Frenchman I ever knew. There is nothing invidious in my saying this, and in this way. I merely speak of the Brossards, father and son, as Frenchmen in this connection, because their admirable qualities of heart and mind were so essentially French ; they would have done equal honor to any country in the world.

I corresponded with him regularly for a few years, and so did Barty ; and then our letters grew fewer and farther between, and finally left off altogether—as nearly always happens in such cases, I think. And I never saw him again ; for when he broke up the school he went to his own province in the southeast, and lived there till twenty years ago, when he died—unmarried, I believe.

Then there was Monsieur Bonzig, and Mlle. Marceline, and others — and three or four boys with whom both

Barty and I were on terms of warm and intimate friendship. None of these boys that I know of have risen to any world-wide fame; and, oddly enough, none of them have ever given sign of life to Barty Josselin, who is just as famous in France for his French literary work as on this side of the Channel for all he has done in English. He towers just as much there as here; and this double eminence now dominates the entire globe, and we are beginning at last to realize everywhere that this bright luminary in our firmament is no planet, like Mars or Jupiter, but, like Sirius, a sun.

Yet never a line from an old comrade in that school where he lived for four years and was so strangely popular—and which he so filled with his extraordinary personality!

So much for Barty Josselin's school life and mine. I fear I may have dwelt on them at too great a length. No period of time has ever been for me so bright and happy as those seven years I spent at the Institution F. Brossard—especially the four years I spent there with Barty Josselin. The older I get, the more I love to recall the trivial little incidents that made for us both the sum of existence in those happy days.

La chasse aux souvenirs d'enfance! what better sport can there be, or more bloodless, at my time of life?

And all the lonely pathetic pains and pleasures of it, now that *he* is gone!

The winter twilight has just set in—"betwixt dog and wolf." I wander alone (but for Barty's old mastiff, who follows me willy-nilly) in the woods and lanes that surround Marsfield on the Thames, the picturesque abode of the Josselins.

Darker and darker it grows. I no longer make out the

familiar trees and hedges, and forget how cold it is and
how dreary.

> "Je marcherai les yeux fixés sur mes pensées,
>> Sans rien voir au dehors, sans entendre aucun bruit—
>> Seul, inconnu, le dos courbé, les mains croisées :
>>> Triste—et le jour pour moi sera comme la nuit."

(This is Victor Hugo, not Barty Josselin.)

It's really far away I am—across the sea ; across the
years, O Posthumus ! in a sunny play-ground that has
been built over long ago, or overgrown with lawns and
flower-beds and costly shrubs.

Up rises some vague little rudiment of a hint of a ghost
of a sunny, funny old French remembrance long forgotten—a brand-new old remembrance—a kind of will-o'-
the-wisp. Chut ! my soul stalks it on tiptoe, while these
earthly legs bear this poor old body of clay, by mere re-
flex action, straight home to the beautiful Elisabethan
house on the hill ; through the great warm hall, up the
broad oak stairs, into the big cheerful music-room like a
studio—ruddy and bright with the huge log-fire opposite
the large window. All is on an ample scale at Marsfield,
people and things ! and I ! sixteen stone, good Lord !

How often that window has been my beacon on dark
nights ! I used to watch for it from the train—a landmark in a land of milk and honey—the kindliest light
that ever led me yet on earth.

I sit me down in my own particular chimney-corner,
in my own cane-bottomed chair by the fender, and stare
at the blaze with my friend the mastiff. An old war-
battered tomcat Barty was fond of jumps up and makes
friends too. There goes my funny little French remembrance, trying to fly up the chimney like a burnt love-
letter. . . .

Barty's eldest daughter (Roberta), a stately, tall Hebe in black, brings me a very sizable cup of tea, just as I like it. A well-grown little son of hers, a very Ganymede, beau comme le jour, brings me a cigarette, and insists on lighting it for me himself. I like that too.

Another daughter of Barty's, "la rossignolle," as we call her—though there is no such word that I know of—goes to the piano and sings little French songs of forty, fifty years ago — songs that she has learnt from her dear papa.

Heavens! what a voice! and how like his, but for the difference of sex and her long and careful training (which he never had); and the accent, how perfect!

Then suddenly :

> "À Saint-Blaize, à la Zuecca . . .
> Vous étiez, vous étiez bien aise !
> À Saint-Blaize, à la Zuecca . . .
> Nous étions, nous étions bien là !
> Mais de vous en souvenir
> Prendrez-vous la peine ?
> Mais de vous en souvenir,
> Et d'y revenir ?
> À Saint-Blaize, à la Zuecca . . .
> Vivre et mourir là !"

So sings Mrs. Trevor (Mary Josselin that was) in the richest, sweetest voice I know. And behold! at last I have caught my little French remembrance, just as the lamps are being lit—and I transfix it with my pen and write it down . . .

And then with a sigh I scratch it all out again, sunny and funny as it is. For it's all about a comical adventure I had with Palaiseau, the sniffer at the fête de St.-Cloud — all about a tame magpie, a gendarme, a blanchisseuse, and a volume of de Musset's poems, and doesn't concern Barty in the least ; for it so happened that Barty wasn't there !

Thus, in the summer of 1851, Barty Josselin and I bade adieu forever to our happy school life—and for a few years to our beloved Paris—and for many years to our close intimacy of every hour in the day.

I remember spending two or three afternoons with him at the great exhibition in Hyde Park just before he went on a visit to his grandfather, Lord Whitby, in Yorkshire —and happy afternoons they were ! and we made the most of them. We saw all there was to be seen there, I think ; and found ourselves always drifting back to the "Amazon" and the "Greek Slave," for both of which Barty's admiration was boundless.

And so was mine. They made the female fashions for 1851 quite deplorable by contrast—especially the shoes, and the way of dressing the hair ; we almost came to the conclusion that female beauty when unadorned is adorned the most. It awes and chastens one so ! and wakes up the knight-errant inside ! even the smartest French boots can't do this ! not the pinkest silken hose in all Paris ! not all the frills and underfrills and wonderfrills that M. Paul Bourget can so eloquently describe !

My father had taken a house for us in Brunswick Square, next to the Foundling Hospital. He was about to start an English branch of the Vougeot-Conti firm in the City. I will not trouble the reader with any details about this enterprise, which presented many difficulties at first, and indeed rather crippled our means.

My mother was anxious that I should go to one of the universities, Oxford or Cambridge ; but this my father could not afford. She had a great dislike to business—

"'QUAND ON PERD, PAR TRISTE OCCURRENCE,
SON ESPÉRANCE,
ET SA GAÎTÉ,
LE REMÈDE AU MÉLANCOLIQUE
C'EST LA MUSIQUE
ET LA BEAUTÉ'"

and so had I ; from different motives, I fancy. I had
the wish to become a man of science—a passion that had
been fired by M. Dumollard, whose special chemistry class
at the Pension Brossard, with its attractive experiments,
had been of the deepest interest to me. I have not described it because Barty did not come in.

Fortunately for my desire, my good father had great
sympathy with me in this ; so I was entered as a student
at the Laboratory of Chemistry at University College,
close by—in October, 1851—and studied there for two
years, instead of going at once into my father's business
in Barge Yard, Bucklersbury, which would have pleased
him even more.

At about the same time Barty was presented with a
commission in the Second Battalion of the Grenadier
Guards, and joined immediately.

Nothing could have been more widely apart than the
lives we led, or the society we severally frequented.

I lived at home with my people ; he in rooms on a second floor in St. James's Street ; he had a semi - grand
piano, and luxurious furniture, and bookcases already
well filled, and nicely colored lithograph engravings on
the walls — beautiful female faces — the gift of Lady
Archibald, who had superintended Barty's installation
with kindly maternal interest, but little appreciation of
high art. There were also foils, boxing-gloves, dumb-
bells, and Indian clubs ; and many weapons, ancient and
modern, belonging more especially to his own martial
profession. They were most enviable quarters. But he
often came to see us in Brunswick Square, and dined
with us once or twice a week, and was made much of—
even by my father, who thoroughly disapproved of everything about him except his own genial and agreeable
self, which hadn't altered in the least.

My father was much away—in Paris and Dijon—and Barty made rain and fine weather in our dull abode, to use a French expression—*il y faisait la pluie et le beau temps.* That is, it rained there when he was away, and he brought the fine weather with him; and we spoke French all round.

The greatest pleasure I could have was to breakfast with Barty in St. James's Street on Sunday mornings, when he was not serving his Queen and country—either alone with him or with two or three of his friends—mostly young carpet warriors like himself; and very charming young fellows they were. I have always been fond of warriors, young or old, and of whatever rank, and wish to goodness I had been a warrior myself. I feel sure I should have made a fairly good one !

Then we would spend an hour or two in athletic exercises and smoke many pipes. And after this, in the summer, we would walk in Kensington Gardens and see the Rank and Fashion. In those days the Rank and Fashion were not above showing themselves in the Kensington Gardens of a Sunday afternoon, crossing the Serpentine Bridge again and again between Prince's Gate and Bayswater.

Then for dinner we went to some pleasant foreign pothouse in or near Leicester Square, where they spoke French—and ate and drank it!—and then back again to his rooms. Sometimes we would be alone, which I liked best : we would read and smoke and be happy; or he would sketch, or pick out accompaniments on his guitar; often not exchanging a word, but with a delightful sense of close companionship which silence almost intensified.

Sometimes we were in very jolly company : more warriors; young Robson, the actor who became so famous;

a big negro pugilist, called Snowdrop; two medical students from St. George's Hospital, who boxed well and were capital fellows; and an academy art student, who died a Royal Academician, and who did not approve of Barty's mural decorations and laughed at the colored lithographs; and many others of all sorts. There used to be much turf talk, and sometimes a little card-playing and mild gambling — but Barty's tastes did not lie that way.

His idea of a pleasant evening was putting on the gloves with Snowdrop, or any one else who chose — or fencing — or else making music; or being funny in any way one could; and for this he had quite a special gift: he had sudden droll inspirations that made one absolutely hysterical—mere things of suggestive look or sound or gesture, reminding one of Robson himself, but quite original; absolute senseless rot and drivel, but still it made one laugh till one's sides ached. And he never failed of success in achieving this.

Among the dullest and gravest of us, and even some of the most high-minded, there is often a latent longing for this kind of happy idiotic fooling, and a grateful fondness for those who can supply it without effort and who delight in doing so. Barty was the precursor of the Arthur Robertses and Fred Leslies and Dan Lenos of our day, although he developed in quite another direction!

Then of a sudden he would sing some little twopenny love-ballad or sentimental nigger melody so touchingly that one had the lump in the throat; poor Snowdrop would weep by spoonfuls!

By-the-way, it suddenly occurs to me that I'm mixing things up—confusing Sundays and week-days; of course our Sunday evenings were quiet and respectable, and I much preferred them when he and I were alone; he was then another person altogether—a thoughtful and intelligent young Frenchman, who loved reading poetry aloud or being read to : especially English poetry—Byron ! He was faithful to his " Don Juan," his Hebrew melodies—his " O'er the glad waters of the deep blue sea." We knew them all by heart, or nearly so, and yet we read them still : and Victor Hugo and Lamartine, and dear Alfred de Musset. . . .

And one day I discovered another Alfred who wrote verses—Alfred the Great, as we called him—one Alfred Tennyson, who had written a certain poem, among others, called " In Memoriam "—which I carried off to Barty's and read out aloud one wet Sunday evening, and the Sunday evening after, and other Sunday evenings ; and other poems by the same hand : " Locksley Hall," " Ulysses," " The Lotos-Eaters," " The Lady of Shalott "—and the chord of Byron passed in music out of sight.

Then Shelley dawned upon us, and John Keats, and Wordsworth—and our Sunday evenings were of a happiness to be remembered forever ; at least they were so to me !

If Barty Josselin were on duty on the Sabbath, it was a blank day for Robert Maurice. For it was not very lively at home—especially when my father was there. He was the best and kindest man that ever lived, but his businesslike seriousness about this world, and his anxiety about the next, and his Scotch Sabbatarianism, were deadly depressing ; combined with the aspect of London on the Lord's day—London east of Russell Square ! Oh, Paris . . Paris . . . and the yellow omnibus that took us both there together, Barty and me, at eight on a Sunday morning in May or June, and didn't bring us back to school till fourteen hours later !

132

I shall never forget one gloomy wintry Sunday—somewhere in 1854 or 5, if I'm not mistaken, towards the end of Barty's career as a Guardsman.

Twice after lunch I had called at Barty's, who was to have been on duty in barracks or at the Tower that morning ; he had not come back ; I called for him at his club, but he hadn't been there either—and I turned my face eastward and homeward with a sickening sense of desolate ennui and deep disgust of London for which I could find no terms that are fit for publication !

And this was not lessened by the bitter reproaches I made myself for being such a selfish and unworthy son and brother. It was precious dull at home for my mother and sister—and my place was *there*.

They were just lighting the lamps as I got to the arcade in the Quadrant—and there I ran against the cheerful Barty. Joy ! what a change in the aspect of everything ! It rained light ! He pulled a new book out of his pocket, which he had just borrowed from some fair lady—and showed it to me. It was called *Maud*.

We dined at Pergolese's, in Rupert Street—and went back to Barty's—and read the lovely poem out loud, taking it by turns ; and that is the most delightful recollection I have since I left the Institution F. Brossard!

Occasionally I dined with him "on guard" at St. James's Palace—and well I could understand all the attractions of his life, so different from mine, and see what a good fellow he was to come so often to Brunswick Square, and seem so happy with us.

The reader will conclude that I was a kind of over-affectionate pestering dull dog, who made this brilliant youth's life a burden to him. It was really not so ; we had very many tastes in common ; and with all his various temptations, he had a singularly constant and affectionate nature — and was of a Frenchness that made French thought and talk and commune almost a daily necessity. We nearly always spoke French when together alone, or with my mother and sister. It would have seemed almost unnatural not to have done so.

I always feel a special tenderness towards young people whose lives have been such that those two languages are exactly the same to them. It means so many things to me. It doubles them in my estimation, and I seem to understand them through and through.

Nor did he seem to care much for the smart society of which he saw so much; perhaps the bar sinister may have made him feel less at his ease in general society than among his intimates and old friends. I feel sure he took this to heart more than any one would have thought possible from his careless manner.

He only once alluded directly to this when we were together. I was speaking to him of the enviable brilliancy of his lot. He looked at me pensively for a minute or two, and said, in English :

"You've got a kink in your nose, Bob—if it weren't for that you'd be a deuced good-looking fellow—like me ; but you ain't."

"Thanks—anything else ?" said I.

"Well, I've got a kink in my birth, you see—and that's as big a kill-joy as I know. I hate it !"

It *was* hard luck. He would have made such a splendid Marquis of Whitby ! and done such honor to the proud old family motto :

"Roy ne puis, prince ne daigne, Rohan je suis !"

Instead of which he got himself a signet-ring, and on it he caused to be engraved a zero within a naught, and round them :

"Rohan ne puis, roi ne daigne. Rien ne suis !"

Soon it became pretty evident that a subtle change was being wrought in him.

He had quite lost his power of feeling the north, and missed it dreadfully ; he could no longer turn his back-somersault with ease and safety ; he had overcome his loathing for meat, and also his dislike for sport—he had, indeed, become a very good shot.

But he could still hear and see and smell with all the keenness of a young animal or a savage. And that must have made his sense of being alive very much more vivid than is the case with other mortals.

He had also corrected his quick impulsive tendency to slap faces that were an inch or two higher up than his own. He didn't often come across one, for one thing—then it would not have been considered "good form" in her Majesty's Household Brigade.

When he was a boy, as the reader may recollect, he was fond of drawing lovely female profiles with black hair and an immense black eye, and gazing at them as he smoked a cigarette and listened to pretty, light music. He developed a most ardent admiration for female beauty, and mixed more and more in worldly and fashionable circles (of which I saw nothing whatever); circles where the heavenly gift of beauty is made more of, perhaps, than is quite good for its possessors, whether female or male.

He was himself of a personal beauty so exceptional that incredible temptations came his way. Aristocratic people all over the world make great allowance for beauty-born frailties that would spell ruin and everlasting disgrace for women of the class to which it is my privilege to belong.

Barty, of course, did not confide his love-adventures to me ; in this he was no Frenchman. But I saw quite

enough to know he was more pursued than pursuing;
and what a pursuer, to a man built like that! no innocent, impulsive young girl, no simple maiden in her
flower—no Elaine.

But a magnificent full-blown peeress, who knew her
own mind and had nothing to fear, for her husband was
no better than herself. But for that, a Guinevere and
Vivien rolled into one, *plus* Messalina!

Nor was she the only light o' love; there are many
naughty "grandes dames de par le monde" whose easy
virtue fits them like a silk stocking, and who live and
love pretty much as they please without loss of caste, so
long as they keep clear of any open scandal. It is one
of the privileges of high rank.

Then there were the ladies gay, frankly of the half-
world, these — laughter-loving hetæræ, with perilously
soft hearts for such as Barty Josselin! There was even
poor, listless, lazy, languid Jenny, "Fond of a kiss and
fond of a guinea!"

His heart was never touched—of that I feel sure; and
he was not vain of these triumphs; but he was a very
reckless youth, a kind of young John Churchill before
Sarah Jennings took him in hand—absolutely non-moral
about such things, rather than immoral.

He grew to be a quite notorious young man about
town; and, most unfortunately for him, Lord (and even
Lady) Archibald Rohan were so fond of him, and so
proud, and so amiably non-moral themselves, that he
was left to go as he might.

He also developed some very rowdy tastes indeed—
and so did I !

It was the fashion for our golden youth in the fifties
to do so. Every night in the Haymarket there was a
kind of noisy saturnalia, in which golden youths joined

hands with youths who were by no means golden, to give much trouble to the police, and fill the pockets of the keepers of night-houses—"Bob Croft's," "Kate Hamilton's," "the Piccadilly Saloon," and other haunts equally well pulled down and forgotten. It was good, in these regions, to be young and big and strong like Barty and me, and well versed in the "handling of one's daddles." I suppose London was the only great city in the world where such things could be. I am afraid that many strange people of both sexes called us Bob and Barty; people the mere sight or hearing of whom would have given my poor dear father fits!

Then there was a little public-house in St. Martin's Lane, kept by big Ben the prize-fighter. In a room at the top of the house there used to be much sparring. We both of us took a high degree in the noble art—especially I, if it be not bragging to say so; mostly on account of my weight, which was considerable for my age. It was in fencing that he beat me hollow: he was quite the best fencer I ever met; the lessons at school of Bonnet's prévôt had borne good fruit in his case.

Then there were squalid dens frequented by touts and betting-men and medical students, where people sang and fought and laid the odds and got very drunk—and where Barty's performances as a vocalist, comic and sentimental (especially the latter), raised enthusiasm that seems almost incredible among such a brutalized and hardened crew.

One night he and I and a medical student called Ticklets, who had a fine bass voice, disguised ourselves as paupers, and went singing for money about Camden Town and Mornington Crescent and Regent's Park. It took us about an hour to make eighteen pence. Barty played the guitar, Ticklets the tambourine, and I the bones. Then we went to the Haymarket, and Barty made five pounds in no time ; most of it in silver donations from unfortunate women—English, of course—who are among the softest-hearted and most generous creatures in the world.

" O lachrymarum fons !"

I forget what use we made of the money—a good one, I feel sure.

I am sorry to reveal all this, but Barty wished it. Forty years ago such things did not seem so horrible as they would now, and the word " bounder " had not been invented.

My sister Ida, when about fourteen (1853), became a pupil at the junior school in the Ladies' College, 48 Bedford Square. She soon made friends — nice young girls, who came to our house, and it was much the livelier. I used to hear much of them, and knew them well before I ever saw them — especially Leah Gibson, who lived in Tavistock Square, and was Ida's special friend ; at last I was quite anxious to see this paragon.

One morning, as I carried Ida's books on her way to school, she pointed out to me three girls of her own age, or less, who stood talking together at the gates of the Foundling Hospital. They were all three very pretty children—quite singularly so—and became great beauties ; one golden-haired, one chestnut-brown, one blueblack. The black-haired one was the youngest and the tallest—a fine, straight, bony child of twelve, with a flat back and square shoulders ; she was very well dressed, and had nice brown boots with brown elastic sides on arched and straight-heeled slender feet, and white stockings on her long legs—a fashion in hose that has long gone out. She also wore a thick plait of black hair all down her back—another departed mode, and one not to be regretted, I think ; and she swung her books round her as she talked, with easy movements, like a strong boy.

"That's Leah Gibson," says my sister ; "the tall one, with the long black plait."

Leah Gibson turned round and nodded to my sister and smiled—showing a delicate narrow face, a clear pale complexion, very beautiful white pearly teeth between very red lips, and an extraordinary pair of large black eyes — rather close together — the blackest I ever saw, but with an expression so quick and penetrating and keen, and yet so good and frank and friendly, that they positively sent a little warm thrill through me—though she was only twelve years old, and not a bit older than her age, and I a fast youth nearly twenty !

And finding her very much to my taste, I said to my sister, just for fun, " Oh—*that's* Leah Gibson, is it ? then some day Leah Gibson shall be Mrs. Robert Maurice !"

From which it may be inferred that I looked on Leah Gibson, at the first sight of her, as likely to become some day an extremely desirable person.

She did.

The Gibsons lived in a very good house in Tavistock Square. They seemed very well off. Mrs. Gibson had a nice carriage, which she kept entirely with her own money. Her father, who was dead, had been a wealthy solicitor. He had left a large family, and to each of them property worth £300 a year, and a very liberal allowance of good looks.

Mr. Gibson was in business in the City.

Leah, their only child, was the darling of their hearts and the apple of their eyes. To dress her beautifully,

THREE LITTLE MAIDS FROM SCHOOL (1853)

to give her all the best masters money could procure, and treat her to every amusement in London—theatres, the opera, all the concerts and shows there were, and give endless young parties for her pleasure — all this seemed the principal interest of their lives.

Soon after my first introduction to Leah, Ida and I received an invitation to a kind of juvenile festivity at the Gibsons', and went, and spent a delightful evening. We were received by Mrs. Gibson most cordially. She was such an extremely pretty person, and so charmingly dressed, and had such winning, natural, genial manners, that I fell in love with her at first sight; she was also very playful and fond of romping; for she was young still, having married at seventeen.

Her mother, Mrs. Bletchley (who was present), was a Spanish Jewess—a most magnificent and beautiful old person in splendid attire, tall and straight, with white hair and thick black eyebrows, and large eyes as black as night.

In Leah the high Sephardic Jewish type was more marked than in Mrs. Gibson (who was not Jewish at all in aspect, and took after her father, the late Mr. Bletchley).

It is a type that sometimes, just now and again, can be so pathetically noble and beautiful in a woman, so suggestive of chastity and the most passionate love combined—love conjugal and filial and maternal—love that implies all the big practical obligations and responsibilities of human life, that the mere term "Jewess" (and especially its French equivalent) brings to my mind some vague, mysterious, exotically poetic image of all I love best in woman. I find myself dreaming of Rebecca of York, as I used to dream of her in the English class at Brossard's, where I so pitied poor Ivanhoe for his misplaced constancy.

If Rebecca at fifty-five was at all like Mrs. Bletchley, poor old Sir Wilfred's regrets must have been all that Thackeray made them out to be in his immortal story of *Rebecca and Rowena.*

Mr. Gibson was a good-looking man, some twelve or fifteen years older than his wife; his real vocation was to be a low comedian; this showed itself on my first introduction to him. He informally winked at me and said :

"Esker voo ker jer dwaw lah vee ? Ah! kel Bonnure !"

This idiotic speech (all the French he knew) was delivered in so droll and natural a manner that I took to him at once. Barty himself couldn't have been funnier!

Well, we had games of forfeits and danced, and Ida played charming things by Mendelssohn on the piano, and Leah sang very nicely in a fine, bold, frank, deep voice, like a choir-boy's, and Mrs. Gibson danced a Spanish fandango, and displayed feet and ankles of which she was very proud, and had every right to be ; and then Mr. Gibson played a solo on the flute, and sang "My Pretty Jane"—both badly enough to be very funny without any conscious effort or straining on his part. Then we supped, and the food was good, and we were all very jolly indeed ; and after supper Mr. Gibson said to me :

"Now, Mister Parleyvoo—can't *you* do something to amuse the company ? You're *big* enough !"

I professed my willingness to do *anything*—and wished I was as Barty more than ever !

"Well, then," says he—"kneel to the wittiest, bow to the prettiest—and kiss the one you love best."

This was rather a large order—but I did as well as I could. I went down on my knees to Mr. Gibson and craved his paternal blessing ; and made my best French bow with my heels together to old Mrs. Bletchley ; and kissed my sister, warmly thanking her in public for having introduced me to Mrs. Gibson : and as far as mere social success is worth anything, I was the Barty of that party !

Anyhow, Mr. Gibson conceived for me an admiration he never failed to express when we met afterwards, and though this was fun, of course, I had really won his heart.

It is but a humble sort of triumph to crow over—and where does Barty Josselin come in ?

Pazienza !

" Well—what do you think of Leah Gibson ?" said my sister, as we walked home together through Torrington Square.

" I think she's a regular stunner," said I—" like her mother and her grandmother before her, and probably her *great*-grandmother too."

And being a poetical youth, and well up in my Byron, I declaimed :

> " She walks in beauty, like the night
> Of cloudless climes and starry skies;
> And all that's best of dark and bright
> Meet in her aspect and her eyes." . . .

Old fogy as I am, and still given to poetical quotations, I never made a more felicitous quotation than that. I little guessed then to what splendor that bony black-eyed damsel would reach in time.

All through this period of high life and low dissipation Barty kept his unalterable good-humor and high spirits—and especially the kindly grace of manner and tact and good-breeding that kept him from ever offending the most fastidious, in spite of his high spirits, and made him many a poor grateful outcast's friend and darling.

I remember once dining with him at Greenwich in very distinguished company ; I don't remember how I came to be invited—through Barty, no doubt. He got me many invitations that I often thought it better not to accept. " Ne sutor ultra crepidam !"

It was a fish dinner, and Barty ate and drank a surprising amount—and so did I, and liked it very much.

We were all late and hurried for the last train, some twenty of us—and Barty, Lord Archibald, and I, and a Colonel Walker Lindsay, who has since become a peer and a Field-Marshal (and is now dead), were all pushed together into a carriage, already occupied by a distinguished clergyman and a charming young lady—probably his daughter ; from his dress, he was either a dean or a bishop, and I sat opposite to him—in the corner.

Barty was very noisy and excited as the train moved off ; he was rather tipsy, in fact—and I was alarmed, on account of the clerical gentleman and his female companion. As we journeyed on, Barty began to romp and play the fool and perform fantastic tricks—to the immense delight of the future Field-Marshal. He twisted two pocket-handkerchiefs into human figures, one on each hand, and made them sing to each other—like Grisi and Mario in the *Huguenots*—and clever drivel of that kind. Lord Archibald and Colonel Lindsay were beside themselves with glee at all this ; they also had dined well.

Then he imitated a poor man fishing in St. James's Park and not catching any fish. And this really was uncommonly good and true to life—with wonderful artistic details, that showed keen observation.

I saw that the bishop and his daughter (if such they were) grew deeply interested, and laughed and chuckled discreetly; the young lady had a charming expression on her face as she watched the idiotic Barty, who got more idiotic with every mile—and this was to be the man who wrote *Sardonyx!*

As the train slowed into the London station, the bishop leant forward towards me and inquired, in a whisper,

" May I ask the name of your singularly delightful young friend ?"

" His name is Barty Josselin," I answered.

" Not of the Grenadier Guards ?"

" Yes."

" Oh, indeed ! a—yes—I've heard of him—"

And his lordship's face became hard and stern—and soon we all got out.

Part Fourth

"La cigale ayant chanté
Tout l'été,
Se trouva fort dépourvue
Quand la bise fut venue." . . .
—LAFONTAINE.

SOMETIMES I went to see Lord and Lady Archibald, who lived in Clarges Street; and Lady Archibald was kind enough to call on my mother, who was charmed with her, and returned her call in due time.

Also, at about this period (1853) my uncle Charles (Captain Blake, late 17th Lancers), who had been Lord Runswick's crony twenty years before, patched up some feud he had with my father, and came to see us in Brunswick Square.

He had just married a charming girl, young enough to be his daughter.

I took him to see Barty, and they became fast friends. My uncle Charles was a very accomplished man, and spoke French as well as any of us; and Barty liked him, and it ended, oddly enough, in Uncle Charles becoming Lord Whitby's land-agent and living in St. Hilda's Terrace, Whitby.

He was a very good fellow and a thorough man of the world, and was of great service to Barty in many ways. But, alas and alas! he was not able to prevent or make up the disastrous quarrel that happened between Barty and Lord Archibald, with such terrible results to my friend—to both.

It is all difficult even to hint at—but some of it must be more than hinted at.

Lord Archibald, like his nephew, was a very passionate admirer of lovely woman. He had been for many years a faithful and devoted husband to the excellent Frenchwoman who brought him wealth—and such affection! Then a terrible temptation came in his way. He fell in love with a very beautiful and fascinating lady, whose birth and principles and antecedents were alike very unfortunate, and Barty was mixed up in all this: it's the saddest thing I ever heard.

The beautiful lady conceived for Barty one of those frantic passions that must lead to somebody's ruin ; it led to his ; but he was never to blame, except for the careless indiscretion which allowed of his being concerned in the miserable business at all, and to this frantic passion he did not respond.

"*Spretæ injuria formæ.*"

So at least *she* fancied ; it was not so. Barty was no laggard in love ; but he dearly loved his uncle Archie, and was loyal to him all through.

> " His honor rooted in dishonor stood,
>   And faith unfaithful kept him falsely true."

Where he was unfaithful was to his beloved and adoring Lady Archibald—his second mother—at miserable cost of undying remorse to himself for ever having sunk to become Lord Archibald's confidant and love-messenger, and bearer of nosegays and *billets doux*, and singer of little French songs. He was only twenty, and thought of such things as jokes ; he had lived among some of the pleasantest, best-bred, and most corrupt people in London.

The beautiful frail lady told the most infamous lies, and stuck to them through thick and thin. The story is not new; it's as old as the Pharaohs. And Barty and his uncle quarrelled beyond recall. The boy was too proud even to defend himself, beyond one simple denial.

Then another thing happened. Lady Archibald died, quite suddenly, of peritonitis—fortunately in ignorance of what was happening, and with her husband and daughter and Barty round her bedside at the end. She died deceived and happy.

Lord Archibald was beside himself with grief; but in six months he married the beautiful lady, and went to the bad altogether — went under, in fact; and Daphne, his daughter of fourteen or fifteen, was taken by the Whitbys.

So now Barty, thoroughly sick of smart society, found himself in an unexpected position — without an allowance, in a crack regiment, and never a penny to look forward to!

For old Lord Whitby, who loved him, was a poor man with a large family; and every penny of Lady Archibald's fortune that didn't go to her husband and daughter went back to her own family of Lonlay-Savignac. She had made no will—no provision for her beloved, her adopted son!

So Barty never went to the Crimea, after all, but sold out, and found himself the possessor of seven or eight hundred pounds—most of which he owed—and with the world before him; but I am going too fast.

In the winter of 1853, just before Christmas, my father fitted up for me a chemical laboratory at the top of the fine old house in Barge Yard, Bucklersbury, where his wine business was carried on, a splendid mansion, with panelled rooms and a carved-oak staircase—once the abode of some Dick Whittington, no doubt a Lord Mayor of London; and I began my professional career, which consisted in analyzing anything I could get to analyze for hire, from a sample of gold or copper ore to a poisoned stomach.

Lord Whitby very kindly sent me different samples of soil from different fields on his estate, and I analyzed them carefully and found them singularly like each other. I don't think the estate benefited much by my scientific investigation. It was my first job, and brought me twenty pounds (out of which I bought two beautiful fans—one for my sister, the other for Leah Gibson—and got a new evening suit for myself at Barty's tailor's).

When this job of mine was finished I had a good deal of time on my hands, and read many novels and smoked many pipes, as I sat by my chemical stove and distilled water, and dried chlorate of potash to keep the damp out of my scales, and toasted cheese, and fried sausages, and mulled Burgundy, and brewed nice drinks, hot or cold—a specialty of mine.

I also made my laboratory a very pleasant place. My father wouldn't permit a piano, nor could I afford one; but I smuggled in a guitar (for Barty), and also a concertina, which I could play a little myself. Barty often came with friends of his, of whom my father did not approve—mostly Guardsmen; also friends of my own—medical students, and one or two fellow-chemists, who were serious, and pleased my father. We often had a capital time: chemical experiments and explosions, and fearful stinks, and poisoned waters of enchanting hue; also oysters, lobsters, dressed crab for lunch—and my Burgundy was good, I promise you, whether white or red!

SOLITUDE

We also had songs and music of every description. Barty's taste had improved. He could sing Beethoven's "Adelaida" in English, German, and Italian, and Schubert's "Serenade" in French—quite charmingly, to his own ingenious accompaniment on the guitar.

We had another vocalist, a little Hebrew art-student, with a heavenly tenor (I've forgotten his name); and Ticklets, the bass; and a Guardsman who could yodel and imitate a woman's voice—one Pepys, whom Barty loved because he was a giant, and, according to Barty, "the handsomest chap in London."

These debauches generally happened when my father was abroad—always, in fact. I'm greatly ashamed of it all now; even then my heart smote me heavily at times when I thought of the pride and pleasure he took in all my scientific appliances, and the money they cost him—twenty guineas for a pair of scales! Poor dear old man! he loved to weigh things in them—a feather, a minute crumb of cork, an infinitesimal wisp of cotton wool!...

However, I've made it all up to him since in many ways; and he has told me that I have been a good son, after all! And that is good to think of now that I am older than he was when he died!

One fine morning, before going to business, I escorted my sister to Bedford Square, calling for Leah Gibson on the way; as we walked up Great Russell Street (that being the longest way round I could think of), we met Barty, looking as fresh as a school-boy, and resplendent as usual. I remember he had on a long blue frock-coat, check trousers, an elaborate waistcoat and scarf, and white hat—as was the fashion—and that he looked singularly out of place (and uncommonly agreeable to the eye) in such an austere and learned neighborhood.

He was coming to call for me in Brunswick Square.

My sister introduced him to her friend, and he looked down at Leah with a surprised glance of delicate fatherly admiration—he might have been fifty.

Then we left the young ladies and went off together citywards ; my father was abroad.

" By Jove, what a stunner that girl is ! I'm blest if I don't marry her some day—you see if I don't !"

" That's just what *I* mean to do," said I. And we had a good laugh at the idea of two such desperadoes, as we thought ourselves, talking like this about a little school-girl.

" We'll toss up," says Barty ; and we did, and he won.

This, I remember, was before his quarrel with Lord Archibald. She was then about fourteen, and her subtle and singular beauty was just beginning to make itself felt.

I never knew till long after how deep had been the impression produced by this glimpse of a mere child on a fast young man about town—or I should not have been amused. For there were times when I myself thought quite seriously of Leah Gibson, and what she might be in the long future ! She looked a year or two older than she really was, being very tall and extremely sedate.

Also, both my father and mother had conceived such a liking for her that they constantly talked of the possibility of our falling in love with each other some day. Castles in Spain !

As for me, my admiration for the child was immense, and my respect for her character unbounded ; and I felt myself such a base unworthy brute that I couldn't bear to think of myself in such a connection — until I had cleansed myself heart and soul (which would take time)!

And as for showing by my manner to her that such an idea had ever crossed my mind, the thought never entered my head.

She was just my dear sister's devoted friend; her petticoat hem was still some inches from the ground, and her hair in a plait all down her back. . . .

Girlish innocence and purity incarnate—that is what she seemed; and what she was. "La plus forte des forces est un cœur innocent," said Victor Hugo—and if you translate this literally into English, it comes to exactly the same, both in rhythm and sense.

When Barty sold out, he first thought he would like to go on the stage, but it turned out that he was too tall to play anything but serious footmen.

Then he thought he would be a singer. We used to go to the opera at Drury Lane, where they gave in English a different Italian opera every night;—and this was always followed by *Acis and Galatea*.

We got our seats in the stalls every evening for a couple of weeks, through the kindness of Mr. Hamilton Braham, whom Barty knew, and who played Polyphemus in Handel's famous serenata.

I remember our first night; they gave *Masaniello*, which I had never seen; and when the tenor sang, "Behold how brightly breaks the morning," it came on us both as a delicious surprise—it was such a favorite song at Brossard's — "*amis! la matinée est belle . . .*" Indeed, it was one of the songs Barty sang on the boulevard for the poor woman, six or seven years back.

The tenor, Mr. Elliot Galer, had a lovely voice; and that was a moment never to be forgotten.

Then came *Acis and Galatea*, which was so odd and old-fashioned we could scarcely sit it out.

"'PILE OU FACE—HEADS OR TAILS?'"

Next night, *Lucia*—charming ; then again *Acis and Galatea*, because we had nowhere else to go.

"Tiens, tiens !" says Barty, as the lovers sang "the flocks shall leave the mountains"; "c'est diantrement joli, ça !—écoute !"

Next night, *La Sonnambula* -- then again *Acis and Galatea*.

"Mais, nom d'une pipe -- elle est *divine*, cette musique là !" says Barty.

And the nights after we could scarcely sit out the Italian opera that preceded what we have looked upon ever since as among the divinest music in the world.

So one must not judge music at a first hearing ; nor poetry ; nor pictures at first sight ; unless one be poet or painter or musician one's self — not even then ! I may live to love thee yet, oh *Tannhäuser !*

Lucy Escott, Fanny Huddart, Elliot Galer, and Hamilton Braham — that was the cast ; I hear their voices now. . . .

One morning Hamilton Braham tried Barty's voice on the empty stage at St. James's Theatre—made him sing "When other lips."

"Sing *out*, man—sing *out!*" said the big bass. And Barty shouted his loudest—a method which did not suit him. I sat in the pit, with half a dozen Guardsmen, who were deeply interested in Barty's operatic aspirations.

It turned out that Barty was neither tenor nor barytone ; and that his light voice, so charming in a room, would never do for the operatic stage ; although his figure, in spite of his great height, would have suited heroic parts so admirably.

Besides, three or four years' training in Italy were needed—a different production altogether.

So Barty gave up this idea and made up his mind to be an artist. He got permission to work in the British Museum, and drew the " Discobolus," and sent his drawing to the Royal Academy, in the hope of being admitted there as a student. He was not.

Then an immense overwhelming homesickness for Paris came over him, and he felt he must go and study art there, and succeed or perish.

My father talked to him like a father, my mother like a mother; we all hung about him and entreated. He was as obdurate as Tennyson's sailor-boy whom the mermaiden forewarned so fiercely !

He was even offered a handsome appointment in the London house of Vougeot-Conti & Co.

But his mind was made up, and to my sorrow, and the sorrow of all who knew him, he fixed the date of his departure for the 2d of May (1856),—this being the day after a party at the Gibsons'—a young dance in honor of Leah's fifteenth birthday, on the 1st—and to which my sister had procured him an invitation.

He had never been to the Gibsons' before. They belonged to a world so different to anything he had been accustomed to—indeed, to a class that he then so much disliked and despised (both as ex-Guardsman and as the descendant of French toilers of the sea, who hate and scorn the bourgeois)—that I was curious to see how he would bear himself there ; and rather nervous, for it would have grieved me that he should look down on people of whom I was getting very fond. It was his theory that all successful business people were pompous and purse-proud and vulgar.

I admit that in the fifties we very often were.

There may perhaps be a few survivals of that period : *old* nouveaux riches, who are still modestly jocose on the subject of each other's millions when they meet, and indulge in pompous little pleasantries about their pet economics, and drop a pompous little *h* now and then, and pretend they only did it for fun. But, dear me, there are other things to be vulgar about in this world besides money and uncertain aspirates.

If to be pompous and pretentious and insincere is to be vulgar, I really think the vulgar of our time are not these old plutocrats—not even their grandsons, who hunt and shoot and yacht and swagger with the best—but those solemn little prigs who have done well at school or college, and become radicals and agnostics before they've even had time to find out what men and women are made of, or what sex they belong to themselves (if any), and loathe all fun and sport and athletics, and rave about pictures and books and music they don't understand, and would pretend to despise if they did—things that were not even *meant* to be understood. It doesn't take three generations to make a prig—worse luck !

At the Gibsons' there was neither pompousness nor insincerity nor pretension of any kind, and therefore no real vulgarity. It is true they were a little bit noisy there sometimes, but only in fun.

When we arrived at that most hospitable house the two pretty drawing-rooms were already crammed with young people, and the dancing was in full swing.

I presented Barty to Mrs. Gibson, who received him with her usual easy cordiality, just as she would have received one of her husband's clerks, or the Prime Minister ; or the Prince Consort himself, for that matter. But she looked up into his face with such frank unabashed admiration that I couldn't help laughing—nor could he !

She presented him to Mr. Gibson, who drew himself

back and folded his arms and frowned ; then suddenly, striking a beautiful stage attitude of surprised emotion, with his hand on his heart, he exclaimed :

"Oh ! Monsewer ! Esker-voo ker jer dwaw lah vee ? —ah ! kel bonnure !"

And this so tickled Barty that he forgot his manners and went into peals of laughter. And from that moment I ceased to exist as the bright particular star in Mr. Gibson's firmament of eligible young men : for in spite of the kink in my nose, and my stolid gravity, which was really and merely the result of my shyness, he had always looked upon me as an exceptionally presentable, proper, and goodly youth, and a most exemplary—that is, if my sister was to be trusted in the matter ; for she was my informant.

I'm afraid Barty was not so immediately popular with the young cavaliers of the party—but all came right in due time. For after supper, which was early, Barty played the fool with Mr. Gibson, and taught him how to do a mechanical wax figure, of which he himself was the showman ; and the laughter, both baritone and soprano, might have been heard in Russell Square. Then they sang an extempore Italian duet together which was screamingly droll—and so forth.

Leah distinguished herself as usual by being attentive to the material wants of the company : comfortable seats, ices, syrups, footstools for mammas, and wraps ; safety from thorough draughts for grandpapas—the inherited hospitality of the clan of Gibson took this form with the sole daughter of their house and home ; she had no "parlor tricks."

We remained the latest. It was a full moon, or nearly so—as usual on a balcony ; for I remember standing on the balcony with Leah.

A belated Italian organ-grinder stopped beneath us and played a tune from *I Lombardi*, called "La mia letizia." Leah's hair was done up for the first time—in two heavy black bands that hid her little ears and framed her narrow chinny face—with a yellow bow plastered on behind. Such was the fashion then, a hideous fashion enough—but we knew no better. To me she looked so lovely in her long white frock—long for the first time—that Tavistock Square became a broad Venetian moonlit lagoon, and the dome of University College an old Italian church, and "La mia letizia" the song of Adria's gondolier.

I asked her what she thought of Barty.

"I really don't know," she said. "He's not a bit romantic, *is* he?"

"No; but he's very handsome. Don't you think so?"

"Oh yes, indeed—much too handsome for a man. It seems such waste. Why, I now remember seeing him when I was quite a little girl, three or four years ago, at the Duke of Wellington's funeral. He had his bearskin on. Papa pointed him out to us, and said he looked like such a pretty girl! And we all wondered who he could be! And so sad he looked! I suppose it was for the Duke.

"I couldn't think where I'd seen him before, and now I remember—and there's a photograph of him in a stall at the Crystal Palace. Have you seen it? Not that he looks like a girl now! Not a bit! I suppose you're very fond of him? Ida is! She talks as much about Mr. Josselin as she does about you! *Barty*, she calls him."

"Yes, indeed; he's like our brother. We were boys at school together in France. My sister calls him *thee* and *thou*; in French, you know."

"A LITTLE WHITE POINT OF INTERROGATION"

"And was he always like that—funny and jolly and good-natured ?"

"Always ; he hasn't changed a bit."

"And is he very sincere ?"

Just then Barty came on to the balcony : it was time to go. My sister had been fetched away already (in her gondola).

So Barty made his farewells, and bent his gallant, irresistible look of mirthful chivalry and delicate middle-aged admiration on Leah's upturned face, and her eyes looked up more piercing and blacker than ever ; and in each of them a little high light shone like a point of interrogation—the reflection of some white window-curtain, I suppose ; and I felt cold all down my back.

(Barty's daughter, Mary Trevor, often sings a little song of De Musset's. It is quite lovely, and begins :

> "Beau chevalier qui partez pour la guerre,
> Qu'allez-vous faire
> Si loin d'ici ?
> Voyez-vous pas que la nuit est profonde,
> Et que le monde
> N'est que souci ?"

It is called "La Chanson de Barberine," and I never hear it but I think of that sweet little white virginal *point d'interrogation,* and Barty going away to France.)

Then he thanked Mrs. Gibson and said pretty things, and finally called Mr. Gibson dreadful French fancy-names : "Cascamèche—moutardier du pape, tromblon-bolivard, vieux coquelicot"; to each of which the delighted Mr. G. answered :

"Voos ayt oon ôter—voos ayt oon ôter !"

And then Barty whisked himself away in a silver cloud of glory. A good exit !

161

Outside was a hansom waiting, with a carpet-bag on the top, and we got into it and drove up to Hampstead Heath, to some little inn called the Bull and Bush, near North-end.

Barty lit his pipe, and said :

" What capital people ! Hanged if they're not the nicest people I ever met !"

" Yes," said I.

And that's all that was said during that long drive.

At North-end we found two or three other hansoms, and Pepys and Ticklets and the little Hebrew tenor art student whose name I've forgotten, and several others.

We had another supper, and made a night of it. There was a piano in a small room opening on to a kind of little terrace, with geraniums, over a bow-window. We had music and singing of all sorts. Even *I* sang — " The Standard - bearer " — and rather well. My sister had coached me ; but I did not obtain an encore.

The next day dawned, and Barty had a wash and changed his clothes, and we walked all over Hampstead Heath, and saw London lying in a dun mist, with the dome and gilded cross of St. Paul's rising into the pale blue dawn ; and I thought what a beastly place London would be without Barty—but that Leah was there still, safe and sound asleep in Tavistock Square !

Then back to the inn for breakfast. Barty, as usual, fresh as paint. Happy Barty, off to Paris !

And then we all drove down to London Bridge to see him safe into the Boulogne steamer. All his luggage was on board. His late soldier-servant was there — a splendid fellow, chosen for his length and breadth as well as his fidelity ; also the Snowdrop, who was lachrymose and in great grief. It was a most affectionate farewell all round.

11

162

"Good-bye, Bob. *I* won that toss—*didn't* I ?"

Oddly enough, *I* was thinking of that, and didn't like it.

"What rot ! it's only a joke, old fellow !" said Barty.

All this about an innocent little girl just fifteen, the daughter of a low - comedy John Gilpin : a still somewhat gaunt little girl, whose budding charms of color, shape, and surface were already such that it didn't matter whether she were good or bad, gentle or simple, rich or poor, sensible or an utter fool.

C'est toujours comme ça !

We watched the steamer pick its sunny way down the Thames, with Barty waving his hat by the man at the wheel ; and I walked westward with the little Hebrew artist, who was so affected at parting with his hero that he had tears in his lovely voice. It was not till I had complimented him on his wonderful B-flat that he got consoled ; and he talked about himself, and his B-flat, and his middle G, and his physical strength, and his eye for color, all the way from the Mansion House to the Foundling Hospital ; when we parted, and he went straight to his drawing-board at the British Museum— an anticlimax !

I found my mother and sister at their late breakfast, and was scolded ; and I told them Barty had got off, and wouldn't come back for long—it might not be for years !

"Thank Heaven !" said my dear mother, and I was not pleased.

Says my sister :

" Do you know, he's actually stolen Leah's photograph, that she gave me for my birthday. He asked me for it and I wouldn't give it him—and it's gone !"

Then I washed and put on my work-a-day clothes, and went straight to Barge Yard, Bucklersbury, and made myself a bed on the floor with my great-coat, and slept all day.

Oh heavens! what a dull book this would be, and how dismally it would drag its weary length along, if it weren't all about the author of *Sardonyx!*

But is there a lost corner anywhere in this planet where English is spoken (or French) in which *The Martian* won't be bought and treasured and spelt over and over again like a novel by Dickens or Scott (or Dumas)—for Josselin's dear sake! What a fortune my publishers would make if I were not a man of business and they were not the best and most generous publishers in the world! And all Josselin's publishers—French, English, German, and what not—down to modern Sanscrit! What millionaires—if it hadn't been for this little busy bee of a Bob Maurice!

Poor Barty! I am here! à bon chat, bon rat!

And what on earth do *I* want a fortune for? Barty's dead, and I've got so much more than I need, who am of a frugal mind—and what I've got is all going to little Josselins, who have already got so much more than *they* need, what with their late father and me; and my sister, who is a widow and childless, and "riche à millions" too! and cares for nobody in all this wide world but little Josselins, who don't care for money in the least, and would sooner work for their living—even break stones on the road—anything sooner than loaf and laze and loll through life. We all have to give most of it away—not that I need proclaim it from the house-tops! It is but a dull and futile hobby, giving away to those who deserve; they soon leave off deserving.

How fortunate that so much money is really wanted by people who don't deserve it any more than I do; and who, besides, are so weak and stupid and lazy and honest—or so incurably dishonest—that they can't make it for themselves! I have to look after a good many of these people. Barty was fond of them, honest or not. They are so incurably prolific; and so was he, poor dear boy! but, oh, the difference! Grapes don't grow on thorns, nor figs on thistles!

I'm a thorn, alas! in my own side, more often than not—and a thistle in the sides of a good many donkeys, whom I feed because they're too stupid or too lazy to feed themselves! But at least I know my place, and the knowledge is more bother to me than all my money, and the race of Maurice will soon be extinct.

When Barty went to foreign parts, on the 2d of May, 1856, I didn't trouble myself about such questions as these.

Life was so horribly stale in London without Barty that I became a quite exemplary young man when I woke up from that long nap on the floor of my laboratory in Barge Yard, Bucklersbury; a reformed character: from sheer grief, I really believe!

I thought of many things — ugly things — very ugly things indeed—and meant to have done with them. I thought of some very handsome things too — a pair of beautiful crown-jewels, each rare as the black tulip—and in each of them a bright little sign like this: ?

I don't believe I ever gave my father another bad quarter of an hour from that moment. I even went to church on Sunday mornings quite regularly; not his own somewhat severe place of worship, it is true! But the Foundling Hospital. There, in the gallery, would I sit with my sister, and listen to Miss Dolby and Miss Louisa Pyne and Mr. Lawler the bass—and a tenor and alto whose names I cannot recall ; and I thought they sang as they ought to have sung, and was deeply moved and comforted—more than by any preachments in the world ; and just in the opposite gallery sat Leah with her mother and I grew fond of nice clean little boys and girls who sing pretty hymns in unison; and afterwards I watched them eat their roast beef, small mites of three and four or five, some of them, and thought how touching it all was—I don't know why ! Love or grief ? or that touch of nature that makes the whole world kin at about 1 P.M. on Sunday ?

One would think that Barty had exerted a bad influence on me, since he seems to have kept me out of all this that was so sweet and new and fresh and wholesome !

He would have been just as susceptible to such impressions as I ; even more so, if the same chance had arisen for him—for he was singularly fond of children, the smaller and the poorer the better, even gutter children ! and their poor mothers loved him, he was so jolly and generous and kind.

Sometimes I got a letter from him in Blaze, my father's shorthand cipher ; it was always brief and bright and hopeful, and full of jokes and funny sketches. And I answered him in Blaze that was long and probably dull.

All that I will tell of him now is not taken from his Blaze letters, but from what he has told me later, by word of mouth—for he was as fond of talking of himself as I of listening — since he was droll and sincere and without guile or vanity ; and would have been just as sympathetic a listener as I, if I had cared to talk about Mr. Robert Maurice, of Barge Yard, Bucklersbury. Besides, I am good at hearing between the words and reading between the lines, and all that—and love to exercise this faculty.

Well, he reached Paris in due time, and took a small bedroom on a third floor in the Rue du Faubourg Poissonnière—over a cheap hatter's — opposite the Conservatoire de Musique.

On the first night he was awoke by a terrible invasion —such malodorous swarms of all sizes, from a tiny brown speck to a full-grown lentil, that they darkened his bed ; and he slept on the tiled floor after making an island of himself by pouring cold water all round him as a kind of moat; and so he slept for a week of nights, until he had managed to poison off most of these invaders with *poudre insecticide . . .* "mort aux punaises !"

In the daytime he first of all went for a swim at the Passy baths—an immense joy, full of the ghosts of bygone times ; then he would spend the rest of his day revisiting old haunts — often sitting on the edge of the stone fountain in the rond-point of the Avenue du Prince Impérial, or de l'Impératrice, or whatever it was — to gaze comfortably at the outside of the old school, which was now a pensionnat de demoiselles : soon to be pulled down and make room for a new house altogether. He did not attempt to invade these precincts of maiden innocence ; but gazed and gazed, and remembered and realized and dreamt: it all gave him unspeakable excitement, and a strange tender wistful melancholy delight for which there is no name. Je connais ça ! I also, ghostlike, have paced round the haunts of my childhood.

When the joy of this faded, as it always must when indulged in too freely, he amused himself by sitting in his bedroom and painting Leah's portrait, enlarged and

in oils ; partly from the very vivid image he had preserved of her in his mind, partly from the stolen photograph. At first he got it very like ; then he lost all the
likeness and could not recover it ; and he worked and
worked till he got stupid over it, and his mental image
faded quite away.

But for a time this minute examination of the photograph (through a powerful lens he bought on purpose),
and this delving search into his own deep consciousness
of her, into his keen remembrance of every detail of
feature and color and shade of expression, made him
realize and idealize and foresee what the face might be
some day—and what its owner might become.

And a horror of his life in London came over him like
a revelation—a blast—a horrible surprise ! Mere sin is
ugly when it's no more ; and *so* beastly to remember,
unless the sinner be thoroughly acclimatized ; and Barty
was only twenty-two, and hated deceit and cruelty in
any form. Oh, poor, weak, frail fellow-sinner—whether
Vivien or Guinevere ! How sadly unjust that loathing
and satiety and harsh male contempt should kill man's
ruth and pity for thee, that wast so kind to man ! what
a hellish after-math !

Poor Barty hadn't the ghost of a notion how to set to
work about becoming a painter, and didn't know a soul
in Paris he cared to go and consult, although there
were many people he might have discovered whom he
had known : old school-fellows, and friends of the Archibald Rohans—who would have been only too glad.

So he took to wandering listlessly about, lunching and
dining at cheap suburban restaurants, taking long walks,
sitting on benches, leaning over parapets, and longing
to tell people who he was, his age, how little money he'd
got, what lots of friends he had in England, what a nice

little English girl he knew, whose portrait he didn't know how to paint—any idiotic nonsense that came into his head, so at least he might talk about something or somebody that interested him.

There is no city like Paris, no crowd like a Parisian crowd, to make you feel your solitude if you are alone in its midst!

At night he read French novels in bed and drank eau sucrée and smoked till he was sleepy; then he cunningly put out his light, and lit it again in a quarter of an hour or so, and exploded what remained of the invading hordes as they came crawling down the wall from above. Their numbers were reduced at last; they were disappearing. Then he put out his candle for good, and went to sleep happy—having at least scored for once in the twenty-four hours. Mort aux punaises!

Twice he went to the Opéra Comique, and saw *Richard Cœur de Lion* and *le Pré aux Clercs* from the gallery, and was disappointed, and couldn't understand why *he* shouldn't sing as well as that—he thought he could sing much better, poor fellow! he had a delightful voice, and charm, and the sense of tune and rhythm, and could please quite wonderfully—but he had no technical knowledge whatever, and couldn't be depended upon to sing a song twice the same! He trusted to the inspiration of the moment—like an amateur.

Of course he had to be very economical, even about candle ends, and almost liked such economy for a change; but he got sick of his loneliness, beyond expression—he was a fish out of water.

Then he took it into his head to go and copy a picture at the Louvre—an old master; in this he felt he could not go wrong. He obtained the necessary permission, bought a canvas six feet high, and sat himself before a picture by Nicolas Poussin, I think : a group of angelic women carrying another woman though the air up to heaven.

They were not very much to his taste, but more so than any others. His chief notion about women in pictures was that they should be very beautiful—since they cannot make themselves agreeable in any other way ; and they are not always so in the works of the great masters. At least, *he* thought not. These are matters of taste, of course.

He had no notion of how to divide his canvas into squares—a device by which one makes it easier to get the copy into proper proportion, it seems. He began by sketching the head of the principal woman roughly in the middle of his canvas, and then he wanted to begin painting it at once—he was so impatient.

Students, female students especially, came and interested themselves in his work, and some *rapins* asked him questions, and tried to help him and give him tips. But the more they told him, the more helpless and hopeless he grew. He soon felt conscious he was becoming quite a funny man again—a centre of interest—in a new line ; but it gave him no pleasure whatever.

After a week of this mistaken drudgery he sat despondent one afternoon on a bench in the Champs Élysées and watched the gay people, and thought himself very down on his luck ; he was tired and hot and miserable—it was the beginning of July. If he had known how, he would almost have shed tears. His loneliness was not to be borne, and his longing to feel once more the north had become a chronic ache.

A tall, thin, shabby man came and sat by his side, and made himself a cigarette, and hummed a tune—a well-known quartier-latin song—about "Mon Aldegonde, ma blonde," and "Ma Rodogune, ma brune."

Barty just glanced at this jovial person and found he didn't look jovial at all, but rather sad and seedy and out at elbows—by no means of the kind that the fair Aldegonde or her dark sister would have much to say to.

Also that he wore very strong spectacles, and that his brown eyes, when turned Barty's way, vibrated with a quick, tremulous motion and sideways, as if they had the "gigs."

Much moved and excited, Barty got up and put out his hand to the stranger, and said :

" Bonjour, Monsieur Bonzig ! comment allez-vous ?"

Bonzig opened his eyes at this well-dressed Briton (for Barty had clothes to last him a French lifetime).

"Pardonnez-moi, monsieur—mais je n'ai pas l'honneur de vous remettre !"

"Je m'appelle Josselin—de chez Brossard !"

"Ah ! Mon Dieu, mon cher, mon très-cher !" said Bonzig, and got up and seized Barty's both hands—and all but hugged him.

"Mais quel bonheur de vous revoir ! Je pense à vous si souvent, et à Ouittebé ! comme vous êtes changé—et quel beau garçon vous êtes ! qui vous aurait reconnu ! Dieu de Dieu—c'est un rêve ! Je n'en reviens pas !" etc., etc. . . .

And they walked off together, and told the other each an epitome of his history since they parted; and dined together cheaply, and spent a happy evening walking up and down the boulevards, and smoking many cigarettes —from the Madeleine to the Porte St.-Martin and back— again and again.

"Non, mon cher Josselin," said Bonzig, in answer to

"'BONJOUR, MONSIEUR BONZIG'"

a question of Barty's—"non, I have not yet seen the sea . . ; it will come in time. But at least I am no longer a damned usher (un sacré pion d'études) ; I am an artist—un peintre de marines—at last ! It is a happy existence. I fear my talent is not very imposing, but my perseverance is exceptional, and I am only forty-five. Anyhow, I am able to support myself—not in splendor, certainly ; but my wants are few and my health is perfect. I will put you up to many things, my dear boy. . . . We will storm the citadel of fame together. . . ."

Bonzig had a garret somewhere, and painted in the studio of a friend, not far from Barty's lodging. This friend, one Lirieux, was a very clever young man—a genius, according to Bonzig. He drew illustrations on wood with surprising quickness and facility and verve, and painted little oil-pictures of sporting life—a garde champêtre in a wood with his dog, or with his dog on a dusty road, or crossing a stream, or getting over a stile, and so forth. The dog was never left out; and these things he would sell for twenty, thirty, even fifty francs. He painted very quick and very well. He was also a capital good fellow, industrious and cultivated and refined, and full of self-respect.

Next to his studio he had a small bedroom which he shared with a younger brother, who had just got a small government appointment that kept him at work all day, in some ministère. In this studio Bonzig painted his marines—still helping himself from *La France Maritime,* as he used to do at Brossard's.

He was good at masts and cordage against an evening sky—"l'heure où le jaune de Naples rentre dans la nature," as he called it. He was also excellent at foam, and far-off breakers, and sea-gulls, but very bad at the human figure — sailors and fishermen and their wives.

Sometimes Lirieux would put one in for him with a few dabs.

As soon as Bonzig had finished a picture, which didn't take very long, he carried it round, still wet, to the small dealers, bearing it very carefully aloft, so as not to smudge it. Sometimes (if there were a sailor by Lirieux) he would get five or even ten francs for it; and then it was ·'Mon Aldegonde" with him all the rest of the day; for success always took the form, in his case, of nasally humming that amorous refrain.

But it very often happened that he was dumb, poor fellow—no supper, no song!

Lirieux conceived such a liking for Barty that he insisted on taking him into his studio as a pupil-assistant, and setting him to draw things under his own eye; and Barty would fill Bonzig's French sea pieces with Whitby fishermen, and Bonzig got to sing "Mon Aldegonde" much oftener than before.

And chumming with these two delightful men, Barty grew to know a clean, quiet happiness which more than made up for lost past splendors and dissipations and gay dishonor. He wasn't even funny; they wouldn't have understood it. Well-bred Frenchmen don't understand English fun — not even in the quartier latin, as a general rule. Not that it's too subtle for them; *that's* not why!

Thus pleasantly August wore itself away, Bonzig and Barty nearly always dining together for about a franc apiece, including the waiter, and not badly. Bonzig knew all the cheap eating - houses in Paris, and what each was specially renowned for — "bonne friture," "fricassée de lapin," "pommes sautées," "soupe aux choux," etc., etc.

Then, after dinner, a long walk and talk and ciga-

174

rettes—or they would look in at a café chantant, a bal de barrière, the gallery of a cheap theatre—then a bock outside a café—et bonsoir la compagnie!

On September the 1st, Lirieux and his brother went to see their people in the south, leaving the studio to Bonzig and Barty, who made the most of it, though greatly missing the genial young painter, both as a companion and a master and guide.

One beautiful morning Bonzig called for Barty at his crémerie, and proposed they should go by train to some village near Paris and spend a happy day in the country, lunching on bread and wine and sugar at some little roadside inn. Bonzig made a great deal of this lunch. It had evidently preoccupied him.

Barty was only too delighted. They went on the impériale of the Versailles train and got out at Ville d'Avray, and found the kind of little pothouse they wanted. And Barty had to admit that no better lunch for the price could be than "small blue wine" sweetened with sugar, and a hunch of bread sopped in it.

Then they had a long walk in pretty woods and meadows, sketching by the way, chatting to laborers and soldiers and farm - people, smoking endless cigarettes of caporal ; and finally they got back to Paris the way they came—so hungry that Barty proposed they should treat themselves for once to a "prix-fixe" dinner at Carmagnol's, in the Passage Choiseul, where they gave you hors-d'œuvres, potage, three courses and dessert and a bottle of wine, for two francs fifty—and everything scrupulously clean.

So to the Passage Choiseul they went ; but just on the threshold of the famous restaurant (which filled the entire arcade with its appetizing exhalations) Bonzig suddenly remembered, to his great regret, that close by there lived a young married couple of the name of Lousteau, who were great friends of his, and who expected him to dine with them at least once a week.

"I haven't been near them for a fortnight, mon cher, and it is just their dinner hour. I am afraid I must really just run in and eat an *aile de poulet* and a *pêche au vin* with them, and give them of my news, or they will be mortally offended. I'll be back with you just when you are *'entre la poire et le fromage'*—so, sans adieu !" and he bolted.

Barty went in and selected his menu ; and waiting for his hors-d'œuvre, he just peeped out of the door and looked up and down the arcade, which was always festive and lively at that hour.

To his great surprise he saw Bonzig leisurely flâning about with his cigarette in his mouth, his hands in his pockets, his long spectacled nose in the air—gazing at the shop windows. Suddenly the good man dived into a baker's shop, and came out again in half a minute with a large brown roll, and began to munch it—still gazing at the shop windows, and apparently quite content.

Barty rushed after and caught hold of him, and breathlessly heaped bitter reproaches on him for his base and unfriendly want of confidence—snatched his roll and threw it away, dragged him by main force into Carmagnol's, and made him order the dinner he preferred and sit opposite.

"Ma foi, mon cher !" said Bonzig—" I own to you that I am almost at the end of my resources for the moment —and also that the prospect of a good dinner in your amiable company is the reverse of disagreeable to me. I thank you in advance, with all my heart !"

"My dear M'sieur Bonzig," says Barty, "you will wound me deeply if you don't look on me like a brother, as I do you ; I can't tell you how deeply you *have* wounded me already ! Give me your word of honor that you will share ma mangeaille with me till I haven't a sou left !"

And so they made it up, and had a capital dinner and a capital evening, and Barty insisted that in future they should always mess together at his expense till better days—and they did.

But Barty found that his own money was just giving out, and wrote to his bankers in London for more. Somehow it didn't arrive for nearly a week ; and they knew at last what it was to dine for five sous each ($2\frac{1}{2}d.$)— with loss of appetite just before the meal instead of after.

Of course Barty might very well have pawned his watch or his scarf-pin ; but whatever trinkets he possessed had been given him by his beloved Lady Archibald—everything pawnable he had in the world, even his guitar ! And he could not bear the idea of taking them to the " Mont de Piété."

So he was well pleased one Sunday morning when his remittance arrived, and he went in search of his friend, that they might compensate themselves for a week's abstinence by a famous déjeuner. But Bonzig was not to be found ; and Barty spent that day alone, and gorged in solitude and guzzled in silence—moult tristement, à l'anglaise.

He was aroused from his first sleep that night by the irruption of Bonzig in a tremendous state of excitement. It seems that a certain Baron (whose name I've forgotten), and whose little son the ex-usher had once coached in early Latin and Greek, had written, begging him to call and see him at his château near Melun ; that Bonzig had walked there that very day—thirty miles ; and found the Baron was leaving next morning for a villa he possessed near Étretat, and wished him to join him there the day after, and stay with him for a couple of months—to coach his son in more classics for a couple of hours in the forenoon.

Bonzig was to dispose of the rest of his time as he liked, except that he was commissioned to paint six "marines" for the baronial dining-room; and the Baron had most considerately given him four hundred francs in advance!

"So, then, to-morrow afternoon at six, my dear Josselin, you dine with *me*, for once — not in the Passage Choiseul this time, good as it is there! But at Babet's, en plein Palais Royal! un jour de séparation, vous comprenez! the dinner will be good, I promise you: a calf's head à la vinaigrette—they are famous for that, at Babet's — and for their Pauillac and their St.-Estèphe; at least, I'm told so! nous en ferons l'expérience. . . . And now I bid you good-night, as I have to be up before the day—so many things to buy and settle and arrange —first of all to procure myself a 'maillot' and a 'peignoir,' and shoes for the beach! I know where to get these things much cheaper than at the seaside. Oh! la mer, la mer! Enfin je vais piquer ma tête [take my header] là dedans—*et pas plus tard qu'après-demain soir.* . . . À demain, très-cher camarade—six heures—chez Babet!"

And, delirious with joyful anticipations, the good Bonzig ran away—all but "piquant sa tête" down the narrow staircase, and whistling "Mon Aldegonde" at the very top of his whistle; and even outside he shouted:

> "Ouïle—mé—sekile rô,
> sekile rô,
> sekile rô . . .
> Ouïle—mé—sekile rô
> Tat brinn my laddé ôme!"

He had to be silenced by a sergent de ville.

And next day they dined at Babet's, and Bonzig was so happy he had to beg pardon for his want of feeling at seeming so exuberant "un jour de séparation! mais venez aussi, Josselin—nous piquerons nos têtes ensemble, et nagerons de conserve. . . ."

But Barty could not afford this little outing, and he was very sad—with a sadness that not all the Pauillac and St.-Estèphe in M. Babet's cellars could have dispelled.

He made his friend a present of a beautiful pair of razors—English razors, which he no longer needed, since he no longer meant to shave—"en signe de mon deuil!" as he said. They had been the gift of Lord Archibald in happier days. Alas! he had forgotten to give his uncle Archie the traditional halfpenny, but he took good care to extract a sou from le Grand Bonzig!

So ended this little episode in Barty's life. He never saw Bonzig again, nor heard from him, and *of* him only once more. That sou was wasted.

It was at Blankenberghe, on the coast of Belgium, that he at last had news of him—a year later—at the café on the plage, and in such an odd and unexpected manner that I can't help telling how it happened.

One afternoon a corner of the big coffee-room was being arranged for private theatricals, in which Barty was to perform the part of a waiter. He had just borrowed the real waiter's jacket and apron, and was dusting the little tables for the amusement of Mlle. Solange, the dame de comptoir, and of the waiter, Prosper, who had on Barty's own shooting-jacket.

Suddenly an old gentleman came in and beckoned to Barty and ordered a demi-tasse and petit-verre. There were no other customers at that hour.

"'DEMI-TASSE—VOILÀ, M'SIEUR'"

Mlle. Solange was horrified ; but Barty insisted on waiting on the old gentleman in person, and helped him to his coffee and pousse - café with all the humorous grace I can so well imagine, and handed him the *Indépendance Belge*, and went back to superintend the arrangements for the coming play.

Presently the old gentleman looked up from his paper and became interested, and soon he grew uneasy, and finally he rose and went up to Barty and bowed, and said (in French, of course):

"Monsieur, I have made a very stupid mistake. I am near - sighted, and that must be my apology. Besides, you have revenged yourself 'avec tant d'esprit,' that you will not bear me *rancune!* May I ask you to accept my card, with my sincere excuses ? . . ."

And lo ! it was Bonzig's famous Baron ! Barty immediately inquired after his lost friend.

"Bonzig ? Ah, monsieur — what a terrible tragedy ! Poor Bonzig, the best of men—he came to me at Étretat. I invited him there from sheer friendship ! He was drowned the very evening he arrived.

"He went and bathed after sunset—on his own responsibility and without mentioning it to any one. How it happened I don't know—nobody knows. He was a good swimmer, I believe, but very blind without his glasses. He undressed behind a rock on the shore, which is against the regulations. His body was not found till two days after, three leagues down the coast.

"He had an aged mother, who came to Étretat. It was harrowing ! They were people who had seen better days," etc., etc., etc.

And so no more of le Grand Bonzig.

Nor did Barty ever again meet Lirieux, in whose existence a change had also been wrought by fortune ; but whether for good or evil I can't say. He was taken to Italy and Greece by a wealthy relative. What happened to him there—whether he ever came back, or succeeded or failed — Barty never heard ! He dropped out of Barty's life as completely as if he had been drowned like his old friend.

These episodes, like many others past and to come in this biography, had no particular influence on Barty Josselin's career, and no reference to them is to be found in anything he has ever written. My only reason for telling them is that I found them so interesting when he told *me*, and so characteristic of himself. He was "bon raconteur." I'm afraid I'm not, and that I've lugged these good people in by the hair of the head; but I'm doing my best. " La plus belle fille au monde ne peut donner que ce qu'elle a !"

I look to my editor to edit me—and to my illustrator to pull me through.

That autumn (1856) my father went to France for six weeks, on business. My sister Ida went with the Gibsons to Ramsgate, and I remained in London with my mother. I did my best to replace my father in Barge Yard, and when he came back he was so pleased with me (and I think with himself also) that he gave me twenty pounds, and said, "Go to Paris for a week, Bob, and see Barty, and give him this, with my love."

And " this " was another twenty-pound note. He had never given me such a sum in my life—not a quarter of it ; and " this " was the first time he had ever tipped Barty.

Things were beginning at last to go well with him. He had arranged to sell the vintages of Bordeaux and

Champagne, as well as those of Burgundy; and was dreaming of those of Germany and Portugal and Spain. Fortune was beginning to smile on Barge Yard, and ours was to become the largest wine business in the world— comme tout un chacun sait.

I started for Paris that very night, and knocked at Barty's bedroom door by six next morning; it was hardly daylight—a morning to be remembered; and what a breakfasting at Babet's, after a rather cold swim in the Passy school of natation, and a walk all round the outside of the school that was once ours!

Barty looked very well, but very thin, and his small sprouting beard and mustache had quite altered the character of his face. I shall distress my lady readers if I tell them the alteration was not an improvement; so I won't.

What a happy week that was to me I leave to the reader's imagination. We took a large double-bedded room at the Hôtel de Lille et d'Albion in case we might want to smoke and talk all night; we did, I think, and had our coffee brought up to us in the morning.

I will not attempt to describe the sensations of a young man going back to his beloved Paris "after five years." Tout ça, c'est de l'histoire ancienne. And Barty and Paris together—that is not for such a pen as mine.

I showed him a new photograph of Leah Gibson—a very large one and an excellent. He gazed at it a long time with his magnifying-glass and without, all his keen perceptions on the alert; and I watched his face narrowly.

"My eyes! She *is* a beautiful young woman, and no mistake!" he said, with a sigh. "You mustn't let her slip through your fingers, Bob!"

"How about that toss?" said I, and laughed.

"Oh, I resign *my* claim ; she's not for the likes o' me. You're going to be a great capitalist—a citizen of credit and renown. I'm Mr. Nobody, of nowhere. Go in and win, my boy ; you have my best wishes. If I can scrape together enough money to buy myself a white waistcoat and a decent coat, I'll be your best man ; or some left-off things of yours might do—we're about of a size, aren't we ? You've become très bel homme, Bob, plutôt bel homme que joli garçon, hein ? That's what women are fond of ; English women especially. I'm nowhere now, without my uniform and the rest. Is it still Skinner who builds for you ? Good old Skinner ! Mes compliments !"

This simple little speech took a hidden weight off my mind and left me very happy. I confided frankly to the good Barty that no Sally in any alley had ever been more warmly adored by any industrious young London apprentice than was Leah Gibson by me !

"Ça y est, alors ! Je te félicite d'avance, et je garde mes larmes pour quand tu seras parti. Allons dîner chez Babet : j'ai soif de boire à ton bonheur !"

Before I left we met an English artist he had known at the British Museum—an excellent fellow, one Walters, who took him under his wing, and was the means of his entering the atelier Troplong in the Rue des Belges as an art student. And thus Barty began his art studies in a proper and legitimate way. It was characteristic of him that this should never have occurred to him before.

So when I parted with the dear fellow things were looking a little brighter for him too.

All through the winter he worked very hard—the first to come, the last to go ; and enjoyed his studio life thoroughly.

Such readers as I am likely to have will not require to

be told what the interior of a French atelier of the kind
is like, nor its domestic economy ; nor will I attempt to
describe all the fun and the frolic, although I heard it
all from Barty in after-years, and very good it was. I
almost felt I'd studied there myself ! He was a prime
favorite—" le Beau Josselin," as he was called.

He made very rapid progress, and had already begun
to work in colors by the spring. He made many friends,
but led a quiet, industrious life, unrelieved (as far as I
know) by any of those light episodes one associates with
student life in Paris. His principal amusements through
the long winter evenings were the café and the brasserie,
mild écarté, a game at billiards or dominoes, and long
talks about art and literature with the usual unkempt
young geniuses of the place and time—French, English,
American.

Then he suddenly took it into his head to go to Antwerp ; I don't know who influenced him in this direction,
but I arranged to meet him there at the end of April—
and we spent a delightful week together, staying at the
" Grand Laboureur" in the Place de Meer. The town
was still surrounded by the old walls and the moat, and
of a picturesqueness that seemed as if it would never
pall.

Twice or three times that week British tourists and
travellers landed at the quai by the Place Verte from
The Baron Osy—and this landing was Barty's delight.

The sight of fair, fresh English girls, with huge crino-
lines, and their hair done up in chenille nets, made him
long for England again, and the sound of their voices
went nigh to weakening his resolve. But he stood firm
to the last, and saw me off by *The Baron*. I felt a
strange "serrement de cœur" as I left him standing
there, so firm, as if he had been put "au piquet" by

M. Dumollard! and so thin and tall and slender—and his boyish face so grave. Good heavens! how much alone he seemed, who was so little built to live alone!

It is really not too much to say that I would have given up to him everything I possessed in the world—every blessed thing! except Leah—and Leah was not mine to give!

Now and again Barty's face would take on a look so ineffably, pathetically, angelically simple and childlike that it moved one to the very depths, and made one feel like father and mother to him in one! It was the true revelation of his innermost soul, which in many ways remained that of a child even in his middle age and till he died. All his life he never quite put away childish things!

I really believe that in bygone ages he would have moved the world with that look, and been another Peter the Hermit!

He became a pupil at the academy under De Keyser and Van Lerius, and worked harder than ever.

He took a room nearly all window on a second floor in the Marché aux Œufs, just under the shadow of the gigantic spire which rings a fragment of melody every seven minutes and a half—and the whole tune at midnight, fortissimo.

He laid in a stock of cigars at less than a centime apiece, and dried them in the sun; they left as he smoked them a firm white ash two inches long; and he grew so fond of them that he cared to smoke nothing else.

He rose before the dawn, and went for a swim more than a mile away—got to the academy at six—worked till eight—breakfasted on a little roll called a pistolet, and a cup of coffee; then the academy again from nine till twelve—when dinner, the cheapest he had ever known, but not the worst. Then work again all the afternoon, copying old masters at the Gallery. Then a cheap supper, a long walk along the quais or ramparts or outside —a game of dominoes, and a glass or two of " Malines" or " Louvain"—then bed, without invading hordes ; the Flemish are as clean as the Dutch ; and there he would soon smoke and read himself to sleep in spite of chimes —which lull you, when once you get " achimatized," as he called it, meaning of course to be funny : a villanous kind of fun—caught, I fear, in Barge Yard, Bucklersbury. It used to rain puns in the City—especially in the Stock Exchange, which is close to Barge Yard.

It was a happy life, and he grew to like it better than any life he had led yet; besides, he improved rapidly, as his facility was great—for painting as for everything he tried his hand at.

He also had a very agreeable social existence.

One morning at the academy, two or three days after his arrival, he was accosted by a fellow-student—one Tescheles—who introduced himself as an old pupil of Troplong's in the Rue des Belges. They had a long chat in French about the old Paris studio. Among other things, Tescheles asked if there were still any English there.

" Oui "—says Barty—" un nommé Valtères " . . .

Barty pronounced this name as if it were French ; and noticed that Tescheles smiled, exclaiming :

" Parbleu, ce bon Valtères—je l'connais bien !"

Next day Tescheles came up to an English student called Fox and said :

" Well, old stick-in-the-mud, how are *you* getting on ?"

" Why, you don't mean to say *you're* an Englishman ?" says Barty to Tescheles.

PETER THE HERMIT AU PIQUET

"Good heavens! you don't mean to say *you* are! fancy your calling poor old Walters *Valtères !*"

And after that they became very intimate, and that was a good thing for Barty.

The polyglot Tescheles was of a famous musical family, of mixed German and Russian origin, naturalized in England and domiciled in France—a true cosmopolite and a wonderful linguist, besides being also a cultivated musician and excellent painter ; and all the musicians, famous or otherwise, that passed through Antwerp made his rooms a favorite resort and house of call. And Barty was introduced into a world as delightful to him as it was new—and to music that ravished his soul with a novel enchantment : Chopin, Liszt, Wagner, Schumann—and he found that Schubert had written a few other songs besides the famous "Serenade"!

One evening he was even asked if he could make music himself, and actually volunteered to sing—and sang that famous ballad of Balfe's which seems destined to become immortal in this country—"When other lips" . . . *alias*, "Then you'll remember me !"

Strange to say, it was absolutely new to this high musical circle, but they went quite mad over it; and the beautiful melody got naturalized from that moment in Belgium and beyond, and Barty was proclaimed the primo tenore of Antwerp—although he was only a barytone !

A fortnight after this Barty heard "When other lips" played by the "Guides" band in the park at Brussels. Its first appearance out of England—and all through him.

Then he belonged to the Antwerp "Cercle Artistique," where he made many friends and was very popular, as I can well imagine.

Thus he was happier than he had ever been in his life ; but for one thing that plagued him now and again : his oft-recurring desire to be conscious once more of the north, which he had not felt for four or five years.

The want of this sensation at certain periods—especially at night—would send a chill thrill of desolation through him like a wave ; a wild panic, a quick agony, as though the true meaning of absolute loneliness were suddenly realized by a lightning flash of insight, and it were to last for ever and ever.

This would pass away in a second or two, but left a haunting recollection behind for many hours. And then all was again sunshine, and the world was made of many friends—and solitude was impossible evermore.

One memorable morning this happiness received a check and a great horror befell him. It was towards the end of summer—just before the vacation.

With a dozen others, he was painting the head of an old man from the life, when he became quite suddenly conscious of something strange in his sight. First he shut his left eye and saw with his right quite perfectly ; then he shut the right, and lo ! whatever he looked at with the left dwindled to a vanishing point and became invisible. No rubbing or bathing of his eye would alter the terrible fact, and he knew what great fear really means, for the first time.

Much kind concern was expressed, and Van Lerius told him to go at once to a Monsieur Noiret, a professor at the Catholic University of Louvain, who had attended *him* for the eyes, and had the reputation of being the first oculist in Belgium.

Barty wrote immediately and an appointment was made, and in three days he saw the great man, half professor, half priest, who took him into a dark chamber lighted by a lamp, and dilated his pupil with atropine, and looked into his eye with the newly discovered " ophthalmoscope."

Professor Noiret told him it was merely a congestion of the retina—for which no cause could be assigned; and that he would be cured in less than a month. That he was to have a seton let into the back of his neck, dry-cup himself on the chest and thighs night and morning, and take a preparation of mercury three times a day. Also that he must go to the seaside immediately—and he recommended Ostend.

Barty told him that he was an impecunious art student, and that Ostend was a very expensive place.

Noiret considerately recommended Blankenberghe, which was cheap; asked for and took his full fee, and said, with a courtly priestly bow :

"If you are not cured, come back in a month. *Au revoir !*"

So poor Barty had the seton put in by a kind of barbersurgeon, and was told how to dress it night and morning; got his medicines and his dry-cupping apparatus, and went off to Blankenberghe quite hopeful.

And there things happened to him which I really think are worth telling; in the first place, because, even if they did not concern Barty Josselin, they should be amusing for their own sake—that is, if I could only tell them as he told me afterwards; and I will do my best !

And then he was nearing the end of the time when he was to remain as other mortals are. His new life was soon to open, the great change to which we owe the Barty Josselin who had changed the world for *us !*"

Besides, this is a biography—not a novel—not literature ! So what does it matter how it's written, so long as it's all true !

Part Fifth

"Ô céleste haine,
    Comment t'assouvir ?
Ô souffrance humaine,
    Qui te peut guérir ?
Si lourde est ma peine
    J'en voudrais mourir—
    Tel est mon désir !

"Navré de comprendre,
    Las de compatir,
Pour ne plus entendre,
    Ni voir, ni sentir,
Je suis prêt à rendre
    Mon dernier soupir—
    Et c'est mon désir !

"Ne plus rien connaître,
    Ni me souvenir—
Ne jamais renaître,
    Ni me rendormir—
Ne plus jamais être,
    Mais en bien finir—
    Voilà mon désir !"—ANON.

BARTY went third class to Bruges, and saw all over it,
and slept at the "Fleur de Blé," and heard new chimes,
and remembered his Longfellow.

Next morning, a very fine one, as he was hopefully
smoking his centime cigar with immense relish near the
little three-horsed wagonette that was to bear him to

Blankenberghe, he saw that he was to have three fellow-passengers, with a considerable amount of very interesting luggage, and rejoiced.

First, a tall man about thirty, in a very smart white summer suit, surmounted by a jaunty little straw hat with a yellow ribbon. He was strikingly handsome, and wore immense black whiskers but no mustache, and had a most magnificent double row of white, pearly teeth, which he showed very much when he smiled, and he smiled very often. He was evidently a personage of importance and very well off, for he gave himself great airs and ordered people about and chaffed them, and it made them laugh instead of making them angry ; and he was obeyed with wonderful alacrity. He spoke French fluently, but with a marked Italian accent.

Next, a very blond lady of about the same age, not beautiful, but rather overdressed, and whose accent, when she spoke French, was very German, and who looked as if she might be easily moved to wrath. Now and then she spoke to the gentleman in a very audible Italian aside, and Barty was able to gather that her Italian was about as rudimentary as his own.

Last and least, a pale, plain, pathetic little girl of six or eight, with a nose rather swollen, and a black plait down her back, and large black eyes, something like Leah Gibson's ; and she never took these eyes off Barty's face.

Their luggage consisted of two big trunks, a guitar and violin (in their cases), and music-books bound together by a rope.

"Vous allez à Blankenberghe, mossié ?" said the Italian, with a winning smile.

Barty answered in the affirmative, and the Italian smiled ecstatic delight.

"Jé souis bienn content—nous férons route ensiemblé. . . ." I will translate : "I call myself Carlo Veronese—first barytone of the theatre of La Scala, Milan. The signora is my second wife ; she is prima donna assoluta of the grand opera, Naples. The little ragazza is my daughter by my first wife. She is the greatest violinist of her age now living—un' prodige, mossié—un' fenomeno !"

Barty, charmed with his new acquaintance, gave the signore his card, and Carlo Veronese invited him graciously to take a seat in the wagonette, as if it were his own private carriage. Barty, who was the most easily impressed person that ever lived, accepted with as much sincere gratitude as if he hadn't already paid for his place, and they started on their sunny drive of eight miles along the dusty straight Belgian chaussée, bordered with poplars on either side, and paved with flagstones all the way to Blankenberghe.

Signor Veronese informed Barty that on their holiday travels they always managed to combine profit with pleasure, and that he proposed giving a grand concert at the Café on the Plage, or the Kursaal, next day ; that he was going to sing Figaro's great song in the *Barbiere,* and the signora would give " *Roberto, toua qué z'aime* " in French (or, rather, " *Ropert, doi que ch'aime,*" as *she* called it, correcting his accent), and the fenomeno, whose name was Marianina, would play an arrangement of the " Carnival of Venice " by Paganini.

"Ma vous aussi, vous êtes mousicien—jé vois ça par la votre figoure !"

Barty modestly disclaimed all pretensions, and said he was only an art student—a painter.

" All the arts are brothers," said the signore, and the little signorina stole her hand into Barty's and left it there.

194

"Listen," said the signore; "why not arrange to live together, you and we? I hate throwing away money on mere pomposity and grandiosity and show. We always take a little furnished apartment, elle et moi. Then I go and buy provisions, bon marché—and she cooks them —and we have our meals better than at the hotel and at half the price! Join us, unless you like to throw your money by the window!"

The Signorina Marianina's little brown hand gave Barty's a little warm squeeze, and Barty was only too delighted to accept an arrangement that promised to be so agreeable and so practically wise.

They arrived at Blankenberghe, and, leaving their luggage at the wagonette station, went in search of lodgings. These were soon found in a large attic at the top of a house, over a bakery. One little mansarde, with a truckle-bed and wash-hand stand, did for the family of Veronese; another, smaller still, for Barty.

Other mansardes also opened on to the large attic, or grenier, where there were sacks of grain and of flour, and a sweet smell of cleanliness. Barty wondered that such economical arrangements could suit his new friends, but was well pleased; a weight was taken off his mind. He feared a style of living he could not have afforded to share, and here were all difficulties smoothed away without any trouble whatever.

They got in their luggage, and Barty went with the signore in search of bread and meat and wine and ground coffee. When they got back, a little stove was ready lighted in the Veronese garret; they cooked the food in a frying-pan, opening the window wide and closing the door, as the signore thought it useless to inform the world by the sense of smell that they did their cooking *en famille;* and Barty enjoyed the meal immensely, and almost forgot his trouble, but for the pain of his seton.

After lunch the signore produced his placards, already printed by hand, and made some paste in an iron pot, and the signora made coffee. And Veronese tuned his guitar and said :

"Jé vais vous canter couelquécose—una piccola cosa da niente !—vous comprenez l'Italien ?"

"Oh yes," said Barty : he had picked up a deal of Italian and many pretty Italian canzonets from his friend old Pergolese, who kept the Italian eating-house in Rupert Street. "Sing me a stornella—je les adore."

And he set himself to listen, with his heart in his mouth from sheer pleasurable anticipation.

The signore sang a pretty little song, by Gordigiani, called "Il vero amore." Barty knew it well.

> "E lo mio amor è andato a soggiornare
> A Lucca bella—e diventar signore. . . ."

Alas for lost illusions ! The signore's voice was a coarse, unsympathetic, strident buffo bass, not always quite in the middle of the note ; nor, in spite of his native liveliness of accent and expression, did he make the song interesting or pretty in the least.

Poor Barty had fallen from the skies ; but he did his best not to show his disenchantment, and this, from a kind and amiable way he always had and a constant wish to please, was not difficult.

Then the signora sang "Ô mon Fernand!" from the *Favorita*, in French, but with a hideous German accent and a screech as of some Teutonic peacock, and without a single sympathetic note ; though otherwise well in tune, and with a certain professional knowledge of what she was about.

And then poor Marianina was made to stand up on six music-books, opposite a small music-easel, and play her "Carnival of Venice" on the violin. Every time she made a false note in the difficult variations, her father, with his long, thick, hairy middle finger, gave her a fierce fillip on the nose, and she had to swallow her tears and play on. Barty was almost wild with angry pity, but dissembled, for fear of making her worse enemies in her father and stepmother.

Not that the poor little thing played badly; indeed, she played surprisingly well for her age, and Barty was sincere in his warm commendation of her talent.

" Et vous ne cantez pas du tout—du tout ?" said Veronese.

" Oh, si, quelquefois !"

" Cantez couelquécoze—zé vous accompagnerai sous la guitare !—n'ayez pas paoure—nous sommes indoulgents, elle et moi—"

" Oh—je m'accompagnerai bien moi-même comme je pourrai—" said Barty, and took the guitar, and sang a little French Tyrolienne called " Fleur des Alpes," which he could always sing quite beautifully ; and the effect was droll indeed.

Marianina wept; the signore went down on his knees in a theatrical manner to him, and called him " maestro " and other big Italian names; the Frau signora, with tears in her eyes, asked permission to kiss his hand, which his modesty refused—he kissed hers instead.

" He was a great genius, a bird of God, who had amused himself by making fools of poor, innocent, humble, wandering minstrels. Oh, would he not be generous as he was great and be one of them for a few days, and take half the profits—more—whatever he liked ?" etc.

And indeed they immediately saw the business side of

"THE CARNIVAL OF VENICE"

the question, and were, to do them justice, immensely liberal in their conditions of partnership—and also most distressingly persistent, with adulations that got more and more fulsome the more he held back.

There was a long discussion. Barty had to be quite brutal at the end—told them he was not a musician, but a painter, and that nothing on earth should induce him to join them in their concert.

And finally, much crestfallen and somewhat huffed, the pair went out to post their placards all over the town, and Barty went for a bath and a long walk—suddenly feeling sad again and horribly one-eyed and maimed, and more wofully northless and homeless and friendless than ever.

Blankenberghe was already very full, and when he got back he saw the famous placards everywhere. And found his friends cooking their dinner, and was pressed to join them; and did so—producing a magnificent pasty and some hot-house grapes and two bottles of wine as a peace-offering—and was forgiven.

And after dinner they all sat on grain-sacks together in the large granary, and made music—with lady's-maids and valets and servants of the house for a most genial and appreciative audience — and had a very pleasant evening; and Barty came to the conclusion that he had mistaken his trade—that he sang devilish well, in fact; and so he did.

Whatever his technical shortcomings might be, he could make any tune sound pretty when he sang it. He had the native gift of ease, pathos, rhythm, humor, and charm — and a delightful sympathetic twang in his voice. His mother must have sung something like that; and all Paris went mad about her. No technical teaching in the world can ever match a genuine inheritance; and that's a fact.

Next morning they all bathed together, and Barty un-heroically and quite obscurely saved a life.

The signore and his fat white signora went dancing out into the sunny waves and right away seawards.

Then came Barty with an all-round shirt-collar round his neck and a white tie on, to conceal his seton, and a pair of blue spectacles for the glare. And behind him Marianina, hopping on and following as best she might. He turned round to encourage her, and she had sudden-ly disappeared ; half uneasy, he went back a step or two, and saw her little pale-brown face gasping just beneath the surface—she had just got out of her depth.

He snatched her out, and she clung to him like a small monkey and cried dreadfully, and was sick all over him and herself. He managed to get her back on shore and washed and dried and consoled her before her people came back—and had the tact not to mention this ad-venture, guessing what fillips she would catch on her poor little pink nose for her stupidity. She looked her gratitude for this reticence of his in the most touching way, with her big black eyes—and had a cunning smile of delight at their common tacit understanding. Her rescuer from a watery grave did not apply for the "mé-daille de sauvetage"!

Barty took an immense walk that day to avoid the common repast ; he was getting very tired of the two senior Veroneses.

The concert in the evening was a tremendous suc-cess. The blatant signore sang his Figaro song very well indeed—it suited him better than little feminine love-ditties. The signora was loud and passionate and dra-matic in "Roberto"; and Belgians make more allowance for a German accent in French than Parisians ; besides, it was not *quite* their own language that was being murdered before them. It *may* be, some day ! I sincerely hope so. Je leur veux du bien.

Poor little Marianina stood on her six music-books and played with immense care and earnestness, just like a frightened but well-trained poodle walking on its hind-legs—one eye on her music and the tail of the other on her father, who accompanied her with his guitar. She got an encore, to Barty's great relief ; and to hers too, no doubt—if she hadn't, fillips on the nose for supper that night ! Then there were more solos and duets, with obbligatos for the violin.

Next day Veronese and his wife were in high feather at the Kursaal, where they had sung the night before.

A very distinguished military foreigner, in attendance on some august personage from Spain or Portugal (and later from Ostend), warmly and publicly complimented the signore on "his admirable rendering of 'Largo al factotum'—which, as his dear old friend Rossini had once told him (the General), he (Rossini) had always modestly looked upon as the one thing he had ever written with which he was *almost* pleased !"

Marianina also received warm commendation from this agreeable old soldier, while quite a fashionable crowd was listening ; and Veronese arranged for another concert that evening, and placarded the town accordingly.

Barty managed to escape any more meals in the Casa Veronese, but took Marianina for one or two pleasant walks, and told her stories and sang to her in the grenier, while she improvised for him clever little obbligatos on her fiddle.

He found a cheap eating-house and picked up a companion or two to chat with. He also killed time with his seton-dressing and self dry-cupping — and hired

French novels and read them as much as he dared with his remaining eye, about which he was morbidly nervous; he always fancied it would get its retina congested like the other, in which no improvement manifested itself whatever — and this depressed him very much. He was a most impatient patient.

To return. The second concert was as conspicuous a failure as the first had been a success : the attendance was small and less distinguished, and there was no enthusiasm. The Frau signora slipped a note and lost her temper in the middle of " Roberto," and sang out of tune and with careless, open contempt of her audience, and this the audience seemed to understand and openly resent. Poor Marianina was frightened, and played very wrong notes under the furious gaze of her papa, and finally broke down and cried, and there were some hisses for him, as well as kind and encouraging applause for the child. Then up jumps Barty and gets on the platform and takes the signore's guitar and twangs it, and smiles all round benignly—immense applause !

Then he pats Marianina's thin pale cheek and wipes her eyes and gives her a kiss. Frantic applause ! Then " Fleur des Alpes !"

Ovation ! encore ! bis ! ter !

And for a third encore he sings a very pretty little Flemish ballad about the rose without a thorn—" Het Roosje uit de Dorne." It is the only Flemish song he knows, and I hope I have spelt it right ! And the audience goes quite crazy with enthusiasm, and everybody goes home happy, even the Veroneses—and Marianina does not get filliped that night.

After this the Veroneses tried humbler spheres for the display of their talents, and in less than a week exhausted every pothouse and beer-tavern and low drinking-shop in Blankenberghe! and at last they took to performing for casual coppers in the open street, and went very rapidly down hill. The signore lost his jauntiness and grew sordid and soiled and shabby and humble; the signora looked like a sulky, dirty, draggle-tailed fury, ready to break out into violence on the slightest provocation; poor Marianina got paler and thinner, and Barty was very unhappy about her. The only things left rosy about her were her bruised nose, and her fingers, that always seemed stiff with cold; indeed, they were blue rather than rosy—and anything but clean.

One evening he bought her a little warm gray cloak that took his fancy; when he went home after dinner to give it her he found the three birds of song had taken flight—sans tambour ni trompette, and leaving no message for him. The baker - landlord had turned them adrift—sent them about their business, sacrificing some of his rent to get rid of them; not a heavy loss, I fancy.

Barty went after them all over the little town, but did not find them; he heard they were last seen marching off with guitar and fiddle in a southerly direction along the coast, and found that their luggage was to be sent to Ostend.

He felt very sorry for Marianina and missed her—and gave the cloak to some poor child in the town, and was very lonely.

One morning as he loafed about dejectedly with his hands in his pockets, he found his way to the little Hôtel de Ville, whence issued sounds of music. He went in. It was like a kind of reading - room and concert - room combined; there was a piano there, and a young lady practising, with her mother knitting by her side; and two or three other people, friends of theirs, lounging about and looking at the papers.

The mamma was a very handsome person of aristocratic appearance. The pretty daughter was practising the soprano part in a duet by Campana, which Barty knew well; it was "Una sera d'amore." The tenor had apparently not kept his appointment, and madame expressed some irritation at this; first to a friend, in French, but with a slight English accent—then in English to her daughter; and Barty grew interested.

After a little while, catching the mamma's eye (which was not difficult, as she very frankly and persistently gazed at him, and with a singularly tender and wistful expression of face), he got up and asked in English if he could be of any use—seeing that he knew the music well and had often sung it. The lady was delighted, and Barty and mademoiselle sang the duet in capital style to the mamma's accompaniment: "guarda che bianca luna," etc.

"What a lovely voice you've got! May I ask your name?" says the mamma.

"Josselin."

"English, of course?"

"Upon my word I hardly know whether I'm English or French!" said Barty, and he and the lady fell into conversation.

It turned out that she was Irish, and married to a Belgian soldier, le Général Comte de Clèves (who was a tremendous swell, it seems—but just then in Brussels).

Barty told Madame de Clèves the story of his eye—he was always very communicative about his eye; and she suddenly buried her face in her hands and wept; and mademoiselle told him in a whisper that her eldest brother had gone blind and died three or four years ago, and that he was extraordinarily like Barty both in face and figure.

Presently another son of Madame de Clèves came in—
an officer of dragoons in undress uniform, a splendid
youth. He was the missing tenor, and made his excuses
for being late, and sang very well indeed.

And Barty became the intimate friend of these good
people, who made Blankenberghe a different place to him
—and conceived for him a violent liking, and introduced
him to all their smart Belgian friends; they were quite
a set—bathing together, making music and dancing, taking excursions, and so forth. And before a fortnight was
over Barty had become the most popular young man in
the town, the gayest of the gay, the young guardsman
once more, throwing dull care to the winds; and in spite
of his impecuniosity (of which he made no secret whatever) the *boute-en-train* of the company. And this led
to many droll adventures—of which I will tell one as a
sample.

A certain Belgian viscount, who had a very pretty
French wife, took a dislike to Barty. He had the reputation of being a tremendous fire-eater. His wife, a light-
hearted little flirt (but with not much harm in her), took
a great fancy to him, on the contrary.

One day she asked him for a wax impression of the
seal-ring he wore on his finger, and the following morning he sealed an empty envelope and stamped it with his
ring, and handed it to her on the Plage. She snatched
it with a quick gesture and slipped it into her pocket
with quite a guilty little coquettish look of mutual understanding.

Monsieur Jean (as the viscount was called) noticed
this, and jostled rudely against Josselin, who jostled
back again and laughed.

Then the whole party walked off to the "tir," or shoot-
ing-gallery on the Plage; some wager was on, I believe,

and when they got there they all began to shoot—at different distances, ladies and gentlemen; all but Barty; it was a kind of handicap.

Monsieur Jean, after a fierce and significant look at Barty, slowly raised his pistol, took a deliberate aim at the small target, and fired—hitting it just half an inch over the bull's-eye; a capital shot. Barty couldn't have done better himself. Then taking another loaded pistol, he presented it to my friend by the butt and said, with a solemn bow:

"À vous, monsieur de la garde."

"Messieurs de la garde doivent toujours tirer les premiers!" said Barty, laughing; and carelessly let off his pistol in the direction of the target without even taking aim. A little bell rang, and there was a shout of applause; and Barty was conscious that by an extraordinary fluke he had hit the bull's-eye in the middle, and saw the situation at once.

Suddenly looking very grave and very sad, he threw the pistol away, and said:

"Je ne tire plus—j'ai trop peur d'avoir la main malheureuse un jour!" and smiled benignly at M. Jean.

A moment's silence fell on the party and M. Jean turned very pale.

Barty went up to Madame Jean:

"Will you forgive me for giving you with my seal an empty envelope? I couldn't think of anything pretty enough to write you—so I gave it up. Tear it and forgive me. I'll do better next time!"

The lady blushed and pulled the letter out of her pocket and held it up to the light, and it was, as Barty said, merely an empty envelope and a red seal. She then held it out to her husband and exclaimed:

"Le cachet de Monsieur Josselin, que je lui avais demandé . . . !"

So bloodshed was perhaps avoided, and Monsieur Jean took care not to jostle Josselin any more. Indeed, they became great friends.

For next day Barty strolled into the Salle d'Armes, Rue des Dunes — and there he found Monsieur Jean fencing with young de Clèves, the dragoon. Both were good fencers, but Barty was the finest fencer I ever met in my life, and always kept it up; and remembering his adventure of the previous day, it amused him to affect a careless nonchalance about such trivial things — "des enfantillages !"

"*You* take a turn with Jean, Josselin!" said the dragoon.

"Oh! I'm out of practice — and I've only got one eye. . . ."

"Je vous en prie, monsieur de la garde !" said the viscount.

"Cette fois, alors, nous allons tirer *ensemble !*" says Barty, and languidly dons the mask with an affected air, and makes a fuss about the glove not suiting him; and then, in spite of his defective sight, which seems to make no difference, he lightly and gracefully gives M. Jean such a dressing as that gentleman had never got in his life—not even from his maître d'armes : and afterwards to young de Clèves the same. Well I knew his way of doing this kind of thing !

So Barty and M. and Madame Jean became quite intimate—and with his usual indiscretion Barty told them how he fluked that bull's-eye, and they were charmed !

"Vous êtes impayable, savez-vous, mon cher !" says M. Jean—"vous avez tous les talents, et un million dans le gosier par-dessus le marché ! Si jamais je puis vous être de service, savez-vous, comptez sur moi pour la vie . . ." said the impulsive viscount when they bade each other good-bye at the end.

"'À VOUS, MONSIEUR DE LA GARDE!'"

"Et plus jamais d'enveloppes vides, quand vous m'écrirez !" says madame.

So frivolous time wore on, and Barty found it pleasant to frivol in such pleasant company — very pleasant indeed ! But when alone in his garret, with his seton-dressing and dry-cuppings, it was not so gay. He had to confess to himself that his eye was getting slowly worse instead of better; darkening day by day; and a little more retina had been taken in by the strange disease—"la peau de chagrin," as he nicknamed this wretched retina of his, after Balzac's famous story. He could still see with the left of it and at the bottom, but a veil had come over the middle and all the rest ; by daylight he could see through this veil, but every object he saw was discolored and distorted and deformed—it was worse than darkness itself ; and this was so distressing, and so interfered with the sight of the other eye, that when the sun went down, the total darkness in the ruined portion of his left retina came as a positive relief. He took all this very desperately to heart and had very terrible forebodings. For he had never known an ache or a pain, and had innocently gloried all his life in the singular perfection of his five wits.

Then his money was coming to an end; he would soon have to sing in the streets, like Veronese, with Lady Archibald's guitar.

Dear Lady Archibald ! When things went wrong with her she would always laugh, and say:

"Les misères du jour font le bonheur du lendemain !"

This he would say or sing to himself over and over again, and go to bed at night quite hopeful and sanguine after a merry day spent among his many friends ; and soon sink into sleep, persuaded that his trouble was a bad dream which next morning would scatter and dispel. But when he woke, it was to find the grim reality sitting by his pillow, and he couldn't dry-cup it away. The very sunshine was an ache as he went out and got his breakfast with his blue spectacles on ; and black care would link its bony arm in his as he listlessly strolled by the much-sounding sea—and cling to him close as he swam or dived; and he would wonder what he had ever done that so serious and tragic a calamity should have befallen so light a person as himself ; who could only dance and sing and play the fool to make people laugh—Rigoletto—Triboulet—a mere grasshopper, no ant or bee or spider, not even a third-class beetle—surely this was not according to the eternal fitness of things !

And thus in the unutterable utterness of his dejection he would make himself such evil cheer that he sickened with envy at the mere sight of any living thing that could see out of two eyes—a homeless irresponsible dog, a hunchback beggar, a crippled organ-grinder and his monkey—till he met some acquaintance ; even but a rolling fisherman with a brown face and honest blue eyes—a pair of them—and then he would forget his sorrow and his envy in chat and jokes and laughter with him over each a centime cigar ; and was set up in good spirits for the day ! Such was Barty Josselin, the most ready lover of his kind that ever existed, the slave of his last impression.

And thus he lived under the shadow of the sword of Damocles for many months ; on and off, for years—indeed, as long as he lived at all. It is good discipline. It rids one of much superfluous self-complacency and puts a wholesome check on our keeping too good a conceit of ourselves ; it prevents us from caring too meanly about mean things—too keenly about our own infinitesimal personalities ; it makes us feel quick sympathy for those who live under a like condition : there are many such weapons dangling over the heads of us poor mortals by just a hair—a panoply, an armory, a very arsenal ! And we grow to learn in time that when the hair gives way and the big thing falls, the blow is not half so bad as the fright had been, even if it kills us ; and more often than not it is but the shadow of a sword, after all ; a bogie that has kept us off many an evil track —perhaps even a blessing in disguise ! And in the end, down comes some other sword from somewhere else and cuts for us the Gordian knot of our brief tangled existence, and solves the riddle and sets us free.

This is a world of surprises, where little ever happens but the unforeseen, which is seldom worth meeting half-way ! And these moral reflections of mine are quite unnecessary and somewhat obvious, but they harm nobody, and are very soothing to make and utter at my time of life. Pity the sorrows of a poor old man and forgive him his maudlin garrulity. . . .

One afternoon, lolling in deep dejection on the top of a little sandy hillock, a "dune," and plucking the long coarse grass, he saw a very tall elderly lady, accompanied by her maid, coming his way along the asphalt path that overlooked the sea—or rather, that prevented the sea from overlooking the land and overflowing it !

She was in deep black and wore a thick veil.

With a little jump of surprise he recognized his aunt Caroline—Lady Caroline Grey—of all his aunts the aunt who had loved him the best as a boy — whom he had loved the best.

She was a Roman Catholic, and very devout indeed—a

widow, and childless now. And between her and Barty a coolness had fallen during the last few years—a heavy raw thick mist of cold estrangement; and all on account of his London life and the notoriety he had achieved there; things of which she disapproved entirely, and thought "unworthy of a gentleman": and who can blame her for thinking so?

She had at first written to him long letters of remonstrance and good advice; which he gave up answering, after a while. And when they met in society, her manner had grown chill and distant and severe.

He hadn't seen or heard of his aunt Caroline for three or four years; but at the sudden sight of her a wave of tender childish remembrance swept over him, and his heart beat quite warmly to her: affliction is a solvent of many things, and first-cousin to forgiveness.

She passed without looking his way, and he jumped up and followed her, and said:

"Oh, Aunt Caroline! won't you even speak to me?"

She started violently, and turned round, and cried: "Oh, Barty, Barty, where have you been all these years?" and seized both his hands, and shook all over.

"Oh. Barty—my beloved little Barty—take me somewhere where we can sit down and talk. I've been thinking of you very much, Barty—I've lost my poor son—he died last Christmas! I was afraid you had forgotten my existence! I was thinking of you the very moment you spoke!"

The maid left them, and she took his arm and they found a seat.

She put up her veil and looked at him: there was a great likeness between them in spite of the difference of age. She had been his father's favorite sister (some ten

years younger than Lord Runswick); and she was very
handsome still, though about fifty-five.

"Oh, Barty, my darling—how things have gone wrong
between us! Is it *all* my doing? Oh, I hope not!..."
And she kissed him.

"How like, how like! And you're getting a little
black and bulgy under the eyes—especially the left one—
and so did *he*, at just about your age! And how thin
you are!"

"I don't think anything need ever go wrong between
us again, Aunt Caroline! I am a very altered person,
and a very unlucky one!"

"Tell me, dear!"

And he told her all his story, from the fatal quarrel
with her brother Lord Archibald—and the true history
of that quarrel; and all that had happened since: he had
nothing to keep back.

She frequently wept a little, for truth was in every
tone of his voice; and when it came to the story of his
lost eye, she wept very much indeed. And his need of affection, of female affection especially, and of kinship, was
so immense that he clung to this most kind and loving
woman as if she'd been his mother come back from the
grave, or his dear Lady Archibald.

This meeting made a great difference to Barty in many
ways — made amends! Lady Caroline meant to pass
the winter at Malines, of all places in the world. The
Archbishop was her friend, and she was friends also with
one or two priests at the seminary there. She was by no
means rich, having but an annuity of not quite three
hundred a year; and it soon became the dearest wish of
her heart that Barty should live with her for a while, and
be nursed by her if he wanted nursing; and she thought
he did. Besides, it would be convenient on account of

"'I AM A VERY ALTERED PERSON!'"

his doctor, M. Noiret, of the University of Louvain, which was near Malines—half an hour by train.

And Barty was only too glad; this warm old love and devotion had suddenly dropped on to him by some happy enchantment out of the skies at a moment of sore need. And it was with a passion of gratitude that he accepted his aunt's proposals.

He well knew, also, how it was in him to brighten her lonely life, almost every hour of it—and promised himself that she should not be a loser by her kindness to Mr. Nobody of Nowhere. He remembered her love of fun, and pretty poetry, and little French songs, and droll chat—and nice cheerful meals tête-à-tête—and he was good at all these things. And how fond she was of reading out loud to him ! The time might soon arrive when that would be a blessing indeed.

Indeed, a new interest had come into his life—not altogether a selfish interest either—but one well worth living for, though it was so unlike any interest that had ever filled his life before. He had been essentially a man's man hitherto, in spite of his gay light love for lovely woman ; a good comrade par excellence, a frolicsome chum, a rollicking boon - companion, a jolly pal ! He wanted quite desperately to love something staid and feminine and gainly and well bred, whatever its age ! some kind soft warm thing in petticoats and thin shoes, with no hair on its face, and a voice that wasn't male !

Nor did her piety frighten him very much. He soon found that she was no longer the over-zealous proselytizing busybody of the Cross—but immensely a woman of the world, making immense allowances. All roads lead to Rome (dit-on !), except a few which converge in the opposite direction ; but even Roman roads lead to this wide tolerance in the end—for those of a rich warm nat-

215

ure who have been well battered by life; and Lady Caroline had been very thoroughly battered indeed: a bad husband — a bad son, her only child! both dead, but deeply loved and lamented; and in her heart of hearts there lurked a sad suspicion that her piety (so deep and earnest and sincere) had not bettered their badness—on the contrary, perhaps! and had driven her Barty from her when he needed her most.

Now that his need of her was so great, greater than it had ever been before, she would take good care that no piety of hers should ever drive him away from her again; she felt almost penitent and apologetic for having done what she had known to be right—the woman in her had at last outgrown the nun.

She almost began to doubt whether she had not been led to selfishly overrate the paramount importance of the exclusive salvation of her own particular soul!

And then his frank, fresh look and manner, and honest boyish voice, so unmistakably sincere, and that mild and magnificent eye, so bright and humorous still, "so like—so like!" which couldn't even see her loving, anxious face. . . . Thank Heaven, there was still one eye left that she could appeal to with both her own!

And what a child he had been, poor dear — the very pearl of the Rohans! What Rohan of them all was ever a patch on this poor bastard of Antoinette Josselin's, either for beauty, pluck, or mother-wit—or even for honor, if it came to that? Why, a quixotic scruple of honor had ruined him, and she was Rohan enough to understand what the temptation had been the other way : she had seen the beautiful bad lady!

And, pure as her own life had been, she was no puritan, but of a church well versed in the deepest knowledge of our poor weak frail humanity ; she has told me all about it, and I listened between the words.

So during the remainder of her stay at Blankenberghe he was very much with Lady Caroline, and rediscovered what a pleasant and lively companion she could be — especially at meals (she was fond of good food of a plain and wholesome kind, and took good care to get it).

She had her little narrownesses, to be sure, and was not hail-fellow-well-met with everybody, like him ; and did not think very much of giddy little viscountesses with straddling loud - voiced Flemish husbands, nor of familiar facetious commercial millionaires, of whom Barty numbered two or three among his adorers ; nor even of the "highly born" Irish wives of Belgian generals and all that. Madame de Clèves was an O'Brien.

These were old ingrained Rohan prejudices, and she was too old herself to alter.

But she loved the good fishermen whose picturesque boats made such a charming group on the sands at sunset, and also their wives and children ; and here she and her nephew were "bien d'accord."

I fear her ladyship would not have appreciated very keenly the rising splendor of a certain not altogether unimportant modern house in Barge Yard, Bucklersbury—and here she would have been wrong. The time has come when we throw the handkerchief at female Rohans, we Maurices and our like. I have not done so myself, it is true ; but not from any rooted antipathy to any daughter of a hundred earls—nor yet from any particular diffidence on my own part.

Anyhow, Lady Caroline loved to hear all Barty had to say of his gay life among the beauty, rank, and fashion of Blankenberghe. She was very civil to the handsome

Irish Madame de Clèves, *née* O'Brien, and listened politely to the family history of the O'Briens and that of the de Clèveses too : and learnt, without indecent surprise, or any emotion of any kind whatever, what she had never heard before—namely, that in the early part of the twelfth century a Rohan de Whitby had married an O'Brien of Ballywrotte; and other prehistoric facts of equal probability and importance.

She didn't believe much in people's twelfth - century reminiscences ; she didn't even believe in those of her own family, who didn't believe in them either, or trouble about them in the least ; and I dare say they were quite right.

Anyhow, when people solemnly talked about such things it made her rather sorry. But she bore up for Barty's sake, and the resigned, half-humorous courtesy with which she assented to these fables was really more humiliating to a sensitive, haughty soul than any mere supercilious disdain; not that she ever wished to humiliate, but she was easily bored, and thought that kind of conversation vulgar, futile, and rather grotesque.

Indeed, she grew quite fond of Madame de Clèves and the splendid young dragoon, and the sweet little black-haired daughter with lovely blue eyes, who sang so charmingly. For they were singularly charming people in every way, the de Clèveses ; and that's a way Irish people often have—as well as of being proud of their ancient blood. There is no more innocent weakness. I have it very strongly — moi qui vous parle — on the maternal side. My mother was a Blake of Derrydown, a fact that nobody would have known unless she now and then accidentally happened to mention it herself, or else my father did. And so I take the opportunity of slipping it in here—just out of filial piety !

So the late autumn of that year found Barty and his
aunt at Malines, or Mechelen, as it calls itself in its native tongue.

They had comfortable lodgings of extraordinary cheap-
ness in one of the dullest streets of that most picturesque
but dead-alive little town, where the grass grew so thick
between the paving-stones here and there that the brewers' dray-horses might have browsed in the "Grand
Brul"—a magnificent but generally deserted thorough-
fare leading from the railway station to the Place
d'Armes, where rose still unfinished the colossal tower
of one of the oldest and finest cathedrals in the world,
whose chimes wafted themselves every half-quarter of
an hour across the dreamy flats for miles and miles, according to the wind, that one might realize how slow
was the flight of time in that particular part of King
Leopold's dominions.

> "'And from a tall tower in the town
> Death looks gigantically down!'"

said Barty to his aunt—quoting (or misquoting) a bard
they were very fond of just then, as they slowly walked
down the "Grand Brul" in solitude together, from the
nineteenth century to the fourteenth in less than twenty
minutes — or three chimes from St. Rombault, or fifty
skrieks from the railway station.

But for these a spirit of stillness and mediæval melancholy brooded over the quaint old city and great archi-
episcopal see and most important railway station in all
Belgium. Magnificent old houses in carved stone with
wrought-iron balconies were to be had for rents that
were almost nominal. From the tall windows of some of
these a frugal, sleepy, priest-ridden old nobility looked
down on broad and splendid streets hardly ever trodden

by any feet but their own, or those of some stealthy Jesuit priest, or Sister of Mercy.

Only during the Kermesse, or at carnival-time, when noisy revellers of either sex and ungainly processions of tipsy masques and mummers waked Mechelen out of its long sleep, and all the town seemed one vast estaminet, did one feel one's self to be alive. Even at night, and in the small hours, frisky masques and dominoes walked the moonlit streets, and made loud old Flemish mediæval love, à la Teniers.

There was a beautiful botanical garden, through which a river flowed under tall trees, and turned the wheels of the oldest flour-mills in Flanders. This was a favorite resort of Barty's—and he had it pretty much to himself.

And for Lady Caroline there were, besides St. Rombault, quite half-a-dozen churches almost as magnificent if not so big, and in them as many as you could wish of old Flemish masters, beginning with Peter Paul Rubens, who pervades the land of his birth very much as Michael Angelo pervades Florence and Rome.

And these dim places of Catholic worship were generously open to all, every day and all day long, and never empty of worshippers, high and low, prostrate in the dust, or kneeling with their arms extended and their heads in the air, their wide-open, immovable, unblinking eyes hypnotized into stone by the cross and the crown of thorns. Mostly peasant women, these : with their black hoods falling from their shoulders, and stiff little close white caps that hid the hair.

Out of cool shadowy recesses of fretted stone and admirably carved wood emanations seemed to rise as from the long-forgotten past—tons of incense burnt hundreds of years ago, and millions of closely packed supplicants, rich and poor, following each other in secula seculorum!

Lady Caroline spent many of her hours haunting these crypts—and praying there.

At the back of their house in the Rue des Ursulines Blanches, Barty's bedroom window overlooked the playground of the convent "des Sœurs Rédemptoristines": all noble ladies, most beautifully dressed in scarlet and ultramarine, with long snowy veils, and who were waited upon by non-noble sisters in garments of a like hue but less expensive texture.

So at least said little Finche Torfs, the daughter of the house—little Frau, as Lady Caroline called her, and who seems to have been one of the best creatures in the world; she became warmly attached to both her lodgers, who reciprocated the feeling in full; it was her chief pleasure to wait on them and look after them at all times of the day, though Lady Caroline had already a devoted maid of her own.

Little Frau's father was a well-to-do burgher with a prosperous ironmongery in the "Petit Brul."

This was his private house, where he pursued his hobby, for he was an amateur photographer, very fond of photographing his kind and simple-minded old wife, who was always attired in rich Brussels silks and Mechelen lace on purpose. She even cooked in them, though not for her lodgers, whose mid-day and evening meals were sent from "La Cigogne," close by, in four large round tins that fitted into each other, and were carried in a wicker-work cylindrical basket. And it was little Frau's delight to descant on the qualities of the menu as she dished and served it. I will not attempt to do so.

But after little Frau had cleared it all away, Barty would descant on the qualities of certain English dishes he remembered, to the immense amusement of Aunt Caroline, who was reasonably fond of what is good to eat.

221

He would paint in words (he was better in words than any other medium—oil, water, or distemper) the boiled leg of mutton, not overdone ; the mashed turnips ; the mealy potato ; the caper-sauce. He would imitate the action of the carver and the sound of the carving-knife making its first keen cut while the hot pink gravy runs down the sides. Then he would wordily paint a French roast chicken and its rich brown gravy and its water-cresses ; the pommes sautées ; the crisp, curly salade aux fines herbes ! And Lady Caroline, still hungry, would laugh till her eyes watered, as well as her mouth.

When it came to the sweets, the apple-puddings and gooseberry-pies and Devonshire cream and brown sugar, there was no more laughing, for then Barty's talent soared to real genius—and genius is a serious thing. And as to his celery and Stilton cheese— But there ! it's lunch-time, and I'm beginning to feel a little peck-ish myself. . . .

Every morning when it was fine Barty and his aunt would take an airing round the town, which was en-closed by a ditch where there was good skating in the winter, on long skates that went very fast, but couldn't cut figures, 8 or 3 !

There were no fortifications or ramparts left. But a few of the magnificent old brick gateways still remained, admitting you to the most wonderful old streets with tall pointed houses—clean little slums, where women sat on their door-steps making the most beautiful lace in the world — odd nooks and corners and narrow ways where it was easy to lose one's self, small as the town really was ; innumerable little toy bridges over toy canals one could have leaped at a bound, overlooked by quaint, irregular little dwellings, of colors that had once been as those of the rainbow, but which time had mellowed into divine harmonies, as it does all it touches—from grand old masters to oak palings round English parks ; from Venice to Mechelen and its lace ; from a disappointed first love to a great sorrow.

Occasionally a certain distinguished old man of soldier-like aspect would pass them on horseback, and gaze at their two tall British figures with a look of curious and benign interest, as if he mentally wished them well, and well away from this drear limbo of penitence and exile and expiation.

They learnt that he was French, and a famous general, and that his name was Changarnier; and they understood that public virtue has to be atoned for.

And he somehow got into the habit of bowing to them with a good smile, and they would smile and bow back again. Beyond this they never exchanged a word, but this little outward show and ceremony of kindly look and sympathetic gesture always gave them a pleasant moment and helped to pass the morning.

All the people they met were to Lady Caroline like people in a dream : silent priests ; velvet-footed nuns, who were much to her taste ; quiet peasant women, in black cloaks and hoods, driving bullock-carts or carts drawn by dogs, six or eight of these inextricably harnessed together and panting for dear life ; blue-bloused men in French caps, but bigger and blonder than Frenchmen, and less given to epigrammatic repartee, with mild, blue, beery eyes, *à fleur de tête,* and a look of health and stolid amiability; sturdy green-coated little soldiers with cock-feathered brigand hats of shiny black, the brim turned up over the right eye and ear that they might the more conveniently take a good aim at the foe before he skedaddled at the mere sight of them ; fat, comfortable burgesses and their wives, so like their ancestors who

223

drink beer out of long glasses and smoke long clay pipes on the walls of the Louvre and the National Gallery that they seemed like old friends; and quaint old heavy children who didn't make much noise!

And whenever they spoke French to you, these good people, they said "savez-vous?" every other second; and whenever they spoke Flemish to each other it sounded so much like your own tongue as it is spoken in the north of England that you wondered why on earth you couldn't understand a single word.

Now and then, from under a hood, a handsome dark face with Spanish eyes would peer out—eloquent of the past history of the Low Countries, which Barty knew much better than I. But I believe there was once a Spanish invasion or occupation of some kind, and I dare say the fair Belgians are none the worse for it to-day. (It might even have been good for some of us, perhaps, if that ill-starred Armada hadn't come so entirely to grief. I'm fond of big, tawny-black eyes.)

All this, so novel and so strange, was a perpetual feast for Lady Caroline. And they bought nice, cheap, savory things on the way home, to eke out the lunch from "la Cigogne."

In the afternoon Barty would take a solitary walk in the open country, or along one of those endless straight *chaussées*, paved in the middle, and bordered by equidistant poplars on either side, and leading from town to town, and the monotonous perspective of which is so desolating to heart and eye; backwards or forwards, it is always the same, with a flat sameness of outlook to right and left, and every 450 seconds the chime would boom and flounder heavily by, with a dozen sharp railway whistles after it, like swordfish after a whale, piercing it through and through.

Barty evidently had all this in his mind when he wrote the song of the seminarist in " Gleams," beginning :

> " Twas April, and the sky was clear,
> An east wind blowing keenly ;
> The sun gave out but little cheer,
> For all it shone serenely.
> The wayside poplars, all arow,
> For many a weary mile did throw
> Down on the dusty flags below
> Their shadows, picked out cleanly."
> Etc., etc., etc.

(Isn't it just like Barty to begin a lyric that will probably last as long as the English language with an innocent jingle worthy of a school-boy ?)

After dinner, in the evening, it was Lady Caroline's delight to read aloud, while Barty smoked his cigarettes and inexpensive cigars—a concession on her part to make him happy, and keep him as much with her as she could ; and she grew even to like the smell so much that once or twice, when he went to Antwerp for a couple of days to stay with Tescheles, she actually had to burn some of his tobacco on a red-hot shovel, for the scent of it seemed to spell his name for her and make his absence less complete.

Thus she read to him *Esmond, Hypatia, Never too Late to Mend, Les Maîtres Sonneurs, La Mare au Diable,* and other delightful books, English and French, which were sent once a week from a circulating library in Brussels. How they blessed thy name, good Baron Tauchnitz !

"Oh, Aunt Caroline, if I could *only* illustrate books ! If I could only illustrate *Esmond* and draw a passable Beatrix coming down the old staircase at Castlewood with her candle !" said Barty, one night.

That was not to be. Another was to illustrate *Es-*

225

mond, a poor devil who, oddly enough, was then living in the next street and suffering from a like disorder.*

As a return, Barty would sing to her all he knew, in five languages—three of which neither of them quite understood — accompanying himself on the piano or guitar. Sometimes she would play for him accompaniments that were beyond his reach, for she was a decently taught musician who could read fairly well at sight; whereas Barty didn't know a single note, and picked up everything by ear. She practised these accompaniments every afternoon, as assiduously as any school-girl.

Then they would sit up very late, as they always had so much to talk about—what had just been read or played or sung, and many other things: the present, the past, and the future. All their old affection for each other had come back, trebled and quadrupled by pity on one side, gratitude on the other—and a little remorse on both. And there were long arrears to make up, and life was short and uncertain.

Sometimes l'Abbé Lefebvre, one of the professors at the séminaire and an old friend of Lady Caroline's, would come to drink tea, and talk politics, which ran high in Mechelen. He was a most accomplished and delightful Frenchman, who wrote poetry and adored Balzac—and even owned to a fondness for good old Paul de Kock, of whom it is said that when the news of his death reached Pius the Ninth, his Holiness dropped a tear and exclaimed :

" Mio caro Paolo di Kocco !"

Now and then the Abbé would bring with him a distinguished young priest, a Dominican—also a professor;

---

* (" Un malheureux, vêtu de noir,
Qui me ressemblait comme un frère . . ."—ED.)

15

Father Louis, of the princely house of Aremberg, who died a Cardinal three years ago.

Father Louis had an admirable and highly cultivated musical gift, and played to them Beethoven and Mozart, Schubert, Chopin, and Schumann—and this music, as long as it lasted (and for some time after), was to Barty as great a source of consolation as of unspeakable delight; and therefore to his aunt also. Though I'm afraid she preferred any little French song of Barty's to all the Schumanns in the world.

First of all, the priest would play the "Moonlight Sonata," let us say; and Barty would lean back and listen with his eyes shut, and almost believe that Beethoven was talking to him like a father, and pointing out to him how small was the difference, really, between the greatest earthly joy and the greatest earthly sorrow : these were not like black and white, but merely different shades of gray, as on moonlit things a long way off! and Time, what a reconciler it was—like distance! and Death, what a perfect resolution of all possible discords, and how certain ! and our own little life, how short, and without importance ! what matters whether it's to-day, this small individual flutter of ours ; or was a hundred years ago ; or will be a hundred years hence ! it has or had to be got through—and it's better past than to come.

"It all leads to the same divine issue, my poor friend," said Beethoven ; "why, just see here—I'm stone-deaf, and can't hear a note of what I'm singing to you ! But it is not about *that* I weep, when I am weeping. It was terrible when it first came on, my deafness, and I could no longer hear the shepherd's pipe or the song of the lark ; but it's well worth going deaf, to hear all that *I* do. I have to write everything down, and read it to myself ; and my tears fall on the ruled paper, and blister the lines,

"THE MOONLIGHT SONATA"

and make the notes run into each other; and when I try
to blot it all out, there's that still left on the page, which,
turned into sound by good father Louis the Dominican,
will tell you, if you can only hear it aright, what is not
to be told in any human speech; not even that of Plato,
or Marcus Aurelius, or Erasmus, or Shakespeare; not
even that of Christ himself, who speaks through me from
His unknown grave, because I am deaf and cannot hear
the distracting words of men—poor, paltry words at their
best, which mean so many things at once that they mean
just nothing at all. It's a Tower of Babel. Just stop
your ears and listen with your heart and you will hear all
that you can see when you shut your eyes or have lost
them — and those are the only realities, mein armer
Barty!"

Then the good Mozart would say:

"Lieber Barty — I'm so stupid about earthly things
that I could never even say Boh to a goose, so I can't
give you any good advice; all my heart overflowed into
my brain when I was quite a little boy and made music
for grown-up people to hear; from the day of my birth
to my fifth birthday I had gone on remembering everything, but learning nothing new—remembering all that
music!

"And I went on remembering more and more till I
was thirty-five; and even then there was such a lot more
of it where that came from that it tired me to try and
remember so much — and I went back thither. And
thither back shall you go too, Barty—when you are
some thirty years older!

"And you already know from me how pleasant life is
there—how sunny and genial and gay; and how graceful
and innocent and amiable and well-bred the natives—and
what beautiful prayers we sing, and what lovely gavottes

and minuets we dance—and how tenderly we make love —and what funny tricks we play ! and how handsome and well dressed and kind we all are—and the likes of you, how welcome ! Thirty years is soon over, Barty, Barty ! Bel Mazetto ! Ha, ha ! good !"

Then says the good Schubert :

" I'm a loud, rollicking, beer-drinking Kerl, I am ! Ich bin ein lustiger Student, mein Pardy ; and full of droll practical jokes ; worse than even you, when you were a young scapegrace in the Guards, and wrenched off knockers, and ran away with a poor policeman's hat ! But I don't put my practical jokes into my music ; if I did, I shouldn't be the poor devil I am ! I'm very hungry when I go to bed, and when I wake up in the morning I have Katzenjammer (from an empty stomach) and a headache, and a heartache, and penitence and shame and remorse ; and know there is nothing in this world or beyond it worth a moment's care but Love, Love, Love ! Liebe, Liebe ! The good love that knows neither concealment nor shame—from the love of the brave man for the pure maiden whom he weds, to the young nun's love of the Lord ! and all the other good loves lie between these two, and are inside them, or come out of them, . . . and that's the love I put into my music. Indeed, my music is the only love I know, since I am not beautiful to the eye, and can only care for tunes ! . . .

" But you, Pardy, are handsome and gallant and gay, and have always been well beloved by man and woman and child, and always will be ; and know how to love back again—even a dog ! however blind you go, you will always have that, the loving heart—and as long as you can hear and sing, you will always have my tunes to fall back upon. . . ."

" And mine !" says Chopin. " If there's one thing

230

sweeter than love, it's the sadness that it can't last; *she* loved me once—and now she loves *tout le monde!* and that's a little sweet melodic sadness of mine that will never fail you, as long as there's a piano within your reach, and a friend who knows how to play me on it for you to hear. You shall revel in my sadness till you forget your own. Oh, the sorrow of my sweet pipings! Whatever becomes of your eyes, keep your two ears for *my* sake; and for your sake too! You don't know what exquisite ears you've got. You are like me—you and I are made of silk, Barty—as other men are made of sackcloth; and their love, of ashes; and their joys, of dust!

" Even the good priest who plays me to you so glibly doesn't understand what I am talking about half so well as *you* do, who can't read a word I write! He had to learn my language note by note from the best music-master in Brussels. It's your mother - tongue! You learned it as you sucked at your sweet young mother's breast, my poor love-child! And all through her, your ears, like your remaining eye, are worth a hatful of the common kind—and some day it will be the same with your heart and brain. . . ."

" Yes"—continues Schumann—" but you'll have to suffer first — like me, who will have to kill myself very soon; because I am going mad—and that's worse than any blindness! and like Beethoven who went deaf, poor demigod! and like all the rest of us who've been singing to you to-night; that's why our songs never pall—because we are acquainted with grief, and have good memories, and are quite sincere. The older you get, the more you will love us and our songs: other songs may come and go in the ear; but ours go ringing in the heart forever !"

In some such fashion did the great masters of tune and tone discourse to Barty through Father Louis's well-trained finger-tips. They always discourse to you a little about yourself, these great masters, always; and always in a manner pleasing to your self-love! The finger-tips (whosesoever's finger-tips they be) have only to be intelligent and well trained, and play just what's put before them in a true, reverent spirit. Anything beyond may be unpardonable impertinence, both to the great masters and yourself.

Musicians will tell you that all this is nonsense from beginning to end; you mustn't believe musicians about music, nor wine-merchants about wine—but vice versa!

When Father Louis got up from the music-stool, the Abbé would say to Barty, in his delightful, pure French :

"And now, mon ami—just for *me*, you know—a little song of autrefois."

"All right, M. l'Abbé—I will sing you the 'Adelaïde,' of Beethoven . . . if Father Louis will play for me."

"Oh, non, mon ami, do not throw away such a beautiful organ as yours on such really beautiful music, which doesn't want it; it would be sinful waste; it's not so much the tune that I want to hear as the fresh young voice ; sing me something French, something light, something amiable and droll; that I may forget the song, and only remember the singer."

"All right, M. l'Abbé," and Barty sings a delightful little song by Gustave Nadaud, called "Petit bonhomme vit encore."

And the good Abbé is in the seventh heaven, and quite forgets to forget the song.

And so, cakes and wine, and good-night—and M. l'Abbé goes humming all the way home. . . .

232

> "Hé, quoi ! pour des peccadilles
> Gronder ces pauvres amours ?
> Les femmes sont si gentilles,
> Et l'on n'aime pas toujours !
> C'est bonhomme
> Qu'on me nomme. . . .
> Ma gaîté, c'est mon trésor !
> Et bonhomme vit encor'—
> Et bonhomme vit encor' !"

An extraordinary susceptibility to musical sound was growing in Barty since his trouble had overtaken him, and with it an extraordinary sensitiveness to the troubles of other people, their partings and bereavements and wants, and aches and pains, even those of people he didn't know; and especially the woes of children, and dogs and cats and horses, and aged folk—and all the live things that have to be driven to market and killed for our eating—or shot at for our fun !

All his old loathing of sport had come back, and he was getting his old dislike of meat once more, and to sicken at the sight of a butcher's shop; and the sight of a blind man stirred him to the depths . . . even when he learnt how happy a blind man can be !

These unhappy things that can't be helped preoccupied him as if he had been twenty, thirty, fifty years older; and the world seemed to him a shocking place, a gray, bleak, melancholy hell where there was nothing but sadness, and badness, and madness.

And bit by bit, but very soon, all his old trust in an all-merciful, all-powerful ruler of the universe fell from him; he shed it like an old skin; it sloughed itself away; and with it all his old conceit of himself as a very fine fellow, taller, handsomer, cleverer than anybody else, " bar two or three "! Such darling beliefs are the best stays we can have ; and he found life hard to face without them.

And he got as careful of his aunt Caroline, and as anxious about her little fads and fancies and ailments, as if he'd been an old woman himself.

Imagine how she grew to dote on him !

And he quite lost his old liability to sudden freaks and fits of noisy fractiousness about trifles—when he would stamp and rave and curse and swear, and be quite pacified in a moment : *" Soupe-au-lait,"* as he was nick-named in Troplong's studio !

Besides his seton and his cuppings, dry and wet, and his blisters on his arms and back, and his mustard poultices on his feet and legs, and his doses of mercury and alteratives, he had also to deplete himself of blood three times a week by a dozen or twenty leeches behind his left ear and on his temple. All this softens and re-laxes the heart towards others, as a good tonic will harden it.

So that he looked a mere shadow of his former self when I went over to spend my Christmas with him.

And his eye was getting worse instead of better ; at night he couldn't sleep for the fireworks it let off in the dark. By day the trouble was even worse, as it so in-terfered with the sight of the other eye — even if he wore a patch, which he hated. He never knew peace but when his aunt was reading to him in the dimly lighted room, and he forgot himself in listening.

Yet he was as lively and droll as ever, with a wan face as eloquent of grief as any face I ever saw; he had it in his head that the right eye would go the same way as the left. He could no longer see the satellites of Jupiter with it : hardly Jupiter itself, except as a luminous blur ;

indeed, it was getting quite near-sighted, and full of spots and specks and little movable clouds—*muscæ volitantes,* as I believe they are called by the faculty. He was always on the lookout for new symptoms, and never in vain ; and his burden was as much as he could bear.

He would half sincerely long for death, of which he yet had such a horror that he was often tempted to kill himself to get the bother of it well over at once. The idea of death *in the dark,* however remote—an idea that constantly haunted him as his own most probable end— so appalled him that it would stir the roots of his hair !

Lady Caroline confided to me her terrible anxiety, which she managed to hide from him. She herself had been to see M. Noiret, who was no longer so confident and cocksure about recovery.

I went to see him too, without letting Barty know. I did not like the man—he was stealthy in look and manner, and priestly and feline and sleek : but he seemed very intelligent, and managed to persuade me that no other treatment was even to be thought of.

I inquired about him in Brussels, and found his reputation was of the highest. What could I do ? I knew nothing of such things ! And what a responsibility for me to volunteer advice !

I could see that my deep affection for Barty was a source of immense comfort to Lady Caroline, for whom I conceived a great and warm regard, besides being very much charmed with her.

She was one of those gentle, genial, kindly, intelligent women of the world, absolutely natural and sincere, in whom it is impossible not to confide and trust.

When I left off talking about Barty, because there was really nothing more to say, I fell into talking about myself : it was irresistible—she *made* one ! I even showed her Leah's last photograph, and told her of my secret aspirations; and she was so warmly sympathetic and said such beautiful things to me about Leah's face and aspect and all they promised of good that I have never forgotten them, and never shall — they showed such a prophetic insight! they fanned a flame that needed no fanning, good heavens! and rang in my ears and my heart all the way to Barge Yard, Bucklersbury—while my eyes were full of Barty's figure as he again watched me depart by the *Baron Osy* from the Quai de la Place Verte in Antwerp; a sight that wrung me, when I remembered what a magnificent figure of a youth he looked as he left the wharf at London Bridge on the Boulogne steamer, hardly more than two short years ago.

When I got back to London, after spending my Christmas holiday with Barty, I found the beginning of a little trouble of my own.

My father was abroad; my mother and sister were staying with some friends in Chiselhurst, and after having settled all business matters in Barge Yard I called at the Gibsons', in Tavistock Square, just after dusk. Mrs. Gibson and Leah were at home, and three or four young men were there, also calling. There had been a party on Christmas-eve.

I'm afraid I did not think much, as a rule, of the young men I met at the Gibsons'. They were mostly in business, like myself; and why I should have felt at all supercilious I can't quite see! But I did. Was it because I was very tall, and dressed by Barty's tailor, in Jermyn Street? Was it because I knew French? Was it because I was a friend of Barty the Guardsman, who had never been supercilious towards anybody in his life? Or was it those maternally ancestral Irish Blakes of Derrydown stirring within me?

236

The simplest excuse I can make for myself is that I was a young snob, and couldn't help it. Many fellows are at that age. Some grow out of it, and some don't. And the Gibsons were by way of spoiling me, because I was Leah's bosom friend's brother, and I gave myself airs in consequence.

As I sat perfectly content, telling Leah all about poor Barty, another visitor was announced—a Mr. Scatcherd, whom I didn't know; but I saw at a glance that it would not do to be supercilious with Mr. Scatcherd. He was quite as tall as I, for one thing, if not taller. His tailor might have been Poole himself; and he was extremely good-looking, and had all the appearance and manners of a man of the world. He might have been a Guardsman. He was not that, it seemed—only a barrister.

He had been at Eton, had taken his degree at Cambridge, and ignored me just as frankly as I ignored Tom, Dick, and Harry — whoever they were; and I didn't like it at all. He ignored everybody but Leah and her mamma : her papa was not there. It turned out that he was the only son of the great wholesale furrier in Ludgate Hill, the largest house of the kind in the world, with a branch in New York and another in Quebec or Montreal. He had been called to the bar to please a whim of his father's.

He had been at the Gibson party on Christmas-eve, and had paid Leah much attention there ; and came to tell them that his mother hoped to call on Mrs. Gibson on the following day. I was savagely glad that he did not succeed in monopolizing Leah ; not even I could do that. She was kind to us all round, and never made any differences in her own house.

Mr. Scatcherd soon took his departure, and it was then that I heard all about him.

ENTER MR. SCATCHERD

There was no doubt that Mr. and Mrs. Gibson were immensely flattered by the civilities of this very important and somewhat consequential young man, and those of his mother, which were to follow; for within a week the Gibsons and Leah dined with Mr. and Mrs. Scatcherd in Portland Place.

On this occasion Mr. Gibson was, as usual, very funny, it seems. Whether his fun was appreciated I doubt, for he confided to me that Mr. Scatcherd, senior, was a pompous and stuck-up old ass. People have such different notions of what is funny. Nobody roared at Mr. Gibson's funniments more than I did; but he was Leah's papa.

> "Let him joke his bellyful;
> I'll bear it all for Sally !"

Young Scatcherd was fond of his joke too—a kind of supersubtly satirical Cambridgy banter that was not to my taste at all; for I am no Cantab, and the wit of the London Stock Exchange is subtle enough for me. His father did not joke. Indeed he was full of useful information, and only too fond of imparting it, and he always made use of the choicest language in doing so; and Mrs. Scatcherd was immensely genteel.

Young Scatcherd became the plague of my life. The worst of it is that he grew quite civil—seemed to take a liking. His hobby was to become a good French scholar, and he practised his French — which was uncommonly good of its English kind—on me. And I am bound to say that his manners were so agreeable (when he wasn't joking), and he was such a thoroughly good fellow, that it was impossible to snub him ; besides, he wouldn't have cared if I had.

Once or twice he actually asked me to dine with him

at his club, and I actually did; and actually he with me, at mine! And we spoke French all through dinner, and I taught him a lot of French school-boy slang, with which he was delighted. Then he came to see me in Barge Yard, and I even introduced him to my mother and sister, who couldn't help being charmed with him. He was fond of the best music only (he had no ear whatever, and didn't know a note), and only cared for old pictures —the National Gallery, and all that; and read no novels but French—Balzac and George Sand—and that only for practice; for he was a singularly pure young man, the purest in all Cambridge, and in those days I thought him a quite unforgivable prig.

So Scatcherd was in my thoughts all day and in my dreams all night—a kind of incubus; and my mother made herself very unhappy about him, on Leah's account and mine; except that now and then she would fancy it was Ida he was thinking of. And that would have pleased my mother very much; and me too!

His mother called on mine, who returned the call— but there was no invitation for us to dine in Portland Place.

Nothing of all this interrupted for a moment the bosom-friendship between my sister and Leah; nothing ever altered the genial sweetness of Leah's manners to me, nor indeed the cordiality of her parents: Mr. Gibson could not get on without that big guffaw of mine, at whatever he looked or said or did; no Scatcherd could laugh as loudly and as readily as I! But I was very wretched indeed, and poured out my woes to Barty in long letters of poetical Blaze, and he would bid me hope and be of good cheer in his droll way; and a Blaze letter from him would hearten me up wonderfully—till I was told of Leah's going to the theatre with Mrs. Scatcherd and her

son, or saw his horses and groom parading up and down
Tavistock Square while he was at the Gibsons', or heard
of his dining there without Ida or me !

Then one fine day in April (the first, I verily believe)
young Scatcherd proposed to Leah—and was refused—
unconditionally refused—to the deep distress and dismay
of her father and mother, who had thoroughly set their
hearts on this match ; and no wonder !

But Leah was an obstinate young woman, it seems, and
thoroughly knew her own mind, though she was so young
—not seventeen.

Was I a happy man ? Ah, wasn't I ! I was sent to
Bordeaux by my father that very week on business—and
promised myself I would soon be quite as good a catch or
match as Scatcherd himself.   I found Bordeaux the sun-
niest, sweetest town I had ever been in—and the Borde-
lais the jolliest men on earth ; and as for the beautiful
Bordelaises—ma foi ! they might have been monkeys, for
me !   There was but one woman among women—one lily
among flowers—everything else was a weed !

Poor Scatcherd ! when I met him, a few days later, he
must have been struck by the sudden warmth of my
friendship—the quick idiomatic cordiality of my French
to him.   This mutual friendship of ours lasted till his
death in '88.   And so did our mutual French !

Except Barty, I never loved a man better ; two years
after his refusal by Leah he married my sister—a happy
marriage, though a childless one ; and except myself,
Barty never had a more devoted friend.   And now to
Barty I will return.

Part Sixth

" From the east to western Ind,
No jewel is like Rosalind.
Her worth, being mounted on the wind,
Through all the world bears Rosalind.
All the pictures, fairest lin'd,
Are but black to Rosalind.
Let no fair be kept in mind,
But the fair of Rosalind.

.　　.　　.　　.　　.

"Thus Rosalind of many parts
By heavenly synod was devis'd,
Of many faces, eyes, and hearts,
To have the touches dearest priz'd."
—As You Like It.

FOR many months Barty and his aunt lived their usual life in the Rue des Ursulines Blanches.

He always looked back on those dreary months as on a long nightmare. Spring, summer, autumn, and another Christmas !

His eye got worse and worse, and so interfered with the sight of the other that he had no peace till it was darkened wholly. He tried another doctor—Monsieur Goyers, professor at the liberal university of Ghent— who consulted with Dr. Noiret about him one day in Brussels, and afterwards told him that Noiret of Louvain, whom he described as a miserable Jesuit, was blinding him, and that he, this Goyers of Ghent, would cure him in six weeks.

"Mettez-vous au régime des viandes saignantes !" had
said Noiret ; and Barty had put himself on a diet of
underdone beef and mutton.

"Mettez - vous au lait !" said Goyers—so he metted
himself at the milk, as he called it—and put himself in
Goyers's hands; and in six weeks got so much worse that
he went back to Noiret and the regimen of the bleeding
meats, which he loathed.

Then, in his long and wretched *désœuvrement,* his mel-
ancholia, he drifted into an indiscreet flirtation with
a beautiful lady—he (as had happened before) being more
the pursued than the pursuer. And so ardent was the
pursuit that one fine morning the beautiful lady found
herself gravely compromised—and there was a bother and
a row.

> "Amour, amour, quand tu nous tiens,
> On peut bien dire 'Adieu Prudence !'"

All this gave Lady Caroline great distress, and ended
most unhappily—in a duel with the lady's husband, who
was a Colonel of Artillery, and meant business !

They fought with swords in a little wood near Laeken.
Barty, who could have run his fat antagonist through a
dozen times during the five minutes they fought, allowed
himself to be badly wounded in the side, just above the
hip, and spent a month in bed. He had hoped to manage for himself a slighter wound, and catch his adver-
sary's point on his elbow.

Afterwards, Lady Caroline, who had so disapproved
of the flirtation, did not, strange to say, so disapprove of
this bloody encounter, and thoroughly approved of the
way Barty had let himself be pinked ! and nursed him
devotedly ; no mother could have nursed him better—
no sister—no wife ! not even the wife of that Belgian
Colonel of Artillery !

BARTY GIVES HIMSELF AWAY

"Il s'est conduit en homme de cœur!" said the good Abbé.

"Il s'est conduit en bon gentilhomme!" said the aristocratic Father Louis, of the princely house of Aremberg.

On the other hand, young de Clèves the dragoon, and Monsieur Jean the Viscount, who had served as Barty's seconds (I was in America), were very angry with him for giving himself away in this "idiotically quixotic manner."

Besides which, Colonel Lecornu was a notorious bully, it seems ; and a fool into the bargain; and belonged to a branch of the service they detested.

The only other thing worth mentioning is that Barty and Father Louis became great friends—almost inseparable during such hours as the Dominican could spare from the duties of his professorate.

It speaks volumes for all that was good in each of them that this should have been so, since they were wide apart as the poles in questions of immense moment: questions on which I will not enlarge, strongly as I feel about them myself—for this is not a novel, but a biography, and therefore no fit place for the airing of one's own opinion on matters so grave and important.

When they parted they constantly wrote to each other —an intimate correspondence that was only ended by the Father's death.

Barty also made one or two other friends in Malines, and was often in Antwerp and Brussels, but seldom for more than a few hours, as he did not like to leave his aunt alone.

One day came, in April, on which she had to leave him.

A message arrived that her father, the old Marquis

SO NEAR AND YET SO FAR

(Barty's grandfather), was at the point of death. He was ninety-six. He had expressed a wish to see her once more, although he had long been childish.

So Barty saw her off, with her maid, by the *Baron Osy.* She promised to be back as soon as all was over. Even this short parting was a pain—they had grown so indispensable to each other.

Tescheles was away from Antwerp, and the disconsolate Barty went back to Malines and dined by himself; and little Frau waited on him with extra care.

It turned out that her mother had cooked for him a special dish of consolation—sausage-meat stewed inside a red cabbage, with apples and cloves, till it all gets mixed up. It is a dish not to be beaten when you are young and Flemish and hungry and happy and well (even then you mustn't take more than one helping). When you are not all this it is good to wash it down with half a bottle of the best Burgundy—and this Barty did (from Vougeot-Conti and Co.).

Then he went out and wandered about in the dark and lost himself in a dreamy dædalus of little streets and bridges and canals and ditches. A huge comet (Encke's, I believe) was flaring all over the sky.

He suddenly came across the lighted window of a small estaminet, and went in.

It was a little beer-shop of the humblest kind—and just started. At a little deal table, brand-new, a middle-aged burgher of prosperous appearance was sitting next to the barmaid, who had deserted her post at the bar—and to whom he seemed somewhat attentive ; for their chairs were close together, and their arms round each other's waists, and they drank out of the same glass.

There was no one else in the room, and Barty was

about to make himself scarce, but they pressed him to come in ; so he sat at another little new deal table on a little new straw-bottomed chair, and she brought him a glass of beer. She was a very handsome girl, with a tall, graceful figure and Spanish eyes. He lit a cigar, and she went back to her beau quite simply—and they all three fell into conversation about an operetta by Victor Massé, which had been performed in Malines the previous night, called *Les Noces de Jeannette*.

The barmaid and her monsieur were trying to remember the beautiful air Jeannette sings as she mends her angry husband's. breeches :

> "Cours, mon aiguille, dans la laine !
> Ne te casse pas dans ma main ;
> Avec de bons baisers demain
> Jean nous paîra de notre peine !"

So Barty sang it to them; and so beautifully that they were all but melted to tears—especially the monsieur, who was evidently very sentimental and very much in love. Besides, there was that ineffable charm of the pure French intonation, so caressing to the Belgian ear, so dear to the Belgian soul, so unattainable by Flemish lips. It was one of Barty's most successful ditties— and if I were a middle-aged burgher of Mechelen, I shouldn't much like to have a young French Barty singing "Cours, mon aiguille" to the girl of my heart.

Then, at their desire, he went on singing things till it was time to leave, and he found he had spent quite a happy evening ; nothing gave him greater pleasure than singing to people who liked it—and he went singing on his way home, dreamily staring at the rare gaslamps and the huge comet, and thinking of his old grandfather who lay dying or dead : "Cours, mon aiguille, it is good to live—it is good to die !"

Suddenly he discovered that when he looked at one lamp, another lamp close to it on the right was completely eclipsed—and he soon found that a portion of his right eye, not far from the centre, was totally sightless.

The shock was so great that he had to lean against a buttress of St. Rombault for support.

When he got home he tested the sight of his eye with a two-franc piece on the green table-cloth, and found there was no mistake—a portion of his remaining eye was stone-blind.

He spent a miserable night, and went next day to Louvain, to see the oculist.

M. Noiret heard his story, arranged the dark room and the lamp, dilated the right pupil with atropine, and made a minute examination with the ophthalmoscope.

Then he became very thoughtful, and led the way to his library and begged Barty to sit down ; and began to talk to him very seriously indeed, like a father—patting the while a small Italian greyhound that lay and shivered and whined in a little round cot by the fire.

M. Noiret began by inquiring into his circumstances, which were not flourishing, as we know—and Barty made no secret of them ; then he asked him if he were fond of music, and was pleased to hear that he was, since it is such an immense resource ; then he asked him if he belonged to the Roman Catholic faith, and again was pleased.

" For "—said he—" you will need all your courage and all your religion to hear and bear what it is my misfortune to have to tell you. I hope you will have more fortitude than another young patient of mine (also an artist) to whom I was obliged to make a similar communication. He blew out his brains on my door-step !"

"I promise you I will not do that. I suppose I am going blind?"

"Hélas! mon jeune ami! I grieve to say that the fatal disease, congestion and detachment of the retina, which has so obstinately and irrevocably destroyed your left eye, has begun its terrible work on the right. We will fight for every inch of the way. But I fear I must not give you any hope, after the careful examination I have just made. It is my duty to be frank with you."

Then he said much about the will of God, and where true comfort was to be found, at the foot of the Cross; in fact, he said all he ought to have said according to his lights, as he fondled his little greyhound—and finally took Barty to the door, which he opened for him, most politely bowing with his black velvet skull-cap; and pocketed his full fee (ten francs) with his usual grace of careless indifference, and gently shut the door on him. There was nothing else to do.

Barty stood there for some time, quite dazed; partly because his pupil was so dilated he could hardly see— partly (he thinks) because he in some way became unconscious; although when he woke from this little seeming trance, which may have lasted for more than a minute, he found himself still standing upright on his legs. What woke him was the *sudden consciousness of the north*, which he hadn't felt for many years; and this gave him extraordinary confidence in himself, and such a wholesome sense of power and courage that he quickly recovered his wits; and when the glad surprise of this had worn itself away he was able to think and realize the terrible thing that had happened. He was almost pleased that his aunt Caroline was away. He felt he could not have faced her with such news—it was a thing easier to write and prepare her for than to tell by word of mouth.

He walked about Louvain for several hours, to tire himself. Then he went to Brussels and dined, and again walked about the lamp-lit streets and up and down the station, and finally went back to Malines by a late train—very nervous—expecting that the retina of his right eye would suddenly go pop—yet hugging himself all the while in his renewed old comfortable feeling of companionship with the north pole, that made him feel like a boy again ; that inexplicable sensation so intimately associated with all the best reminiscences of his innocent and happy childhood.

He had been talking to himself like a father all day, though not in the same strain as M. Noiret ; and had almost arrived at framing the programme of a possible existence—singing at cafés with his guitar—singing anywhere : he felt sure of a living for himself, and for the little boy who would have to lead him about—if the worst came to the worst.

If but the feeling of self-orientation which was so necessary to him could only be depended upon, he felt that in time he would have pluck enough to bear anything. Indeed, total eclipse was less appalling, in its finality, than that miserable sword of Damocles which had been hanging over him for months—robbing him of his manhood—poisoning all the springs of life.

Why not make life-long endurance of evil a study, a hobby, and a pride ; and be patient as bronze or marble, and ever wear an invincible smile at grief, even when in darkness and alone ? Why not, indeed !

And he set himself then and there to smile invincibly, meaning to keep on smiling for fifty years at least—the blind live long.

"HÉLAS! MON JEUNE AMI . . . ."

So he chatted to himself, saying *Sursum cor! sursum corda!* all the way home ; and walking down the Grand Brul, he had a little adventure which absolutely gave him a hearty guffaw and sent him almost laughing to bed.

There was a noisy squabble between some soldiers and civilians on the opposite side of the way, and a group of men in blouses were looking on. Barty stood leaning against a lamp-post, and looked on too.

Suddenly a small soldier rushed at the blouses, brandishing his short straight sword (or *coupe-choux,* as it is called in civilian slang), and saying :

"Ça ne vous regarde pas, savez-vous ! allez-vous en bien vite, ou je vous . . ."

The blouses fled like sheep.

Then as he caught sight of Barty he reached at him.

"Ça ne vous regarde pas, savez-vous ! . . . "

(It doesn't concern you.)

"Non—c'est moi qui regarde, savez-vous !" said Barty.

"Qu'est-ce que vous regardez ?"

"Je regarde la lune et les étoiles. Je regarde la comète !"

"Voulez-vous bien vous en aller bien vite ?"

"Une autre fois !" says Barty.

"Allez-vous en, je vous dis !"

"Après-demain !"

"Vous . . . ne . . . voulez . . . pas . . . vous . . . en . . . aller ?" says the soldier, on tiptoe, his chest against Barty's stomach, his nose almost up to Barty's chin, glaring up like a fiend and poising his *coupe-choux* for a death-stroke.

"*Non,* sacré petit pousse - cailloux du diable !" roars Barty.

"Eh bien, restez ou vous êtes !" and the little man

plunged back into the fray on the opposite side—and no blood was shed after all.

Barty dreamt of this adventure, and woke up laughing at it in the small hours of that night. Then, suddenly, in the dark, he remembered the horror of what had happened. It overwhelmed him. He realized, as in a sudden illuminating flash, what life meant for him henceforward—life that might last for so many years.

Vitality is at its lowest ebb at that time of night; though the brain is quick to perceive, and so clear that its logic seems inexorable.

It was hell. It was not to be borne a moment longer. It must be put an end to at once. He tried to feel the north, but could not. He would kill himself then and there, while his aunt was away; so that the horror of the sight of him, after, should at least be spared her.

He jumped out of bed and struck a light. Thank Heaven, he wasn't blind yet, though he saw all the bogies, as he called them, that had made his life a burden to him for the last two years — the retina floating loose about his left eye, tumbling and deforming every lighted thing it reflected—and also the new dark spot in his right.

He partially dressed, and stole up-stairs to old Torfs's photographic studio. He knew where he could find a bottle full of cyanide of potassium, used for removing finger-stains left by silver nitrate; there was enough of it to poison a whole regiment. That was better than taking a header off the roof. He seized a handful of the stuff, and came down and put it into a tumbler by his bedside and poured some water over it.

Then he got his writing-case and a pen and ink, and jumped into bed; and there he wrote four letters: one to Lady Caroline, one to Father Louis, one to Lord Archibald, and one to me in Blaze.

The cyanide was slow in melting. He crushed it angrily in the glass with his penholder—and the scent of bitter-almonds filled the room. Just then the sense of the north came back to him in full ;- but it only strengthened his resolve and made him all the calmer.

He lay staring at the tumbler, watching little bubbles, revelling in what remained of his exquisite faculty of minute sight—with a feeling of great peace ; and thought prayerfully ; lost himself in a kind of formless prayer without words—lost himself completely. It was as if the wished-for dissolution were coming of its own accord ; Nirvana — an ecstasy of conscious annihilation — the blessed end, the end of all ! as though he were passing

> ". . . . du sommeil au songe—
> Du songe à la mort."

It was not so. . . .

He was aroused by a knock at the door, which was locked. It was broad daylight.

"Il est dix heures, savez-vous ?" said little Frau outside—"voulez-vous votre café dans votre chambre ?"

"O Christ !" said Barty — and jumped out of bed. " It's all got to be done now !"

But something very strange had happened.

The tumbler was still there, but the cyanide had disappeared ; so had the four letters he had written. His pen and ink were on the table, and on his open writing-case lay a letter in Blaze—in his own handwriting. The north was strong in him. He called out to Finche Torfs to leave his coffee in the drawing-room, and read his blaze letter—and this is what he read :

"My dear Barty,—Don't be in the least alarmed on reading this hasty scrawl, after waking from the sleep you meant to sleep forever. There is no sleep without a live body to sleep in—no such thing as everlasting sleep. Self-destruction seems a very simple thing—more often a duty than not; but it's not to be done! It is quite impossible not to be, when once you have been.

"If I were to let you destroy your body, as you were so bent on doing, the strongest interest I have on earth would cease to exist.

"I love you, Barty, with a love passing the love of woman; and have done so from the day you were born. I loved your father and mother before you—and theirs; ça date de loin, mon pauvre ami! and especially I love your splendid body and all that belongs to it—brain, stomach, heart, and the rest; even your poor remaining eye, which is worth all the eyes of Argus!

"So I have used your own pen and ink and paper, your own right hand and brain, your own cipher, and the words that are yours, to write you this—in English. I like English better than French.

"Listen. Monsieur Noiret is a fool; and you are a poor self-deluded hypochondriac.

"I am convinced your right eye is safe for many years to come—probably for the rest of your life.

"You have quite deceived yourself in fancying that the symptom you perceived in your right eye threatens the disease which has destroyed your left—for the sight of that, alas! is irretrievably gone; so don't trouble about it any more. It will always be charming to *look at*, but it will never *see* again. Some day I will tell you how you came to lose the use of it. I think I know.

"M. Noiret is new to the ophthalmoscope. The old humbug never saw your right retina at all—nor your left one either, for that matter. He only pretended, and judged entirely by what you told him; and you didn't tell him very clearly. He's a Belgian, you know, and a priest, and doesn't think very quick.

"*I* saw your retina, although but with *his* eye. There is no sign of congestion or coming detachment whatever. That blind portion you discovered is in *every* eye. It is called the '*punctum cæcum.*' It is where the optic nerve enters the retina and spreads out. It is only with one eye shut that an ordinary person can find it, for each eye supplements this defect of the other. To-morrow morning try the experiment on little Finche Torfs; on any one you meet. You will find it in everybody.

"So don't trouble about either eye any more. I'm not infallible, of course; it's only *your* brain I'm using now. But your brain is infinitely better than that of poor M. Noiret, who doesn't know what his eye really perceives, and takes it for something else! Your brain is the best brain I know, although you are not aware of this, and have never even used it, except for trash and nonsense. But you *shall*—some day. *I'll* take care of that, and the world shall wonder.

"Trust me. Live on, and I will never desert you again, unless you again force me to by your conduct. I have come back to you in the hour of your need.

"I have managed to make you, in your sleep, throw away your poison where it will injure nobody but the rats, and no one will be a bit the wiser. I have made you burn your touching letters of farewell; you will find the ashes inside the stove. Yours is a good heart!

"Now take a cold bath and have a good breakfast, and go to Antwerp or Brussels and see people and amuse yourself.

"Never see M. Noiret again. But when your aunt

comes back you must both clear out of this depressing priestly hole ; it doesn't suit either of you, body or mind. Go to Düsseldorf, in Prussia. Close by, at a village called Riffrath, lives an old doctor, Dr. Hasenclever, who understands a deal about the human heart and something about the human body ; and even a little about the human eye, for he is a famous oculist. He can't cure, but he'll give you things that at least will do you no harm. He won't rid you of the eye that remains ! You will meet some pleasant English people, whom I particularly wish you to meet, and make friends, and have a holiday from trouble, and begin the world anew.

"As to who *I* am, you shall know in time. My power to help you is very limited, but my devotion to you (for very good reasons) has no limits at all.

"Take it that my name is Martia. When you have finished reading this letter look at yourself in your looking-glass and say (loud enough for your own ears to hear you):

"'I trust you, Martia !'

"Then I will leave you for a while, and come back at night, as in the old days. Whenever the north is in you, there am I; seeing, hearing, smelling, tasting, feeling with your five splendid wits by day—sleeping your lovely sleep at night; but only able to think with *your* brain, it seems, and then only when you are fast asleep. I only found it out just now, and saved your earthly life, mon beau somnambule ! It was a great surprise to me !

"Don't mention this to any living soul till I give you leave. You will only hear from me on great occasions.

"MARTIA."

"P. S.—Always leave something to write with by your bedside at night, in case the great occasion should arise. On ne sait pas ce qui peut arriver !"

Bewildered, beside himself, Barty ran to his looking-glass, and stared himself out of countenance, and almost shouted :

"I trust you, Martia !"

And ceased suddenly to feel the north.

Then he dressed and went to breakfast. Little Frau thought he had gone mad, for he put a five-franc piece upon the carpet, and made her stand a few feet off from it and cover her left eye with her hand.

"Now follow the point of my stick with your right eye," says he, "and tell me if the five-franc piece disappears."

And he slowly drew with the point of his stick an imaginary line from the five-franc piece to the left of her, at right angles to where she stood. When the point of the stick was about two feet from the coin, she said :

"Tiens, tiens, I no longer see the piece !"

When the point of the stick had got a foot farther on, she said, "Now I can see the piece again quite plain."

Then he tried the same experiment on her left eye, rightwards, with the same result. Then he experimented with equal success on her father and mother, and found that every eye at No. 36 Rue des Ursulines Blanches had exactly the same blind spot as his own.

Then off he went to Antwerp to see his friends with a light heart—the first light heart he had known for many months; but when he got there he was so preoccupied with what had happened that he did not care to see anybody.

He walked about the ramparts and along the Scheldt, and read and re-read that extraordinary letter.

Who and what could Martia be ?

The reminiscence of some antenatal incarnation of his own soul? the soul of some ancestor or ancestress—

of his mother, perhaps? or, perhaps, some occult portion of himself—of his own brain in unconscious cerebration during sleep?

As a child and a small boy, and even as a very young man, he had often dreamt at night of a strange, dim land by the sea, a land unlike any land he had ever beheld with the waking eye, where beautiful aquatic people, mermen and mermaids and charming little mer-children (of which he was one) lived an amphibious life by day, diving and sporting in the waves.

Splendid caverns, decorated with precious stones, and hung with soft moss, and shining with a strange light; heavenly music, sweet, affectionate caresses—and then total darkness; and yet one knew who and what and where everything and everybody was by some keener sense than that of sight.

It all seemed strange and delightful, but so vague and shadowy it was impossible to remember anything clearly; but ever pervading all things was that feeling of the north which had always been such a comfort to him.

Was this extraordinary letter the result of some such forgotten dream he may have had during the previous night, and which may have prompted him to write it in his sleep? some internal knowledge of the anatomy of his own eye which was denied to him when awake?

Anyhow, it was evidently true about that blind spot in the retina (the *punctum cæcum*), and that he had been frightening himself out of his wits for nothing, and that his right eye was really sound; and, all through this wondrous yet simple revelation, it was time this old hysterical mock-disease should die.

Once more life was full of hopes and possibilities, and with such inarticulate and mysterious promptings as he often felt within his soul, and such a hidden gift to guide them, what might he not one day develop into ?

Then he went and found Tescheles, and they dined together with a famous pianist, Louis Brassin, and afterwards there was music, and Barty felt the north, and his bliss was transcendent as he went back to Malines by the last train—talking to Martia (as he expressed it to himself) in a confidential whisper which he made audible to his own ear (that she, if it was a she, might hear too) ; almost praying, in a fervor of hope and gratitude ; and begging for further guidance ; and he went warmly to sleep, hugging close within himself, somewhere about the region of the diaphragm, an ineffable imaginary something which he felt to be more precious than any possession that had ever yet been his—more precious even than the apple of his remaining eye ; and when he awoke next morning he felt he had been most blissfully dreaming all night long, but could not remember anything of his dreams, and on a piece of paper he had left by his bedside was written in pencil, in his own blaze :

" You must depend upon yourself, Barty, not on me. Follow your own instincts when you feel you can do so without self-reproach, and all will be well with you.—M."

His instincts led him to spend the day in Brussels, and he followed them ; he still wanted to walk about and muse and ponder, and Brussels is a very nice, gay, and civilized city for such a purpose — a little Paris, with charming streets and shops and a charming arcade, and very good places to eat and drink in, and hear pretty music.

He did all this, and spent a happy day.

He came to the conclusion that the only way to keenly appreciate and thoroughly enjoy the priceless gift of sight in one eye was to lose that of the other; in the kingdom of the blind the one-eyed is king, and he fully revelled in the royalty that was now his, he hoped, for evermore; but wished for himself as limited a kingdom and as few subjects as possible.

Then back to Malines by the last train—and the sensation of the north, and a good-night; but no message in the morning — no message from Martia for many mornings to come.

He received, however, a long letter from Lady Caroline.

The old Marquis had died without pain, and with nearly all his family round him; but perfectly childish, as he had been for two or three years. He was to be buried on the following Monday.

Barty wrote a long letter in reply, telling his aunt how much better he had suddenly become in health and spirits; how he had thought of things, and quite reconciled himself at last to the loss of his left eye, and meant to keep the other and make the best of it he could; how he had heard of a certain Doctor Hasenclever, a famous oculist near Düsseldorf, and would like to consult him; how Düsseldorf was such a healthy town, charming and gay, full of painters and soldiers, the best and nicest people in the world — and also very cheap. Mightn't they try it?

He was very anxious indeed to go back to his painting, and Düsseldorf was as good a school as any, etc., etc., etc. He wrote pages — of the kind he knew she would like, for it was of the kind he liked writing to her; they understood each other thoroughly, he and Lady Caroline, and well he knew that she could only be quite happy in doing whatever he had most at heart.

How he longed to tell her everything! but that must

not be. I can imagine all the deep discomfort to poor Barty of having to be discreet for the first time in his life, of having to keep a secret—and from his beloved Aunt Caroline of all people in the world !

That was a happy week he spent—mostly in Antwerp among the painters. He got no more letters from Martia, not for many days to come; but he felt the north every night as he sank into healthy sleep, and woke in the morning full of hope and confidence in himself—at last *sans peur et sans reproche.*

One day in Brussels he met M. Noiret, who naturally put on a very grave face; they shook hands, and Barty inquired affectionately after the little Italian greyhound, and asked what was the French for *"punctum cæcum."*

Said Noiret: "Ça s'appelle *le point caché*—c'est une portion de la rétine avec laquelle on ne peut pas voir. . . ."

Barty laughed and shook hands again, and left the Professor staring.

Then he was a great deal with Father Louis. They went to Ghent together, and other places of interest; and to concerts in Brussels.

The good Dominican was very sorrowful at the prospect of soon losing his friend. Poor Barty ! The trial it was to him not to reveal his secret to this singularly kind and sympathetic comrade ; not even under the seal of confession ! So he did not confess at all ; although he would have confessed anything to Father Louis, even if Father Louis had not been a priest. There are the high Catholics, who understand the souls of others, and all the difficulties of the conscience, and do not proselytize in a hurry; and the low Catholics, the converts of the day before yesterday, who will not let a body be !

Father Louis was a very high Catholic indeed.

The Lady Caroline Grey, 12A Seamore Place, London, to M. Josselin, 36 Rue des Ursulines Blanches, Malines :

"MY DEAR LITTLE BARTY, — Your nice long letter made me very happy — happy beyond description ; it makes me almost jealous to think that you should have suddenly got so much better in your health and spirits while I was away : you won't want me any more ! That doesn't prevent my longing to get back to you. You must put up with your poor old aunty for a little while yet.

"And now for *my* news — I couldn't write before. Poor papa was buried on Monday, and we all came back here next day. He has left you £200 : c'est toujours ça ! Everything seems in a great mess. Your Uncle Runswick* is going to be very poor indeed ; he is going to let Castle Rohan, and live here all the year round. Poor fellow, he looks as old as his father did ten years ago, and he's only sixty-three ! If Algy could only make a good marriage ! At forty that's easier said than done.

"Archibald and his wife are at a place called Monte Carlo, where there are gaming-tables : she gambles fearfully, it seems ; and they lead a cat-and-dog life. She is *plus que coquette*, and extravagant to a degree ; and he is quite shrunk and premature old, and almost shabby, and drinks more brandy than he ought.

"Daphne is charming, and is to come out next spring ; she will have £3000 a year, lucky child ; all out of chocolate. What nonsense we've all talked about trade ! we shall all have to take to it in time. The Lonlay-Savignac people were wise in their generation.

"And what do you think ? Young Digby-Dobbs wants

---

* The new Marquis of Whitby.

to marry her, out of the school-room ! He'll be Lord Frognal, you know; and very soon, for his father is drinking himself to death.

"He's in your old regiment, and a great favorite ; not yet twenty—he only left Eton last Christmas twelvemonth. She says she won't have him at any price, because he stammers.

"She declares you haven't written to her for three months, and that you owe her an illustrated letter in French, with priests and nuns, and dogs harnessed to a cart.

"And now for news that will delight you : She is to come abroad with me for a twelvemonth, and wishes to go with you and me to Düsseldorf first ! *Isn't* that a happy coincidence ? We would all spend the summer there, and then Italy for the winter ; you too, if you can (so you must be economical with that £200).

"I have already heard wonders about Dr. Hasenclever, even before your letter came ; he cured General Baines, who was given up by everybody here, Lady Palmerston told me ; she was here yesterday, by-the-bye, and the Duchess of Bermondsey, and both inquired most kindly after you.

"The Duchess looked as handsome as ever, and as proud as a peacock ; for last year she presented her niece, Julia Royce, 'the divine Julia,' the greatest beauty ever seen, I am told—with many thousands a year, if you please — Lady Jane Royce's daughter, an only child, and her father's dead. She's six feet high, so you would go mad about her. She's already refused sixty offers, good ones ; among them little Lord Orrisroot, the hunchback, who'll have £1000 a day (including Sundays) when he comes into the title—and that can't be very far off, for the wicked old Duke of Deptford has got creeping paralysis, like his father and grandfather before him, and is now quite mad, and thinks himself a postman, and rat-tats all day long on the furniture. Lady Jane is furious with her for not accepting ; and when Julia told her, she slapped her face before the maid !

"There's another gigantic beauty that people have gone mad about—a Polish pianist, who's just married young Harcourt, who's a grandson of that old scamp the Duke of Towers.

"Talking of beauties, whom do you think I met yesterday in the Park ? Whom but your stalwart friend Mr. Maurice (*he* wasn't the beauty), with his sister, your old Paris playfellow, and the lovely Miss Gibson. He introduced them both, and I was delighted with them, and we walked together by the Serpentine; and after five minutes I came to the conclusion that Miss Gibson is as beautiful as it is possible for a dark beauty to be, and as nice as she looks. She isn't dark really, only her eyes and hair ; her complexion is like cream : she's a freak of nature. Lucky young Maurice if she is to be his fate— and both well off, I suppose.

"Upon my word, if you were King Cophetua and she the beggar-maid, I would give you both my blessing. But how is it you never fell in love with the fair *Ida?* You never told me how handsome she is. She too complained of you as a correspondent, and declares that she gets one letter in return for three she writes you.

"I have bought you some pretty new songs, among others one by Charles Kingsley, which is lovely ; about three fishermen and their wives : it reminds one of our dear Whitby ! I can play the accompaniment in perfection, and all by heart !

"Give my kindest remembrances to Father Louis and the dear Abbé Lefebvre, and say kind things from me to the Torfses. Martha sends her love to little Frau, and so do I.

" We hope to be in Antwerp in a fortnight, and shall put up at the Grand Laboureur. I shall go to Malines, of course, to say good-bye to people.

" Tell the Torfses to get my things ready for moving. There will be five of us: I and Martha, and Daphne and two servants of her own; for Daphne's got to take old Mrs. Richards, who won't be parted from her.

" Good-bye for the present. My dear boy, I thank God on my knees night and morning for having given you back to me in my old age.

" Your ever affectionate aunt,

" Caroline.

" P. S.—You remember pretty little Kitty Hardwicke you used to flirt with, who married young St. Clair, who's now Lord Kidderminster? She's just had three at a birth; she had twins only last year; the Queen's delighted. Pray be careful about never getting wet feet—"

One stormy evening in May, Mrs. Gibson drove Ida and Leah and me and Mr. Babbage, a middle-aged but very dapper War Office clerk (who was a friend of the Gibson family), to Chelsea, that we might explore Cheyne Walk and its classic neighborhood. I rode on the box by the coachman.

We alighted by the steamboat pier and explored, I walking with Leah.

We came to a very narrow street, quite straight, the narrowest street that could call itself a street at all, and rather long; we were the only people in it. It has since disappeared, with all that particular part of Chelsea.

Suddenly we saw a runaway horse without a rider

coming along it at full gallop, straight at us, with a most demoralizing sharp clatter of its iron hoofs on the stone pavement.

"Your backs to the wall!" cried Mr. Babbage, and we flattened ourselves to let the maddened brute go by, bridle and stirrups flying—poor Mrs. Gibson almost faint with terror.

Leah, instead of flattening herself against the wall, put her arms round her mother, making of her own body a shield for her, and looked round at the horse as it came tearing up the street, striking sparks from the flag-stones.

Nobody was hurt, for a wonder: but Mrs. Gibson was quite overcome. Mr. Babbage was very angry with Leah, whose back the horse actually grazed, as he all but caught his hoofs in her crinoline and hit her with a stirrup on the shoulder.

I could only think of Leah's face as she looked round at the approaching horse, with her protecting arms round her mother. It was such a sudden revelation to me of what she really was, and its expression was so hauntingly impressive that I could think of nothing else. Its mild, calm courage, its utter carelessness of self, its immense tenderness—all blazed out in such beautiful lines, in such beautiful white and black, that I lost all self-control; and when we walked back to the pier, following the rest of the party, I asked her to be my wife.

She turned very pale again, and the flesh of her chin quivered as she told me that was *quite impossible—and could never be.*

I asked her if there was anybody else, and she said there was nobody, but that she did not wish ever to marry; that, beyond her parents and Ida, she loved and respected me more than anybody else in the whole world, but that she could never marry me. She was much agitated, and said the sweetest, kindest things, but put all hope out of the question at once.

It was the greatest blow I have ever had in my life.

Three days after, I went to America; and before I came back I had started in New York the American branch of the house of Vougeot-Conti, and laid the real foundation of the largest fortune that has ever yet been made by selling wine, and of the long political career about which I will say nothing in these pages.

On my voyage out I wrote a long blaze letter to Barty, and poured out all my grief, and my resignation to the decree which I felt to be irrevocable. I reminded him of that playful toss-up in Southampton Row, and told him that, having surrendered all claims myself, the best thing that could happen to me was that she should some day marry *him* (which I certainly did not think at all likely).

So henceforward, reader, you will not be troubled by your obedient servant with the loves of a prosperous merchant of wines. Had those loves been more successful, and the wines less so, you would never have heard of either.

Whether or not I should have been a happier man in the long-run I really can't say—mine has been, on the whole, a very happy life, as men's lives go; but I am bound to admit, in all due modesty, that the universe would probably have been the poorer by some very splendid people, and perhaps by some very splendid things it could ill have spared ; and one great and beautifully borne sorrow the less would have been ushered into this world of many sorrows.

It was a bright May morning (a year after this) when Barty and his aunt Caroline and his cousin Daphne and their servants left Antwerp for Düsseldorf on the Rhine.

At Malines they had to change trains, and spent half an hour at the station waiting for the express from Brussels and bidding farewell to their Mechlin friends, who had come there to wish them God-speed : the Abbé Lefebvre, Father Louis, and others ; and the Torfses, père et mère ; and little Frau, who wept freely as Lady Caroline kissed her and gave her a pretty little diamond brooch. Barty gave her a gold cross and a hearty shake of the hand, and she seemed quite heart-broken.

Then up came the long, full train, and their luggage was swallowed, and they got in, and the two guards blew their horns, and they left Malines behind them—with a mixed feeling of elation and regret.

They had not been very happy there, but many people had been very kind ; and the place, with all its dreariness, had a strange, still charm, and was full of historic beauty and romantic associations.

Passing Louvain, Barty shook his fist at the Catholic University and its scientific priestly professors, who condemned one so lightly to a living death. He hated the aspect of the place, the very smell of it.

At Verviers they left the Belgian train ; they had reached the limits of King Leopold's dominions. There was half an hour for lunch in the big refreshment-room, over which his Majesty and the Queen of the Belgians presided from the wall—nearly seven feet high each of them, and in their regal robes.

Just as the Rohans ordered their repast another English party came to their table and ordered theirs—a distinguished old gentleman of naval bearing and aspect ; a still young middle-aged lady, very handsome, with blue spectacles ; and an immensely tall, fair girl, very fully developed, and so astonishingly beautiful that it almost took one's breath away merely to catch sight of her ; and people were distracted from ordering their mid-day meal merely to stare at this magnificent goddess, who was evidently born to be a mother of heroes.

These British travellers had a valet, a courier, and two maids, and were evidently people of consequence.

Suddenly the lady with the blue spectacles (who had seated herself close to the Rohan party) got up and came round the table to Barty's aunt and said :

" You don't remember me, Lady Caroline ; Lady Jane Royce !"

And an old acquaintance was renewed in this informal manner—possibly some old feud patched up.

Then everybody was introduced to everybody else, and they all lunched together, a scramble !

It turned out that Lady Jane Royce was in some alarm about her eyes, and was going to consult the famous Dr. Hasenclever, and had brought her daughter with her, just as the London season had begun.

Her daughter was the "divine Julia" who had refused so many splendid offers — among them the little hunchback Lord who was to have a thousand a day, "including Sundays"; a most unreasonable young woman, and a thorn in her mother's flesh.

The elderly gentleman, Admiral Royce, was Lady Jane's uncle-in-law, whose eyes were also giving him a little anxiety. He was a charming old stoic, by no means pompous or formal, or a martinet, and declared he remembered hearing of Barty as the naughtiest boy in the Guards ; and took an immediate fancy to him in consequence.

They had come from Brussels in the same train that had brought the Rohans from Malines, and they all journeyed together from Verviers to Düsseldorf in the same first-class carriage, as became English swells of the first water — for in those days no one ever thought of going first-class in Germany except the British aristocracy and a few native royalties.

The divine Julia turned out as fascinating as she was fair, being possessed of those high spirits that result from youth and health and fancy-freedom, and no cares to speak of. She was evidently also a very clever and accomplished young lady, absolutely without affectation of any kind, and amiable and frolicsome to the highest degree—a kind of younger Barty Josselin in petticoats ; oddly enough, so like him in the face she might have been his sister.

Indeed, it was a lively party that journeyed to Düsseldorf that afternoon in that gorgeously gilded compartment, though three out of the six were in deep mourning ; the only person not quite happy being Lady Jane, who, in addition to her trouble about her eyes (which was really nothing to speak of), began to fidget herself miserably about Barty Josselin ; for that wretched young detrimental was evidently beginning to ingratiate himself with the divine Julia as no young man had ever been known to do before, keeping her in fits of laughter, and also laughing at everything she said herself.

Alas for Lady Jane ! it was to escape the attentions of a far less dangerous detrimental, and a far less ineligible one, that she had brought her daughter with her all the way to Riffrath — "from Charybdis to Scylla," as we used to say at Brossard's, putting the cart before the horse, *more Latino!*

I ought also to mention that a young Captain Graham-Reece was a patient of Dr. Hasenclever's just then—and Captain Graham-Reece was heir to the octogenarian Earl of Ironsides, who was one of the four wealthiest peers in the United Kingdom, and had no direct descendants.

When they reached Düsseldorf they all went to the Breidenbacher Hotel, where rooms had been retained for them, all but Barty, who, as became his humbler means, chose the cheaper hotel Domhardt, which overlooks the market-place adorned by the statue of the Elector that Heine has made so famous.

He took a long evening walk through the vernal Hof Gardens and by the Rhine, and thought of the beauty and splendor of the divine Julia; and sighed, and remembered that he was Mr. Nobody of Nowhere, *pictor ignotus*, with only one eye he could see with, and possessed of a fortune which invested in the 3 per cents would bring him in just £6 a year—and made up his mind he would stick to his painting and keep as much away from her divinity as possible.

"O Martia, Martia!" he said, aloud, as he suddenly felt the north at the right of him, "I hope that you are some loving female soul, and that you know my weakness—namely, that one woman in every ten thousand has a face that drives me mad; and that I can see just as well with one eye as with two, in spite of my *punctum cæcum!* and that when that face is all but on a level with mine, good Lord! then am I lost indeed! I am but a poor penniless devil, without a name; oh, keep me from that ten-thousandth face, and cover my retreat!"

Next morning Lady Jane and Julia and the Admiral left for Riffrath—and Barty and his aunt and cousin went in search of lodgings; sweet it was, and bright and sunny, as they strolled down the broad Allée Strasse; a regiment of Uhlans came along on horseback, splendid fellows, the band playing the "Lorelei."

In the fulness of their hearts Daphne and Barty squeezed each other's hand to express the joy and elation they felt at the pleasantness of everything. She was his little sister once more, from whom he had so long been parted, and they loved each other very dearly.

"Que me voilà donc bien contente, mon petit Barty—et toi ? la jolie ville, hein ?"

"C'est le ciel, tout bonnement—et tu vas m'apprendre l'allemand, n'est-ce-pas, m'amour ?"

"Oui, et nous lirons *Heine* ensemble ; tiens, à propos ! regarde le nom de la rue qui fait le coin ! *Bolker Strasse!* c'est là qu'il est né, le pauvre Heine ! Ôte ton chapeau !"

(Barty nearly always spoke French with Daphne, as he did with my sister and me, and said " thee and thou.")

They found a furnished house that suited them in the Schadow Strasse, opposite Geissler's, where for two hours every Thursday and Sunday afternoon you might sit for sixpence in a pretty garden and drink coffee, beer, or Maitrank, and listen to lovely music, and dance in the evening under cover to strains of Strauss, Lanner, and Gungl, and other heavenly waltz-makers ! With all their faults, they know how to make the best of their lives, these good Vaterlanders, and how to dance, and especially how to make music—and also how to fight ! So we won't quarrel with them, after all !

Barty found for himself a cheap bedroom, high up in an immense house tenanted by many painters—some of them English and some American. He never forgot the delight with which he awoke next morning and opened his window and saw the silver Rhine among the trees, and the fir-clad hills of Grafenberg, and heard the gay painter fellows singing as they dressed ; and he called out to the good-humored slavy in the garden below :

"Johanna, mein Frühstück, bitte !"

A phrase he had carefully rehearsed with Daphne the evening before.

And, to his delight and surprise, Johanna understood the mysterious jargon quite easily, and brought him what he wanted with the most good-humored grin he had ever seen on a female face.

Coffee and a roll and a pat of butter.

First of all, he went to see Dr. Hasenclever at Riffrath, which was about half an hour by train, and then half an hour's walk—an immensely prosperous village, which owed its prosperity to the famous doctor, who attracted patients from all parts of the globe, even from America. The train that took Barty thither was full of them; for some chose to live in Düsseldorf.

The great man saw his patients on the ground-floor of the König's Hotel, the principal hotel in Riffrath, the hall of which was always crowded with these afflicted ones—patiently waiting each his turn, or hers; and there Barty took his place at four in the afternoon; he had sent in his name at 10 A.M., and been told that he would be seen after four o'clock. Then he walked about the village, which was charming, with its gabled white houses, ornamented like the cottages in the Richter albums by black beams—and full of English, many of them with green shades or blue spectacles or a black patch over one eye; some of them being led, or picking their way by means of a stick, alas!

Barty met the three Royces, walking with an old gentleman of aristocratic appearance, and a very nice-looking young one (who was Captain Graham-Reece). The Admiral gave him a friendly nod—Lady Jane a nod that almost amounted to a cut direct. But the divine Julia gave him a look and a smile that were warm enough to make up for much maternal frigidity.

Later on, in a tobacconist's shop, he again met the Admiral, who introduced him to the aristocratic old gentleman, Mr. Beresford Duff, secretary to the Admiralty—who evidently knew all about him, and inquired quite affectionately after Lady Caroline, and invited him to come and drink tea at five o'clock : a new form of hospitality of his own invention—it has caught on !

Barty lunched at the König's Hotel table d'hôte, which was crowded, principally with English people, none of whom he had ever met or heard of. But from these he heard a good deal of the Royces and Captain Graham-Reece and Mr. Beresford Duff, and other smart people who lived in furnished houses or expensive apartments away from the rest of the world, and were objects of general interest and curiosity among the smaller British fry.

Riffrath was a microcosm of English society, from the lower middle class upwards, with all its respectabilities and incompatibilities and disabilities—its narrownesses and meannesses and snobbishnesses, its gossipings and backbitings and toadyings and snubbings—delicate little social things of England that foreigners don't understand !

The sensation of the hour was the advent of Julia, the divine Julia ! Gossip was already rife about her and Captain Reece. They had taken a long walk in the woods together the day before—with Lady Jane and the Admiral far behind, out of ear-shot, almost out of sight !

In the afternoon, between four and five, Barty had his interview with the doctor—a splendid, white-haired old man, of benign and intelligent aspect, almost mesmeric, with his assistant sitting by him.

He used no new-fangled ophthalmoscope, but asked many questions in fairly good French, and felt with his fingers, and had many German asides with the assistant. He told Barty that he had lost the sight of his left eye forever ; but that with care he would keep that of the right one for the rest of his life—barring accidents, of course. That he must never eat cheese nor drink beer. That he (the doctor) would like to see him once a week or fortnight or so for a few months yet—and gave him a prescription for an eye-lotion and dismissed him happy.

Half a loaf is so much better than no bread, if you can only count upon it !

Barty went straight to Mr. Beresford Duff's, and there found a very agreeable party, including the divine Julia, who was singing little songs very prettily and accompanying herself on a guitar.

" ' You ask me why I look so pale ?' " sang Julia, just Barty entered : and red as a rose was she.

Lady Jane didn't seem at all overjoyed to see Barty, but Julia did, and did not disguise the seeming.

There were eight or ten people there, and they all appeared to know about him, and all that concerned or belonged to him. It was the old London world over again, in little ! the same tittle-tattle about well-known people, and nothing else—as if nothing else existed ; a genial, easy-going, good-natured world, that he had so often found charming for a time, but in which he was never quite happy and had no proper place of his own, all through that fatal bar-sinister—la barre de bâtardise ; a world that was his and yet not his, and in whose midst his position was a false one, but where every one took him for granted at once as one of *them,* so long as he never trespassed beyond that sufferance ; that there must be no love-making to lovely young heiresses by the bastard of Antoinette Josselin was taken for granted also !

Before Barty had been there half an hour two or three

"YOU ASK ME WHY I LOOK SO PALE?"

people had evidently lost their hearts to him in friendship ; among them, to Lady Jane's great discomfiture, the handsome and amiable Graham-Reece, the cynosure of all female eyes in Riffrath ; and when Barty (after very little pressing by Miss Royce) twanged her guitar and sang little songs—French and English, funny and sentimental—he became, as he had so often become in other scenes, the Rigoletto of the company ; and Riffrath was a kingdom in which he might be court jester in ordinary if he chose, whenever he elected to honor it with his gracious and facetious musical presence.

So much for his début in that strange little overgrown busy village ! What must it be like now ?

Dr. Hasenclever has been gathered to his fathers long ago, and nobody that I know of has taken his place. All those new hotels and lodging-houses and smart shops— what can they have been turned into ? Barracks ? prisons ? military hospitals and sanatoriums ? How dull !

Lady Caroline and Daphne and Barty between them added considerably to the gayety of Düsseldorf that summer—especially when Royces and Reeces and Duffs and such like people came there from Riffrath to lunch, or tea, or dinner, or for walks or drives or rides to Grafenberg or Neanderthal, or steamboatings to Neuss.

There were one or two other English families in Düsseldorf, living there for economy's sake, but yet of the world—of the kind that got to be friends with the Rohans ; half-pay old soldiers and sailors and their families, who introduced agreeable and handsome Uhlans and hussars—from their Serene Highnesses the Princes Fritz and Hans von Eselbraten - Himmelsblutwürst - Silberschinken, each passing rich on £200 a year, down to poor Lieutenants von this or von that, with nothing but their pay and their thirty-two quarterings.

Also a few counts and barons, and princes not serene, but with fine German fortunes looming for them in the future, though none amounting to £1000 a day, like little Lord Orrisroot's !

Soon there was hardly a military heart left whole in the town; Julia had eaten them all up, except one or two that had been unconsciously nibbled by little Daphne.

Barty did not join in these aristocratic revels; he had become a pupil of Herr Duffenthaler, and worked hard in his master's studio with two brothers of the brush— one English, the other American; delightful men who remained his friends for life.

Indeed, he lived among the painters, who all got to love "der schöne Barty Josselin" like a brother.

Now and then, of an evening, being much pressed by his aunt, he would show himself at a small party in Schadow Strasse, and sing and be funny, and attentive to the ladies, and render himself discreetly useful and agreeable all round—and make that party go off. Lady Caroline would have been far happier had he lived with them altogether. But she felt herself responsible for her innocent and wealthy little niece.

It was an article of faith with Lady Caroline that no normal and properly constituted young woman could see much of Barty without falling over head and ears in love with him—and this would never do for Daphne. Besides, they were first-cousins. So she acquiesced in the independence of his life apart from them. She was not responsible for the divine Julia, who might fall in love with him just as she pleased, and welcome ! That was Lady Jane's lookout, and Captain Graham-Reece's.

But Barty always dined with his aunt and cousin on Thursdays and Sundays, after listening to the music in

Geissler's Garden, opposite, and drinking coffee with them there, and also with Prince Fritz and Prince Hans, who always joined the party and smoked their cheap cigars ; and sometimes the divine Julia would make one of the party too, with her mother and uncle and Captain Reece ; and the good painter fellows would envy from afar their beloved but too fortunate comrade ; and the hussars and Uhlans, von this and von that, would find seats and tables as near the princely company as possible.

And every time a general officer entered the garden, up stood every officer of inferior rank till the great man had comfortably seated himself somewhere in the azure sunshine of Julia's forget-me-not warm glance.

And before the summer had fulfilled itself, and the roses at Geissler's were overblown, it became evident to Lady Caroline, if to none other, that Julia had eyes for no one else in the world but Barty Josselin. I had it from Lady Caroline herself.

But Barty Josselin had eyes only (such eyes as they were) for his work at Herr Duffenthaler's, and lived laborious days, except on Thursday and Sunday afternoons, and shunned delights, except to dine at the Runsberg Speiserei with his two fellow-pupils, and Henley and Armstrong and Bancroft and du Maurier and others, all painters, mostly British and Yankee ; and an uncommonly lively and agreeable repast that was ! And afterwards, long walks by moon or star light, or music at each other's rooms, and that engrossing technical shop talk that never palls on those who talk it. No Guardsman's talk of turf or sport or the ballet had ever been so good as this, in Barty's estimation ; no agreeable society gossip at Mr. Beresford Duff's Riffrath tea-parties !

Once in every fortnight or so Barty would report him-

"'YOU DON'T MEAN TO SAY YOU'RE GOING TO PAINT FOR HIRE!'"

self to Dr. Hasenclever, and spend the day in Riffrath and lunch with the good old Beresford Duff, who was very fond of him, and who lamented over his loss of caste in devoting himself professionally to art.

"God bless me—my dear Barty, you don't mean to say you're going to paint for *hire!*"

"Indeed I am, if any one will hire me. How else am I to live?"

"Well, *you* know best, my dear boy; but I should have thought the Rohans might have got you something better than *that*. It's true, Buckner does it, and Swinton, and Francis Grant! But *still*, you know . . . there *are* other ways of getting on for a fellow like you. Look at Prince Gelbioso, who ran away with the Duchess of Flitwick! He didn't sing a bit better than you do, and as for looks, you beat him hollow, my dear boy; yet all London went mad about Prince Gelbioso, and so did she; and off she bolted with him, bag and baggage, leaving husband and children and friends and all! and she'd got ten thousand a year of her own; and when the Duke divorced her they were married, and lived happily ever after — in Italy; and some of the best people called upon 'em, by George! . . . just to spite the Duke!"

Barty felt it would seem priggish or even insincere if he were to disclaim any wish to emulate Prince Gelbioso; so he merely said he thought painting easier on the whole, and not so risky; and the good Beresford Duff talked of other things—of the divine Julia, and what a good thing it would be if she and Graham-Reece could make a match of it.

"Two of the finest fortunes in England, by George! they *ought* to come together, if only just for the fun of the thing! Not that she is a bit in love with him—I'll eat my hat if she is ! What a pity *you* ain't goin' to be Lord Ironsides, Barty !"

Barty frankly confessed *he* shouldn't much object, for one.

" But, 'ni l'or ni la grandeur ne nous rendent heureux,' as we used to be taught at school."

"Ah, that's all gammon ; wait till you're *my* age, my young friend, and as poor as *I* am," said Beresford Duff. And so the two friends talked on, Mentor and Telemachus—and we needn't listen any further.

Part Seventh

> "Old winter was gone
> In his weakness back to the mountains hoar,
> And the spring came down
> From the planet that hovers upon the shore
> Where the sea of sunlight encroaches
> On the limits of wintry night;
> If the land, and the air, and the sea
> Rejoice not when spring approaches,
> We did not rejoice in thee,
> Ginevra !"
>
> —SHELLEY.

RIFFRATH, besides its natives and its regular English colony of residents, had a floating population that constantly changed. And every day new faces were to be found drinking tea with Mr. Beresford Duff—and all these faces were well known in society at home, you may be sure; and Barty made capital caricatures of them all, which were treasured up and carried back to England ; one or two of them turn up now and then at a sale at Christie's and fetch a great price. I got a little pen-and-ink outline of Captain Reece there, drawn before he came into the title. I had to give forty-seven pounds ten for it, not only because it was a speaking likeness of the late Lord Ironsides as a young man, but on account of the little " B. J." in the corner.

And only the other evening I sat at dinner next to the Dowager Countess. Heavens ! what a beautiful creature she still is, with her prematurely white hair and her long thick neck!

And after dinner we talked of Barty—she with that delightful frankness that always characterized her through life, I am told :

"Dear Barty Josselin! how desperately in love I was with that man, to be sure ! Everybody was—he might have thrown the handkerchief as he pleased in Riffrath, I can tell you, Sir Robert ! He was the handsomest man I ever saw, and wore a black pork-pie hat and a little yellow Vandyck beard and mustache ; just the color of Turkish tobacco, like his hair ! All that sounds odd now, doesn't it ? Fashions have changed—but not for the better ! And what a figure ! and such fun he was ! and always in such good spirits, poor boy ! and now he's dead, and it's one of the greatest names in all the world ! Well, if he'd thrown that handkerchief at me just about then, I should have picked it up—and you're welcome to tell all the world so, Sir Robert !"

And next day I got a kind and pretty little letter :

"DEAR SIR ROBERT,—I was quite serious last night. Barty Josselin was *mes premières amours!* Whether he ever guessed it or not, I can't say. If not, he was very obtuse ! Perhaps he feared to fall, and didn't feel fain to climb in consequence. I all but proposed to him, in fact ! Anyhow, I am proud my girlish fancy should have fallen on such a man !

"I told him so myself only last year, and we had a good laugh over old times ; and then I told his wife, and she seemed much pleased. I can understand his preference, and am old enough to forgive it and laugh— although there is even now a tear in the laughter. You

know his daughter, Julia Mainwaring, is my godchild ;
sometimes she sings her father's old songs to me :

> " ' Petit chagrin de notre enfance
> Coûte un soupir !'

"Do you remember ?

"Poor Ironsides knew all about it when he married
me, and often declared I had amply made up to him
for that and many other things—over and over again.
Il avait bien raison ; and made of me a very happy wife
and a most unhappy widow.

"Put this in your book, if you like.

> "Sincerely yours,
> "JULIA IRONSIDES."

Thus time flowed smoothly and pleasantly for Barty
all through the summer. In August the Royces left, and
also Captain Reece—they for Scotland, he for Algiers—
and appointed to meet again in Riffrath next spring.

In October Lady Caroline took her niece to Rome,
and Barty was left behind to his work, very much to her
grief and Daphne's.

He wrote to them every Monday, and always got a
letter back on the Saturday following.

Barty spent the winter hard at work, but with lots of
play between, and was happy among his painter fellows
—and sketching and caricaturing, and skating and sleigh-
ing with the English who remained in Düsseldorf, and
young von this and young von that. I have many of
his letters describing this genial, easy life—letters full of
droll and charming sketches.

He does not mention the fair Julia much, but there is
no doubt that the remembrance of her much preoccupied
him, and kept him from losing his heart to any of the

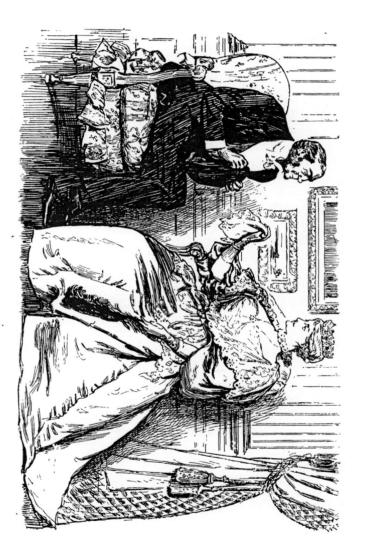

"HE MIGHT HAVE THROWN THE HANDKERCHIEF AS HE PLEASED"

fair damsels, English and German, whom he skated and danced with, and sketched and sang to.

As a matter of fact, he had never yet lost his heart in his life—not even to Julia. He never said much about his love-making with Julia to me. But his aunt did—and I listened between the words, as I always do. His four or five years' career in London as a thoroughgoing young rake had given him a very deep insight into woman's nature—an insight rare at his age, for all his perceptions were astonishingly acute, and his unconscious faculty of sympathetic observation and induction and deduction immense.

And, strange to say, if that heart had never been touched, it had never been corrupted either, and probably for that very reason—that he had never been in love with these sirens. It is only when true love fades away at last in the arms of lust that the youthful, manly heart is wrecked and ruined and befouled.

He made up his mind that art should be his sole mistress henceforward, and that the devotion of a lifetime would not be price enough to pay for her favors, if but she would one day be kind. He had to make up for so much lost time, and had begun his wooing so late! Then he was so happy with his male friends! Whatever void remained in him when his work was done for the day could be so thoroughly filled up by Henley and Bancroft and Armstrong and du Maurier and the rest that there was no room for any other and warmer passion. Work was a joy by itself; the rest from it as great a joy; and these alternations were enough to fill a life. To how many great artists had they sufficed! and what happy lives had been led, with no other distraction, and how glorious and successful! Only the divine Julia, in all the universe, was worthy to be weighed in the scales with

289

these, and she was not for the likes of Mr. Nobody of Nowhere.

Besides, there was the faithful Martia. Punctually every evening the ever-comforting sense of the north filled him as he jumped into bed; and he whispered his prayers audibly to this helpful spirit, or whatever it might be, that had given him a sign and saved him from a cowardly death, and filled his life and thoughts as even no Julia could.

And yet, although he loved best to forgather with those of his own sex, woman meant much for him! There *must* be a woman somewhere in the world—a needle in a bottle of hay—a nature that could dovetail and fit in with his own; but what a life-long quest to find her! She must be young and beautiful, like Julia—rien que ça!—and as kind and clever and simple and well-bred and easy to live with as Aunt Caroline, and, heavens! how many things besides, before poor Mr. Nobody of Nowhere could make her happy, and be made happy by her!

So Mr. Nobody of Nowhere gave it up, and stuck to his work, and made much progress, and was well content with things as they were.

He had begun late, and found many difficulties in spite of his great natural facility. His principal stock in trade was his keen perception of human beauty, of shape and feature and expression, male or female—of face or figure or movement; and a great love and appreciation of human limbs, especially hands and feet.

With a very few little pen-strokes he could give the most marvellously subtle likenesses of people he knew—beautiful or ordinary or plain or hideous; and the beauty of the beautiful people, just hinted in mere outline, was so keen and true and fascinating that this

19

extraordinary power of expressing it amounted to real genius.

It is a difficult thing, even for a master, to fully render with an ordinary steel pen and a drop of common ink (and of a size no bigger than your little finger nail) the full face of a beautiful woman, let us say; or a child, in sadness or merriment or thoughtful contemplation; and make it as easily and unmistakably recognizable as a good photograph, but with all the subtle human charm and individuality of expression delicately emphasized in a way that no photograph has ever achieved yet.

And this he could always do in a minute from sheer memory and unconscious observation; and in another few minutes he would add on the body, in movement or repose, and of a resemblance so wonderful and a grace so enchanting, or a humor so happily, naïvely droll, that one forgot to criticise the technique, which was quite that of an amateur; indeed, with all the success he achieved as an artist, he remained an amateur all his life. Yet his greatest admirers were among the most consummate and finished artists of their day, both here and abroad.

It was with his art as with his singing : both were all wrong, yet both gave extraordinary pleasure ; one almost feared that regular training would mar the gift of God, so much of the charm we all so keenly felt lay in the very imperfections themselves — just as one loved him personally as much for his faults as for his virtues.

" Il a les qualités de ses défauts, le beau Josselin," said M. Taine one day.

"Mon cher," said M. Renan, "ses défauts sont ses meilleures qualités."

So he spent a tranquil happy winter, and wrote of his happiness and his tranquillity to Lady Caroline and

Daphne and Ida and me; and before he knew where he was, or we, the almond-trees blossomed again, and then the lilacs and limes and horse-chestnuts and syringas; and the fireflies flew in and out of his bedroom at night, and the many nightingales made such music in the Hof gardens that he could scarcely sleep for them; and other nightingales came to make music for him too—most memorable music! Stockhausen, Jenny Ney, Joachim, Madame Schumann; for the triennial Musik festival was held in Düsseldorf that year (a month later than usual); and musical festivals are things they manage uncommonly well in Germany. Barty, unseen and unheard, as becomes a chorus-singer, sang in the choruses of Gluck's *Iphigenia*, and heard and saw everything for nothing.

But, before this, Captain Reece came back to Riffrath, and, according to appointment, Admiral Royce and Lady Jane, and Julia, lovelier than ever; and all the sweetness she was so full of rose in her heart and gathered in her eyes as they once more looked on Barty Josselin.

He steeled and stiffened himself like a man who knew that the divine Julias of this world were for his betters—not for him! Nevertheless, as he went to bed, and thought of the melting gaze that had met his, he was deeply stirred; and actually, though the north was in him, he forgot, for the first time in all that twelvemonth, for the first time since that terrible night in Malines, to say his prayers to Martia—and next morning he found a letter by his bedside in pencil-written blaze of his own handwriting:

"BARTY MY BELOVED,—A crisis has come in your affairs, which are mine; and, great as the cost is to me, I must write again, at the risk of betraying what amounts to a sacred trust; a secret that I have innocently surprised, the secret of a noble woman's heart.

"One of the richest girls in England, one of the healthiest and most beautiful women in the whole world, a bride fit for an emperor, is yours for the asking. It is my passionate wish, and a matter of life and death to me, that you and Julia Royce should become man and wife; when you are, you shall both know why.

"Mr. Nobody of Nowhere—as you are so fond of calling yourself—you shall be such, some day, that the best and highest in the land will be only too proud to be your humble friends and followers ; no woman is too good for you—only one good enough ! and she loves you : of that I feel sure—-and it is impossible you should not love her back again.

"I have known her from a baby, and her father and mother also ; I have inhabited her, as I have inhabited you, although I have never been able to give her the slightest intimation of the fact. You are both, physically, the most perfect human beings I was ever in ; and in heart and mind the most simply made, the most richly gifted, and the most admirably balanced ; and I have inhabited many thousands, and in all parts of the globe.

"You, Barty, are the only one I have ever been able to hold communication with, or make to feel my presence; it was a strange chance, that—a happy accident ; it saved your life. I am the only one, among many thousands of homeless spirits, who has ever been able to influence an earthly human being, or even make him feel the magnetic current that flows through us all, and by which we are able to exist ; all the rappings and table-turnings are mere hysterical imaginations, or worse — the cheapest form of either trickery or self-deception that can be. Barty, your unborn children are of a moment to me be-

yond anything you can realize or imagine, and Julia
must be their mother; Julia Royce, and no other woman
in the world.

"It is in you to become so great when you are ripe
that she will worship the ground you walk upon; bat
you can only become as great as that through her and
through me, who have a message to deliver to mankind
here on earth, and none but you to give it a voice—not
one. But I must have my reward, and that can only
come through your marriage with Julia.

"When you have read this, Barty, go straight to Riffrath, and see Julia if you can, and be to her as you
have so often been to any women you wished to please,
and who were not ·worth pleasing. Her heart is her own
to give, like her fortune; she can do what she likes with
them both, and will—her mother notwithstanding, and
in the teeth of the whole world.

"Poor as you are, maimed as you are, irregularly born
as you are, it is better for her that she should be your
wife than the wife of any man living, whoever he be.

"Look at yourself in the glass, and say at once,

"'Martia, I'm off to Riffrath as soon as I've swallowed
my breakfast!'

"And then I'll go about my business with a light
heart and an easy mind.

"MARTIA."

Much moved and excited, Barty looked in the glass
and did as he was bid, and the north left him; and Johanna brought him his breakfast, and he started for
Riffrath.

All through this winter that was so happily spent by
Barty in Düsseldorf things did not go very happily in

London for the Gibsons. Mr. Gibson was not meant for business; nature intended him as a rival to Keeley or Buckstone.

He was extravagant, and so was his wife; they were beth given to frequent and most expensive hospitalities; and he to cards, and she to dressing herself and her daughter more beautifully than quite became their position in life. The handsome and prosperous shop in Cheapside—the "emporium," as he loved to call it—was not enough to provide for all these luxuries; so he took another in Conduit Street, and decorated it and stocked it at immense expense, and called it the "Universal Fur Company," and himself the "Head of a West End firm."

Then he speculated, and was not successful, and his affairs got into tangle.

And a day came when he found he could not keep up these two shops and his private house in Tavistock Square as well; the carriage was put down first—a great distress to Mrs. Gibson; and finally, to her intense grief, it became necessary to give up the pretty house itself.

It was decided that their home in future most be over the new emporium in Conduit Street; Mrs. Gibson had a properly constituted English shopkeeper's wife's horror of living over her husband's shop—the idea almost broke her heart; and as a little consolation, while the necessary changes were being wrought for their altered mode of life, Mr. Gibson treated her and Leah and my sister to a trip up the Rhine—and Mrs. Bletchley, the splendid old Jewess (Leah's grandmother), who suffered, or fancied she suffered, in her eyesight, took it into her head that she would like to see the famous Dr. Hasenclever in Riffrath, and elected to journey with them—at all events as far as Düsseldorf. I would have escorted them, but that my father was ill, and I had to replace him in Barge Yard ; besides, I was not yet quite cured of my unhappy passion, though in an advanced stage of convalescence ; and I did not wish to put myself under conditions that might retard my complete recovery, or even bring on a relapse. I wished to love Leah as a sister ; in time I succeeded in doing so ; she has been fortunate in her brother, though I say it who shouldn't—and, O heavens ! haven't I been fortunate in my sister Leah ?

My own sister Ida wrote to Barty to find rooms and meet them at the station, and fixed the day and hour of their arrival ; and commissioned him to take seats for Gluck's *Iphigenia*.

She thought more of *Iphigenia* than of the Drachenfels or Ehrenbreitstein ; and was overjoyed at the prospect of once more being with Barty, whom she loved as well as she loved me, if not even better. He was fortunate in his sister, too !

And the Rhine in May did very well as a background to all these delights.

So Mr. Babbage (the friend of the family) and I saw them safely on board the *Baron Osy* ("the Ank-works package," as Mrs. Gamp called it), which landed them safely in the Place Verte at Antwerp ; and then they took train for Düsseldorf, changing at Malines and Verviers ; and looked forward eagerly, especially Ida, to the meeting with Barty at the little station by the Rhine.

Barty, as we know, started for Riffrath at Martia's written command, his head full of perplexing thoughts.

Who was Martia ? What was she ? " A disembodied conscience ?" Whose ? Not his own, which counselled the opposite course.

He had once seen a man at a show with a third rudimentary leg sticking out behind, and was told this extra limb belonged to a twin, the remaining portions of whom had not succeeded in getting themselves begotten and born. Could Martia be a frustrated and undeveloped twin sister of his own, that interested herself in his affairs, and could see with his eyes and hear with his ears, and had found the way of communicating with him during his sleep—and was yet apart from him, as phenomenal twins are apart from each other, however closely linked—and had, moreover, not managed to have any part of her body born into this world at all ?

She wrote like him ; her epistolary style was his very own, every turn of phrase, every little mannerism. The mystery of it overwhelmed him again, though he had grown somewhat accustomed to the idea during the last twelvemonth. *Why* was she so anxious he should marry Julia ? Had he, situated as he was, the right to win the love of this splendid creature, in the face of the world's opposition and her family's—he, a beggar and a bastard ? Would it be right and honest and fair to her ?

And then, again, was he so desperately in love with her, after all, that he should give up the life of art and toil he had planned for himself and go through existence as the husband of a rich and beautiful woman belonging, first of all, to the world and society, of which she was so brilliant an ornament that her husband must needs remain in the background forever, even if he were a gartered duke or a belted earl ?

What success of his own would he ever hope to achieve, handicapped as he would be by all the ease and luxury she would bring him ? He had grown to love the poverty which ever lends such strenuousness to endeavor. He thought of an engraving he had once taken a fancy to in

Brussels, and purchased and hung up in his bedroom. *I* have it now! It is after Gallait, and represents a picturesquely poor violinist and his violin in a garret, and underneath is written "Art et liberté."

Then he thought of Julia's lovely face and magnificent body — and all his manhood thrilled as he recalled the look in her eyes when they met his the day before.

This was the strongest kind of temptation by which his nature could ever be assailed—he knew himself to be weak as water when that came his way, the ten-thousandth face (and the figure to match)! He had often prayed to Martia to deliver him from such a lure. But here was Martia on the side of the too sweet enemy!

The train stopped for a few minutes at Neanderthal, and he thought he could think better if he got out and walked in that beautiful valley an hour or two—there was no hurry; he would take another train later, in time to meet Julia at Beresford Duff's, where she was sure to be. So he walked among the rocks, the lonely rocks, and sat and pondered in the famous cave where the skull was found—that simple prehistoric cranium which could never have been so pathetically nonplussed by such a dilemma as this when it was a human head!

And the more he pondered the less he came to a conclusion. It seemed as though there were the "tug of war" between Martia and all that he felt to be best in himself—his own conscience, his independence as a man, his sense of honor. He took her letter out of his pocket to re-read, and with it came another letter; it was from my sister, Ida Maurice. It told him when they would arrive in Düsseldorf.

He jumped up in alarm—it was that very day. He had quite forgotten!

He ran off to the station, and missed a train, and had

298

to wait an hour for another ; but he got himself to the Rhine station in Düsseldorf a few minutes before the train from Belgium arrived.

Everything was ready for the Gibson party—lodgings and tea and supper to follow—he had seen to all that before ; so there he walked up and down, waiting, and still revolving over and over again in his mind the troublous question that so bewildered and oppressed him. Who was Martia ? what was she—that he should take her for a guide in the most momentous business of his life ; and what were her credentials ?

And what was love ? Was it love he felt for this young goddess with yellow hair and light-blue eyes so like his own, who towered in her full-blown frolicsome splendor among the sons and daughters of men, with her moist, ripe lips so richly framed for happy love and laughter—that royal milk-white fawn that had only lain in the roses and fed on the lilies of life ?

"Oh, Mr. Nobody of Nowhere ! be at least a man ; let no one ever call you the basest thing an able-bodied man can become, a fortune-hunting adventurer !"

Then a bell rang, and the smoke of the coming train was visible—ten minutes late. The tickets were taken, and it slowed into the station and stopped. Ida's head and face were seen peering through one of the second-class windows, on the lookout, and Barty opened the door and there was a warm and affectionate greeting between them ; the meeting was joy to both.

Then he was warmly greeted by Mrs. Gibson, who introduced him to her mother; then he was conscious of somebody he had not seen yet because she stood at his blind side (indeed, he had all but forgotten her existence) ; namely, the presence of a very tall and most beautiful dark-haired young lady, holding out her slen-

der gloved hand and gazing up into his face with the
most piercing and strangest and blackest eyes that ever
were ; yet so soft and quick and calm and large and kind
and wise and gentle that their piercingness was but an
added seduction ; one felt they could never pierce too
deep for the happiness of the heart they pronged and
riddled and perforated through and through !

Involuntarily came into Barty's mind, as he shook the
slender hand, a little song of Schubert's he had just
learnt :

"Du dist die Ruh', der Friede mild!"

And wasn't it odd ?—all his doubts and perplexities
resolved themselves at once, as by some enchantment,
into a lovely, unexpected chord of extreme simplicity ;
and Martia was gently but firmly put aside, and the
divine Julia quietly relegated to the gilded throne which
was her fit and proper apanage.

Barty saw to the luggage, and sent it on, and they all
went on foot behind it.

The bridge of boats across the Rhine was open in the
middle to let a wood-raft go by down stream. This raft
from some distant forest was so long they had to wait
nearly twenty minutes ; and the prow of it had all but
lost itself in the western purple and gold and dun of sky
and river while it was still passing the bridge.

All this was new and delightful to the Londoners,
who were also delighted with the rooms Barty had taken
for them in the König's Allee and the tea that awaited
them there. Leah made tea, and gave a cup to Barty.
That was a good cup of tea, better even than the tea Julia
was making (that very moment, no doubt) at Beresford
Duff's.

Then the elder ladies rested, and Barty took Leah

and Ida for a walk in the Hof gardens. They were charmed with everything — especially the fire-flies at dusk. Leah said little; she was not a very talkative person outside her immediate family circle. But Ida and Barty had much to say.

Then home to supper at the Gibsons' lodgings, and Barty sat opposite Leah, and drank in the beauty of her face, which had so wonderfully ripened and accentuated and individualized itself since he had seen her last, three years before.

As he discreetly gazed, whenever she was not looking his way, saying to himself, like Geraint: "'Here by God's rood is the one maid for me,'" he suddenly felt the north, and started with a kind of terror as he remembered Martia. He bade the company a hasty good-night, and went for a long walk by the Rhine, and had a long talk with his Egeria.

"Martia," said he, in a low but audible voice, "it's no good, I *can't;* c'est plus fort que moi. I can't sell myself to a woman for gold; besides, I can't fall in love with Julia; I don't know why, but I *can't;* I will never marry her. I don't deserve that she should care for me; perhaps she doesn't, perhaps you're quite mistaken, and if she does, it's only a young girl's fancy. What does a girl of that age really know about her own heart? and how base I should be to take advantage of her innocence and inexperience!"

And then he went on in a passionate and eager voice to explain all he had thought of during the day and still further defend his recalcitrancy.

"Give me at least your reasons, Martia; tell me, for God's sake, who you are and what! Are you *me?* are you the spirit of my mother? Why do you love me, as you say you do, with a love passing the love of woman?

301

What am I to you ? Why are you so bent on worldly things ?"

This monologue lasted more than an hour, and he threw himself on to his bed quite worn out, and slept at once, in spite of the nightingales, who filled the starlit, breezy, balmy night with their shrill, sweet clamor.

Next morning, as he expected, he found a letter :

"Barty, you are ruining me and breaking my life, and wrecking the plans of many years—plans made before you were born or thought of.

"Who am I, indeed ? Who is this demure young black-eyed witch that has come between us, this friend of Ida Maurice's ?

"She's the cause of all my misery, I feel sure ; with Ida's eyes I saw you look at her ; you never yet looked at Julia like that !—never at any woman before !

"Who is she ? No mate for a man like you, I feel sure. In the first place, she is not rich ; I could tell that by the querulous complaints of her middle-class mother. She's just fit to be some pious Quaker's wife, or a Sister of Charity, or a governess, or a hospital nurse, or a nun—no companion for a man destined to move the world !

"Barty, you don't *know* what you are ; you have never *thought;* you have never yet looked *within!*

"Barty, with Julia by your side and me at your back, you will be a leader of men, and sway the destinies of your country, and raise it above all other nations, and make it the arbiter of Europe—of the whole world—and your seed will ever be first among the foremost of the earth.

"Will you give up all this for a pair of bright black eyes and a pretty white skin ? Isn't Julia white enough for you ?

"A painter ? What a trade for a man built like you ! Take the greatest of them ; what have they ever really mattered ? What do they matter now, except to those who want to imitate them and can't, or to those who live by buying cheap the fruits of their long labors, and selling them dear as so much wall furniture for the vulgar rich ? Besides, you will never be a great painter ; you've begun too late !

"Think of yourself ten years hence—a king among men, with the world at your feet, and at those of the glorious woman who will have smoothed your path to greatness and fame and power ! Mistress and wife—goddess and queen in one !

"Think of the poor struggling painter, painting his poor little pictures in his obscure corner to feed half a dozen hungry children and the anxious, careworn wife, whose beauty has long faded away in the petty, sordid, hopeless domestic struggle, just as her husband's little talent has long been wasted and used up in wretched pot-boilers for mere bread ; think of poverty, debt, and degradation, and all the miserable ugliness of life—the truest, tritest, and oldest story in the world ! Love soon flies out of the window when these wolves snarl at the door.

"Think of all this, Barty, and think of the despair you are bringing on one lost lonely soul who loves you as a mother loves her first-born, and has founded such hopes on you ; dismiss this pretty little middle-class puritan from your thoughts and go back to Julia.

"I will not hurry your decision ; I will come back in exactly a week from to-night. I am at your mercy.

"MARTIA."

This letter made Barty very unhappy. It was a strange dilemma.

What is it that now and again makes a woman in a single moment take such a powerful grip of a man's fancy that he can never shake himself free again, and never wants to ?

Tunes can be like that, sometimes. Not the pretty little tinkling tunes that please everybody at once ; the pleasure of them can fade in a year, a month—even a week, a day ! But those from a great mint, and whose charm will last a man his lifetime !

Many years ago a great pianist, to amuse some friends (of whom I was one), played a series of waltzes by Schubert which I had never heard before—the " Soirées de Vienne," I think they were called. They were lovely from beginning to end ; but one short measure in particular was full of such extraordinary enchantment for me that it has really haunted me through life. It is as if it were made on purpose for me alone, a little intimate aside à mon intention—the gainliest, happiest thought I had ever heard expressed in music. For nobody else seemed to think those particular bars were more beautiful than all the rest ; but, oh ! the difference to me !

And said I to myself : " That's Leah ; and all the rest is some heavenly garden of roses she's walking in !"

Tempo di valsa :

> *Rum*—tiddle-iddle *um* tum tum,
> *Tid*dle-tiddle-iddle-iddle *um*-tum, tum
> *Tum* tiddle-iddle-iddle *um* tum, tum
> *Tid*dle-iddle, iddle-*hay!* . . . etc., etc.

That's how the little measure begins, and it goes on just for a couple of pages. I can't write music, unfortunately, and I've nobody by me at just this moment who can ; but if the reader is musical and knows the " Soirées de Vienne," he will guess the particular waltz I mean.

Well, the Düsseldorf railway station is not a garden of

roses ; but when Leah stepped out of that second-class carriage and looked straight at Barty, *dans le blanc des yeux*, he fitted her to the tune *he* loved best just then (not knowing the " Soirées de Vienne"), and it's one of the tunes that last forever :

" Du bist die Ruh', der Friede mild!"

Barty's senses were not as other men's senses. With his one eye he saw much that most of *us* can't see with two ; I feel sure of this. And he suddenly saw in Leah's face, now she was quite grown up, that which bound him to her for life—some veiled promise, I suppose ; we can't explain these things.

Barty escorted the Gibson party to Riffrath, and put down Mrs. Bletchley's name for Dr. Hasenclever, and then took them to the woods of Hammerfest, close by, with which they were charmed. On the way back to the hotel they met Lady Jane and Miss Royce and the good Beresford Duff, who all bowed to Barty, and Julia's blue glance crossed Leah's black one.

" Oh, what a lovely girl!" said Leah to Barty. " What a pity she's so tall ; why, I'm sure she's half a head taller than even I, and they make *my* life a burden to me at home because I'm such a giantess ! Who is she ? You know her well, I suppose ?"

" She's a Miss Julia Royce, a great heiress. Her father's dead ; he was a wealthy Norfolk Squire, and she was his only child."

" Then I suppose she's a very aristocratic person ; she looks so, I'm sure!"

" Very much so indeed," said Barty.

" Dear me ! it seems unfair, doesn't it, having everything like that ; no wonder she looks so happy!"

DR. HASENCLEVER AND MRS. BLETCHLEY

Then they went back to the hotel to lunch ; and in the afternoon Mrs. Bletchley saw the doctor, who gave her a prescription for spectacles, and said she had nothing to fear ; and was charming to Leah and to Ida, who spoke French so well, and to the pretty and lively Mrs. Gibson, who lost her heart to him and spoke the most preposterous French he had ever heard.

He was fond of pretty English women, the good German doctor, whatever French they spoke.

They were quite an hour there. Meanwhile Barty went to Beresford Duff's, and found Julia and Lady Jane drinking tea, as usual at that hour.

"Who are your uncommonly well - dressed friends, Barty ?" said Mr. Duff. "I never met any of them that *I* can remember."

"Well—they're just from London—the elder lady is a Mrs. Bletchley."

"Not one of the Berkshire Bletchleys, eh ?"

"Oh no—she's the widow of a London solicitor."

"Dear me ! And the lovely, tall, black-eyed *damigella* —who's she ?"

"She's a Miss Gibson, and her father's a furrier in Cheapside."

"And the pretty girl in blue with the fair hair ?"

"She's the sister of a very old friend of mine, Robert Maurice—he's a wine merchant."

"You don't say so ! Why, I took them for people of condition !" said Mr. Beresford Duff, who was a trifle old-fashioned in his ways of speech. "Anyhow, they're uncommonly nice to look at."

"Oh yes," said the not too priggishly grammatical Lady Jane ; "nowadays those sort of people dress like duchesses, and think themselves as good as any one."

"They're good enough for *me*, at all events," said Barty, who was not pleased.

"I'm sure Miss Gibson's good enough for *anybody in the world!*" said Julia. "She's the most beautiful girl I ever saw!" and she gave Barty a cup of tea.

Barty drank it, and felt fond of Julia, and bade them all good-bye, and went and waited in the hall of the König's Hotel for his friends, and took them back to Düsseldorf.

Next day the Gibsons started for their little trip up the Rhine, and Barty was left to his own reflections, and he reflected a great deal; not about what he meant to do himself, but about how he should tell Martia what he meant to do.

As for himself, his mind was thoroughly made up : he would break at once and forever with a world he did not properly belong to, and fight his own little battle unaided, and be a painter—a good one, if he could. If not, so much the worse for him. Life is short.

When he would have settled his affairs and paid his small debts in Düsseldorf, he would have some ten or fifteen pounds to the good. He would go back to London with the Gibsons and Ida Maurice. There were no friends for him in the world like the Maurices. There was no woman for him in the world like Leah, whether she would ever care for him or not.

Rich or poor, he didn't mind! she was Leah ; she had the hands, the feet, the lips, the hair, the eyes! That was enough for him! He was absolutely sure of his own feelings ; absolutely certain that this path was not only the pleasant path he liked, but the right one for a man in his position to follow : a thorny path indeed, but the thorns were thorns of roses!

All this time he was busily rehearsing his part in the

chorus of *Iphigenia ;* he had applied for the post of second tenor chorister ; the conditions were that he should be able to read music at sight. This he could not do, and his utter incapacity was tested at the Mahlcasten, before a crowd of artists, by the conductor. Barty failed signally, amid much laughter ; and he impudently sang quite a little tune of his own, an improvisation.

The conductor laughed too ; but Barty was admitted all the same ; his voice was good, and he must learn his part by heart—that was all ; anybody could teach him.

The Gibsons came back to Düsseldorf in time for the performance, which was admirable, in spite of Barty. From his coign of vantage, amongst the second tenors, he could see Julia's head with its golden fleece ; Julia, that rose without a thorn—

"Het Roosje uit de dorne !"

She was sitting between Lady Jane and the Captain.

He looked in vain for the Gibsons, as he sang his loudest, yet couldn't hear himself sing (he was one of a chorus of avenging furies, I believe).

But there were three vacant seats in the same row as the Royces'. Presently three ladies, silken hooded and cloaked—one in yellow, one in pink, and one in blue—made their way to the empty places, just as the chorus ceased, and sat down. Just then Orestes (Stockhausen) stood up and lifted his noble barytone.

"Die Ruhe kehret mir zurück "—

And the yellow-hooded lady unhooded a shapely little black head, and it was Leah's.

"*Prosit omen !*" thought Barty—and it seemed as if his whole heart melted within him.

He could see that Leah and Julia often looked at each

other ; he could also see, during the intervals, how many
double-barrelled opera-glasses were levelled at both ; it
was impossible to say which of these two lovely women
was the loveliest ; probably most votes would have been
for Julia, the fair-haired one, the prima donna assoluta,
the soprano, the Rowena, who always gets the biggest sal-
ary and most of the applause.

The brunette, the contralto, the Rebecca, dazzles less,
but touches the heart all the more deeply, perhaps ; anyhow, Barty had no doubt as to which of the two voices
was the voice for him. His passion was as that of Brian
de Bois-Guilbert for mere strength, except that he was
bound by no vows of celibacy. There were no moonlit
platonics about Barty's robust love, but all the chivalry
and tenderness and romance of a knight-errant underlay
its vigorous complexity. He was a good knight, though
not Sir Galahad !

Also he felt very patriotic, as a good knight should
ever feel, and proud of a country which could grow such
a rose as Julia, and such a lily as Leah Gibson.

Next to Julia sat Captain Reece, romantic and handsome as ever, with manly love and devotion expressed in
every line of his face, every movement of his body ; and
the heaviest mustache and the most beautiful brown
whiskers in the world. He was either a hussar or a
lancer ; I forget which.

"By my halidom," mentally ejaculated Barty, "I sincerely wish thee joy and life-long happiness, good Sir
Wilfred of Ivanhoe. Thou art a right fit mate for her,
peerless as she may be among women ! A benison on you
both from your poor Wamba, the son of Witless."

As he went home that night, after the concert, to his
tryst with Martia, the north came back to him—through
the open window as it were, with the fire-flies and fra-

grances, and the song of fifty nightingales. It was for him a moment of deep and harassing emotion and keen anxiety. He leaned over the window-sill and looked out on the starlit heavens, and whispered aloud the little speech he had prepared :

"Martia, I have done my best. I would make any sacrifice to obey you, but I cannot give up my freedom to love the woman that attracts me as I have never been attracted before. I would sooner live a poor and unsuccessful struggler in the art I have chosen, with her to help me live, than be the mightiest man in England without her—even with Julia, whom I admire as much, and even more !

"One can't help these things. They may be fancies, and one may live to repent them ; but while they last they are imperious, not to be resisted. It's an instinct, I suppose ; perhaps even a form of insanity ! But I love Leah's little-finger nail better than Julia's lovely face and splendid body and all her thousands.

"Besides, I will not drag Julia down from her high position in the world's eye, even for a day, nor owe anything to either man or woman except love and fidelity ! It grieves me deeply to disappoint you, though I cannot understand your motives. If you love me as you say you do, you ought to think of my happiness and honor before my worldly success and prosperity, about which I don't care a button, except for Leah's sake.

"Besides, I know myself better than you know me. I'm not one of those hard, strong, stern, purposeful, Napoleonic men, with wills of iron, that clever, ambitious women conceive great passions for !

"I'm only a 'funny man'—a *gringalet-jocrisse !* And now that I'm quite grown up, and all my little funniments are over, I'm only fit to sit and paint, with my one

"'MARTIA, I HAVE DONE MY BEST'"

eye, in my little corner, with a contented little wife, who won't want me to do great things and astonish the world. There's no place like home ; faire la popotte ensemble au coin du feu—c'est le ciel !

" And if I'm half as clever as you say, it 'll all come out in my painting, and I shall be rich and famous, and all off my own bat. I'd sooner be Sir Edwin Landseer than Sir Robert Peel, or Pam, or Dizzy !

" Even to retain your love and protection and interest in me, which I value almost as much as I value life itself, I can't do as you wish. Don't desert me, Martia. I may be able to make it all up to you some day ; after all, you can't foresee and command the future, nor can I. It wouldn't be worth living for if we could ! It would all be discounted in advance !

" I may yet succeed in leading a useful, happy life ; and that should be enough for you if it's enough for me, since I am your beloved, and as you love me as your son. . . . Anyhow, my mind is made up for good and all, and . . ."

Here the sensation of the north suddenly left him, and he went to his bed with the sense of bereavement that had punished him all the preceding week : desperately sad, all but heart-broken, and feeling almost like a culprit, although his conscience, whatever that was worth, was thoroughly at ease, and his intent inflexible.

A day or two after this he must have received a note from Julia, making an appointment to meet him at the Ausstellung, in the Allee Strasse, a pretty little picture-gallery, since he was seen there sitting in deep conversation with Miss Royce in a corner, and both seeming much moved ; neither the Admiral nor Lady Jane was with them, and there was some gossip about it in the British colony both in Düsseldorf and Riffrath.

Barty, who of late years has talked to me so much, and with such affectionate admiration, of "Julia Countess," as he called her, never happened to have mentioned this interview; he was very reticent about his love-makings, especially about any love that was made to him.

I made so bold as to write to Julia, Lady Ironsides, and ask her if it were true they had met like this, and if I might print her answer, and received almost by return of post the following kind and characteristic letter:

"96 GROSVENOR SQUARE.

"DEAR SIR ROBERT,—You're quite right; I did meet him, and I've no objection whatever to telling you how it all happened—and you may do as you like.

"It happened just like this (you must remember that I was only just out, and had always had my own way in everything).

"Mamma and I and Uncle James (the Admiral) and Freddy Reece (Ironsides, you know) went to the Musikfest in Düsseldorf. Barty was singing in the chorus. I saw him opening and shutting his mouth and could almost fancy I heard him, poor dear boy.

"Leah Gibson, as she was then, sat near to me, with her mother and your sister. Leah Gibson looked like—well, *you* know what she looked like in those days. By-the-way, I can't make out how it is you weren't over head and ears in love with her yourself! I thought her the loveliest girl I had ever seen, and felt very unhappy.

"We slept at the hotel that night, and on the way back to Riffrath next morning Freddy Reece proposed to me.

"I told him I couldn't marry him—but that I loved him as a sister, and all that; I really was very fond of him indeed, but I didn't want to marry him; I wanted

314

to marry Barty, in fact ; and make him rich and famous, as I felt sure he would be some day, whether I married him or not.

"But there was that lovely Leah Gibson, the furrier's daughter !

"When we got home to Riffrath mamma found she'd got a cold, and had a fancy for a French thing called a 'loch '; I think her cold was suddenly brought on by my refusing poor Freddy's offer !

"I went with Grissel, the maid (who knew about *lochs*), to the Riffrath chemist's, but he didn't even know what we meant—so I told mamma I would go and get a *loch* in Düsseldorf next day if she liked, with Uncle James. Mamma was only too delighted, for next day was Mr. Josselin's day for coming to Riffrath ; but he didn't, for I wrote to him to meet me at twelve at a little picture-gallery I knew of in the Allee Strasse—as I wanted to have a talk with him.

"Uncle James had caught a cold too, so I went with Grissel ; and found a chemist who'd been in France, and knew what a loch was and made one for me ; and then I went to the gallery, and there was poor Barty sitting on a crimson velvet couch, under a picture of Milton dictating *Paradise Lost* to his daughters (I bought it afterwards, and I've got it now).

"We said how d'ye do, and sat on the couch together, and I felt dreadfully nervous and ashamed.

"Then I said :

"'You must think me very odd, Mr. Josselin, to ask you to meet me like this !'

"'I think it's a very great honor !' he said ; 'I only wish I deserved it.'

"And then he said nothing for quite five minutes, and I think he felt as uncomfortable as I did.

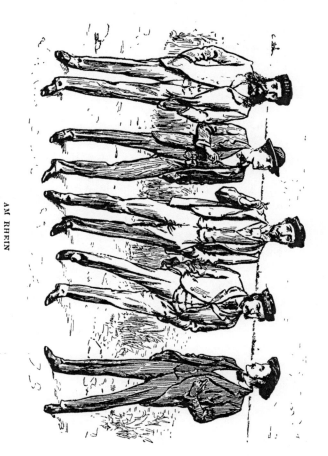

AM RHEIN
"LED WE NOT THERE A JOLLY LIFE
BETWIXT THE SUN AND SHADE?"

" ' Captain Graham-Reece has asked me to be his wife, and I refused,' I said.

" ' Why did you refuse ?   He's one of the best fellows I've ever met,' said Barty.

" ' He's to be so rich, and so am I,' I said.

" No answer.

" ' It would be right for me to marry a *poor* man—man with brains and no money, you know, and help him to make his way.'

" ' Reece has plenty of brains too,' said Barty.

" ' Oh, Mr. Josselin—don't misunderstand me '—and then I began to stammer and look foolish.

" ' Miss Royce—I've only got £15 in the world, and with that I mean to go to London and be an artist ; and comfort myself during the struggle by the delightful remembrance of Riffrath and Reece and yourself—and the happy hope of meeting you both again some day, when I shall no longer be the poor devil I am now, and am quite content to be ! And when you and he are among the great of the earth, if you will give me each a commission to paint your portraits I will do my very best !' (and he smiled his irresistible smile). ' You will be kind, I am sure, to Mr. Nobody of Nowhere, the famous portrait-painter—who doesn't even bear his father's name—as he has no right to it.'

" I could have flung my arms round his neck and kissed him ! What did *I* care about his father's name ?

" ' Will you think me dreadfully bold and indiscreet, Mr. Josselin, if I—if I—' (I stammered fearfully.)

" ' If you *what*, Miss Royce ?'

" ' If I—if I ask you if you—if you—think Miss Gibson the most beautiful girl you ever saw ?'

" ' Honestly, I think *you* the most beautiful girl I ever saw !'

317

" ' Oh, that's *nonsense,* Mr. Josselin, although I ought to have known you would say that ! I'm not fit to tie her shoes. What I mean is—a—a—oh ! forgive me—are you very *fond* of her, as I'm sure she deserves, you know ?'

" ' Oh yes, Miss Royce, very fond of her indeed ; she's poor, she's of no family, she's Miss Nobody of Nowhere, you know ; she's all that I am, except that she has a right to her honest father's name—'

" ' Does she *know* you're very fond of her ?'

" ' No ; but I hope to tell her so some day.'

" Then we were silent, and I felt very red, and very much inclined to cry, but I managed to keep in my tears.

" Then I got up, and so did he—and he made some joke about Grissel and the loch-bottle ; and we both laughed quite naturally and looked at the pictures, and he told me he was going back to London with the Gibsons that very week, and thanked me warmly for my kind interest in him, and assured me he thoroughly deserved it—and talked so funnily and so nicely that I quite forgave myself. I really don't think he guessed for one moment what I had been driving at all the while ; I got back all my self-respect ; I felt so grateful to him that I was fonder of him than ever, though no longer so idiotically in love. He was not for me. He had somehow laughed me into love with him, and laughed me out of it.

" Then I bade him good-bye, and squeezed his hand with all my heart, and told him how much I should like some day to meet Miss Gibson and be her friend if she would let me.

" Then I went back to Riffrath and took mamma her loch ; but she no longer wanted it, for I told her I had changed my mind about Freddy, and that cured her like magic ; and she kissed me on both cheeks and called me her dear, darling, divine Julia.   Poor, sweet mamma !

"I had given her many a bad quarter of an hour, but this good moment made up for them all.

"She was eighty-two last birthday, and can still read Josselin's works in the cheap edition without spectacles —thanks, no doubt, to the famous Doctor Hasenclever ! She reads nothing else !

"Et voilà comment ça s'est passé.

"It's I that 'll be the proud woman when I read this letter, printed, in your life of Josselin.

"Yours sincerely,

"JULIA IRONSIDES.

"P. S.—I've actually just told mamma—and I'm still her dear, darling, divine Julia !"

Charming as were Barty's remembrances of Düsseldorf, the most charming of all was his remembrance of going aboard the little steamboat bound for Rotterdam, one night at the end of May, with old Mrs. Bletchley, Mrs. Gibson and her daughter, and my sister Ida.

The little boat was crowded ; the ladies found what accommodation they could in what served for a ladies' cabin, and expostulated and bribed their best ; fortunately for them, no doubt, there were no English on board to bribe against them.

Barty spent the night on deck, supine, with a carpet-bag for a pillow ; we will take the full moon for granted. From Düsseldorf to Rotterdam there is little to see on either side of a Rhine steamboat, except the Rhine— especially at night.

Next day, after breakfast, he made the ladies as comfortable as he could on the after-deck, and read to them

"'DOES SHE *KNOW* YOU'RE VERY FOND OF HER?'"

from *Maud*, from the *Idylls of the King*, from the *Mill on the Floss*. Then windmills came into sight—Dutch windmills ; then Rotterdam, almost too soon. They went to the big hotel on the Boompjes and fed, and then explored Rotterdam, and found it a most delightful city.

Next day they got on board the steamboat bound for St. Katharine's wharf ; the wind had freshened and they soon separated, and met at breakfast next morning in the Thames.

Barty declared he smelt Great Britain as distinctly as one can smell a Scotch haggis, or a Welsh rabbit, or an Irish stew, and the old familiar smell made him glad. However little you may be English, if you are English at all you are more English than anything else, *et plus royaliste que le Roi !*

According to Heine, an Englishman loves liberty as a good husband loves his wife ; that is also how he loves the land of his birth ; at all events, England has a kind of wifely embrace for the home-coming Briton, especially if he comes home by the Thames.

It is not unexpected, nor madly exciting, perhaps ; but it is singularly warm and sweet if the conjugal relations have not been strained in the meanwhile. And as the Thames narrows itself, the closer, the more genial, the more grateful and comforting this long-anticipated and tenderly intimate uxorious dalliance seems to grow.

Barty felt very happy as he stood leaning over the bulwarks in the sunshine, between Ida and Leah, and looked at Rotherhithe, and promised himself he would paint it some day, and even sell the picture !

Then he made himself so pleasant to the custom-house officers that they all but forgot to examine the Gibson luggage.

321

Was I delighted to grasp his hand at St. Katharine's wharf, after so many months ?   Ah ! . . .

Mr. Gibson was there, funny as ever, and the Gibsons went home with him to Conduit Street in a hired fly. Alas ! poor Mrs. Gibson's home-coming was the saddest part for her of the delightful little journey.

And Barty and Ida and I went our own way in a four-wheeler to eat the fatted calf in Brunswick Square, washed down with I will not say what vintage.   There were so many available from all the wine-growing lands of Europe that I've forgotten which was chosen to celebrate the wanderers' return !

Let us say Romané-Conti, which is the " cru " that Barty loved best.

Next morning Barty left us early, with a portfolio of sketches under his arm, and his heart full of sanguine expectation, and spent the day in Fleet Street, or thereabouts, calling on publishers of illustrated books and periodicals, and came back to us at dinner-time very fagged, and with a long and piteous but very droll story of his ignominious non-success : his weary waitings in dull, dingy, little business back rooms, the patronizing and snubbing he and his works had met with, the sense that he had everything to learn—he, who thought he was going to take the publishing world by storm.

Next day it was just the same, and the day after, and the day after that—every day of the week he spent under our roof.

Then he insisted on leaving us, and took for himself a room in Newman Street—a studio by day, a bedroom by night, a pleasant smoking-room at all hours, and very soon a place of rendezvous for all sorts and conditions of jolly fellows, old friends and new, from

Guardsmen to young stars of the art world, mostly idle apprentices.

Gradually boxing-gloves crept in, and foils and masks, and the faithful Snowdrop (whose condition three or four attacks of delirium tremens during Barty's exile had not improved).

And fellows who sang, and told good stories, and imitated popular actors—all as it used to be in the good old days of St. James's Street.

But Barty was changed all the same. These amusements were no longer the serious business of life for him. In the midst of all the racket he would sit at his small easel and work. He declared he couldn't find inspiration in silence and solitude, and, bereft of Martia, he could not bear to be alone.

Then he looked up other old friends, and left cards and got invitations to dinners and drums. One of his first visits was to his old tailor in Jermyn Street, to whom he still owed money, and who welcomed him with open arms—almost hugged him—and made him two or three beautiful suits; I believe he would have dressed Barty for nothing, as a mere advertisement. At all events, he wouldn't hear of payment "for many years to come! The finest figure in the whole Household Brigade!—the idea!"

Soon Barty got a few sketches into obscure illustrated papers, and thought his fortune was made. The first was a little sketch in the manner of John Leech, which he took to the *British Lion,* just started as a rival to *Punch.* The *British Lion* died before the sketch appeared, but he got a guinea for it, and bought a beautiful volume of Tennyson, illustrated by Millais, Holman Hunt, Rossetti, and others, and made a sketch on the flyleaf of a lovely female with black hair and black eyes, and gave it to Leah Gibson. It was his old female face of ten years ago ; yet, strange to say, the very image of Leah herself (as it had once been that of his mother).

The great happiness of his life just then was to go to the opera with Mrs. Gibson and Leah and Mr. Babbage (the family friend), who could get a box whenever he liked, and then to sup with them afterwards in Conduit Street, over the Emporium of the " Universal Fur Company," and to imitate Signor Giuglini for the delectation of Mr. Gibson, whose fondness for Barty soon grew into absolute worship !

And Leah, so reserved and self-contained in general company, would laugh till the tears ran down her cheeks ; and the music of her laughter, which was deep and low, rang more agreeably to Barty's ear than even the ravishing strains of Adelina Patti—the last of the great prime donne of our time, I think — whose voice still stirs me to the depths, with vague remembrance of fresh girlish innocence turned into sound.

Long life to her and to her voice ! Lovely voices should never fade, nor pretty faces either !

Sometimes I replaced Mr. Babbage and escorted Mrs. Gibson to the opera, leaving Leah to Barty ; for on fine nights we walked there, and the ladies took off their bonnets and shawls in the box, which was generally on the upper tier, and we looked down on Scatcherd and my mother and sister in the stalls. Then back to Conduit Street to supper. It was easy with half an eye to see the way things were going. I can't say I liked it. No man would, I suppose. But I reconciled myself to the inevitable, and bore up like a stoic.

L'amitié est l'amour sans ailes ! A happy intimate friendship, a wingless love that has lasted more than thirty years without a break, is no bad substitute for

tumultuous passions that have missed their mark! I
have been as close a friend to Barty's wife as to Barty
himself, and all the happiness I have ever known has
come from them and theirs.

Walking home, poor Mrs. Gibson would confide to me
her woes and anxieties, and wail over the past glories of
Tavistock Square and all the nice people who lived
there, and in Russell Square and Bedford Street and
Gower Street, many of whom had given up calling on
her now that she lived over a shop. Not all the liveliness of Bond Street and Regent Street combined (which
Conduit Street so broadly and genially connected with
each other) could compensate her for the lost gentility,
the aristocratic dulness and quiet and repose, "almost
equal to that of a West End square."

Then she believed that business was not going on well,
since Mr. Gibson talked of giving up his Cheapside
establishment; he said it was too much for him to look
after. But he had lost much of his fun, and seemed
harassed and thin, and muttered in his sleep; and the
poor woman was full of forebodings, some of which were
to be justified by the events that followed.

About this time Leah, who had forebodings too, took
it into her head to attend a class for book-keeping, and
in a short time thoroughly mastered the science in all
its details. I'm afraid she was better at this kind of
work than at either drawing or music, both of which she
had been so perseveringly taught. She could read off
any music at sight quite glibly and easily, it is true—
the result of hard plodding—but could never play to
give real pleasure, and she gave it up. And with singing it was the same; her voice was excellent and had
been well trained, but when she heard the untaught
Barty she felt she was no singer, and never would be,

and left off trying. Yet nobody got more pleasure out
of the singing of others—especially Barty's and that of
young Mr. Santley, who was her pet and darling, and
whom she far preferred to that sweetest and suavest of
tenors, Giuglini, about whom we all went mad. I agreed
with her. Giuglini's voice was like green chartreuse in
a liqueur-glass ; Santley's like a bumper of the very best
burgundy that ever was ! Oh that high G ! Romané-
Conti, again ; and in a quart-pot ! En veux-tu ? en
voilà !

And as for her drawing, it was as that of all intelligent young ladies who have been well taught, but have
no original talent whatever ; nor did she derive any
special pleasure from the masterpieces in the National
Gallery ; the Royal Academy was far more to her taste ;
and to mine, I frankly admit ; and, I fear, to Barty's
taste also, in those days. Enough of the Guardsman
still remained in him to quite unfit his brain and ear
and eye for what was best in literature and art. He was
mildly fond of the "Bacchus and Ariadne," and Rembrandt's portrait of himself, and a few others; as he was
of the works of Shakespeare and Milton. But Mantegna
and Botticelli and Signorelli made him sad, and almost
morose.

The only great things he genuinely loved and revered
were the Elgin Marbles. He was constantly sketching
them. And I am told that they have had great influence
on his work and that he owes much to them. I have
grown to admire them immensely myself in consequence,
though I used to find that part of the British Museum a
rather dreary lounge in the days when Barty used to
draw there.

I am the proud possessor of a Velasquez, two Titians,
and a Rembrandt ; but, as a rule, I like to encourage

the art of my own time and country and that of modern France.

And I suppose there's hardly a great painter living, or recently dead, some of whose work is not represented on my walls, either in London, Paris, or Scotland ; or at Marsfield, where so much of my time is spent; although the house is not mine, it's my real home ; and thither I have always been allowed to send my best pictures, and my best bric-à-brac, my favorite horses and dogs, and the oldest and choicest liquors that were ever stored in the cellars of Vougeot-Conti & Co. Old bachelor friends have their privileges, and Uncle Bob has known how to make himself at home in Marsfield.

Barty soon got better off, and moved into better lodgings in Berners Street ; a sitting-room and bedroom at No. 12B, which has now disappeared.

And there he worked all day, without haste and without rest, and at last in solitude ; and found he could work twice as well with no companion but his pipe and his lay figure, from which he made most elaborate studies of drapery, in pen and ink; first in the manner of Sandys and Albert Dürer ! later in the manner of Millais, Walker, and Keene.

Also he acquired the art of using the living model for his little illustrations. It had become the fashion ; a new school had been founded with *Once a Week* and the *Cornhill Magazine*, it seems ; besides those already named, there were Lawless, du Maurier, Poynter, not to mention Holman Hunt and F. Leighton ; and a host of new draughtsmen, most industrious apprentices, whose talk and example soon weaned Barty from a mixed and somewhat rowdy crew.

And all became more or less friends of his ; a very good thing, for they were admirable in industry and

327

talent, thorough artists and very good fellows all round.
Need I say they have all risen to fame and fortune—as
becomes poetical justice ?

He also kept in touch with his old brother officers,
and that was a good thing too.

But there were others he got to know, rickety, un-
wholesome geniuses, whose genius (such as it was) had
allied itself to madness ; and who were just as conceited
about the madness as about the genius, and took more
pains to cultivate it. It brought them a quicker kudos,
and was so much more visible to the naked eye.

At first Barty was fascinated by the madness, and
took the genius on trust, I suppose. They made much
of him, painted him, wrote music and verses about him,
raved about his Greekness, his beauty, his yellow hair,
and his voice and what not, as if he had been a woman.
He even stood that, he admired them so! or rather, this
genius of theirs.

He introduced me to this little clique, who called
themselves a school, and each other " master ": " the
neo-priapists," or something of that sort, and they worshipped the tuberose.

They disliked me at sight, and I them, and we did not
dissemble !

Like Barty, I am fond of men's society ; but at least I
like them to be unmistakably men of my own sex, manly
men, and clean ; not little misshapen troglodytes with
foul minds and perverted passions, or self-advertising
little mountebanks with enlarged and diseased vanities ;
creatures who would stand in a pillory sooner than not be
stared at or talked about at all.

Whatever their genius might be, it almost made me
sick—it almost made me kick, to see the humorous and
masculine Barty prostrate in admiration before these

inspired epicenes, these gifted epileptoids, these anæmic little self-satisfied nincompoops, whose proper place, it seemed to me, was either Earlswood, or Colney Hatch, or Broadmoor. That is, if their madness was genuine, which I doubt. He and I had many a quarrel about them, till he found them out and cut them for good and all—a great relief to me; for one got a bad name by being friends with such nondescripts.

" Dis-moi qui tu hantes, je te dirai ce que tu es !"

Need I say they all died long ago, without leaving the ghost of a name?—and nobody cared. Poetical justice again! How encouraging it is to think there are no such people now, and that the breed has been thoroughly stamped out !*

Barty never succeeded as an illustrator on wood. He got into a way of doing very slight sketches of pretty people in fancy dress and coloring them lightly, and sold them at a shop in the Strand, now no more. Then he made up little stories, which he illustrated himself, something like the picture-books of the later Caldecott, and I found him a publisher, and he was soon able to put aside a few pounds and pay his debts.

* Editor.

Part Eighth

"And now I see with eyes serene
The very pulse of the machine;
A being breathing thoughtful breath,
A traveller betwixt life and death;
The reason firm, the temperate will,
Endurance, foresight, strength, and skill;
A perfect woman, nobly planned
To warn and comfort and command;
And yet a spirit too and bright
With something of an angel-light."
—WORDSWORTH.

WHEN Barty had been six months in England, poor Mr. Gibson's affairs went suddenly smash. My father saved him from absolute bankruptcy, and there was lamentation and wailing for a month or so in Conduit Street; but things were so managed that Mr. Gibson was able to keep on the "West End firm," and make with it a new start.

He had long been complaining of his cashier, and had to dismiss him and look out for another; but here his daughter came in and insisted on being cashier herself— (to her mother's horror).

So she took her place at a railed-in desk at the back of the shop, and was not only cashier and bookkeeper, but overseer of all things in general, and was not above seeing any exacting and importunate customer whom the shopmen couldn't manage.

She actually liked her work, and declared she had

found her real vocation, and quite ceased to regret Tavistock Square.

Her authority in the emporium was even greater than her father's, who was too fond of being funny. She awed the shopmen into a kind of affectionate servility, and they were prostrate as before a goddess, in spite of her never-failing politeness to them.

Customers soon got into a way of asking to see Miss Gibson, especially when they were accompanied by husbands or brothers or male friends; and Miss Gibson soon found she sold better than any shopman, and became one of the notables in the quarter.

All Mr. Gibson's fun came back, and he was as proud of his daughter as if she'd been proposed to by an earl. But Mrs. Gibson couldn't help shedding tears over Leah's loss of caste—Leah, on whose beauty and good breeding she had founded such hopes; it is but fair to add that she was most anxious to keep the books herself, so that her daughter might be spared this degradation; for no "gentleman," she felt sure, would ever propose to her daughter now.

But she was mistaken.

One night Barty and I dined at a little cagmag he used to frequent, where he fared well—so he said—for a shilling, which included a glass of stout. It was a disgusting little place, but he liked it, and therefore so did I.

Then we called for Mrs. Gibson and Leah, and took them to the Princess's to see Fechter in Ruy Blas, and escorted them home, and had supper with them, a very good supper—nothing ever interfered with the luxuriously hospitable instincts of the Gibsons—and a very merry one. Barty imitated Fechter to the life.

"I 'av ze garrb of a *lacquais*—you 'av ze sôle of *wawn!*"

331

This he said to Mr. Gibson, who was in fits of delight. Mr. Gibson had just come home from his club, and the cards had been propitious ; Leah was more reserved than usual, and didn't laugh at Barty, for a wonder, but gazed at him with love in her eyes.

When we left them, Barty took my arm and walked home with me, down Oxford Street and up Southampton Row, and talked of Ruy Blas and Fechter, whom he had often seen in Paris.

Just where a little footway leads from the Row to Queen Square and Great Ormond Street, he stopped and said :

" Bob, do you remember how we tossed up for Leah Gibson at this very spot ?"

" I should think I did," said I.

" Well, you had a fair field and no favor, old boy, didn't you ?"

" Oh yes, I've long resigned any pretensions, as I wrote you more than a year ago; you may go in and win—si le cœur t'en dit !"

" Well, then, your congratulations, please. I asked her to marry me as we crossed Regent Circus, Oxford Street, on the way home ; a hansom came by and scattered and splashed us. Then we came together again, and just opposite Peter Robinson's, she asked me if my mind was quite made up—if I was sure I wouldn't ever change. I swore by the eternal gods, and she said she would be my wife; so there we are, an engaged couple."

I must ask the reader to believe that I was equal to the occasion, and said what I ought to have said.

. . . .

Mrs. Gibson was happy at last; she was satisfied that Barty was a "gentleman," in spite of the kink in his birth; and as for his prospects, money was a thing that

332

never entered Mrs. Gibson's head, and she loved Barty as a son — was a little bit in love with him herself, I believe ; she was not yet forty, and as pretty as she could be.

Besides, a week after, who should call upon her over the shop—there was a private entrance of course—but the Right Honorable Lady Caroline Grey and her niece, Miss Daphne Rohan, granddaughter of the late and niece of the present Marquis of Whitby !

And Mrs. Gibson felt as much at home with them in five minutes as if she'd known them all her life.

Leah was summoned from below, and kissed and congratulated by the two aristocratic relatives of Barty's, and relieved of her shyness in a very short time indeed.

As a matter of fact, Lady Caroline, who knew her nephew well, and thoroughly understood his position, was really well pleased ; she had never forgotten her impression of Leah when she met her in the park with Ida and me a year back, and we all walked by the Serpentine together—a certain kind of beauty seems to break down all barriers of rank ; and she knew Leah's character both from Barty and me, and from her own native shrewdness of observation. She had been delighted to hear from Barty of Leah's resolute participation in her father's troubles, and in his attempt—so successful through her—to rehabilitate his business. To her old-fashioned aristocratic way of looking at things, there was little to choose between a respectable West End shopkeeper and a medical practitioner or dentist or solicitor or architect—or even an artist, like Barty himself. Once outside the Church, the Army and Navy, or a Government office, what on earth did it matter *who* or *what* one was, or wasn't ? The only thing she couldn't stand was that

"LEAH WAS SUMMONED FROM BELOW"

horrid form of bourgeois gentility, the pretension to seem something better than you really are. Mrs. Gibson was so naïvely honest in her little laments over her lost grandeur that she could hardly be called vulgar about it.

Mr. Gibson didn't appear; he was overawed, and distrusted himself. I doubt if Lady Caroline would have liked anything in the shape of jocose familiarity; and I fear her naturalness and simplicity and cordiality of manner, and the extreme plainness of her attire, might have put him at his ease almost a trifle too much.

Whether her ladyship would have been so sympathetic about this engagement if Barty had been a legitimate Rohan—say a son of her own—is perhaps to be doubted; but anyhow she had quite made up her mind that Leah was a quite exceptional person, both in mind and manners. She has often said as much to me, and has always had as high a regard for Barty's wife as for any woman she knows, and has still—the Rohans are a long-lived family. She has often told me she never knew a better, sincerer, nobler, or more sensible woman than Barty's wife.

Besides which, as I have been told, the ancient Yorkshire house of Rohan has always been singularly free from aristocratic hauteur; perhaps their religion may have accounted for this, and also their poverty.

This memorable visit, it must be remembered, happened nearly forty years ago, when social demarcations in England were far more rigidly defined than at present; then, the wife of a costermonger with a donkey did not visit the wife of a costermonger who had to wheel his barrow himself.

We are more sensible in these days, as all who like Mr. Chevalier's admirable coster-songs are aware. Old Europe itself has become less tolerant of distinctions of rank:

even Austria is becoming so. It is only in southeastern
Bulgaria—and even of this I am not absolutely sure—that
the navvy who happens to be of noble birth refuses to
work in the same gang with the navvy who isn't; and
that's what I call real "esprit de corps," without which
no aristocracy can ever hope to hold its own in these degenerate days.

Noblesse oblige !

Why, I've got a Lord Arthur in my New York agency,
and two Hon'bles in Barge Yard, and another at Cape
Town; and devilish good men of business they are, besides being good fellows all round. They hope to become
partners some day; and, by Jove ! they shall. Now I've
said it, I'll stick to it.

The fact is, I'm rather fond of noble lords : why
shouldn't I be ? I might have been one myself any day
these last ten years; I might now, if I chose; but there !
Charles Lamb knew a man who wanted to be a tailor
once, but hadn't got the spirit. I find I haven't got the
spirit to be a noble lord. Even Barty might have been a
lord—he, a mere man of letters !—but he refused every
honor and distinction that was ever offered to him,
either here or abroad — even the Prussian order of
Merit !

Alfred Tennyson was a lord, so what is there to make
such a fuss about. Give me lords who can't help themselves, because they were born so, and the stupider the
better ; and the older—for the older they are the grander
their manners and the manners of their womankind.

Take, for instance, that splendid old dow, Penelope,
Duchess of Rumtifoozleland—I always give nicknames to
my grand acquaintances; not that she's particularly old
herself, but she belongs to an antiquated order of things
that is passing away—for she was a Fitztartan, a daughter

of the ducal house of Comtesbois (pronounced County Boyce); and she's very handsome still.

Have you ever been presented to her Grace, O reader?

If so, you must have been struck by the grace of her Grace's manner, as with a ducal gesture and a few courtly words she recognizes the value of whatever immense achievements yours must have been to have procured you such an honor as such an introduction, and expresses her surprise and. regret that she has not known you before. The formula is always the same, on every possible occasion. I ought to know, for I've had the honor of being presented to her Grace seven times this year.

Now this lofty forgetting of your poor existence—or mine—is not aristocratic hauteur or patrician insolence; it is *bêtise pure et simple,* as they call it in France. She was a daughter of the house of Comtesbois, and the Fitztartans were not the inventors of gunpowder, nor was she.

But for a stately, magnificent Grande Dame of the ancient régime, to meet for the seventh time, and be presented to—for the seventh time—with all due ceremony in the midst of a distinguished conservative crowd—say at a ball at Buckingham Palace—give me Penelope, Dowager Duchess of Rumtifoozleland!

(This seems a somewhat uncalled-for digression. But, anyhow, it shows that when it pleases me to do so I move in the very best society—just like Barty Josselin.)

.   .   .   .

So here was Mr. Nobody of Nowhere taking unto himself a wife from among the daughters of Heth; from the class he had always disliked, the buyers cheap and the sellers dear—whose sole aim in life is the making of money, and who are proud when they succeed and ashamed when they fail—and getting actually fond of his future father and mother in law, as I was!

337

When I laughed to him about old Gibson—John Gilpin, as we used to call him—being a tradesman, he said :

"Yes ; but what an *unsuccessful* tradesman, my dear fellow !" as if that in itself atoned or made amends for everything.

"Besides, he's Leah's father ! And as for Mrs. Gilpin, she's a *dear*, although she's always on pleasure bent ; at all events, she's not of a frugal mind ; and she's so pretty and dresses so well—and what a foot !—and she's got such easy manners, too ; she reminds me of dear Lady Archibald ! that's a mother-in-law I shall get on with. . . . I wish she didn't make such a fuss about living over the shop ; I call that being above one's business in every way."

"Je suis au - dessus de mes affaires," as old Bonzig proudly said when he took a garret over the Mont de Piété, in the Rue des Averses.

.   .   .   .

Barty's courtship didn't last long—only five or six months—during which he made lots of money by sketching little full-length portraits of people in outline and filling up with tints in water-color. He thus immortalized my father and mother, and Ida Scatcherd and her husband, and the old Scatcherds, and lots of other people. It was not high art, I suppose ; he was not a high artist ; but it paid well, and made him more tolerant of trade than ever.

He took the upper part of a house in Southampton Row, and furnished it almost entirely with weddinggifts ; among other things, a beautiful semi-grand piano by Érard—the gift of my father. Everything was charming there and in the best taste.

Leah was better at furnishing a house than at drawing and music-making ; it was an occupation she revelled in.

22

It is not perhaps for me to say that their cellar might hold its own with that of any beginners in their rank of life !

Well, and so they were married at Marylebone Church, and I was Barty's best man (he was to have been mine, and for that very bride). Nobody else was there but the family, and Ida, whose husband was abroad ; the sun shone, though it was not yet May — and then we breakfasted ; and John Gilpin made a very funny speech, though with tears in his voice ; and as for poor Maman-belle-mère, as Barty called her, she was a very Niobe.

They went for a fortnight to Boulogne. I wished them joy from the bottom of my heart, and flung a charming little white satin slipper of Mrs. Gibson's ; it alighted on the carriage—*our* carriage, by-the-way ; we had just started one, and now lived at Lancaster Gate.

It was a sharp pang—almost unbearable, but, also, almost the last. The last was when she came back and I saw how radiant she looked. And as for Barty, he was like

> " the herald Mercury,
> New lighted on a heaven-kissing hill !"

and he had shaved off his beard and mustache to please his wife.

．　　　．　　　．　　　．　　　．　　　．　　　．

" From George du Maurier, Esqre., A.R.W.S., Hampstead Heath, to the Right Honble. Sir Robert Maurice, Bart., M.P.:

" MY DEAR MAURICE,—In answer to your kind letter, I shall be proud and happy to illustrate your biography of Barty Josselin ; but as for editing it, *vous plaisantez, mon ami ; un amateur comme moi !* who'll edit the editor ?　*Quis custodiet ?* . . .

" You're mistaken about Malines. I only got back there a week or two before he left it. I remember often seeing him there, arm in arm with his aunt, Lady Caroline Grey, and being told that he was a *monsieur anglais, qui avait mal aux yeux* (like me) ; but in Düsseldorf, during the following winter, I knew him very well indeed.

" We, and the others you tell me you mention, had a capital time in Düsseldorf. I remember the beautiful Miss Royce they were all so mad about, and also Miss Gibson, whom I admired much the most of the two, although she wasn't quite so tall—you know my craze for lovely giantesses.

" Josselin and I came to London at about the same time, and there again I saw much of him, and was immensely attracted by him, of course—as we all were, in the very pleasant little artistic clique you tell me you describe ; but somehow I was never very intimate with him — none of us were, except, perhaps, Charles Keene.

" He went a great deal into smart society, and a little of the guardsman still clung to him, and this was an unpardonable crime in those Bohemian days.

" He was once seen walking between two well-known earls, in the Burlington Arcade, arm in arm !

" Z—— (to whom a noble lord was as a red rag to a bull) all but cut him for this, and we none of us approved of his swell friends, Guardsmen and others. How we've all changed, especially Z——, who hasn't missed a levée for twenty years, nor his wife a drawing-room !

" Josselin and I acted in a little French musical farce together at Cornelys's ; he had a charming voice and sang beautifully, as you know.

"Then he married, and a year after I did the same ; and though we lived near each other for a little while, we didn't meet very often, beyond dining together once or twice at each other's houses. They lived very much in the world.

" It will be very difficult to draw his wife. I really think Mrs. Josselin was the most beautiful woman I ever saw ; but she used to be very reserved in those early days, and I never felt quite at my ease with her. I'm sure she was sweetness and kindness itself; she was certainly charming at her own dinner-table, where she was less shy.

" Millais's portrait of her is very good, and so is Watts's ; but the best idea of her is to be got from Josselin's little outlines in ' The

Discreet Princess,' and these are out of print. If you have any, please lend them to me, and I will faithfully return them. I have more than once tried to draw her in *Punch*, from memory, but never with success.

" I used to call her ' *La belle dame sans merci.*'

" I've often, however, drawn Josselin, as you must remember, and people have recognized him at once. Thanks for all his old sketches of school, etc., which will be very useful.

" I wish I had known the Josselins better. But when one lives in Hampstead one has to forego many delightful friendships ; and then he grew to be such a tremendous swell! Good heavens !— *Sardonyx*, etc. I never could muster courage even to write and congratulate him.

" It never occurred to any of us, either in Düsseldorf or London, to think him what is called *clever;* he never said anything very witty or profound. But he was always funny in a good-natured, jovial manner, and made me laugh more than any one else.

" As for satire, good heavens ! that seemed not in him. He was always well dressed, always in high spirits and a good temper, and very demonstrative and caressing ; putting his arm round one, and slapping one on the back or lifting one up in the air; a kind of jolly, noisy, boisterous boon - companion — rather uproarious, in fact, and with no disdain for a good bottle of wine or a good bottle of beer. His artistic tastes were very catholic, for he was prostrate in admiration before Millais, Burne-Jones, Fred Walker, and Charles Keene, with the latter of whom he used to sing old English duets. Oddly enough, Charles Keene had for Josselin's little amateur pencillings the most enthusiastic admiration — probably because they were the very antipodes of his own splendid work. I believe he managed to get some little initial letters of Josselin's into *Punch* and *Once a Week ;* but they weren't signed, and made no mark, and I've forgotten them.

" Josselin didn't really get his foot in the stirrup till a year or two after his marriage.

" And that was by his illustrations to his own *Sardonyx*, which are almost worthy of the letter-press, I think ; though still somewhat lacking in freedom and looseness, and especially in the sense of tone. The feeling for beauty and character in them (especially that of women and children) is so utterly beyond anything else of the kind that has ever been attempted, that technical considerations

"BETWEEN TWO WELL-KNOWN EARLS"

no longer count. I think you will find all of us, in or outside the Academy, agreed upon this point.

"I saw very little of him after he bought Marsfield; but I sometimes meet his sons and daughters, *de par le monde.*

"And what a pleasure that is to an artist of my particular bent you can readily understand. I would go a good way to see or talk to any daughter of Josselin's ; and to hear Mrs. Trevor sing, what miles ! I'm told the grandchildren are splendid—chips of the old block too.

"And now, my dear Maurice, I will do my best ; you may count upon that, for old-times' sake, and for Josselin's, and for that of '*La belle dame sans merci,*' whom I used to admire so enthusiastically. It grieves me deeply to think of them both gone—and all so sudden !

" Sincerely yours,

"GEORGE DU MAURIER.

"P. S.—Very many thanks for the Château Yquem and the Steinberger Cabinet; *je tâcherai de ne pas en abuser trop !*

"I send you a little sketch of Graham-Reece (Lord Ironsides), taken by me on a little bridge in Düsselthal, near Düsseldorf. He stood for me there in 1860. It was thought very like at the time."

.   .   .   .

When the Josselins came back from their honeymoon and were settled in Southampton Row many people of all kinds called on the newly married pair ; invitations came pouring in, and they went very much into the world. They were considered the handsomest couple in London that year, and became quite the fashion, and were asked everywhere, and made much of, and raved about, and had a glorious time till the following season, when somebody else became the fashion, and they had grown tired of being lionized themselves, and discovered they were people of no social importance whatever, as Leah had long perceived ; and it did them good.

Barty was in his element. The admiration his wife excited filled him with delight ; it was a kind of reflected

343

glory, that pleased him more than any glory he could possibly achieve for himself.

I doubt if Leah was quite so happy. The grand people, the famous people, the clever, worldly people she met made her very shy at first, as may be easily imagined.

She was rather embarrassed by the attentions many smart men paid her as to a very pretty woman, and not always pleased or edified. Her deep sense of humor was often tickled by this new position in which she found herself, and which she put down entirely to the fact that she was Barty's wife.

She never thought much of her own beauty, which had never been made much of at home, where beauty of a very different order was admired, and where she was thought too tall, too pale, too slim, and especially too quiet and sedate.

Dimpled little rosy plumpness for Mr. and Mrs. John Gilpin, and the never-ending lively chatter, and the ever-ready laugh that results from an entire lack of the real sense of humor and a laudable desire to show one's pretty teeth.

Leah's only vanity was her fondness for being very well dressed ; it had become a second nature, especially her fondness for beautiful French boots and shoes, an instinct inherited from her mother.

For these, and for pretty furniture and hangings, she had the truly æsthetic eye, and was in advance of her time by at least a year.

She shone most in her own home — by her great faculty of making others at home there, too, and disinclined to leave it. Her instinct of hospitality was a true inheritance ; she was good at the ordering of all such things —food, wines, flowers, waiting, every little detail of the dinner-table, and especially who should be asked to meet whom, and which particular guests should be chosen to sit by each other. All things of which Barty had no idea whatever.

I remember their first dinner-party well, and how pleasant it was. How good the fare, and how simple; and how quick the hired waiting—and the wines! how— (but I won't talk of that); and how lively we all were, and how handsome the women. Lady Caroline and Miss Daphne Rohan, Mr. and Mrs. Graham-Reece, Scatcherd and my sister; G. du Maurier (then a bachelor) and myself—that was the party, a very lively one.

After dinner du Maurier and Barty sang capital songs of the quartier latin, and told stories of the atelier, and even danced a kind of cancan together—an invention of their own—which they called "*le dernier des Abencerrages.*" We were in fits of laughter, especially Lady Caroline and Mrs. Graham-Reece. I hope D. M. has not forgotten that scene, and will do justice to it in this book.

There was still more of the Bohemian than the Guardsman left in Barty, and his wife's natural tastes were far more in the direction of Bohemia than of fashionable West End society, as it was called by some people who were not in it, whatever it consists of; there was more of her father in her than her mother, and she was not sensitive to the world's opinion of her social status.

Sometimes Leah and Barty and I would dine together and go to the gallery of the opera, let us say, or to see Fechter and Miss Kate Terry in the *Duke's Motto*, or Robson in Shylock, or the *Porter's Knot*, or whatever was good. Then on the way home to Southampton Row Barty would buy a big lobster, and Leah would make a salad of it, with innovations of her own devising which were much appreciated; and then we would feast, and

" LE DERNIER DES ABENCERRAGES "

afterwards Leah would mull some claret in a silver saucepan, and then we (Barty and I) would drink and smoke and chat of pleasant things till it was very late indeed and I had to be turned out neck and crop.

And the kindness of the two dear people ! Once, when my father and mother were away in the Isle of Wight and the Scatcherds in Paris, I felt so seedy I had to leave Barge Yard and go home to Lancaster Gate. I had felt pretty bad for two or three days. Like all people who are never ill, I was nervous and thought I was going to die, and sent for Barty.

In less than twenty minutes Leah drove up in a hansom. Barty was in Hampton Court for the day, sketching. When she had seen me and how ill I looked, off she went for the doctor, and brought him back with her in no time. He saw I was sickening for typhoid, and must go to bed at once and engage two nurses.

Leah insisted on taking me straight off to Southampton Row, and the doctor came with us. There I was soon in bed and the nurses engaged, and everything done for me as if I'd been Barty himself—all this at considerable inconvenience to the Josselins.

And I had my typhoid most pleasantly. And I shall never forget the joys of convalescence, nor what an angel that woman was in a sick - room—nor what a companion when the worst was over ; nor how she so bore herself through all this forced intimacy that no unruly regrets or jealousies mingled in my deep affection and admiration for her, and my passionate gratitude. She was such a person to tell all one's affairs to, even dry business affairs ! such a listener, and said such sensible things, and sometimes made suggestions that were invaluable ; and of a discretion ! a very tomb for momentous secrets.

How on earth Barty would have ever managed to get through existence without her is not to be conceived. Upon my word, I hardly see how I should have got on myself without these two people to fill my life with ; and in all matters of real importance to me she was the nearest of the two, for Barty was so light about things, and couldn't listen long to anything that was at all intricate. Such matters bored him, and that extraordinary good sense which underlies all his brilliant criticism of life was apt to fail him in practical matters ; he was too headstrong and impulsive, and by no means discreet.

It was quite amusing to watch the way his wife managed him without ever letting him suspect what she was doing, and how, after his raging and fuming and storming and stamping—for all his old fractiousness had come back—she would gradually make him work his way round — of his own accord, as he thought — to complete concession all along the line, and take great credit to himself in consequence ; and she would very gravely and slowly give way to a delicate little wink in my direction, but never a smile at what was all so really funny. I've no doubt she often got me to do what she thought right in just the same way—*à mon insu*—and shot her little wink at Barty.

.   .   .   .

In due time—namely, late in the evening of December 31, 1862—Barty hailed a hansom, and went first to summon his good friend Dr. Knight, in Orchard Street ; and then he drove to Brixton, and woke up and brought back with him a very respectable, middle - aged, and motherly woman whose name was Jones ; and next morning, which was a very sunny, frosty one, my dear little god-daughter was ushered into this sinful world, a fact which was chronicled the very next day in Leah's diary by the simple entry :

"Jan. 1 —Roberta was born and the coals came in."

When Roberta was first shown to her papa by the nurse, he was in despair and ran and shut himself up in his studio, and, I believe, almost wept. He feared he had brought a monster into the world. He had always thought that female babies were born with large blue eyes framed with long lashes, a beautiful complexion of the lily and the rose, and their shining, flaxen curls already parted in the middle. And this little bald, wrinkled, dark-red, howling lump of humanity all but made him ill. But soon the doctor came and knocked at the door, and said :

"I congratulate you, old fellow, on having produced the most magnificent little she I ever saw in my life— bar none ; she might be shown for money."

And it turned out that this was not the coarse, unfeeling chaff poor Barty took it for at first, but the pure and simple truth.

So, my blessed Roberta, pride of your silly old god- father's heart and apple of his eye, mother of Cupid and Ganymede and Aurora and the infant Hercules, think of your poor young father weeping in solitude at the first sight of you, because you were so hideous in his eyes !

You were not so in mine. Next day—you had improved, no doubt—I took you in my arms and thought well of you, especially your little hands that were very prehen- sile, and your little feet turned in, with rosy toes and lit- tle pink nails like shiny gems ; and I was complimented by Mrs. Jones on the skill with which I dandled you. I have dandled your sons and daughters, Roberta, and may I live to dandle theirs !

So then Barty dried his tears, if he really shed them—
and he swears he did—and went and sat by his wife's
bedside, and felt unutterably, as I believe all good men
do under similar circumstances; and lo!—proh!—to his
wonderment and delight, in the middle of it all, the
sense of the north came back like a tide, like an overwhelming avalanche. He declared he all but fainted in
the double ineffability of his bliss.

That night he arranged by his bedside writing materials chosen with extra care, and before he went to bed
he looked out of window at the stars, and filled his
lungs with the clean, frozen, virtuous air of Bloomsbury,
and whispered a most passionate invocation to Martia,
and implored her forgiveness, and went to sleep hugging
the thought of her to his manly breast, now widowed for
quite a month to come.

Next morning there was a long letter in bold, vigorous
Blaze :

"MY MORE THAN EVER BELOVED BARTY,—It is for
me to implore pardon, not for *you!* Your first-born is
proof enough to me how right you were in letting your
own instinct guide you in the choice of a wife.

"Ah ! and well now I know her worth and your good-
fortune. I have inhabited her for many months, little
as she knows it, dear thing !

"Although she was not the woman I first wanted for
you, and had watched so many years, she is all that I
could wish, in body and mind, in beauty and sense and
goodness of heart and intelligence, in health and strength,
and especially in the love with which she has so easily,
and I trust so lastingly, filled your heart—for that is
the most precious thing of all to me, as you shall know
some day, and why ; and you will then understand and

forgive me for seeming such a shameless egotist and caring so desperately for my own ends.

"Barty, I will never doubt you again, and we will do great things together. They will not be quite what I used to hope, but they will be worth doing, and all the doing will be yours. All I can do is to set your brains in motion—those innocent brains that don't know their own strength any more than a herd of bullocks which any little butcher boy can drive to the slaughter-house.

"As soon as Leah is well enough you must tell her all about me—all you know, that is. She won't believe you at first, and she'll think you've gone mad; but she'll have to believe you in time, and she's to be trusted with any secret, and so will you be when once you've shared it with her.

"(By-the-way, I wish you weren't so slipshod and colloquial in your English, Barty—Guardsman's English, I suppose—which I have to use, as it's yours; your French is much more educated and correct. You remember dear M. Durosier at the Pension Brossard? he taught you well. You must read, and cultivate a decent English style, for the bulk of our joint work must be in English, I think; and I can only use your own words to make you immortal, and your own way of using them.)

"We will be simple, Barty — as simple as Lemuel Gulliver and the good Robinson Crusoe—and cultivate a fondness for words of one syllable, and if that doesn't do we'll try French.

"Now listen, or, rather, read :

"First of all, I will write out for you a list of books, which you must study whenever you feel I'm inside you —and this more for me than for yourself. Those marked with a cross you must read constantly and carefully at home, the others you must read at the British Museum.

351

"Get a reading ticket at once, and read the books in the order I put down. Never forget to leave paper and pencil by your bedside. Leah will soon get accustomed to your quiet somnambulism ; I will never trouble your rest for more than an hour or so each night, but you can make up for it by staying in bed an hour or two longer. You will have to work during the day from the pencil notes in Blaze you will have written during the night, and in the evening, or at any time you are conscious of my presence, read what you have written during the day, and leave it by your bedside when you go to bed, that I may make you correct and alter and suggest — during your sleep.

"Only write on one side of a page, leaving a margin and plenty of space between the lines, and let it be in copybooks, so that the page on the left-hand side be left for additions and corrections from my Blaze notes, and so forth ; you'll soon get into the way of it.

"Then when each copybook is complete — I will let you know — get Leah to copy it out ; she writes a very good, legible business hand. All will arrange itself. . . .

"And now, get the books and begin reading them. I shall not be ready to write, nor will you, for more than a month.

"Keep this from everybody but Leah ; don't even mention it to Maurice until I give you leave—not but what's he's to be thoroughly trusted. You are fortunate in your wife and your friend—I hope the day will come when you will find you have been fortunate in your

"MARTIA."

Here follows a list of books, but it has been more or less carefully erased ; and though some of the names are

still to be made out, I conclude that Barty did not wish
them to be made public.

. . . .

Before Roberta was born, Leah had reserved herself
an hour every morning and every afternoon for what she
called the cultivation of her mind — the careful reading
of good standard books, French and English, that she
might qualify herself in time, as she said, for the intellectual society in which she hoped to mix some day ; she
built castles in the air, being somewhat of a hero-worship-
per in secret, and dreamt of meeting her heroes in the
flesh, now that she was Barty's wife.

But when she became a mother there was not only
Roberta who required much attention, but Barty himself
made great calls upon her time besides.

To his friends' astonishment he had taken it into his
head to write a book. Good heavens ! Barty writing a
book ! What on earth could the dear boy have to write
about ?

He wrote much of the book at night in bed, and corrected and put it into shape during the daytime ; and
finally Leah had to copy it all out neatly in her best
handwriting, and this copying out of Barty's books became to her an all but daily task for many years—a happy
labor of love, and one she would depute to no one else ;
no hired hand should interfere with these precious pro-
ductions of her husband's genius. So that most of the
standard works, English and French, that she grew to
thoroughly master were of her husband's writing — not
a bad education, I venture to think !

Besides, it was more in her nature and in the circumstances of her life that she should become a woman of
business and a woman of the world rather than a reader
of books — one who grew to thoroughly understand life

as it presented itself to her; and men and women, and especially children ; and the management of a large and much frequented house ; for they soon moved away from Southampton Row.

She quickly arrived at a complete mastery of all such science as this—and it is a science; such a mastery as I have never seen surpassed by any other woman, of whatever world. She would have made a splendid Marchioness of Whitby, this daughter of a low-comedy John Gilpin ; she would have beaten the Whitby record !

She developed into a woman of the world in the best sense—full of sympathy, full of observation and quick understanding of others' needs and thoughts and feelings ; absolutely sincere, of a constant and even temper, and a cheerfulness that never failed—the result of her splendid health ; without caprice, without a spark of vanity, without selfishness of any kind—generous, open-handed, charitable to a fault ; always taking the large and generous view of everything and everybody ; a little impulsive perhaps, but not often having to regret her impulses ; of unwearied devotion to her husband, and capable of any heroism or self-sacrifice for his sake ; of that I feel sure.

No one is perfect, of course. Unfortunately, she was apt to be somewhat jealous at first of his singularly catholic and very frankly expressed admiration of every opposite type of female beauty ; but she soon grew to see that there was safety in numbers, and she was made to feel in time that her own type was the arch-type of all in his eyes, and herself the arch-representative of that type in his heart.

She was also jealous in her friendships, and was not happy unless constantly assured of her friends' warm love—Ida's, mine, even that of her own father and mother. Good heavens! had ever a woman less cause for doubt or complaint on that score!

Then, like all extremely conscientious people who always know their own mind and do their very best, she did not like to be found fault with; she secretly found such fault with herself that she thought that was fault-finding enough. Also, she was somewhat rigid in sticking to the ways she thought were right, and in the selection of these ways she was not always quite infallible. *On a les défauts de ses qualités;* and a little obstinacy is often the fault of a very noble quality indeed!

Though somewhat shy and standoffish during the first year or two of her married life, she soon became *"joliment dégourdie,"* as Barty called it; and I can scarcely conceive any position in which she would have been awkward or embarrassed for a moment, so ready was she always with just the right thing to say—or to withhold, if silence were better than speech; and her fit and proper place in the world as a great man's wife—and a good and beautiful woman—was always conceded to her with due honor, even by the most impertinent among the highly placed of her own sex, without any necessity for self-assertion on her part whatever—without assumption of any kind.

It was a strange and peculiar personal ascendency she managed to exert with so little effort, an ascendency partly physical, no doubt; and the practice of it had begun in the West End emporium of the "Universal Fur Company, Limited."

How admirably she filled the high and arduous position of wife to such a man as Barty Josselin is well known to the world at large. It was no sinecure! but

"SARDONYX"

she gloried in it; and to her thorough apprehension and management of their joint lives and all that came of them, as well as to her beauty and sense and genial warmth, was due her great popularity for many years in an immense and ever-widening circle, where the memory of her is still preserved and cherished as one of the most remarkable women of her time.

With all this power of passionate self-surrender to her husband in all things, little and big, she was not of the type that cannot see the faults of the beloved one, and Barty was very often frankly pulled up for his short-comings, and by no means had it all his own way when his own way wasn't good for him. She was a person to reckon with, and incapable of the slightest flattery, even to Barty, who was so fond of it from her, and in spite of her unbounded admiration for him.

Such was your mother, my dear Roberta, in the bloom of her early twenties and ever after; till her death, in fact—on the day following his!

.   .   .   .

Somewhere about the spring of 1863 she said to me:

"Bob, Barty has written a book. Either I'm an idiot, or blinded by conjugal conceit, or else Barty's book —which I've copied out myself in my very best hand-writing—is one of the most beautiful and important books ever written. Come and dine with me to-night; Barty's dining in the City with the Fishmongers—you shall have what you like best: pickled pork and pease-pudding, a dressed crab and a Welsh rabbit to follow, and draught stout—and after dinner I will read you the beginning of *Sardonyx*—that's what he's called it—and I should like to have your opinion."

I dined with her as she wished. We were alone, and she told me how he wrote every night in bed, in a kind of ecstasy—between two and four, in Blaze—and then elaborated his work during the day, and made sketches for it.

And after dinner she read me the first part of *Sardonyx;* it took three hours.

Then Barty came home, having dined well, and in very high spirits.

"Well, old fellow! how do you like *Sardonyx?*"

I was so moved and excited I could say nothing—I couldn't even smoke. I was allowed to take the precious manuscript away with me, and finished it during the night.

Next morning I wrote to him out of the fulness of my heart.

I read it aloud to my father and mother, and then lent it to Scatcherd, who read it to Ida. In twenty-four hours our gay and genial Barty—our Robin Goodfellow and Merry Andrew, our funny man—had become for us a demi-god ; for all but my father, who looked upon him as a splendid but irretrievably lost soul, and mourned over him as over a son of his own.

And in two months *Sardonyx* was before the reading world, and the middle-aged reader will remember the wild enthusiasm and the storm it raised.

All that is ancient history, and I will do no more than allude to the unparalleled bitterness of the attacks made by the Church on a book which is now quoted again and again from every pulpit in England—in the world—and has been translated into almost every language under the sun.

Thus he leaped into fame and fortune at a bound, and at first they delighted him. He would take little Roberta on to the top of his head and dance "La Paladine" on his hearth-rug, singing :

"Rataplan, Rataplan,
I'm a celebrated man—"

in imitation of Sergeant Bouncer in *Cox and Box*.

But in less than a year celebrity had quite palled, and all his money bored him—as mine does me. He had a very small appetite for either the praise or the pudding which were served out to him in such excess all through his life. It was only his fondness for the work itself that kept his nose so constantly to the grindstone.

Within six months of the *Sardonyx* Barty wrote *La quatrième Dimension* in French, which was published by Dollfus-Moïs frères, in Paris, with if possible a greater success; for the clerical opposition was even more virulent. The English translation, which is admirable, is by Scatcherd.

Then came *Motes in a Moonbeam, Interstellar Harmonics*, and *Berthe aux grands Pieds* within eighteen months, so that before he was quite thirty, in the space of two years, Barty had produced five works—three in English and two in French—which, though merely novels and novelettes, have had as wide and far-reaching an influence on modern thought as the *Origin of Species,* that appeared about the same time, and which are such, for simplicity of expression, exposition, and idea, that an intelligent ploughboy can get all the good and all the pleasure from them almost as easily as any philosopher or sage.

Such was Barty's début as a man of letters. This is not the place to criticise his literary work, nor am I the proper person to do so; enough has been written already about Barty Josselin during his lifetime to fill a large library—in nearly every language there is. I tremble to think of what has yet to follow!

"'RATAPLAN, RATAPLAN'"

Sardonyx came of age nearly twelve years ago—what a coming of age that was the reader will remember well. I shall not forget its celebration at Marsfield ; it happened to coincide with the birth of Barty's first grandchild, at that very house.

I will now go back to Barty's private life, which is the sole object of this humble attempt at book-making on my part.

During the next ten years Barty's literary activity was immense. Beautiful books followed each other in rapid succession—and so did beautiful little Bartys, and Leah's hands were full.

And as each book, English or French, was more beautiful than the last ; so was each little Barty, male or female. All over Kensington and Campden Hill—for they took Gretna Lodge, next door to Cornelys, the sculptor's— the splendor of these little Bartys, their size, their beauty, their health and high spirits, became almost a joke, and their mother became almost a comic character in consequence—like the old lady who lived in a shoe.

Money poured in with a profusion few writers of good books have ever known before, and every penny not wanted for immediate household expenses was pounced upon by Scatcherd or by me to be invested in the manner we thought best : nous avons eu la main heureuse !

The Josselins kept open house, and money was not to be despised, little as Barty ever thought of money.

Then every autumn the entire smalah migrated to the coast of Normandy, or Picardy, or Brittany, or to the Highlands of Inverness, and with them the Scatcherds and the chronicler of these happy times—not to mention cats, dogs, and squirrels, and guinea-pigs, and white mice, and birds of all kinds, from which the children would not be parted, and the real care of which, both at home and abroad, ultimately devolved on poor Mrs. Josselin—who was not so fond of animals as all that—so that her life was full to overflowing of household cares.

Another duty had devolved upon her also : that of answering the passionate letters that her husband received by every post from all parts of the world—especially America—and which he could never be induced to answer himself. Every morning regularly he would begin his day's work by writing "Yours truly—B. Josselin" on quite a score of square bits of paper, to be sent through the post to fair English and American autograph collectors who forwarded stamped envelopes, and sometimes photographs of themselves, that he might study the features of those who loved him at a respectful distance, and who so frankly told their love ; all of which bored Barty to extinction, and was a source of endless amusement to his wife.

But even *she* was annoyed when a large unstamped or insufficiently stamped parcel arrived by post from America, enclosing a photograph of her husband to which his signature was desired, and containing no stamps to frank it on its return journey !

And the photographers he had to sit to ! and the interviewers, male and female, to whom he had to deny himself ! Life was too short !

How often has a sturdy laborer or artisan come up to him, as he and I walked together, with :

"I should very much like to shake you by the hand, Mr. Josselin, if I might make so bold, sir !"

And such an appeal as this would please him far more than the most fervently written outpourings of the female hearts he had touched.

They, of course, received endless invitations to stay

at country-houses all over the United Kingdom, where they might have been lionized to their hearts' content, if such had been their wish ; but these they never accepted. They never spent a single night away from their own house till most of their children were grown up—or ever wanted to ; and every year they got less and less into the way of dining out, or spending the evening from home— and I don't wonder ; no gayer or jollier home ever was than that they made for themselves, and each other, and their intimate friends ; not even at Cornelys's, next door, was better music to be heard ; for Barty was friends with all the music - makers, English and foreign, who cater for us in and out of the season ; even *they* read his books, and understood them; and they sang and played better for Barty—and for Cornelys, next door—than even for the music-loving multitude who filled their pockets with British gold.

And the difference between Barty's house and that of Cornelys was that at the former the gatherings were smaller and more intimate—as became the smaller house —and one was happier there in consequence.

Barty gave himself up entirely to his writing, and left everything else to his wife, or to me, or to Scatcherd. She was really a mother to him, as well as a passionately loving and devoted helpmeet.

To make up for this, whenever she was ill, which didn't often happen—except, of course, when she had a baby—he forgot all his writing in his anxiety about her ; and in his care of her, and his solicitude for her ease and comfort, he became quite a motherly old woman, a better nurse than Mrs. Jones or Mrs. Gibson—as practical and sensible and full of authority as Dr. Knight himself.

And when it was all over, all his amiable carelessness came back, and with it his genius, his school-boy high spirits, his tomfooling, his romps with his children, and his utter irresponsibility, and absolute disdain for all the ordinary business of life ; and the happy, genial temper that never seemed to know a moment's depression or nourish an unkind thought.

Poor Barty ! what would he have done without us all, and what should we have done without Barty ? As Scatcherd said of him, " He's having his portion in this life."

But it was not really so.

Then, in 1870, he bought that charming house, Mansfield, by the Thames, which he rechristened Marsfield ; and which he—with the help of the Scatcherds and myself, for it became our hobby—made into one of the most delightful abodes in England. It was the real home for all of us ; I really think it is one of the loveliest spots on earth. It was a bargain, but it cost a lot of money ; altogether, never was money better spent—even as a mere investment. When I think of what it is worth now ! Je suis homme d'affaires !

What a house-warming that was on the very day that France and Germany went to war ; we little guessed what was to come for the country we all loved so dearly, or we should not have been so glad.

I am conscious that all this is rather dull reading. Alas ! Merry England is a devilish dull place compared to foreign parts—and success, respectability, and domestic bliss are the dullest things to write—or read—about that I know—and with middle age to follow too !

It was during that first summer at Marsfield that Barty told me the extraordinary story of Martia, and I really thought he had gone mad. For I knew him to be the most truthful person alive.

Even now I hardly know what to think, nor did Leah— nor did Barty himself up to the day of his death.

He showed me all her letters, *which I may deem it advisable to publish some day:* not only the Blaze suggestions for his books, and all her corrections; things to occupy him for life—all, of course, in his own handwriting; but many letters about herself, also written in sleep and by his own hand; and the style is Barty's—not the style in which he wrote his books, and which is not to be matched; but that in which he wrote his Blaze letters to me.

If her story is true—and I never read a piece of documentary evidence more convincing—these letters constitute the most astonishing revelation ever yet vouchsafed to this earth.

But her story cannot be true!

That Barty's version of his relations with "The Martian" is absolutely sincere it is impossible to doubt. He was quite unconscious of the genesis of every book he ever wrote. His first hint of every one of them was the elaborately worked out suggestion he found by his bedside in the morning—written by himself in his sleep during the preceding night, with his eyes wide open, while more often than not his wife anxiously watched him at his unconscious work, careful not to wake or disturb him in any way.

Roughly epitomized, Martia's story was this:

For an immense time she had gone through countless incarnations, from the lowest form to the highest, in the cold and dreary planet we call Mars, the outermost of the four inhabited worlds of our system, where the sun seems no bigger than an orange, and which but for its moist, thin, rich atmosphere and peculiar magnetic conditions that differ from ours would be too cold above ground for human or animal or vegetable life. As it is, it is only inhabited now in the neighborhood of its equator, and even there during its long winter it is colder and more desolate than Cape Horn or Spitzbergen—except that the shallow, fresh-water sea does not freeze except for a few months at either pole.

All these incarnations were forgotten by her but the last; nothing remained of them all but a vague consciousness that they had once been, until their culmination in what would be in Mars the equivalent of a woman on our earth.

Man in Mars is, it appears, a very different being from what he is here. He is amphibious, and descends from no monkey, but from a small animal that seems to be something between our seal and our sea-lion.

According to Martia, his beauty is to that of the seal as that of the Theseus or Antinous to that of an orang-outang. His five senses are extraordinarily acute, even the sense of touch in his webbed fingers and toes; and in addition to these he possesses a sixth, that comes from his keen and unintermittent sense of the magnetic current, which is far stronger in Mars than on the earth, and far more complicated, and more thoroughly understood.

When any object is too delicate and minute to be examined by the sense of touch and sight, the Martian shuts his eyes and puts it against the pit of his stomach, and knows all about it, even its inside.

In the absolute dark, or with his eyes shut, and when he stops his ears, he is more intensely conscious of what immediately surrounds him than at any other time, except that all color-perception ceases; conscious not only of material objects, but of what is passing in his fellow-Martian's mind—and this for an area of many hundreds of cubic yards.

In the course of its evolutions this extraordinary faculty—which exists on earth in a rudimentary state, but only among some birds and fish and insects and in the lower forms of animal life—has developed the Martian mind in a direction very different from ours, since no inner life apart from the rest, no privacy, no concealment is possible except at a distance involving absolute isolation; not even thought is free ; yet in some incomprehensible way there is, as a matter of fact, a really greater freedom of thought than is conceivable among ourselves : absolute liberty in absolute obedience to law, a paradox beyond our comprehension.

Their habits are as simple as those we attribute to the cave - dwellers during the prehistoric periods of the earth's existence.   But their moral sense is so far in advance of ours that we haven't even a terminology by which to express it.

In comparison, the highest and best of us are monsters of iniquity and egoism, cruelty and corruption ; and our planet (a very heaven for warmth and brilliancy and beauty, in spite of earthquakes and cyclones and tornadoes) is a very hell through the creatures that people it—a shambles, a place of torture, a grotesque and impure pandemonium.

These exemplary Martians wear no clothes but the exquisite fur with which nature has endowed them, and which constitutes a part of their immense beauty, according to Martia.

They feed exclusively on edible moss and roots and submarine seaweed, which they know how to grow and prepare and preserve.   Except for heavy-winged bat-like birds, and big fish, which they have domesticated and use for their own purposes in an incredible manner (incarnating a portion of themselves and their consciousness at will in their bodies), they have cleared Mars of all useless and harmful and mutually destructive forms of animal life. A sorry fauna, the Martian—even at its best—and a flora beneath contempt, compared to ours.

They are great engineers and excavators, great irrigators, great workers in delicate metal, stone, marble, and precious gems (there is no wood to speak of); great sculptors and decorators of the beautiful caves, so fancifully and so intricately connected, in which they live, and which have taken thousands of years to design and excavate and ventilate and adorn, and which they warm and light up at will in a beautiful manner by means of the tremendous magnetic current.

This richly parti-colored light is part of their mental and moral life in a way it is not in us to apprehend, and has its exact equivalent in sound—and vice versa.

They have no language of words, and do not need it, since they can only be isolated in thought from each other by a distance greater than that which any vocal sound can traverse; but their organs of voice and hearing are far more complex and perfect than ours, and their atmosphere infinitely more conductive of phonal vibrations.

It seems that everything which can be apprehended by the eye or hand is capable of absolute sonorous translation : light, color, texture, shape in its three dimensions, weight, and density. The phonal expression and comprehension of all these are acquired by the Martian baby almost as soon as it knows how to swim or dive, or move upright and erect on dry land or beneath it; and the mechanical translation of such expression by means of wind and wire and sounding texture and curved surface of extraordinary elaboration is the principal business of the Martian life—an art by which all the combined past experience and future aspirations of the race receive the fullest utterance.   Here again personal magnetism plays an enormous part.

And it is by means of this long and patiently evolved and highly trained faculty that the race is still developing towards perfection with constant strain and effort—although the planet is far advanced in its decadence and within measurable distance of its unfitness for life of any kind.

All is so evenly and harmoniously balanced, whether above ground or beneath, that existence is full of joy in spite of the tremendous strain of life, in spite also of a dreariness of outlook, on barren nature, which is not to be matched by the most inhospitable regions of the earth ; and death is looked upon as the crowning joy of all, although life is prolonged by all the means in their power.

For when the life of the body ceases and the body itself is burned and its ashes scattered to the winds and waves, the infinitesimal, imponderable, and indestructible something *we* call the *soul* is known to lose itself in a sunbeam and make for the sun, with all its memories about it, that it may then receive further development, fitting it for other systems altogether beyond conception ; and the longer it has lived in Mars the better for its eternal life in the future.

But it often, on its journey sunwards, gets entangled in other beams, and finds its way to some intermediate planet—Mercury, Venus, or the Earth ; and putting on flesh and blood and bone once more, and losing for a space all its knowledge of its own past, it has to undergo another mortal incarnation—a new personal experience, beginning with its new birth ; a dream and a forgetting, till it awakens again after the pangs of dissolution, and finds itself a step further on the way to freedom.

Martia, it seems, came to our earth in a shower of

shooting-stars a hundred years ago. She had not lived her full measure of years in Mars ; she had elected to be suppressed, through some unfitness, physical or mental or moral, which rendered it inexpedient that she should become a mother of Martians, for they are very particular about that sort of thing in Mars : we shall have to be so here some day, or else we shall degenerate and become extinct ; or even worse !

Many Martian souls come to our planet in this way, it seems, and hasten to incarnate themselves in as promising unborn though just begotten men and women as they find, that they may the sooner be free to hie them sunwards with all their collected memories.

According to Martia, most of the best and finest of our race have souls that have lived forgotten lives in Mars. But Martia was in no hurry ; she was full of intelligent curiosity, and for ten years she went up and down the earth, revelling in the open air, lodging herself in the brains and bodies of birds, beasts, and fishes, insects, and animals of all kinds—like a hermit crab in a shell that belongs to another—but without the slightest inconvenience to the legitimate owners, who were always quite unconscious of her presence, although she made what use she could of what wits they had.

Thus she had a heavenly time on this sunlit earth of ours—now a worm, now a porpoise, now a sea-gull or a dragon-fly, now some fleet-footed, keen-eyed quadruped that did not live by slaying, for she had a horror of bloodshed.

She could only go where these creatures chose to take her, since she had no power to control their actions in the slightest degree ; but she saw, heard, smelled and touched and tasted with their organs of sense, and was as conscious of their animal life as they were themselves.

Her description of this phase of her earthly career is full of extraordinary interest, and sometimes extremely funny—though quite unconsciously so, no doubt. For instance, she tells how happy she once was when she inhabited a small brown Pomeranian dog called "Schnapfel," in Cologne, and belonging to a Jewish family who dealt in old clothes near the Cathedral; and how she loved them and looked up to them—how she revelled in fried fish and the smell of it—and in all the stinks in every street of the famous city—all except one, that arose from Herr Johann Maria Farina's renowned emporium in the Julichs Platz, which so offended the canine nostrils that she had to give up inhabiting that small Pomeranian dog forever, etc.

Then she took to man, and inhabited man and woman, and especially child, in all parts of the globe for many years; and, finally, for the last fifty or sixty years or so, she settled herself exclusively among the best and healthiest English she could find.

She took a great fancy to the Rohans, who are singularly well endowed in health of mind and body, and physical beauty, and happiness of temper. She became especially fond of the ill-fated but amiable Lord Runswick—Barty's father. Then through him she knew Antoinette, and loved her so well that she determined to incarnate herself at last as their child; but she had become very cautious and worldly during her wandering life on earth, and felt that she would not be quite happy either as a man or a woman in Western Europe unless she were reborn in holy wedlock — a concession she made to our British prejudices in favor of respectability; she describes herself as the only Martian Philistine and snob.

Evil communications corrupt good manners, and poor

371

Martia, to her infinite sorrow and self-reproach, was conscious of a sad lowering of her moral tone after this long frequentation of the best earthly human beings — even the best English.

She grew to admire worldly success, rank, social distinction, the perishable beauty of outward form, the lust of the flesh and the pride of the eye—the pomps and vanities of this wicked world—and to basely long for these in her own person !

Then when Barty was born she loved to inhabit his singularly well constituted little body better than any other, and to identify herself with his happy child-life, and enjoy his singularly perfect senses, and sleep his beautiful sleep, and revel in the dreams he so completely forgot when he woke—reminiscent dreams, that she was actually able to weave out of the unconscious brain that was his: absolutely using his dormant organs of memory for purposes of her own, to remember and relive her own past pleasures and pains, so sensitively and highly organized was he ; and to her immense surprise she found she could make him feel her presence even when awake by means of the magnetic sense that pervaded her strongly as it pervades all Martian souls, till they reincarnate themselves among us and forget.

And thus he was conscious of the north whenever she enjoyed the hospitality of his young body.

She stuck to him for many years, till he offended her taste by his looseness of life as a Guardsman (for she was extremely straitlaced) ; and she inhabited him no more for some time, though she often watched him through the eyes of others, and always loved him and lamented sorely over his faults and follies.

Then one memorable night, in the energy of her despair at his resolve to slip that splendid body of his, she was able to influence him in his sleep, and saved his life; and all her love came back tenfold.

She had never been able to impose a fraction of her will on any being, animal or human, that she had ever inhabited on earth until that memorable night in Malines, where she made him write at her dictation.

Then she conceived an immense desire that he should marry the splendid Julia, whom she had often inhabited also, that she might one day be a child of his by such a mother, and go through her earthly incarnation in the happiest conceivable circumstances; but herein she was balked by Barty's instinctive preference for Leah, and again gave him up in a huff.

But she soon took to inhabiting Leah a great deal, and found her just as much to her taste for her own future earthly mother as the divine Julia herself, and made up her mind she would make Barty great and famous by a clever management of his very extraordinary brains, of which she had discovered the hidden capacity, and influence the earth for its good—for she had grown to love the beautiful earth, in spite of its iniquities —and finally be a child of Barty and Leah, every new child of whom seemed an improvement on the last, as though practice made perfect.

Such is, roughly, the story of Martia.

There is no doubt—both Barty and Leah agreed with me in this—that it is an easy story to invent, though it is curiously convincing to read in the original shape, with all its minute details and their verisimilitude; but even then there is nothing in it that the author of *Sardonyx* could not have easily imagined and made more convincing still.

He declared that all through life on awaking from his night's sleep he always felt conscious of having had extraordinary dreams—even as a child—but that he forgot them in the very act of waking, in spite of strenuous efforts to recall them. But now and again on sinking into sleep the vague memory of those forgotten dreams would come back and they were all of a strange life under new conditions — just such a life as Martia had described—where arabesques of artificial light and interwoven curves of subtle sound had a significance undreamt of by mortal eyes or ears, and served as conductors to a heavenly bliss unknown to earth—revelations denied to us here, or we should be very different beings from what we most unhappily are.

He thought it quite possible that his brain in sleep had at last become so active through the exhausting and depleting medical régime that he went through in Malines that it actually was able to dictate its will to his body, and that everything might have happened to him as it did then and afterwards without any supernatural or ultranatural agency whatever—without a Martia!

He might, in short, have led a kind of dual life, and Martia might be a simple fancy or invention of his brain in an abnormal state of activity during slumber; and both Leah and I inclined to this belief (but for a strange thing which happened later, and which I will tell in due time). Indeed, it all seems so silly and far-fetched, so "out of the question," that one feels almost ashamed at bringing this Martia into a serious biography of a great man—un conte à dormir debout! But you must wait for the end.

Anyhow, the singular fact remains that in some way inexplicable to himself Barty has influenced the world in a direction which it never entered his thoughts even to conceive, so far as he remembered.

Think of all he has done.

He has robbed Death of nearly all its terrors ; even for the young it is no longer the grisly phantom it once was for ourselves, but rather of an aspect mellow and benign; for to the most sceptical he (and only he) has restored that absolute conviction of an indestructible germ of Immortality within us, born of remembrance made perfect and complete after dissolution : he alone has built the golden bridge in the middle of which science and faith can shake hands over at least one common possibility—nay, one common certainty for those who have read him aright.

There is no longer despair in bereavement — all bereavement is but a half parting ; there is no real parting except for those who survive, and the longest earthly life is but a span. Whatever the future may be, the past will be ours forever, and that means our punishment and our reward and reunion with those we loved. It is a happy phrase, that which closes the career of *Sardonyx*. It has become as universal as the Lord's Prayer !

To think that so simple and obvious a solution should have lain hidden all these æons, to turn up at last as though by chance in a little illustrated story-book ! What a nugget !

Où avions-nous donc la tête et les yeux ?

Physical pain and the origin of evil seem the only questions with which he has not been able to grapple. And yet if those difficulties are ever dealt with and mastered and overcome for us it can only be by some follower of Barty's methods.

It is true, no doubt, that through him suicide has become the normal way out of our troubles when these are beyond remedy. I will not express any opinion as to the ethical significance of this admitted result of his teaching, which many of us still find it so hard to reconcile with their conscience.

Then, by a dexterous manipulation of our sympathies that amounts to absolute conjuring, he has given the death-blow to all cruelty that serves for our amusement, and killed the pride and pomp and circumstance of glorious sport, and made them ridiculous with his lusty laugh ; even the bull-fights in Spain are coming to an end, and all through a Spanish translation of *Life-blood*. All the cruelties of the world are bound to follow in time, and this not so much because they are cruel as because they are ridiculous and mean and ugly, and would make us laugh if they didn't make us cry.

And to whom but Barty Josselin do we owe it that our race is on an average already from four to six inches taller than it was thirty years ago, men and women alike; that strength and beauty are rapidly becoming the rule among us, and weakness and ugliness the exception?

He has been hard on these ; he has been cruel to be kind, and they have received notice to quit, and been generously compensated in advance, I think ! Who in these days would dare to enter the holy state of wedlock unless they were pronounced physically, morally, and mentally fit—to procreate their kind—not only by their own conscience, but by the common consent of all who know them ? And that beauty, health, and strength are a part of that fitness, and old age a bar to it, who would dare deny ?

I'm no Adonis myself. I've got a long upper lip and an Irish kink in my nose, inherited perhaps from some maternally ancestral Blake of Derrydown, who may have been a proper blackguard ! And that kink should be now, no doubt, the lawful property of some ruffianly cattle-houghing moonlighter, whose nose—which should have been mine—is probably as straight as Barty's. For in Ireland are to be found the handsomest and ugliest people in all Great Britain, and in Great Britain the handsomest and ugliest people in the whole world.

Anyhow, I have known my place. I have not perpetuated that kink, and with it, possibly, the base and cowardly instincts of which it was meant to be the outward and visible sign—though it isn't in my case—that my fellow-men might give me a wide berth.

Leah's girlish instinct was a right one when she said me nay that afternoon by the Chelsea pier—for how could she see inside me, poor child ? How could Beauty guess the Beast was a Prince in disguise ? It was no fairy-tale !

Things have got mixed up ; but they're all coming right, and all through Barty Josselin.

And what vulgar pride and narrownesses and meannesses and vanities and uglinesses of life, in mass and class and individual, are now impossible ! — and all through Barty Josselin and his quaint ironies of pen and pencil, forever trembling between tears and laughter, with never a cynical spark or a hint of bitterness.

How he has held his own against the world ! how he has scourged its wickedness and folly, this gigantic optimist, who never wrote a single line in his own defence !

How quickly their laugh recoiled on those early laughers ! and how Barty alone laughed well because he laughed the last, and taught the laughers to laugh on his side ! People thought he was always laughing. It was not so.

Part Ninth

"Cara deûm soboles, magnum Jovis incrementum."
—VIRGIL.

THE immense fame and success that Barty Josselin achieved were to him a source of constant disquiet. He could take neither pride nor pleasure in what seemed to him not his ; he thought himself a fraud.

Yet only the mere skeleton of his work was built up for him by his demon ; all the beauty of form and color, all the grace of movement and outer garb, are absolutely his own.

It has been noticed how few eminent men of letters were intimate with the Josselins, though the best among them—except, of course, Thomas Carlyle—have been so enthusiastic and outspoken in their love and admiration of his work.

He was never at his ease in their society, and felt himself a kind of charlatan.

The fact is, the general talk of such men was often apt to be over his head, as it would have been over mine, and often made him painfully diffident and shy. He needn't have been; he little knew the kind of feeling he inspired among the highest and best.

Why, one day at the Marathonœum, the first and foremost of them all, the champion smiter of the Philistines, the apostle of culture and sweetness and light, told me that, putting Barty's books out of the question, he always got more profit and pleasure out of Barty's society than that of any man he knew.

" It does me good to be in the same room with him; the freshness of the man, his voice, his aspect, his splendid vitality and mother-wit, his boyish spirit, and the towering genius behind it all. I only wish to goodness I was an intimate friend of his as you are ; it would be a liberal education to me !"

But Barty's reverence and admiration for true scholarship and great literary culture in others amounted to absolute awe, and filled him with self-distrust.

There is no doubt that until he was universally accepted, the crudeness of his literary method was duly criticised with great severity by those professional literary critics who sometimes carp with such a big mouth at their betters, and occasionally kill the Keatses of this world !

In writing, as in everything else, he was an amateur, and more or less remained one for life; but the greatest of his time accepted him at once, and laughed and wept, and loved him for his obvious faults as well as for his qualities. Tous les genres sont bons, hormis le genre ennuyeux ! And Barty was so delightfully the reverse of a bore !

Dear me ! what matters it how faultlessly we paint or write or sing if no one will care to look or read or listen ? He is all fault that hath no fault at all, and we poor outsiders all but yawn in his face for his pains.

They should only paint and write and sing for each other, these impeccables, who so despise success and revile the successful. How do they live, I wonder ? Do they take in each other's washing, or review each other's books ?

It edifies one to see what a lot of trouble these deriders of other people's popularity will often take to advertise themselves, and how they yearn for that popular acclaim they so scornfully denounce.

Barty was not a well-read man by any means; his scholarship was that of an idle French boy who leaves school at seventeen, after having been plucked for a cheap French degree, and goes straightway into her Majesty's Household Brigade.

At the beginning of his literary career it would cut him to the quick to find himself alluded to as that inspired Anglo-Gallic buffoon, the ex-Guardsman, whose real vocation, when he wasn't twaddling about the music of the spheres, or writing moral French books, was to be Mr. Toole's understudy.

He was even impressed by the smartness of those second-rate decadents, French and English, who so gloried in their own degeneracy—as though one were to glory in scrofula or rickets; those unpleasant little anthropoids with the sexless little muse and the dirty little Eros, who would ride their angry, jealous little tilt at him in the vain hope of provoking some retort which would have lifted them up to glory! Where are they now? He has improved them all away! Who ever hears of decadents nowadays?

Then there were the grubs of Grub Street, who sometimes manage to squirt a drop from their slime-bags on to the swiftly passing boot that scorns to squash them. He had no notion of what manner of creatures they really were, these gentles! He did not meet them at any club he belonged to—it was not likely. Clubs have a way of blackballing grubs—especially grubs that are out of the common grubby; nor did he sit down to dinner with them at any dinner-table, or come across them at any house he was by way of frequenting; but he imagined they were quite important persons because they did not sign their articles! and he quite mistook their place in the economy of creation. C'était un naïf, le beau Josselin!

Big fleas have little fleas, and they've got to put up with them! There is no "poudre insecticide" for literary vermin—and more's the pity! (Good heavens! what would the generous and delicate-minded Barty say, if he were alive, at my delivering myself in this unworthy fashion about these long-forgotten assailants of his, and at my age too—he who never penned a line in retaliation! He would say I was the most unseemly grub of them all, and he would be quite right; so I am just now, and ought to know better—but it amuses me.)

Then there were the melodious bardlets who imitate those who imitate those who imitate the forgotten minor poets of the olden time and log-roll each other in quaint old English. They did not log-roll Barty, whom they thought coarse and vulgar, and wrote to that effect in very plain English that was not old, but quite up to date.

"How splendidly they write verse!" he would say, and actually once or twice he would pick up one or two of their cheap little archaic mannerisms and proudly use them as his own, and be quite angry to find that Leah had carefully expunged them in her copy.

"A *fair* and *gracious* garden indeed!" says Leah. "I *won't* have you use such ridiculous words, Barty—you mean a *pretty* garden, and you shall say so; or even a *beautiful* garden if you like!—and no more '*manifolds*,' and '*there-anents*,' and '*in veriest sooths*,' and '*waters wan*,' and '*wan waters*,' and all that. I won't stand it; they don't suit your style at all!"

She and Scatcherd and I between us soon laughed him out of these innocent little literary vagaries, and he remained content with the homely words he had inherited

381

from his barbarian ancestors in England (they speak good English, our barbarians), and the simple phrasing he had learnt from M. Durosier's classe de littérature at the Institution Brossard.

One language helps another; even the smattering of a dead language is better than no extra language at all, and that's why, at such cost of time and labor and paternal cash, we learn to smatter Greek and Latin, I suppose. "Arma virumque cano"—"Tityre tu patulæ"—"Mæcenas atavis"—"Μῆνιν ἄειδε"—and there you are! It sticks in the memory, and it's as simple as "How d'ye do?"

Anyhow, it is pretty generally admitted, both here and in France, that for grace and ease and elegance and absolute clearness combined, Barty Josselin's literary style has never been surpassed and very seldom equalled; and whatever his other faults, when he was at his ease he had the same graceful gift in his talk, both French and English.

It might be worth while my translating here the record of an impression made by Barty and his surroundings on a very accomplished Frenchman, M. Paroly, of the *Débats*, who paid him a visit in the summer of 1869, at Campden Hill.

I may mention that Barty hated to be interviewed and questioned about his literary work—he declared he was afraid of being found out.

But if once the interviewer managed to evade the lynx-eyed Leah, who had a horror of him, and get inside the studio, and make good his footing there, and were a decently pleasant fellow to boot, Barty would soon get over his aversion—utterly forget he was being interviewed—and talk as to an old friend; especially if the reviewer were a Frenchman or an American.

The interviewer is an insidious and wily person, and

often presents himself to the soft-hearted celebrity in such humble and pathetic guise that one really hasn't the courage to snub him. He has come such a long way for such a little thing! it is such a lowly function he plies at the foot of that tall tree whose top you reached at a single bound! And he is supposed to be a "gentleman," and has no other means of keeping body and soul together! Then he is so prostrate in admiration before your Immensity. . . .

So you give way, and out comes the little note-book, and out comes the little cross-examination.

As a rule, you are none the worse and the world is none the better; we know all about you already—all, at least, that we want to know ; we have heard it all before, over and over again. But a poor fellow-creature has earned his crust, and goes home the happier for having talked to you about yourself and been treated like a man and a brother.

But sometimes the reviewer is very terrible indeed in his jaunty vulgarization of your distinguished personality, and you have to wince and redden, and rue the day you let him inside your house, and live down those light familiar paragraphs in which he describes you and the way you dress and how you look and what jolly things you say ; and on what free and easy terms *he* is with you, of all people in the. world!

But the most terrible of all is the pleasant gentleman from America, who has yearned to know you for *so* many years, and comes perhaps with a letter of introduction— or even without!—not to interview you or write about you (good heavens! he hates and scorns that modern pest, the interviewer), but to sit at your feet and worship at your shrine, and tell you of all the good you have done him and his, all the happiness you have given them all—"the debt of a lifetime!"

And you let yourself go before him, and so do your family, and so do your old friends ; is *he* not also a friend, though not an old one ? You part with him almost in sorrow, he's so nice ! And in three weeks some kind person sends you from the other side such a printed account of you and yours—so abominably true, so abominably false—that the remembrance of it makes you wake up in the dead of night, and most unjustly loathe an entire continent for breeding and harboring such a shameless type of press reptile !

I feel hard-hearted towards the interviewer, I own. I wish him, and those who employ him, a better trade ; and a better taste to whoever reads what he writes. But Barty could be hard-hearted to nobody, and always regretted having granted the interview when he saw the published outcome of it.

Fortunately, M. Paroly was decently discreet.

" I've got a Frenchman coming this afternoon—a tremendous swell," said Barty, at lunch.

Leah. " Who is he ?"

Barty. " M. Paroly, of the *Débats.*"

Leah. " What is he when he's at home ?"

Barty. " A famous journalist ; as you'd know if you'd read the French newspapers sometimes, which you never do."

Leah. " Haven't got the time. He's coming to interview you, I suppose, and make French newspaper copy out of you."

Barty. " Why shouldn't he come just for the pleasure of making my acquaintance ?"

Leah. " And mine—I'll be there and talk to him, too !"

Barty. " My dear, he probably doesn't speak a word

of English; and your French, you know! You never *would* learn French properly, although you've had me to practise on for so many years—not to mention Bob and Ida."

Leah. "How unkind of you, Barty! When have I had time to trouble about French ? Besides, you always laugh at my French accent and mimic it—and *that's* not encouraging !"

Barty. "My dear, I *adore* your French accent; it's so unaffected ! I only wish I heard it a little oftener."

Leah. "You shall hear it this afternoon. At what o'clock is he coming, your Monsieur Paroly ?"

Barty. "At four-thirty."

Leah. "Oh, Barty, *don't* give yourself away — don't talk to him about your writings, or about yourself; or about your family. He'll vulgarize you all over France. Surely you've not forgotten that nice 'gentleman' from America who came to see you, and who told you that *he* was no interviewer, not *he!* but came merely as a friend and admirer — a distant but constant worshipper for many years ! and how you talked to him like a long-lost brother, in consequence ! ' There's nobody in the world like the best Americans,' you said. You adored them *all,* and wanted to be an American yourself—till a month after, when he published every word you said, and more, and what sort of cravat you had on, and how silent and cold and uncommunicative your good, motherly English wife was—you, the brilliant and talkative Barty Josselin, who should have mated with a countrywoman of his own! and how your bosom friend was a huge, overgrown everyday Briton with a broken nose ! *I* saw what he was at, from the low cunning in his face as he listened ; and felt that every single unguarded word you dropped was a dollar in his pocket ! How we've all had to live down that

385

dreadfully facetious and grotesque and familiar article
he printed about us all in those twenty American newspapers that have got the largest circulation in the world!
and how you stamped and raved, Barty, and swore that
never another American 'gentleman' should enter your
house! What names you called him : 'cad !' 'sweep !'
' low-bred, little Yankee penny-a-liner !' Don't you remember ? Why, he described you as a quite nice-looking man somewhat over the middle height !"

"Oh yes ; damn him, *I* remember !" said Barty, who
was three or four inches over six feet, and quite openly
vain of his good looks.

Leah. " Well, then, pray be cautious with this Monsieur Paroly you think so much of because he's French.
Let *him* talk—interview *him*—ask him all about his family, if he's got one—his children, and all that ; play a
game of billiards with him—talk French politics—dance
' La Paladine '—make him laugh—make him smoke one
of those strong Trichinopoli cigars Bob gave you for the
tops of omnibuses—make him feel your biceps—teach
him how to play cup and ball—give him a sketch—then
bring him in to tea. Madame Cornelys will be there,
and Julia Ironsides, and Ida, who'll talk French by the
yard. Then we'll show him the St. Bernards and Minerva, and I'll give him an armful of Gloire de Dijon
roses, and shake him warmly by the hand, so that he
won't feel ill-natured towards us ; and we'll get him out
of the house as quick as possible."

Thus prepared, Barty awaited M. Paroly, and this is
a free rendering of what M. Paroly afterwards wrote
about him :

" With a mixture of feelings difficult to analyze and

define, I bade adieu to the sage and philosopher of Cheyne Row, and had myself transported in my hansom to the abode of the other great *sommité littéraire* in London, the light one — M. Josselin, to whom we in France also are so deeply in debt.

" After a longish drive through sordid streets we reached a bright historic vicinity and a charming hill, and my invisible Jehu guided me at the great trot by verdant country lanes. We turned through lodge gates into a narrow drive in a well-kept garden where there was a lawn of English greenness, on which were children and nurses and many dogs, and young people who played at the lawn-tennis.

" The door of the house was opened by a charming young woman in black with a white apron and cap, like a waitress at the Bouillon Duval, who guided me through a bright corridor full of pictures and panoplies, and then through a handsome studio to a billiard-room, where M. Josselin was playing at *the* billiard to himself all alone.

" M. Josselin receives me with jovial cordiality; he is enormously tall, enormously handsome, like a drum-major of the Imperial Guard, except that his lip and chin are shaved and he has slight whiskers; very well dressed, with thick curly hair, and regular features, and a singularly sympathetic voice : he is about thirty-five.

" I have to decline a game of billiards, and refuse a cigar, a very formidable cigar, very black and very thick and very long. I don't smoke, and am no hand at a cue. Besides, I want to talk about *Étoiles Mortes*, about *Les Trépassées de François Villon*, about *Déjanire et Dalila!*

" M. Josselin speaks French as he writes it, in absolute perfection ; his mother, he tells me, was from Nor-

"I'M DEFENDING MY LIEGE FRO MADAME TUSSOT IN."

mandy—the daughter of fisherfolk in Dieppe; he was at school in Paris, and has lived there as an art student.

"He does not care to talk about *Les Trépassées* or *Les Étoiles*, or any of his immortal works.

"He asks me if I'm a good swimmer, and can do *la coupe* properly; and leaning over his billiard-table he shows me how it ought to be done, and dilates on the merits of that mode of getting through the water. He confides to me that he suffers from a terrible nostalgia—a consuming desire to do *la coupe* in the swimming-baths of Passy against the current; to take a header *à la hussarde* with his eyes open and explore the bed of the Seine between Grenelle and the Île des Cygnes—as he used to do when he was a school-boy—and pick up mussels with his teeth.

"Then he explains to me the peculiar virtues of his stove, which is almost entirely an invention of his own, and shows me how he can regulate the heat of the room to the fraction of a degree centigrade, which he prefers to Fahrenheit—just as he prefers metres and centimetres to inches and feet—and ten to twelve!

"After this he performs some very clever tricks with billiard-balls; juggles three of them in each hand simultaneously, and explains to me that this is an exceptional achievement, as he only sees out of one eye, and that no acrobat living could do the same with one eye shut.

"I quite believe him, and wonder and admire, and his face beams with honest satisfaction—and this is the man who wrote *La quatrième Dimension!*

"Then he tells me some very funny French school-boy stories; he delights in my hearty laughter; they are capital stories, but I had heard them all before — when I was at school.

"'And now, M. Josselin,' I say, 'à propos of that last

story you've just told me; in the *Trépassées de François Villon* you have omitted "la très-sage Héloïse" altogether.'

"'Oh, have I? How stupid of me!—Abélard and all that! Ah well—there's plenty of time—nous allons arranger tout ça! All that sort of thing comes to me in the night, you know, when I'm half asleep in bed—a—a—I mean after lunch in the afternoon, when I take my siesta.'

"Then he leads me into his studio and shows me pencil studies from the life, things of ineffable beauty of form and expression — things that haunt the memory.

"'Show me a study for Déjanire,' I say.

"'Oh! I'll draw Déjanire for you,' and he takes a soft pencil and a piece of smooth card-board, and in five minutes draws me an outline of a naked woman on a centaur's back, a creature of touching beauty no other hand in the world could produce — so aristocratically delicately English and of to-day—so severely, so nobly and classically Greek. C'est la chasteté même—mais ce n'est pas Déjanire!

"He gives me this sketch, which I rechristen Godiva, and value as I value few things I possess.

"Then he shows me pencil studies of children's heads, from nature, and I exclaim:

"'O Heaven, what a dream of childhood! Childhood is never so beautiful as that.'

"'Oh yes it is, in England, I assure you,' says he. 'I'll show you *my* children presently; and you, have you any children?'

"'Alas! no,' I reply; 'I am a bachelor.'

"I remark that from time to time, just as the moon veils itself behind a passing cloud, the radiance of his brilliant and jovial physiognomy is eclipsed by the expression of a sadness immense, mysterious, infinite ; this is followed by a look of angelic candor and sweetness and gentle heroism, that moves you strangely, even to the heart, and makes appeal to all your warmest and deepest sympathies—the look of a very masculine Joan of Arc ! You don't know why, but you feel you would make any sacrifice for a man who looks at you like that, follow him to the death—lead a forlorn hope at his bidding.

" He does not exact from me anything so arduous as this, but passing round my neck his powerful arm, he says :

" ' Come and drink some tea ; I should like to present you to my wife.'

" And he leads me through another corridor to a charming drawing-room that gives on to the green lawn of the garden.

" There are several people there taking the tea.

" He presents me first to Madame Josselin. If the husband is enormously handsome, the wife is a beauty absolutely divine ; she, also, is very tall — très élégante ; she has soft wavy black hair, and eyes and eyebrows d'un noir de jais, and a complexion d'une blancheur de lis, with just a point of carmine in the cheeks. She does not say much—she speaks French with difficulty ; but she expresses with her smiling eyes so cordial and sincere a welcome that one feels glad to be in the same room with her, one feels it is a happy privilege , it does one good—one ceases to feel one may possibly be an intruder—one almost feels one is wanted there.

" I am then presented to three or four other ladies ; and it would seem that the greatest beauties of London have given each other rendezvous in Madame Josselin's salon — this London, where are to be found the most beautiful women in the world and the ugliest.

"First, I salute the Countess of Ironsides — ah, mon Dieu, la Diane chasseresse—la Sapho de Pradier! Then Madame Cornelys, the wife of the great sculptor, who lives next door — a daughter of the ancient gods of Greece! Then a magnificent blonde, an old friend of theirs, who speaks French absolutely like a Frenchwoman, and says thee and thou to M. Josselin, and introduces me to her brother, un vrai type de colosse bon enfant, d'une tenue irréprochable [thank you, M. Paroly], who also speaks the French of France, for he was at school there—a school-fellow of our host.

"There are two or three children, girls, more beautiful than anything or anybody else in the house — in the world, I think! They give me tea and cakes, and bread and butter; most delicious tartines, as thin as wafers, and speak French well, and relate to me the biographies of their animals, une vraie ménagerie which I afterwards have to visit—immense dogs, rabbits, hedgehogs, squirrels, white mice, and a gigantic owl, who answers to the name of Minerva.

" I find myself, ma foi, very happy among these wonderful people, and preserve an impression of beauty, of bonhomie, of naturalness and domestic felicity quite unlike anything I have ever been privileged to see—an impression never to be forgotten.

"But as for *Étoiles Mortes* and *Les Trépassées de François Villon*, I really have to give them up; the beautiful big dogs are more important than all the books in the world, even the master's — even the master himself!

"However, I want no explanation to see and understand how M. Josselin has written most of his chefs-d'œuvre from the depths of a happy consciousness habituated to all that is most graceful and charming and seductive in real life — and a deeply sympathetic, poignant, and compassionate sense of the contrast to all this.

"Happy mortal, happy family, happy country where grow (poussent) such people, and where such children flourish! The souvenir of that so brief hour spent at Gretna Lodge is one of the most beautiful souvenirs of my life—and, above all, the souvenir of the belle châtelaine who filled my hansom with beautiful roses culled by her own fair hand, which gave me at parting that cordial English pressure so much more suggestive of *Au revoir* than *Adieu!*

"It is with sincere regret one leaves people who part with one so regretfully.

"ALPHONSE PAROLY."

.   .   .   .

Except that good and happy women have no history, I should almost like to write the history of Barty's wife, and call it the history of the busiest and most hard-working woman in Great Britain.

Barty left everything to her — to the very signing of cheques. He would have nothing to do with any business of any kind.

He wouldn't even carve at lunch or dinner. Leah did, unless *I* was there.

It is but fair to say he worked as hard as any man I know. When he was not writing or drawing, he was thinking about drawing or writing; when they got to Marsfield, he hardly ever stirred outside the grounds.

There he would garden with gardeners or cut down trees, or do carpenter's work at his short intervals of rest, or groom a horse.

How often have I seen him suddenly drop a spade or axe or saw or curry-comb, and go straight off to a thatched

393

gazebo he had built himself, where writing materials were left, and write down the happy thought that had occurred ; and then, pipe in mouth, back to his gardening or the rest !

I also had a gazebo close to his, where I read bluebooks and wrote my endless correspondence with the help of a secretary—only too glad, both of us, to be disturbed by festive and frolicsome young Bartys of either sex—by their dogs—by their mother !

Leah's province it was to attend to all the machinery by which life was carried on in this big house, and social intercourse, and the education of the young, and endless hospitalities.

She would even try to coach her boys in Latin and Euclid during their preparation times for the school where they spent the day, two miles off. Such Latin ! such geometry ! She could never master the ablative absolute, nor what used to be called at Brossard's *le que retranché,* nor see the necessity of demonstrating by $A + B$ what was sufficiently obvious to her without.

"Who helps you in your Latin, my boy?" says the master, with a grin.

"My father," says Geoffrey, too loyal to admit it was his mother who had coached him wrong.

"Ah, I suppose he helps you with your Euclid also ?" says the master, with a broader grin still.

"Yes, sir," says Geoffrey.

"Your father's French, I suppose ?"

"I dare say, sir," says Geoffrey.

"Ah, I thought so !"

All of which was very unfair to Barty, whose Latin, like that of most boys who have been brought up at a French school, was probably quite as good as the English school-master's own, except for its innocence of quantities; and Blanchet and Legendre are easier to learn than Euclid, and stick longer in the memory; and Barty remembered well.

Then, besides the many friends who came to the pleasant house to stay, or else for lunch or tea or dinner, there were pious pilgrims from all parts of the world, as to a shrine—from Paris, from Germany, Italy, Norway, and Sweden; from America especially. Leah had to play the hostess almost every day of her life, and show off her lion and make him roar and wag his tail and stand on his hind legs—a lion that was not always in the mood to tumble and be shown off, unless the pilgrims were pretty and of the female sex.

Barty was a man's man par excellence, and loved to forgather with men. The only men he couldn't stand were those we have agreed to call in modern English the Philistines and the prigs—or both combined, as they can sometimes be; and this objection of his would have considerably narrowed his circle of male acquaintances but that the Philistines and the prigs, who so detest each other, were so dotingly fond of Barty, and ran him to earth in Marsfield.

The Philistines loved him for his world-wide popularity; the prigs in spite of it! They loved him for himself alone—because they couldn't help it, I suppose—and lamented over him as over a fallen angel.

He was happiest of all with the good denizens of Bohemia, who have known want and temptation and come unscathed out of the fire, but with their affectations and insincerities and conventionalities all burnt away.

Good old Bohemia—alma mater dolorosa; stern old gray she-wolf with the dry teats—marâtre au cœur de pierre! It is not a bad school in which to graduate, if you can do so without loss of principle or sacrifice of the delicate bloom of honor and self-respect.

Next to these I think he loved the barbarians he belonged to on his father's side, who, whatever their faults, are seldom prigs or Philistines; and then he loved the proletarians, who had good, straightforward manners and no pretension—the laborer, the skilled artisan, especially the toilers of the sea.

In spite of his love of his own sex, he was of the kind that can go to the devil for a pretty woman.

He did not do this; he married one instead, fortunately for himself and for his children and for her, and stuck to her and preferred her society to any society in the world. Her mere presence seemed to have an extraordinarily soothing influence on him; it was as though life were short, and he could never see enough of her in the allotted time and space; the chronic necessity of her nearness to him became a habit and a second nature— like his pipe, as he would say.

Still, he was such a slave to his own æsthetic eye and ever-youthful heart that the sight of lovely woman pleased him more than the sight of anything else on earth; he delighted in her proximity, in the rustle of her garments, in the sound of her voice; and lovely woman's instinct told her this, so that she was very fond of Barty in return.

He was especially popular with sweet. pretty young girls, to whom his genial, happy, paternal manner always endeared him. They felt as safe with Barty as with any father or uncle, for all his facetious love-making; he made them laugh, and they loved him for it, and they forgot his Apolloship, and his Lionhood, and his general Immensity, which he never remembered himself.

It is to be feared that women who lacked the heavenly gift of good looks did not interest him quite so much, whatever other gifts they might possess, unless it were the gift of making lovely music. The little brown nightingale outshone the brilliant bird of paradise if she were a true nightingale; if she were very brown indeed, he would shut his eyes and listen with all his ears, rapt, as in a heavenly dream. And the closed lids would moisten, especially the lid that hid the eye that couldn't see—the emotional one!—although he was the least lachrymose of men, since it was with such a dry eye he wrote what I could scarcely read for my tears.

But his natural kindliness and geniality made him always try and please those who tried to please him, beautiful or the reverse, whether they succeeded or not; and he was just as popular with the ducks and geese as with the swans and peacocks and nightingales and birds of paradise. The dull, commonplace dames who prosed and buzzed and bored, the elderly intellectual virgins who knew nothing of life but what they had read—or written—in "Tendenz" novels, yet sadly rebuked him, more in sorrow than in anger, for this passage or that in his books, about things out of their ken altogether, etc.

His playful amenity disarmed the most aggressive bluestocking, orthodox or Unitarian, Catholic or Hebrew—radicals, agnostics, vegetarians, teetotalers, anti-vaccinationists, anti-vivisectionists—even anti-things that don't concern decent women at all, whether married or single.

It was only when his privacy was invaded by some patronizing, loud-voiced nouvelle-riche with a low-bred physiognomy that no millions on earth could gild or refine, and manners to match; some foolish, fashionable, would-be worldling, who combined the arch little coquetries and impertinent affectations of a spoilt beauty with the ugliness of an Aztec or an Esquimau; some silly, titled old frump who frankly ignored his tea-making wife and

daughters and talked to *him* only—and only about her
grotesque and ugly self—and told him of all the famous
painters who had wanted to paint her for the last hundred years—it was only then he grew glum and reserved
and depressed and made an unfavorable impression on
the other sex.

What it must have cost him not to express his disgust
more frankly ! for reticence on any matter was almost a
torture to him.

Most of us have a mental sanctum to which we retire
at times, locking the door behind us ; and there we think
of high and beautiful things, and hold commune with
our Maker ; or count our money, or improvise that repartee the gods withheld last night, and shake hands
with ourselves for our wit ; or caress the thought of some
darling, secret wickedness or vice ; or revel in dreams of
some hidden hate, or some love we mustn't own ; and
curse those we have to be civil to whether we like them
or not, and nurse our little envies till we almost get to
like them.

There we remember all the stupid and unkind things
we've ever said or thought or done, and all the slights
that have ever been put on us, and secretly plan the
revenge that never comes off — because time has softened our hearts, let us hope, when opportunity serves at
last !

That Barty had no such holy of holies to creep into I
feel pretty sure—unless it was the wifely heart of Leah ;
whatever came into his head came straight out of his
mouth ; he had nothing to conceal, and thought aloud,
for all the world to hear ; and it does credit, I think, to
the singular goodness and guilelessness of his nature that
he could afford to be so outspoken through life and yet
give so little offence to others as he did.   His indiscretion

did very little harm, and his naïve self-revelation only made him the more lovable to those who knew him well.

They were poor creatures, the daws who pecked at that manly heart, so stanch and warm and constant.

As for Leah, it was easy to see that she looked upon her husband as a fixed star, and was well pleased to tend and minister and revolve, and shine with no other light than his; it was in reality an absolute adoration on her part. But she very cleverly managed to hide it from him ; she was not the kind of woman that makes a doormat of herself for the man she loves. She kept him in very good order indeed.

It was her theory that female adoration is not good for masculine vanity, and that he got quite enough of it outside his own home ; and she would make such fun of him and his female adorers all over the world that he grew to laugh at them himself, and to value a pat on the back and a hearty " Well done, Barty !" from his wife more than

> " The blandishments of all the womankind
> In Europe and America combined."

Gentle and kind and polite as she was, however, she could do battle in defence of her great man, who was so backward at defending himself ; and very effective battle too.

As an instance among many, illustrating her method of warfare : Once at an important house a very immense personage (who had an eye for a pretty woman) had asked to be introduced to her and had taken her down to supper ; a very immense personage indeed, whose fame had penetrated to the uttermost ends of the earth and deservedly made his name a beloved household word wherever our tongue is spoken, so that it was in every

Englishman's mouth all over the world—as Barty's is now.

Leah was immensely impressed, and treated his elderly Immensity to a very full measure of the deference that was his due ; and such open homage is not always good for even the Immensest Immensities—it sometimes makes them give themselves immense airs. So that this particular Immensity began mildly but firmly to patronize Leah. This she didn't mind on her own account, but when he said, quite casually :

"By-the-way, I forget if I *know* your good husband; *do* I ?"

—she was not pleased, and immediately answered :

"I really can't say ; I don't think I ever heard him mention your name !"

This was not absolutely veracious on Leah's part ; for to Barty in those days this particular great man was a god, and he was always full of him. But it brought the immense one back to his bearings at once, and he left off patronizing and was almost humble.

Anyhow, it was a lie so white that the recording angel will probably delete what there is of it with a genial smile, and leave a little blank in its place.

.   .   .   .

In an old diary of Leah's I find the following entry :

"March 6th, 1874.—Mamma and Ida Scatcherd came to stay. In the evening our sixth daughter and eighth child was born."

Julia (Mrs. Mainwaring) was this favored person — and is still. Julia and her predecessors have all lived and flourished up to now.

The Josselins had been exceptionally fortunate in their children ; each new specimen seemed an even finer specimen than the last. The health of this remarkable family had been exemplary—measles, and mumps, and whooping-cough their only ailments.

During the month of Leah's confinement Barty's nocturnal literary activity was unusually great. Night after night he wrote in his sleep, and accumulated enough raw material to last him a lifetime; for the older he grew and the more practised his hand the longer it took him to give his work the shape he wished; he became more fastidious year by year as he became less of an amateur.

One morning, a day or two before his wife's complete recovery, he found a long personal letter from Martia by his bedside—a letter that moved him very deeply, and gave him food for thought during many weeks and months and years :

"My Beloved Barty,—The time has come at last when I must bid you farewell.

"I have outstayed my proper welcome on earth as a disembodied conscience by just a hundred years, and my desire for reincarnation has become an imperious passion not to be resisted.

"It is more than a desire—it is a duty as well, a duty far too long deferred.

"Barty, I am going to be your next child. I can conceive no greater earthly felicity than to be a child of yours and Leah's. I should have been one long before, but that you and I have had so much to do together for this beautiful earth—a great debt to pay : you, for being as you are ; I, for having known you.

"Barty, you have no conception what you are to me and always have been.

"I am to you but a name, a vague idea, a mysterious inspiration; sometimes a questionable guide, I fear.

"'I DON'T THINK I EVER HEARD HIM MENTION YOUR NAME'"

You don't even believe all I have told you about myself
—you think it all a somnambulistic invention of your
own ; and so does your wife, and so does your friend.

"O that I could connect myself in your mind with the
shape I wore when I was last a living thing ! No shape
on earth, not either yours or Leah's or that of any child
yet born to you both, is more beautiful to the eye that has
learned how to see than the fashion of that lost face and
body of mine.

"*You* wore the shape once, and so did your father
and mother, for you were Martians. Leah was a Martian,
and wore it too ; there are many of them here—they are
the best on earth, the very salt thereof. I mean to be
the best of them all, and one of the happiest. Oh, help
me to that !

"Barty, when I am a splendid son of yours or a sweet
and lovely daughter, all remembrance of what I was before will have been wiped out of me until I die. But
you will remember, and so will Leah, and both will love
me with such a love as no earthly parents have ever felt
for any child of theirs yet.

"Think of the poor loving soul, lone, wandering, but
not lost, that will so trustfully look up at you out of
those gleeful innocent eyes !

" How that soul has suffered both here and elsewhere
you don't know, and never will, till the secrets of all
hearts shall be disclosed ; and I am going to forget it
myself for a few decades—sixty, seventy, eighty years
perhaps ; such happy years, I hope—with you for my
father and Leah for my mother during some of them at
least—and sweet grandchildren of yours, I hope, for my
sons and daughters ! Why, life to me now will be almost a holiday.

"Oh, train me up the way I should go ! Bring me up

403

to be healthy and chaste and strong and brave—never to
know a mean ambition or think an ungenerous thought
—never to yield to a base or unworthy temptation.

"If I'm a boy—and I want to be a boy very much
(although, perhaps, a girl would be dearer to your heart)
—don't let me be either a soldier or a sailor, however
much I may wish it as a Josselin or a Rohan; don't
bring me up to buy or sell like a Gibson, or deal in law
like a Bletchley.

"Bring me up to invent, or make something useful,
if it's only pickles or soap, but not to buy and sell them;
bring me up to build or heal or paint or write or make
music—to help or teach or please.

"If I'm a girl, bring me up to be as much like Leah
as you can, and marry me to just such another as yourself, if you can find him. Whether I'm a girl or a boy,
call me Marty, that my name may rhyme with yours.

"When my conscience re-embodies itself, I want it
never to know another pang of self-reproach. And when
I'm grown up, if you think it right to do so, tell me who
and what I once was, that I may love you both the more;
tell me how fondly I loved you when I was a bland and
fleeting little animalcule, without a body, but making
my home in yours—so that when you die I may know
how irrevocably bound up together we must forever be,
we three; and rejoice the more in your death and Leah's
and my own. Teach me over again all I've ever taught
you, Barty—over and over again!

"Alas! perhaps you don't believe all this! How can
I give you a sign?

"There are many ways; but a law, of necessity inexorable, forbids it. Such little entity as I possess would
cease to be; it was all but lost when I saved your life—
and again when I told you that you were the beloved of

Julia Royce. It would not do for us Martians to meddle with earthly things; the fat would soon be in the fire, I can tell you!

"Try and trust me, Barty, and give me the benefit of any doubt.

"You have work planned out for many years to come, and are now yourself so trained that you can do without me. You know what you have still to say to mankind; never write a line about which you are not sure.

"For another night or two you will be my host, and this splendid frame of yours my hostelry; on y est très bien. Be hospitable still for a little while — make the most of me; hug me tight, squeeze me warm!

"As soon as Leah is up and about and herself again you will know me no more, and no more feel the north.

"Ah! you will never realize what it is for me to bid you good-bye, my Barty, my Barty! All that is in your big heart and powerful brain to feel of grief belongs to me, now that you are fast asleep. And your genius for sorrow, which you have never really tested yet, is as great as any gift you possess.

"Happy Barty, who have got to forty years without sounding the great depths, and all through me! what will you do without your poor devoted unknown Martia to keep watch over you and ward — to fight for you like a wild-cat, if necessary?

"Leah must be your wild-cat now. She has it in her to be a tigress when you are concerned, or any of her children! Next to you, Leah is the darling of my heart; for it's your heart I make use of to love her with.

"I want you to tell the world all about your Martia some day. They may disbelieve, as you do; but good fruit will come of it in the future. Martians will have a freer hand with you all, and that will be a good thing

405

for the earth ; they were trained in a good hard school
—they are the Spartans of our universe.

"Such things will come to pass, before many years are
over, as are little dreamt of now, and all through your
wanting to swallow that dose of cyanide at No. 36 Rue
des Ursulines Blanches, and my having the gumption to
prevent you !

"It's a good seed that we have sown, you and I. It
was not right that this beautiful planet should go much
longer drifting through space without a single hope that
is not an illusion, without a single hint of what life
should really be, without a goal.

"Why such darkness under so bright a sun ! such
blindness to what is so patent ! such a deaf ear to the
roaring of that thunderous harmony which you call the
eternal silence!—you of the earth, earthy, who can hear
the little trumpet of the mosquito so well that it makes
you fidget and fret and fume all night, and robs you of
your rest. Then the sun rises and frightens the mos-
quitoes away, and you think that's what the sun is for
and are thankful ; but why the deuce a mosquito should
sting you, you can't make out !—mystery of mysteries !

"At the back of your brain is a little speck of perishable matter, Barty ; it is no bigger than a needle's point,
but it is bigger in you than in anybody else I know, except in Leah ; and in your children it is bigger still—
almost as big as the point of a pin !

"If they pair well, and it is in them to do so if they
follow their inherited instinct, their children and their
children's children will have that speck still bigger.
When that speck becomes as big as a millet-seed in your
remote posterity, then it will be as big as in a Martian,
and the earth will be a very different place, and man of
earth greater and even better than the Martian by all the

greatness of his ampler, subtler, and more complex brain; his sense of the Deity will be as an eagle's sense of the sun at noon in a cloudless tropical sky; and he will know how to bear that effulgence without a blink, as he stands on his lonely summit, ringed by the azure world.

"Indeed, there will be no more Martians in Mars by that time; they are near the end of their lease; all good Martians will have gone to Venus, let us hope; if not, to the Sun itself!

"Man has many thousands of years before him yet ere his little ball of earth gets too cold for him; the little speck in his brain may grow to the size of a pea, a cherry, a walnut, an egg, an orange! He will have in him the magnetic consciousness of the entire solar system, and hold the keys of time and space as long and as far as the sun shines for us all — and then there will be the beginning of everything. And all through that little episode in the street of those White Ursulines! And the seed of Barty and Leah will overflow to the uttermost ends of the earth, and finally blossom and bear fruit for ever and ever beyond the stars.

"What a beginning for a new order of things! what a getting up-stairs! what an awakening! what an annunciation!

"Do you remember that knock at the door?

"'Il est dix heures, savez-vous? Voulez-vous votre café dans votre chambre?'

"She little knew, poor little Frau! humble little Finche Torfs, lowly Flemish virgin, who loved you as the moth loves the star; vilain mangeur de cœurs que vous êtes!

"Barty, I wish your wife to hear nothing of this till the child who once was your Martia shall have seen the light of day with eyes of its own; tell her that I have left you at last, but don't tell her why or how; tell her some day, years hence, if you think she will love me the better for it ; not otherwise.

"When you wake, Barty, I shall still be inside you ; say to me in your mezza voce all the kind things you can think of — such things as you would have said to your mother had she lived till now, and you were speeding her on a long and uncertain journey.

"How you would have loved your mother ! She was most beautiful, and of the type so dear to you. Her skin was almost as white as Leah's, her eyes almost as black, her hair even blacker; like Leah, she was tall and slim and lithe and graceful. She might have been Leah's mother, too, for the likeness between them. How often you remind me of her when you laugh or sing, and when you're funny in French; those droll, quick gestures and quaint intonations, that ease and freedom and deftness as you move ! And then you become English in a moment, and your big, burly, fair-haired father has come back with his high voice, and his high spirits, and his frank blue eyes, like yours, so kind and brave and genial.

"And *you*, dear, what a baby you were—a very prince among babies ; ah ! if I can only be like that when I begin again !

"The people in the Tuileries garden used to turn round and stare and smile at you when Rosalie with the long blue streamers bore you along as proudly as if Louis Philippe were your grandfather and she the royal wetnurse ; and later, after that hideous quarrel about nothing, and the fatal fight by the 'mare aux biches,' how the good fisher people of Le Pollet adored you ! 'Un vrai petit St. Jean ! il nous portera bonheur, bien sûr !'

"You have been thoroughly well loved all your life, my Barty, but most of all by me—never forget that !

"I have been your father and your mother when they

sat and watched your baby-sleep; I have been Rosalie when she gave you the breast ; I have been your French grandfather and grandmother quarrelling as to which of the two should nurse you as they sat and sunned themselves on their humble doorstep in the Rue des Guignes!

"I have been your doting wife when you sang to her, your children when you made them laugh till they cried. I've been Lady Archibald when you danced the Dieppoise after tea, in Dover, with your little bare legs; and Aunt Caroline, too, as she nursed you in Malines after that silly duel where you behaved so well ; and I've been by turns Mérovée Brossard, Bonzig, old Laferté, Mlle. Marceline, Finche Torfs, poor little Marianina, Julia Royce, Father Louis, the old Abbé, Bob Maurice—all the people you've ever charmed, or amused, or been kind to —a legion; good heavens! I have been them all ! What a snowball made up of all these loves I've been rolling after you all these years ! and now it has all got to melt away in a single night, and with it the remembrance of all I've ever been during ages untold.

"And I've no voice to bid you good-bye, my beloved; no arms to hug you with, no eyes to weep—I, a daughter of the most affectionate, and clinging, and caressing race of·little people in existence ! Such eyes as I once had, too; such warm, soft, furry arms, and such a voice—it would have wanted no words to express all that I feel now ; that voice — nous savons notre orthographie en musique là bas !

"How it will please, perhaps, to remember even this farewell some day, when we're all together again, with nothing to come between !

"And now, my beloved, there is no such thing as good-bye; it is a word that has no real meaning ; but it is so English and pretty and sweet and child-like and nonsensical that I could write it over and over again—just for fun !

"So good-bye ! good-bye ! good-bye ! till I wake up once more after a long living sleep of many years, I hope; a sleep filled with happy dreams of you, dear, delightful people, whom I've got to live with and love, and learn to lose once more; and then—no more good-byes !

"MARTIA."

.   .   .   .

So much for Martia—whoever or whatever it was that went by that name in Barty's consciousness.

After such close companionship for so many years, the loss of her—or it—was like the loss of a sixth and most valuable sense, worse almost than the loss of his sight would have been; and with this he was constantly threatened, for he most unmercifully taxed his remaining eye, and the field of his vision had narrowed year by year.

But this impending calamity did not frighten him as in the old days. His wife was with him now, and as long as she was by his side he could have borne anything—blindness, poverty, dishonor—anything in the world. If he lost her, he would survive her loss just long enough to put his affairs in order, and no more.

But most distressfully he missed the physical feeling of the north—even in his sleep. This strange bereavement drew him and Leah even more closely together, if that were possible; and she was well content to reign alone in the heart of her fractious, unreasonable but most affectionate, humorous, and irresistible great man. Although her rival had been but a name and an idea, a mere abstraction in which she had never really believed, she did not find it altogether displeasing to herself that the lively Martia was no more ; she has almost told me as much.

And thus began for them both the happiest and most beautiful period of their joint lives, in spite of sorrows yet to come. She took such care of him that he might have been as blind as Belisarius himself, and he seemed almost to depend upon her as much—so wrapt up was he in the work of his life, so indifferent to all mundane and practical affairs. What eyesight was not wanted for his pen and pencil he reserved to look at her with—at his beloved children, and the things of beauty in and outside Marsfield : pictures, old china, skies, hills, trees, and river; and what wits remained he kept to amuse his family and his friends—there was enough and to spare.

The older he grew the more he teemed and seethed and bubbled and shone—and set others shining round him— even myself. It is no wonder Marsfield became such a singularly agreeable abode for all who dwelt there, even for the men-servants and the maid-servants, and the birds and the beasts, and the stranger within its gates — and for me a kind of earthly paradise.

.   .   .   .

And now, gentle reader, I want very badly to talk about myself a little, if you don't mind—just for half a dozen pages or so, which you can skip if you like. Whether you do so or not, it will not hurt you—and it will do me a great deal of good.

I feel uncommonly sad, and very lonely indeed, now that Barty is gone; and with him my beloved comrade Leah.

The only people left to me that I'm really fond of—except my dear widowed sister, Ida Scatcherd—are all so young. They're Josselins, of course—one and all—and they're all that's kind and droll and charming, and I adore them. But they can't quite realize what this sort of bereavement means to a man of just my age, who has

"'I'M A PHILISTINE, AND AM NOT ASHAMED'"

still got some years of life before him, probably — and is yet an old man.

The Right Honorable Sir Robert Maurice, Bart., M.P., etc., etc., etc. That's me. I take up a whole line of manuscript. I might be a noble lord if I chose, and take up two !

I'm a liberal conservative, an opportunist, a pessi-optimist, an in-medio-tutissimist, and attend divine service at the Temple Church.

I'm a Philistine, and not ashamed ; so was Molière— so was Cervantes. So, if you like, was the late Martin Farquhar Tupper—and those who read him ; we're of all sorts in Philistia, the great and the small, the good and the bad.

I'm in the sixties—sound of wind and limb—only two false teeth—one at each side, bicuspids, merely for show. I'm rather bald, but it suits my style ; a little fat, perhaps—a pound and a half over sixteen stone ! but I'm an inch and a half over six feet, and very big-boned. Altogether, diablement bien conservé ! I sleep well, the sleep of the just ; I have a good appetite and a good digestion, and a good conceit of myself still, thank Heaven —though nothing like what it used to be ! One can survive the loss of one's self-respect ; but of one's vanity, never.

What a prosperous and happy life mine has been, to be sure, up to a few short months ago — hardly ever an ache or a pain !—my only real griefs, my dear mother's death ten years back, and my father's in 1870. Yes, I have warmed both hands at the fire of life, and even burnt my fingers now and then, but not severely.

One love disappointment. The sting of it lasted a couple of years, the compensation more than thirty ! I loved her all the better, perhaps, that I did not marry her. I'm afraid it is not in me to love a very good wife of my own as much as I really ought !

And I love her children as well as if they'd been mine, and her grandchildren even better. They are irresistible, these grandchildren of Barty's and Leah's—mine wouldn't have been a patch on them ; besides, I get all the fun and none of the bother and anxiety. Evidently it was my true vocation to remain single—and be a tame cat in a large, warm house, where there are lots of nice children.

O happy Bob Maurice ! O happy sexagenarian !

"O me fortunatum, mea si bona nôrim !" (What would Père Brossard say at this ? he would give me a twisted pinch on the arm—and serve me right !)

I'm very glad I've been successful, though it's not a very high achievement to make a very large fortune by buying and selling that which put into a man's mouth is said to steal away his brains !

But it does better things than this. It reconciles and solves and resolves mental discords, like music. It makes music for people who have no ear—and there are so many of these in the world that I'm a millionaire, and Franz Schubert died a pauper. So I prefer to drink beer—as *he* did ; and I never miss a Monday Pop if I can help it.

I have done better things, too. I have helped to govern my country and make its laws ; but it all came out of wine to begin with—all from learning how to buy and sell . We're a nation of shopkeepers, although the French keep better shops than ours, and more of them.

I'm glad I'm successful because of Barty, although success, which brings the world to our feet, does not always endear us to the friend of our bosom. If I had been a failure Barty would have stuck to me like a brick, I feel sure, instead of my sticking to him like a leech ! And the sight of his success might have soured me—that eternal chorus of praise, that perpetual feast of pudding in which I should have had no part but to take my share as a mere guest, and listen and look on and applaud, and wish I'd never been born !

As it is, I listened and looked on and clapped my hands with as much pride and pleasure as if Barty had been my son—and my share of the pudding never stuck in my throat !

I should have been always on the watch to take him down a peg when he was pleased with himself—to hold him cheap and overpraise some duffer in his hearing—so that I might save my own self-esteem ; to pay him bad little left-handed compliments, him and his, whenever I was out of humor ; and I should have been always out of humor, having failed in life.

And then I should have gone home wretched—for I have a conscience—and woke up in the middle of the night and thought of Barty ; and what a kind, genial, jolly, large-minded, and generous-hearted old chap he was and always had been—and buried my face in my pillow, and muttered :

" Ach ! what a poor, mean, jealous beast I am—un fruit sec ! un malheureux raté !"

With all my success, this life-long exclusive cultivation of Barty's society, and that of his artistic friends, which has somehow unfitted me for the society of my brother-merchants of wine—and most merchants of everything else—has not, I regret to say, quite fitted me to hold my own among the "leaders of intellectual modern thought," whose company I would fain seek and keep in preference to any other.

My very wealth seems to depress and disgust them, as it does me—and I'm no genius, I admit, and a poor conversationalist.

To amass wealth is an engrossing pursuit — and now
that I have amassed a good deal more than I quite know
what to do with, it seems to me a very ignoble one. It
chokes up everything that makes life worth living; it
leaves so little time for the constant and regular practice
of those ingenuous arts which faithfully to have learned
is said to soften the manners, and make one an agreeable
person all round.

It is even more *abrutissant* than the mere pursuit of
sport or pleasure.

How many a noble lord I know who's almost as beastly
rich as myself, and twice as big a fool by nature, and perhaps not a better fellow at bottom—yet who can command the society of all there is of the best in science,
literature, and art!

Not but what they will come and dine with me fast
enough, these shining lights of culture and intellect—my
food is very good, although I say it, and I get noble
lords to meet them.

But they talk their real talk to each other—not to me—
and to the noble lords who sit by them at my table, and
who try to understand what they say. With me they fall
back on politics and bimetallism, for all the pains I've
taken to get up the subjects that interest them, and keep
myself posted in all they've written and done. Precious
little they know about bimetallism or politics!

Is it only on account of their pretty manners that my
titled friends are such favorites with these highly intellectual guests of mine — and with me? If so, then
pretty manners should come before everything else in the
world, and be taught instead of Latin and Greek.

But if it's only because they're noble lords, then I'm
beginning to think with Mr. Labouchere that it's high
time the Upper House were abolished, and its denizens

wafted into space, since they make such snobs of us all—
including your humble servant, of course, who at least
is not quite so snobbish as to know himself for a damned
snob and pretend he isn't one.

Anyhow, I'm glad my life has been such a success.
But would I live it all over again ? Even the best of it?
The "forty year" ?

Taking one consideration with another, most decidedly
not.

I have only met two men of my own age who would
live their lives over again. They both cared more for
their meals than for anything else in the world—and they
have always had four of these every day ; sometimes even
five! plenty of variety, and never a meal to disagree with
them! affaire d'estomac! They simply want to eat all
those meals once more. They lived to feed, and to re-
feed would re-live !

My meals have never disagreed with me either—but I
have always found them monotonous ; they have always
been so simple and so regular when I've had the ordering
of them! Fried soles, chops or steaks, and that sort of
thing, and a pint of lager-beer—no wine for me, thank
you ; I sell it—and all this just to serve as a mere foundation for a smoke—and a chat with Barty, if possible !

Hardly ever an ache or a pain, and I wouldn't live it
all over again ! yet I hope to live another twenty years,
if only to take Leah's unborn great-grandchildren to the
dentist's, and tip them at school, and treat them to the
pantomime and Madame Tussaud's, as I did their mothers and grandmothers before them—or their fathers and
grandfathers.

This seems rather inconsistent ! For would I care,
twenty years hence, to re-live these coming twenty years?
Evidently not—it's out of the question.

417

So why don't I give up at once ? I know how to do it, without pain, without scandal, without even invalidating my life-insurance, about which I don't care a rap !

Why don't I ? why don't *you*, O middle-aged reader— with all the infirmities of age before you and all the pleasures of youth behind ? Anyhow, we don't, either you or I—and so there's an end on't.

O Pandora ! I have promised myself that I would take a great-grandchild of Barty's on a flying-machine from Marsfield to London and back in half an hour— and that great-grandchild can't well be born for several years—perhaps not for another twenty !

And now, gentle reader, I've had my little say, and I'm a good deal better, thanks, and I'll try not to talk about myself any more.

Except just to mention that in the summer of 1876 I contested East Rosherville in the Conservative interest and was successful—and owed my success to the canvassing of Barty and Leah, who had no politics of their own whatever, and would have canvassed for me just as conscientiously if I'd been a Radical, probably more so ! For if Barty had permitted himself any politics at all, he would have been a red-hot Radical, I fear—and his wife would have followed suit. And so, perhaps, would I !

27

Part Tenth

> "Je suis allé de bon matin
> Cueillir la violette,
> Et l'aubépine, et le jasmin,
> Pour célébrer ta fête.
> J'ai lié de ma propre main
> Bouton de rose et romarin
> Pour couronner ta blonde tête.
>
> "Mais de ta royale beauté
> Sois humble, je te prie.
> Ici tout meurt, la fleur, l'été,
> La jeunesse et la vie :
> Bientôt, bientôt ce jour sera,
> Ma belle, où l'on te portera
> Dans un linceul, pâle et flétrie."
> —*A Favorite Song of* MARY TREVOR'S.

THAT was a pleasant summer.

First of all we went to Ste. Adresse, a suburb of Hâvre, where there is very good bathing—with rafts, *périssoires, pique-têtes* to dive from—all those aquatic delights the French are so clever at inventing, and which make a "station balnéaire" so much more amusing than a mere British watering-place.

We made a large party and bathed together every morning ; and Barty and I taught the young ones to dive and do "la coupe" in the true orthodox form, with that free horizontal sweep of each alternate arm that gives it such distinction.

It was very good fun to see those rosy boys and girls taking their "hussardes" neatly without a splash from the little platform at the top of the pole, and solemnly performing "la coupe" in the wake of their papa ; one on his back. Right out to sea they went, I bringing up the rear—and the faithful Jean-Baptiste in attendance with his boat, and Leah inside it—her anxious eyes on the stretch to count those curly heads again and again. She was a good mathematician, and the tale always came right in the end ; and home was reached at last, and no one a bit the worse for a good long swim in those well-aired, sunlit waves.

Once we went on the top of the diligence to Étretat for the day, and there we talked of poor Bonzig and his first and last dip in the sea ; and did " la coupe " in the waters that had been so fatal to him, poor fellow !

Then we went by the steamer *Jean Bart* to Trouville and Deauville, and up the Seine in a steam-launch to Rouen.

In the afternoons and evenings we took long country walks and caught moths, or went to Hàvre by tramway and cleared out all the pastry-cooks in the Rue de Paris, and watched the transatlantic steamers, out or home, from that gay pier which so happily combines business with pleasure—utile dulci, as Père Brossard would have said—and walked home by the charming Côte d'Ingouville, sacred to the memory of Modeste Mignon.

And then, a little later on, I was a good Uncle Bob, and took the whole party to Auteuil, near Paris, and hired two lordly mansions next door to each other in the Villa Montmorency, and turned their gardens into one.

Altogether, with the Scatcherds and ourselves, eight children, governesses, nurses, and other servants, and dogs and the smaller animals, we were a very large party, and a very lively one. I like this sort of thing better than anything else in the world.

I hired carriages and horses galore, and for six weeks we made ourselves thoroughly comfortable and at home in Paris and around.

That was the happiest holiday I ever had since the vacation Barty and I spent at the Lafertés' in the Gué des Aulnes when we were school-boys.

And such was our love for the sport he called "*la chasse aux souvenirs*" that one day we actually went there, travelling by train to La Tremblaye, where we spent the night.

It was a sad disenchantment!

The old Lafertés were dead, the young ones had left that part of the country; and the house and what remained of the gardens now belonged to another family, and had become formal and mean and business-like in aspect, and much reduced in size.

Much of the outskirts of the forest had been cleared and was being cleared still, and cheap little houses run up for workmen; an immense and evil-smelling factory with a tall chimney had replaced the old home-farm, and was connected by a single line of rails with the station of La Tremblaye. The clear, pellucid stream where we used to catch crayfish had been canalized—" s'est encanaillé," as Barty called it — its waters fouled by barge traffic and all kinds of horrors.

We soon found the haunted pond that Barty was so fond of—but quite in the open, close to an enormous brick-field, and only half full; and with all its trees cut down, including the tree on which they had hanged the gay young Viscount who had behaved so badly to Séraphine Doucet, and on which Séraphine Doucet afterwards hanged herself in remorse.

No more friendly charcoal-burners, no more wolves or boars or cerfs—dix-cors ; and as for were-wolves, the very memory of them had died out.

There seems no greater desecration to me than cutting down an old and well-remembered French forest I have loved ; and solving all its mystery, and laying bare the nakedness of the land in a way so brutal and expeditious and unexpected. It reminds one of the manner in which French market-women will pluck a goose before it's quite dead ; you bristle with indignation to see it, but you mustn't interfere.

La Tremblaye itself had become a flourishing manufacturing town, and to our jaundiced and disillusioned eyes everybody and everything was as ugly as could be— and I can't say we made much of a bag in the way of souvenirs.

We were told that young Laferté was a barrister at Angers, prosperous and married. We deliberated whether we would hunt him up and talk of old times. Then we reflected how curiously cold and inhospitable Frenchmen can sometimes be to old English friends in circumstances like these—and how little they care to talk of old times and all that, unless it's the Englishman who plays the host.

Ask a quite ordinary Frenchman to come and dine with you in London, and see what a genial and charming person he can be—what a quick bosom friend, and with what a glib and silver tongue to praise the warmth of your British welcome.

Then go and call on him when you find yourself in Paris—and you will soon learn to leave quite ordinary Frenchmen alone, on their own side of the Channel.

Happily, there are exceptions to this rule !

Thus the sweet Laferté remembrance, which had so

often come back to me in my dreams, was forever spoiled by this unlucky trip.

It had turned that leaf from the tablets of my memory into a kind of palimpsest, so that I could no longer quite make out the old handwriting for the new, which would not be obliterated, and these were confused lines it was hard to read between—with all my skill!

Altogether we were uncommonly glad to get back to the Villa Montmorency—from the distorted shadows of a nightmare to happy reality.

There, all was fresh and delightful; as boys we had often seen the outside walls of that fine property which had come to the speculative builder at last, but never a glimpse within; so that there was no desecration for us in the modern laying out of that beautiful double garden of ours, whatever there might have been for such ghosts of Montmorencys as chose to revisit the glimpses of the moon.

We haunted Auteuil, Passy, Point du Jour, Suresnes, Courbevoie, Neuilly, Meudon—all the familiar places. Especially we often haunted the neighborhood of the rond point de l'Avenue du Bois de Boulogne.

One afternoon, as he and I and Leah and Ida were driving round what once was our old school, we stopped in the lane not far from the porte-cochère, and Barty stood up on the box and tried to look over the wall.

Presently, from the grand stone loge which had replaced Jaurion's den, a nice old concierge came out and asked if we desired anything. We told him how once we had been at school on that very spot, and were trying to make out the old trees that had served as bases in "la balle au camp," and that if we really desired anything just then it was that we might become school-boys once more!

"Ah, ma foi ! je comprends ça, messieurs—moi aussi, j'ai été écolier, et j'aimais bien la balle au camp," said the good old man, who had been a soldier.

He informed us the family were away, but that if we liked to come inside and see the garden he was sure his master would have no objection. We jumped at this kind offer and spent quite an hour there, and if I were Barty I could so describe the emotions of that hour that the reader would feel quite as tearfully grateful to me as to Barty Josselin for Chapters III. and IV. in *Le Fil de la Vierge,* which are really founded, *mutatis mutandis,* on this self-same little adventure of ours.

Nothing remained of our old school—not even the outer walls; nothing but the big trees and the absolute ground they grew out of. Beautiful lawns, flower - beds, conservatories, summer-houses, ferns, and evergreen shrubs made the place seem even larger than it had once been— the very reverse of what usually happens—and softened for us the disenchantment of the change.

Here, at least, was no desecration of a hallowed spot. When the past has been dead and buried a long while ago there is no sweeter decking for its grave than a rich autumn tangle, all yellow and brown and pale and hectic red, with glossy evergreens and soft, damp moss to keep up the illusion of spring and summer all the year round.

Much to the amusement of the old concierge and his wife, Barty insisted on climbing into a huge horse-chestnut tree, in which was a natural seat, very high up, where, well hidden by the dense foliage, he and I used to color pipes for boys who couldn't smoke without feeling sick.

Nothing would suit him now but that he must smoke a pipe there while we talked to the good old couple below.

" Moi aussi, je fumais quand c'était défendu ; que

voulez-vous ? Il faut bien que jeunesse se passe, n'est ce pas ?" said the old soldier.

"Ah, dame !" said his old wife, and sighed.

Every tree in this enchanted place had its history— every corner, every square yard of soil. I will not inflict these histories on the reader ; I will restrain myself with all my might, and merely state that just as the old school had been replaced by this noble dwelling the noble dwelling itself has now been replaced, trees and garden and all, by a stately palace many stories high, which rears itself among so many other stately palaces that I can't even identify the spot where once stood the Institution F. Brossard !

Later, Barty made me solemnly pledge my word that if he and Leah should pre-decease me I would see to their due cremating and the final mingling of their ashes ; that a portion of these—say half—should be set apart to be scattered on French soil, in places he would indicate in his will, and that the lion's share of that half should be sprinkled over the ground that once was our play-ground, with—or without—the legitimate owner's permission.

(Alas! and ah me! These instructions would have been carried out to the letter but that the place itself is no more ; and, with a conviction that I should be merely acting just as they would have wished, I took it on myself to mingle with their ashes those of a very sweet and darling child of theirs, dearer to them and to me and to us all than any creature ever born into this cruel universe ; and I scattered a portion of these precious remains to the four winds, close by the old spot we so loved.)

.   .   .   .

Yes, that was a memorable holiday ; the charming fête de St. Cloud was in full swing — it was delightful to haunt it once more with those dear young people so little dreamt of when Barty and I first got into scrapes there, and were duly punished by Latin verbs to conjugate in our best handwriting for Bonzig or Dumollard.

Then he and I would explore the so changed Bois de Boulogne for the little "Mare aux Biches," where his father had fallen under the sword of Lieutenant Rondelys ; but we never managed to find it : perhaps it had evaporated ; perhaps the does had drunk it all up, before they, too, had been made to vanish, before the German invader—or inside him ; for he was fond of French venison, as well as of French clocks ! He was a most omnivorous person.

Then Paris had endless charms for us both, and we relieved ourselves at last of that long homesickness of years, and could almost believe we were boys again, as we dived into such old and well-remembered streets as yet remained.

There were still some slums we had loved ; one or two of them exist even now. Only the other day I saw the Rue de Cléry, the Rue de la Lune, the Rue de la Montagne — all three on the south side of the Boulevard Bonne Nouvelle : they are still terrible to look at from the genial Boulevard, even by broad daylight—the houses so tall, so irregular, the streets so narrow and winding and black. They seemed to us boys terrible, indeed, between eight and nine on a winter's evening, with just a lamp here and there to make their darkness visible. Whither they led I can't say ; we never dared explore their obscure and mysterious recesses. They may have ended in the *cour des miracles* for all we knew—it was nearly fifty years ago—and they may be quite virtuous abodes of poverty to-day ; but they seemed to us then strange, labyrinthine abysses of crime and secret dens of infamy, where dreadful deeds were done in the dead of

long winter nights. Evidently, to us in those days, whoever should lose himself there would never see daylight
again; so we loved to visit them after dark, with our
hearts in our mouths, before going back to school.

We would sit on posts within call of the cheerful Boulevard, and watch mysterious women hurry up and down in
the cold, out of darkness into light and back again, poor
creatures—dingy moths, silent but ominous night-jars,
forlorn women of the town—ill-favored and ill-dressed,
some of them all but middle-aged, in common caps and
aprons, with cotton umbrellas, like cooks looking for a
situation.

They never spoke to us, and seemed to be often brutal-
ly repulsed by whatever men they did speak to—mostly
men in blouses.

"Ô dis-donc, *Hôr*tense! qu'y *faît* froid! quand donc qu'y
s'ra *ônze* heures, q'nous allions nous *coûcher*?"

So said one of them to another one cold, drizzly night,
in a raucous voice, with low intonations of the gutter.
The dimly felt horror and despair and pathos of it sent us
away shivering to our Passy omnibus as fast as our legs
could carry us.

That phrase has stuck in my memory ever since.
Thank Heaven! the eleventh hour must have struck
long ago, and Hortense and her friend must be fast asleep
and well out of the cold by now—they need walk those
evil streets no more. . . .

When we had exhausted it all, and we felt homesick
for England again, it was good to get back to Marsfield,
high up over the Thames—so beautiful in its rich October
colors which the river reflected—with its old trees that
grew down to the water's edge, and brooded by the boat-
house there in the mellow sunshine.

And then again when it became cold and dreary, at

Christmas-time there was my big house at Lancaster Gate, where Josselins were fond of spending some of the winter months, and where I managed to find room for them all—with a little squeezing during the Christmas holidays when the boys came home from school. What good times they were!

    .   .   .   .   .

"On May 24th, at Marsfield, Berks, the wife of Bartholomew Josselin, of a daughter"—or, as Leah put it in her diary, "our seventh daughter and ninth child—to be called Martia, or Marty for short."

It seems that Marty, prepared by her first ablution for this life, and as she lay being powdered on Mrs. Jones's motherly lap, was of a different type to her predecessors—much whiter, and lighter, and slighter; and she made no exhibition of that lusty lung-power which had so characterized the other little Barties on their introduction to this vale of tears.

Her face was more regularly formed and more highly finished, and in a few weeks grew of a beauty so solemn and pathetic that it would sometimes make Mrs. Jones, who had lost babies of her own, shed motherly tears merely to look at her.

Even *I* felt sentimental about the child; and as for Barty, he could talk of nothing else, and made those rough and hasty silver-point studies of her head and face—mere sketches—which, being full of obvious faults, became so quickly famous among æsthetic and exclusive people who had long given up Barty as a writer on account of his scandalous popularity.

Alas! even those silver-points have become popular now, and their photogravures are in the shop-windows of sea-side resorts and in the back parlors of the lower middle-class; so that the æsthetic exclusives who are up to date have had to give up Barty altogether. No one is sacred in these days—not even Shakespeare and Michael Angelo.

We shall be hearing Schumann and Wagner on the piano-organ, and "*nous autres*" of the cultured classes will have to fall back on Balfe and Byron and Landseer.

In a few months little Marty became famous for this extra beauty all over Henley and Maidenhead.

She soon grew to be the idol of her father's heart, and her mother's, and Ida's. But I really think that if there was one person who idolized her more than all the rest, it was I, Bob Maurice.

She was extremely delicate, and gave us much anxiety and many alarms, and Dr. Knight was a very constant visitor at Marsfield Lodge. It was fortunate, for her sake, that the Josselins had left Campden Hill and made their home in Marsfield.

Nine of these children—including one not yet born then—developed there into the finest and completest human beings, take them for all in all, that I have ever known; nine—a good number!

"Numero Deus impare gaudet."

Or, as poor Rapaud translated this (and was pinched black and blue by Père Brossard in consequence):

"Le numéro deux se réjouit d'être impair!" (Number two takes a pleasure in being odd!)

The three sons—one of them now in the army, as becomes a Rohan; and one a sailor, as becomes a Josselin; and one a famous actor, the true Josselin of all—are the very types of what I should like for the fathers of my grandchildren, if I had marriageable daughters of my own.

And as for Barty's daughters, they are all—but one— so well known in society and the world—so famous, I may say—that I need hardly mention them here; all but Marty, my sweet little "maid of Dove."

When Barty took Marsfield he and I had entered what I have ever since considered the happiest decade of a successful and healthy man's life—the forties.

" Wait till you get to *forty year !*"

So sang Thackeray, but with a very different experience to mine. He seemed to look upon the fifth decade as the grave of all tender illusions and emotions, and exult!

My tender illusions and emotions became realties— things to live by and for. As Barty and I " dipped our noses in the Gascon wine "—Vougeot - Conti & Co.—I blessed my stars for being free of Marsfield, which was, and is still, my real home, and for the warm friendship of its inhabitants who have been my real family, and for several years of unclouded happiness all round.

Even in winter what a joy it was, after a long solitary walk, or ride, or drive, or railway journey, to suddenly find myself at dusk in the midst of all that warmth and light and gayety ; what a contrast to the House of Commons; what a relief after Barge Yard or Downing Street; what tea that was, what crumpets and buttered toast, what a cigarette ; what romps and jokes, and really jolly good fun; and all that delightful untaught music that afterwards became so cultivated! Music was a special inherited gift of the entire family, and no trouble or expense was ever spared to make the best and the most of it.

Roberta became the most finished and charming amateur pianist I ever heard, and as for Mary *la rossignolle* —Mrs. Trevor—she's almost as famous as if she had made singing her profession, as she once so wished to do. She married happily instead, a better profession still ; and though her songs are as highly paid for as any—except, perhaps, Madame Patti's—every penny goes to the poor.

She can make a nigger melody sound worthy of Schubert and a song of Schumann go down with the common herd as if it were a nigger melody, and obtain a genuine encore for it from quite simple people.

Why, only the other night she and her husband dined with me at the Bristol, and we went to Baron Schwartzkind's in Piccadilly to meet Royal Highnesses.

Up comes the Baron with:

"Ach, Mrs. Drefor! vill you not zing zomzing? ze Brincess vould be so jarmt."

"I'll sing as much as you like, Baron, if you promise me you'll send a checque for £50 to the Foundling Hospital to-morrow morning," says Mary.

"*I'll* send *another* fifty, Baron," says Bob Maurice. And the Baron had to comply, and Mary sang again and again, and the Princess was more than charmed.

She declared herself enchanted, and yet it was Brahms and Schumann that Mary sang; no pretty little English ballad, no French, no Italian.

> " Aus meinen Thränen spriessen
>   Viel' blühende Blumen hervor ;
> Und meine Seufze werden
>   Ein Nachtigallen Chor. . . ."

So sang Mary, and I declare some of the royal eyes were moist.

They all sang and played, these Josselins; and tumbled and acted, and were droll and original and fetching, as their father had been and was still; and, like him, amiable and full of exuberant life ; and, like their mother, kind and appreciative and sympathetic and ever thoughtful of others, without a grain of selfishness or conceit.

"'I DON'T THINK I EVER HEARD HIM MENTION YOUR NAME'"

They were also great athletes, boys and girls alike; good swimmers and riders, and first-rate oars. And though not as good at books and lessons as they might have been, they did not absolutely disgrace themselves, being so quick and intelligent.

Amid all this geniality and liveliness at home and this beauty of surrounding nature abroad, little Marty seemed to outgrow in a measure her constitutional delicacy.

It was her ambition to become as athletic as a boy, and she was persevering in all physical exercises—and threw stones very straight and far, with a quite easy masculine sweep of the arm; I taught her myself.

It was also her ambition to draw, and she would sit for an hour or more on a high stool by her father, or on the arm of his chair, and watch him at his work in silence. Then she would get herself paper and pencil, and try and do likewise; but discouragement would overtake her, and she would have to give it up in despair, with a heavy sigh and a clouded look on her lovely little pale face; and yet they were surprisingly clever, these attempts of hers.

Then she took to dictating a novel to her sisters and to me: it was all about an immense dog and three naughty boys, who were awful dunces at school and ran away to sea, dog and all; and performed heroic deeds in Central Africa, and grew up there, "booted and bearded, and burnt to a brick!" and never married or fell in love, or stooped to any nonsense of that kind.

This novel, begun in the handwriting of all of us, and continued in her own, remained unfinished; and the precious MS. is now in my possession. I have read it oftener than any other novel, French or English, except, perhaps, *Vanity Fair !*

I may say that I had something to do with the devel-

433

opment of her literary faculty, as I read many good books to her before she could read quite comfortably for herself : *Evenings at Home, The Swiss Family Robinson, Gulliver, Robinson Crusoe,* books by Ballantyne, Marryat, Mayne Reid, Jules Verne, etc., and *Treasure Island, Tom Sawyer, Huckleberry Finn, The Wreck of the Grosvenor,* and then her father's books, or some of them.

But even better than her famous novel were the stories she improvised to me in a small boat which I often rowed up-stream while she steered—one story, in particular, that had no end ; she would take it up at any time.

She had imagined a world where all trees and flowers and vegetation (and some birds) were the size they are now ; but men and beasts no bigger than Lilliputians, with houses and churches and buildings to match—and a family called Josselin living in a beautiful house called Marsfield, as big as a piano organ.

Endless were the adventures by flood and field of these little people : in the huge forest and on the gigantic river which it took them nearly an hour to cross in a steam-launch when the wind was high, or riding trained carrier - pigeons to distant counties, and the coasts of Normandy, Brittany, and Picardy, where everything was on a similar scale.

It would astonish me to find how vivid and real she could make these imaginations of hers, and to me how fascinating—oddly enough she reserved them for me only, and told no one else.

There was always an immensely big strong man, one Bobby Maurice, a good-natured giant, nearly three inches high and over two ounces in weight, who among other feats would eat a whole pea at a sitting, and hold out an

28

acorn at arm's-length, and throw a pepper-corn over two
yards—which has remained the record.

Then, coming back down-stream, she would take the
sculls and I the tiller, and I would tell her (in French)
all about our school adventures at Brossard's and
Bonzig, and the Lafertés, and the Revolution of February; and in that way she picked up a lot of useful
and idiomatic Parisian which considerably astonished
Fräulein Werner, the German governess, who yet knew
French almost as well as her own language—almost as
well as Mr. Ollendorff himself.

She also changed one of the heroes in her famous
novel, *Tommy Holt*, into a French boy, and called him
Rapaud!

She was even more devoted to animals than the rest
of the family : the beautiful Angora, Kitty, died when
Marty was five, from an abscess in her cheek, where
she'd been bitten by a strange bull-terrier; and Marty
tearfully wrote her epitaph in a beautiful round hand—

> "Here lies Kitty, full of grace ;
> Died of an *abbess* in her face !"

This was her first attempt at verse-making, and here's
her last, from the French of Sully-Prudhomme :

> "If you but knew what tears, alas !
> One weeps for kinship unbestowed,
> In pity you would sometimes pass
> My poor abode !

> "If you but knew what balm, for all
> Despond, lies in an angel's glance,
> Your looks would on my window fall
> As though by chance !

435

> " If you but knew the heart's delight
> To feel its fellow-heart is by,
> You'd linger, as a sister might,
> These gates anigh !

> "If you but knew how oft I yearn
> For one sweet voice, one presence dear,
> Perhaps you'd even simply turn
> And enter here !''

She was only just seventeen when she wrote them, and, upon my word, I think they're almost as good as the original !

Her intimate friendship with Chucker-out, the huge St. Bernard, lasted for nearly both their lives, alas ! It began when they both weighed exactly the same, and I could carry both in one arm. When he died he turned the scale at sixteen stone, like me.

It has lately become the fashion to paint big dogs and little girls, and engravings of these pictures are to be seen in all the print-sellers' shops. It always touches me very much to look at these works of art, although —and I hope it is not libellous to say so—the big dog is always hopelessly inferior in beauty and dignity and charm to Chucker-out, who was champion of his day. And as for the little girls— *Ah, mon Dieu!*

Such pictures are not high art of course, and that is why I don't possess one, as I've got an æsthetic character to keep up ; but why they shouldn't be I can't guess. Is it because no high artist—except Briton Riviere—will stoop to so easily understood a subject ?

A great master would not be above painting a small child or a big dog separately—why should he be above putting them both in the same picture ? It would be too obvious, I suppose—like a melody by Mozart, or Handel's "Harmonious Blacksmith," or Schubert's Serenade, and other catchpenny tunes of the same description.

I was also very intimate with Chucker-out, who made more of me than he even did of his master.

One night I got very late to Marsfield by the last train, and, letting myself in with my key, I found Chucker-out waiting for me in the hall, and apparently in a very anxious frame of mind, and extremely demonstrative, wanting to say something more than usual—to confide a trouble, to confess !

We went up into the big music-room, which was still lighted, and lay on a couch together ; he, with his head on my knees, whimpering softly as I smoked and read a paper.

Presently Leah came in and said :

"Such an unfortunate thing happened ; Marty and Chucker - out were playing on the slope, and he knocked her down and sprained her knee."

As soon as Chucker-out heard Marty's name he sat up and whined piteously, and pawed me down with great violence ; pawed three buttons off my waistcoat and broke my watch-chain—couldn't be comforted ; the misadventure had been preying on his mind for hours.

I give this subject to Mr. Briton Riviere, who can paint both dogs and children, and everything else he likes. I will sit for him myself, if he wishes, and as a Catholic priest ! He might call it a confession—and an absolution ! or, "The Secrets of the Confessional."

The good dog became more careful in future, and restrained his exuberance even going down - stairs with Marty on the way to a ramble in the woods, which excited him more than anything ; if he came down - stairs with anybody else, the violence of his joy was such that one had to hold on by the banisters. He was a dear, good beast, and a splendid body - guard for Marty in her solitary woodland rambles—never left her side for a second. I have often watched him from a distance, unbeknown to both ; he was proud of his responsibility—almost fussy about it.

I have been fond of many dogs, but never yet loved a dog as I loved big Chucker-out—or *Choucroûte*, as Coralie, the French maid, called him, to Fräulein Werner's annoyance (Choucroûte is French for sauerkraut) ; and I like to remember him in his splendid prime, guarding his sweet little mistress, whom I loved better than anything else on earth. She was to me a kind of pet Marjorie, and said such droll and touching things that I could almost fill a book with them. I kept a diary on purpose, and called it Martiana.

She was tall, but lamentably thin and slight, poor dear, with her mother's piercing black eyes and the very fair curly locks of her papa — a curious and most effective contrast—and features and a complexion of such extraordinary delicacy and loveliness that it almost gave one pain in the midst of the keen pleasure one had in the mere looking at her.

Heavens ! how that face would light up suddenly at catching the unexpected sight of some one she was fond of ! How often it has lighted up at the unexpected sight of " Uncle Bob"! The mere remembrance of that sweet illumination brightens my old age for me now ; and I could almost wish her back again, in my senile selfishness and inconsistency. Pazienza !

Sometimes she was quite embarrassing in her simplicity, and reminded me of her father.

Once in Dieppe—when she was about eight—she and I had gone through the Établissement to bathe, and people had stared at her even more than usual and whispered to each other.

"I bet you don't know why they all stare so, Uncle Bob ?"

"I give it up," said I.

"It's because I'm so *handsome*—we're *all* handsome, you know, and I'm the handsomest of the lot, it seems ! *You*'re *not* handsome, Uncle Bob. But oh ! aren't you *strong !* Why, you could tuck a piou-piou under one arm and a postman under the other and walk up to the castle with them and pitch them into the sea, *couldn't* you? And that's better than being handsome, *isn't* it ? I wish *I* was like that."

And here she cuddled and kissed my hand.

When Mary began to sing (under Signor R.) it was her custom of an afternoon to lock herself up alone with a tuning-fork in a large garret and practise, as she was shy of singing exercises before any one else.

Her voice, even practising scales, would give Marty extraordinary pleasure, and me, too. Marty and I have often sat outside and listened to Mary's rich and fluent vocalizings ; and I hoped that Marty would develop a great voice also, as she was so like Mary in face and disposition, except that Mary's eyes were blue and her hair very black, and her health unexceptionable.

Marty did not develop a real voice, although she sang very prettily and confidentially to me, and worked hard at the piano with Roberta ; she learned harmony and composed little songs, and wrote words to them, and Mary or her father would sing them to her and make her happy beyond description.

Happy ! she was always happy during the first few years of her life—from five or six to twelve.

I like to think her happiness was so great for this

brief period, that she had her full share of human felicity just as if she had lived to the age of the Psalmist.

It seemed everybody's business at Marsfield to see that Marty had a good time. This was an easy task, as she was so easy to amuse; and when amused, herself so amusing to others.

As for me, it is hardly too much to say that every hour I could spare from business and the cares of state was spent in organizing the amusement of little Marty Josselin, and I was foolish enough to be almost jealous of her own father and mother's devotion to the same object.

Unlike her brothers and sisters, she was a studious little person, and fond of books—too much so indeed, for all she was such a tomboy ; and all this amusement was designed by us with the purpose of winning her away from the too sedulous pursuit of knowledge. I may add that in temper and sweetness of disposition the child was simply angelic, and could not be spoiled by any spoiling.

It was during these happy years at Marsfield that Barty, although bereft of his Martia ever since that farewell letter, managed, nevertheless, to do his best work, on lines previously laid down for him by her.

For the first year or two he missed the feeling of the north most painfully—it was like the loss of a sense—but he grew in time accustomed to the privation, and quite resigned ; and Marty, whom he worshipped—as did her mother—compensated him for the loss of his demon.

Inaccessible Heights, Floréal et Fructidor, The Infinitely Little, The Northern Pactolus, Pandore et sa Boîte, Cancer and Capricorn, Phœbus et Séléné followed each other in leisurely succession. And he also found time for those controversies that so moved and amused the world ; among others, his famous and triumphant confutation of Canon ——, on one hand, and Professor ——, the famous scientist, on the other, which has been compared to the classic litigation about the oyster, since the oyster itself fell to Barty's share, and a shell to each of the two disputants.

Orthodox and agnostic are as the poles asunder, yet they could not but both agree with Barty Josselin, who so cleverly extended a hand to each, and acted as a conductor between them.

That irresistible optimism which so forces itself upon all Josselin's readers, who number by now half the world, and will probably one day include the whole of it—when the whole of it is civilized—belonged to him by nature, by virtue of his health and his magnificent physique and his happy circumstances, and an admirably balanced mind, which was better fitted for his particular work and for the world's good than any special gift of genius in one direction.

His literary and artistic work never cost him the slightest effort. It amused him to draw and write more than did anything else in the world, and he always took great pains, and delighted in taking them ; but himself he never took seriously for one moment — never realized what happiness he gave, and was quite unconscious of the true value of all he thought and wrought and taught !

He laughed good-humoredly at the passionate praise that for thirty years was poured upon him from all quarters of the globe, and shrugged his shoulders at the coarse invective of those whose religious susceptibilities he had so innocently wounded ; left all published insults unanswered ; never noticed any lie printed about himself —never wrote a paragraph in explanation or self-defence, but smoked many pipes and mildly wondered.

Indeed he was mildly wondering all his life : at his luck—at all the ease and success and warm domestic bliss that had so compensated him for the loss of his left eye and would almost have compensated him for the loss of both.

"It's all because I'm so deuced good-looking !" says Barty—"and so's Leah !"

And all his life he sorrowed for those who were less fortunate than himself. His charities and those of his wife were immense—he gave all the money, and she took all the trouble.

"C'est papa qui paie et maman qui régale," as Marty would say ; and never were funds distributed more wisely.

But often at odd moments the Weltschmerz, the sorrow of the world, would pierce this man who no longer felt sorrows of his own—stab him through and through—bring the sweat to his temples—fill his eyes with that strange pity and trouble that moved you so deeply when you caught the look ; and soon the complicated anguish of that dim regard would resolve itself into gleams of a quite celestial sweetness—and a heavenly message would go forth to mankind in such simple words that all might read who ran. . . .

All these endowments of the heart and brain, which in him were masculine and active, were possessed in a passive form by his wife ; instead of the buoyant energy and boisterous high spirits, she had patience and persistency that one felt to be indomitable, and a silent sympathy that never failed, and a fund of cheerfulness and good sense on which any call might be made by life without fear of bankruptcy; she was of those who could play a losing game and help others to play it—and she never had a losing game to play !

These gifts were inherited by their children, who, moreover, were so fed on their father's books—so imbued with them—that one felt sure of their courage, endurance, and virtue, whatever misfortunes or temptations might assail them in this life.

One felt this especially with the youngest but one, Marty, who, with even more than her due share of those gifts of the head and heart they had all inherited from their two parents, had not inherited their splendid frames and invincible health.

Roderick, *alias* Mark Tapley, *alias* Chips, who is now the sailor, was, oddly enough, the strongest and the hardiest of the whole family, and yet he was born two years after Marty. She always declared she brought him up and made a man of him, and taught him how to throw stones, and how to row and ride and swim ; and that it was entirely to her he owed it that he was worthy to be a sailor—her ideal profession for a man.

He was devoted to her, and a splendid little chap, and in the holidays he and she and I were inseparable, and of course Chucker-out, who went with us wherever it was—Hâvre, Dieppe, Dinard, the Highlands, Whitby, etc.

Once we were privileged to settle ourselves for two months in Castle Rohan, through the kindness of Lord Whitby; and that was the best holiday of all—for the young people especially. And more especially for Barty himself, who had such delightful boyish recollections of that delightful place, and found many old friends among the sailors and fisher people—who remembered him as a boy.

Chips and Marty and I and the faithful Chucker-out were never happier than on those staiths where there is always such an ancient and fishlike smell ; we never tired of watching the miraculous draughts of silver herring being disentangled from the nets and counted into baskets, which were carried on the heads of the stalwart, scaly fishwomen, and packed with salt and ice in innumerable barrels for Billingsgate and other great markets; or else the sales by auction of huge cod and dark-gray dog-fish as they lay helpless all of a row on the wet flags amid a crowd of sturdy mariners looking on, with their hands in their pockets and their pipes in their mouths.

Then over that restless little bridge to the picturesque old town, and through its long, narrow street, and up the many stone steps to the ruined abbey and the old church on the East Cliff; and the old churchyard, where there are so many stones in memory of those who were lost at sea.

It was good to be there, in such good company, on a sunny August morning, and look around and about and down below : the miles and miles of purple moor, the woods of Castle Rohan, the wide North Sea, which turns such a heavenly blue beneath a cloudless sky ; the two stone piers, with each its lighthouse, and little people patiently looking across the waves for Heaven knows what ! the busy harbor full of life and animation ; under our feet the red roofs of the old town and the little clock tower of the market-place ; across the stream the long quay with its ale-houses and emporiums and jet shops and lively traffic ; its old gabled dwellings and their rotting wooden balconies. And rising out of all this, tier upon tier, up the opposite cliff, the Whitby of the visitors, dominated by a gigantic windmill that is—or was—almost as important a landmark as the old abbey itself.

To the south the shining river ebbs and flows, between its big ship-building yards and the railway to York, under endless moving craft and a forest of masts, now straight on end, now slanting helplessly on one side when there's

not water enough to float their keels ; and the long row
of Cornish fishing-smacks, two or three deep.

How the blue smoke of their cooking wreathes up-
ward in savory whiffs and whirls ! They are good cooks,
these rovers from Penzance, and do themselves well, and
remind us that it is time to go and get lunch at the hotel.

We do, and do ourselves uncommonly well also ; and
afterwards we take a boat, we four (if the tide serves),
and row up for a mile or so to a certain dam at Ruswarp,
and there we take another boat on a lovely little secluded
river, which is quite independent of tides, and where for
a mile or more the trees bend over us from either side as
we leisurely paddle along and watch the leaping salmon-
trout, pulling now and then under a drooping ash or
weeping-willow to gaze and dream or chat, or read out
loud from *Sylvia's Lovers ;* Sylvia Robson once lived in
a little farm - house near Upgang, which we know well,
and at Whitby every one reads about Sylvia Robson ; or
else we tell stories, or inform each other what a jolly
time we're having, and tease old Chucker-out, who gets
quite excited, and we admire the discretion with which
he disposes of his huge body as ballast to trim the boat,
and remains perfectly still in spite of his excitement for
fear he should upset us. Indeed, he has been learning
all his life how to behave in boats, and how to get in and
out of them.

And so on till tea - time at five, and we remember
there's a little inn at Sleights, where the scones are good ;
or, better still, a leafy garden full of raspberry-bushes at
Cock Mill, where they give excellent jam with your tea,
and from which there are three ways of walking back to
Whitby when there's not enough water to row—and
which is the most delightful of those three ways has
never been decided yet.

Then from the stone pier we watch a hundred brown-sailed Cornish fishing-smacks follow each other in single file across the harbor bar and go sailing out into the west as the sun goes down—a most beautiful sight, of which Marty feels all the mystery and the charm and the pathos, and Chips all the jollity and danger and romance.

Then to the trap, and home all four of us *au grand trot*, between the hedge-rows and through the splendid woods of Castle Rohan; there at last we find all the warmth and light and music and fun of Marsfield, and many good things besides : supper, dinner, tea—all in one; and happy, healthy, hungry, indefatigable boys and girls who've been trapesing over miles and miles of moor and fell, to beautiful mills and dells and waterfalls—too many miles for slender Marty or little Chips ; or even Bob and Chucker-out — who weigh thirty - two stone between them, and are getting lazy in their old age, and fat and scant of breath.

Whitby is an ideal place for young people; it almost makes old people feel young themselves there when the young are about ; there is so much to do.

I, being the eldest of the large party, chummed most of the time with the two youngest and became a boy again ; so much so that I felt myself almost a sneak when I tactfully tried to restrain such exuberance of spirits on their part as might have led them into mischief : indeed it was difficult not to lead them into mischief myself ; all the old inventiveness (that had got me and others into so many scrapes at Brossard's) seemed to come back, enhanced by experience and maturity.

At all events, Marty and Chips were happier with me than without—of that I feel quite sure, for I tested it in many ways.

I always took immense pains to devise the kinds of excursion that would please them best, and these never seemed to fail of their object; and I was provident and well skilled in all details of the commissariat (Chips was healthily alimentative); I was a very *Bradshaw* at trains and times and distances, and also, if I am not bragging too much, and making myself out an Admirable Crichton, extremely weatherwise, and good at carrying small people pickaback when they got tired.

Marty was well up in local folk-lore, and had mastered the history of Whitby and St. Hilda, and Sylvia Robson; and of the old obsolete whaling-trade, in which she took a passionate interest; and fixed poor little Chips's mind with a passion for the Polar regions (he is now on the coast of Senegambia).

We were much on the open sea ourselves, in cobles; sometimes the big dog with us—"Joomboa," as the fishermen called him; and they marvelled at his good manners and stately immobility in a boat.

One afternoon—a perfect afternoon—we took tea at Runswick, from which charming little village the Whitbys take their second title, and had ourselves rowed round the cliffs to Staithes, which we reached just before sunset; Chips and his sister also taking an oar between them, and I another. There, on the brink of the little bay, with the singularly quaint and picturesque old village behind it, were fifty fishing-boats side by side waiting to be launched, and all the fishing population of Staithes were there to launch them—men, women and children; as we landed we were immediately pressed into the service.

Marty and Chips, wild with enthusiasm, pushed and yo-ho'd with the best; and I also won some commendation by my hearty efforts in the common cause. Soon the coast was clear of all but old men and boys, women and children, and our four selves; and the boats all sailed westward, in a cluster, and lost themselves in the golden haze. It was the prettiest sight I ever saw, and we were all quite romantic about it.

Chucker-out held a small court on the sands, and was worshipped and fed with stale fish by a crowd of good-looking and agreeable little lasses and lads who called him "Joomboa," and pressed Chips and Marty for biographical details about him, and were not disappointed. And I smoked a pipe of pipes with some splendid old salts, and shared my Honeydew among them.

Nous étions bien, là !

So sped those happy weeks—with something new and exciting every day—even on rainy days, when we wore waterproofs and big india-rubber boots and sou'westers, and Chucker-out's coat got so heavy with the soak that he could hardly drag himself along : and we settled, we three at least, that we would never go to France or Scotland—never any more—never anywhere in the world but Whitby, jolly Whitby—

Ah me ! l'homme propose. . . .

Marty always wore a red woollen fisherman's cap that hung down behind over the waving masses of her long, thick yellow hair—a blue jersey of the elaborate kind women knit on the Whitby quay—a short, striped petticoat like a Boulogne fishwife's, and light brown stock-ings on her long, thin legs.

I have a photograph of her like that, holding a shrimp-ing-net; with a magnifying-glass, I can see the little high-light in the middle of each jet-black eye—and every detail and charm and perfection of her childish face. Of all the art-treasures I've amassed in my long life, that is to me the most beautiful, far and away—but I can't look at it yet for more than a second at a time . . .

"O tempo passato, perchè non ritorni?"

As Mary is so fond of singing to me sometimes, when she thinks I've got the blues. As if I haven't always got the blues!

All Barty's teaching is thrown away on me, now that he's not here himself to point his moral—

"Et je m'en vais
Au vent mauvais
Qui m'emporte
Deçà, delà,
Pareil à la
Feuille morte . . ."

Heaven bless thee, Mary dear, rossignolet de mon âme! Would thou wert ever by my side! fain would I keep thee for myself in a golden cage, and feed thee on the tongues of other nightingales, so thou mightst warble every day, and all day long. By some strange congenital mystery the native tuning of thy voice is such, for me, that all the pleasure of my past years seems to go forever ringing in every single note. Thy dear mother speaks again, thy gay young father rollicks and jokes and sings, and little Marty laughs her happy laugh.

Da capo, e da capo, Mary—only at night shouldst thou cease from thy sweet pipings, that I might smoke myself to sleep, and dream that all is once more as it used to be.

.   .   .   .

The writing, such as it is, of this life of Barty Josselin—which always means the writing of so much of my own—has been to me, up to the present moment, a great source of consolation, almost of delight, when the pen was in my hand and I dived into the past.

But now the story becomes such a record of my own

449

personal grief that I have scarcely the courage to go on ;
I will get through it as quickly as I can.

It was at the beginning of the present decade that the
bitter thing arose—medio de fonte leporum ; just as all
seemed so happy and secure at Marsfield.

One afternoon in May I arrived at the house, and nobody was at home; but I was told that Marty was in the
wood with old Chucker-out, and I went thither to find
her, loudly whistling a bar which served as a rallying sig-
nal to the family.   It was not answered, but after a long
hunt I found Marty lying on the ground at the foot of a
tree, and Chucker-out licking her face and hands.

She had been crying, and seemed half-unconscious.

When I spoke to her she opened her eyes and said :

"Oh, Uncle Bob, I *have* hurt myself so!   I fell down
that tree.   Do you think you could carry me home?"

Beside myself with terror and anxiety, I took her up as
gently as I could, and made my way to the house.   She
had hurt the base of her spine as she fell on the roots of
the tree ; but she seemed to get better as soon as Sparrow, the nurse, had undressed her and put her to bed.

I sent for the doctor, however, and he thought, after
seeing her, that I should do well to send for Dr. Knight.

Just then Leah and Barty came in, and we telegraphed
for Dr. Knight, who came at once.

Next day Dr. Knight thought he had better have
Sir —— ——, and there was a consultation.

Marty kept her bed for two or three days, and then
seemed to have completely recovered but for a slight internal disturbance, brought on by the concussion, and
which did not improve.

One day Dr. Knight told me he feared very much that
this would end in a kind of ataxia of the lower limbs—it
might be sooner or later; indeed, it was Sir —— ——'s

29

opinion that it would be sure to do so in the end—that spinal paralysis would set in, and that the child would become a cripple for life, and for a life that would not be long.

I had to tell this to her father and mother.

.   .   .   .

Marty, however, recovered all her high spirits. It was as if nothing had happened or could happen, and during six months everything at Marsfield went on as usual but for the sickening fear that we three managed to conceal in our hearts, even from each other.

At length, one day as Marty and I were playing lawn-tennis, she suddenly told me that her feet felt as if they were made of lead, and I knew that the terrible thing had come. . . .

I must really pass over the next few months.

In the summer of the following year she could scarcely walk without assistance, and soon she had to go about in a bath-chair.

Soon, also, she ceased to be conscious when her lower limbs were pinched and pricked till an interval of about a second had elapsed, and this interval increased every month. She had no natural consciousness of her legs and feet whatever unless she saw them, although she could move them still and even get in and out of bed, or in and out of her bath-chair, without much assistance, so long as she could see her lower limbs. Often she would stumble and fall down, even on a grassy lawn. In the dark she could not control her movements at all.

She was also in constant pain, and her face took on permanently the expression that Barty's often wore when he thought he was going blind in Malines, although, like him in those days, she was always lively and droll, in spite of this heavy misfortune, which seemed to break every heart at Marsfield except her own.

For, alas! Barty Josselin, who has so lightened for us the sorrow of mere bereavement, and made quick-coming death a little thing — for some of us, indeed, a lovely thing—has not taught us how to bear the sufferings of those we love, the woful ache of pity for pangs we are powerless to relieve and can only try to share.

Endeavor as I will, I find I cannot tell this part of my story as it should be told; it should be a beautiful story of sweet young feminine fortitude and heroic resignation —an angel's story.

During the four years that Martia's illness lasted the only comfort I could find in life was to be with her— reading to her, teaching her blaze, rowing her on the river, driving her, pushing or dragging her bath-chair; but, alas! watching her fade day by day.

Strangely enough, she grew to be the tallest of all her sisters, and the most beautiful in the face; she was so wasted and thin she could hardly be said to have had a body or limbs at all.

I think the greatest pleasure she had was to lie and be sung to by Mary or her father, or played to by Roberta, or chatted to about domestic matters by Leah, or read to by me. She took the keenest interest in everything that concerned us all; she lived out of herself entirely, and from day to day, taking short views of life.

It filled her with animation to see the people who came to the house and talk with them; and among these she made many passionately devoted friends.

There were also poor children from the families of laborers in the neighborhood, in whom she had always taken a warm interest. She now organized them into regular classes, and taught and amused them and told them stories, sang funny songs to them, and clothed and fed them with nice things, and they grew to her an immense hobby and constant occupation.

She also became a quite surprising performer on the banjo, which her father had taught her when she was quite a little girl, and invented charming tunes and effects and modulations that had never been tried on that humble instrument before. She could have made a handsome living out of it, crippled as she was.

She seemed the busiest, drollest, and most contented person in Marsfield; she all but consoled us for the dreadful thing that had happened to herself, and laughingly pitied us for pitying her.

So much for the teaching of Barty Josselin, whose books she knew by heart, and constantly read and reread.

And thus, in spite of all, the old, happy, resonant cheerfulness gradually found its way back to Marsfield, as though nothing had happened ; and poor broken Marty, who had always been our idol, became our goddess, our prop and mainstay, the angel in the house, the person for every one to tell their troubles to—little or big — their jokes, their good stories ; there was never a laugh like hers, so charged with keen appreciation of the humorous thing, the relish of which would come back to her again and again at any time—even in the middle of the night when she could not always sleep for her pain ; and she would laugh anew.

Ida Scatcherd and I, with good Nurse Sparrow to help, wished to take her to Italy—to Egypt—but she would not leave Marsfield, unless it were to spend the winter months with all of us at Lancaster Gate, or the autumn in the Highlands or on the coast of Normandy.

And indeed neither Barty nor Leah nor the rest could

have got on without her; they would have had to come, too — brothers, sisters, young husbands, grandchildren, and all.

Never but once did she give way. It was one June evening, when I was reading to her some favorite short poems out of Browning's *Men and Women* on a small lawn surrounded with roses, and of which she was fond.

The rest of the family were on the river, except her father and mother, who were dressing to go and dine with some neighbors; for a wonder, as they seldom dined away from home.

The carriage drove up to the door to fetch them, and they came out on the lawn to wish us good-night.

Never had I been more struck with the splendor of Barty and his wife, now verging towards middle age, as they bent over to kiss their daughter, and he cut capers and cracked little jokes to make her laugh.

Leah's hair was slightly gray and her magnificent figure somewhat matronly, but there were no other signs of autumn; her beautiful white skin was still as delicate as a baby's, her jet-black eyes as bright and full, her teeth just as they were thirty years back.

Tall as she was, her husband towered over her, the finest and handsomest man of his age I have ever seen. And Marty gazed after them with her heart in her eyes as they drove off.

"How splendid they are, Uncle Bob!"

Then she looked down at her own shrunken figure and limbs—her long, wasted legs and her thin, slight feet that were yet so beautifully shaped.

And, hiding her face in her hands, she began to cry:

"And I'm their poor little daughter—oh dear, oh dear!"

455

She wept silently for a while, and I said nothing, but endured an agony such as I cannot describe.

Then she dried her eyes and smiled, and said :

"What a goose I am," and, looking at me—

"Oh! Uncle Bob, forgive me ; I've made you very unhappy—it shall never happen again !"

Suddenly the spirit moved me to tell her the story of Martia.

Leah and Barty and I had often discussed whether she should be told this extraordinary thing, in which we never knew whether to believe or not, and which, if there were a possibility of its being true, concerned Marty so directly.

They settled that they would leave it entirely to me— to tell her or not, as my own instinct would prompt me, should the opportunity occur.

My instinct prompted me to do so now. I shall not forget that evening.

The full moon rose before the sun had quite set, and I talked on and on. The others came in to dinner. She and I had some dinner brought to us out there, and on I talked — and she could scarcely eat for listening. I wrapped her well up, and lit pipe after pipe, and went on talking, and a nightingale sang, but quite unheard by Marty Josselin.

She did not even hear her sister Mary, whose voice went lightly up to heaven through the open window :

"Oh that we two were maying!"

And when we parted that night she thanked and kissed me so effusively I felt that I had been happily inspired.

"I believe every word of it's true ; I know it, I feel it ! Uncle Bob, you have changed my life ; I have often desponded when nobody knew—but never again! Dear papa! Only think of him! As if any human being alive could write what he has written without help from above or outside. Of course it's all true; I sometimes think I can almost remember things. . . . I'm sure I can."

Barty and Leah were well pleased with me when they came home that night.

That Marty was doomed to an early death did not very deeply distress them. It is astonishing how lightly they thought of death, these people for whom life seemed so full of joy; but that she should ever be conscious of the anguish of her lot while she lived was to them intolerable —a haunting preoccupation.

To me, a narrower and more selfish person, Marty had almost become to me life itself—her calamity had made her mine forever; and life without her had become a thing not to be conceived: her life was my life.

That life of hers was to be even shorter than we thought, and I love to think that what remained of it was made so smooth and sweet by what I told her that night.

I read all Martia's blaze letters to her, and helped her to read them for herself, and so did Barty. She got to know them by heart—especially the last; she grew to talk as Martia wrote; she told me of strange dreams she had often had—dreams she had told Sparrow and her own brothers and sisters when she was a child—wondrous dreams, in their seeming confirmation of what seemed to us so impossible. Her pains grew slighter and ceased.

And now her whole existence had become a dream—a tranquil, happy dream; it showed itself in her face, its transfigured, unearthly beauty—in her cheerful talk, her eager sympathy; a kind of heavenly pity she seemed to feel for those who had to go on living out their normal length of days. And always the old love of fun and frolic and pretty tunes.

Her father would make her laugh till she cried, and the same fount of tears would serve when Mary sang Brahms and Schubert and Lassen to her—and Roberta played Chopin and Schumann by the hour.

So she might have lived on for a few years—four or five—even ten. But she died at seventeen, of mere influenza, very quickly and without much pain. Her father and mother were by her bedside when her spirit passed away, and Dr. Knight, who had brought her into the world.

She woke from a gentle doze and raised her head, and called out in a clear voice :

"Barty—Leah—come to me, come !"

And fell back dead.

Barty bowed his head and face on her hand, and remained there as if asleep. It was Leah who drew her eyelids down.

An hour later Dr. Knight came to me, his face distorted with grief.

"It's all over ?" I said.

"Yes, it's all over."

"And Leah ?"

"Mrs. Josselin is with her husband. She's a noble woman ; she seems to bear it well."

"And Barty ?"

"Barty Josselin is no more."

THE END

GLOSSARY

GLOSSARY

[First figure indicates Page; second figure, Line.]

3, 26. *odium theologicum* — theological hatred.

3, 27. *sæva indignatio*—fierce indignation.

5, 1. " *De Paris à Versailles*," etc.—
" From Paris to Versailles, lon, là,
From Paris to Versailles—
There are many fine walks,
Hurrah for the King of France !
There are many fine walks,
Hurrah for the schoolboys !"

5, 2. *salle d'études des petits*—study-room of the smaller boys.

6, 11. *parloir*—parlor.

6, 14. *e da capo*—and over again.

6, 16. *le Grand Bonzig*—the Big Bonzig.

6, 17. *estrade*—platform.

8, 2. *à la malcontent*—convict style.

8, 5. *ceinture de gymnastique*—a wide gymnasium belt.

8, 16. *marchand de coco* — licorice-water seller.

8, 17. *Orphéonistes*—members of musical societies.

8, 32. *exceptis excipiendis*—exceptions being made.

9, 10. " *Infandum, regina, jubes renovare* " (" *dolorem* "), etc.
" Thou orderest me, O queen, to renew the unutterable grief."

9, 17. " *Mouche-toi donc, animal ! tu me dégoûtes, à la fin !*"—" Blow your nose, you beast, you disgust me !"

9, 20. " *Taisez-vous, Maurice—ou je vous donne cent vers à copier !*"—
" Hold your tongue, Maurice, or I will give you a hundred lines to copy !"

10, 20. " *Oui, m'sieur !*"—" Yes, sir !"

10, 25. " *Moi, m'sieur ?*"—" I, sir ?"

10, 26. " *Oui, vous !*"—" Yes, you !"

10, 27. " *Bien, m'sieur !*"—" Very well, sir !"

10, 31. " *Le Roi qui passe !*"—" There goes the King !"

12, 3. " *Fermez les fenêtres, ou je vous mets tous au pain sec pour un mois !*"
—" Shut the windows, or I will put you all on dry bread for a month !"

13, 1. " *Soyez diligent et attentif, mon ami ; à plus tard !*"—" Be diligent and attentive, my friend ; I will see you later !"

13, 6. *en cinquième*—in the fifth class.

13, 11. *le nouveau*—the new boy.

14, 8. " *Fermez votre pupitre* "—" Shut your desk."

14, 34. *jocrisse*—effeminate man.

15, 1. *paltoquet*—clown.
petit polisson—little scamp.

15, 32. *lingère*—seamstress.

16, 13. *quatrième*—fourth class.

16, 21. " *Notre Père, . . . les replis les plus profonds de nos cœurs* "—" Our Father, who art in heaven," Thou whose searching glance penetrates even to the inmost recesses of our hearts."

16, 24. " *au nom du Père, du Fils, et du St. Esprit, ainsi soit-il !*"—" in the name of the Father, the Son, and the Holy Ghost, so be it !"

18, 21. *concierge*—janitor.
croquets—crisp almond cakes.

18, 22. *blom - boudingues* — plum puddings.
pains d'épices—gingerbreads.
sucre-d'orge—barley sugar.

462

18, 23. *nougat*—almond cake.
   pâte de guimauve—marshmallow paste.
   pralines—burnt almonds.
   dragées—sugar-plums.
18, 30. *le père et la mère*—father and mother.
19, 2. *corps de logis*—main buildings.
19, 13. *la table des grands*—the big boys' table.
   la table des petits—the little boys' table.
19, 27. *brouet noir des Lacédémoniens*—the black broth of the Spartans.
20, 25. *A la retenue*—To be kept in.
20, 29. *barres traversières*—crossbars.
20, 30. *la raie*—leap-frog.
21, 14. *rentiers*—stockholders.
21, 20. *Classe d'Histoire de France au moyen âge*—Class of the History of France during the Middle Ages.
21, 27. *trente-septième légère* — thirty-seventh light infantry
22, 13 *nous avons changé tout cela!*—we have changed all that!
22, 16 *représentant du peuple*—representative of the people
22, 19. *les nobles*—the nobles.
22, 27. *par parenthèse* — by way of parenthesis.
22, 30. *lingerie*—place where linen is kept.
24, 30. *Berthe aux grands pieds*—Bertha of the big feet. (She was the mother of Charlemagne, and is mentioned in the poem that Du Maurier elsewhere calls " that never to be translated, never to be imitated lament, the immortal ' Ballade des Dames du Temps Jadis ' " of François Villon)
25, 23. *Allée du Bois de Boulogne*—Lane of the Bois de Boulogne.
25, 28. *pensionnat*—boarding-school.
28, 4. *la belle Madame de Ronsvic*—the beautiful Lady Runswick.
28, 33. *deuxième Spahis*—second Spahi regiment.
30, 4. *Mare aux Biches* — The Roes Pool.
30, 14. *la main si malheureuse* — such an unfortunate hand.

31. 2 *La Dieppoise* — a dance of Dieppe.
31, 5. " *Beuvons, donc,*" etc.
   " Let's drink, drink, drink then
      Of this, the best wine in the world...
   Let's drink, drink, drink then
      Of this, the very best wine !
   For if I didn't drink it,
      I might get the pip !
   Which would make me...."
31, 13. " *Ah, mon Dieu! quel amour d'enfant! Oh! gardons-le!*"—" Ah, my Lord ! what a love of a child ! Oh ! let us keep him !"
32, 5. *cæteris paribus* — other things being equal.
34, 19. *à propos*—seasonable.
35. 3. *chaire*—master's raised desk.
35, 6. *recueillement*—contemplation.
35, 11. " *Non, m'sieur, je n'dors pas. J' travaille.*" — " No, sir, I'm not asleep. I'm working."
36, 1. *à la porte*—to leave the room.
36, 14. *On demande Monsieur Josselin au parloir*—Mr. Josselin is wanted in the parlor.
36, 24. *pensum*—a task.
36, 31. *maître de mathématiques (et de cosmographie)* — teacher of mathematics (and cosmography).
37, 17. *Mes compliments*—My compliments.
38, 5. " *Quelquefois je sais . . . . il n'y a pas à s'y tromper!*"—" Sometimes I know — sometimes I don't — but when I know, I know, and there is no mistake about it !"
38, 18. *A l'amandier!*"—" At the almond-tree !"
38, 21. *la balle au camp* — French baseball.
39, 6. *aussi simple que bonjour* — as easy as saying good-day.
40, 17. " *C'était pour Monsieur Josselin!*"—" It was for Mr. Josselin !"
41, 11. *quorum pars magna fui* — of which I was a great part.
41, 16 *bourgeois gentilhomme*—citizen gentleman. (The title of one of Molière's comedies in which M. Jourdain is the principal character.)

463

42, 29. *Dis donc*—Say now.

43, 4. " *Ma foi, non ! c'est pas pour ça !* "—" My word no! it isn't for that !"

43, 5. " *Pourquoi, alors ?*" — " Why, then ?"

43, 21. *Jolivet trois*—the third Jolivet.

44, 2. *au rabais*—at bargain sales.

44, 32. " *Comme c'est bête, de s'battre, hein ?*"—" How stupid it is to fight, eh ?"

45, 9. *tuum et meum*—thine and mine.

45, 19. *magnifique*—magnificent.

45, 32. *La quatrième Dimension*—The fourth Dimension.

46, 14. *Étoiles mortes*—Dead Stars.

46, 15. *Les Trépassées de François Villon*—The Dead of François Villon.

46, 29. *École des Ponts et Chaussées*—School of Bridges and Roads.

47, 8. *en cachette*—in hiding. *Quelle sacrée pose !* — What a damned bluff !

47, 12. " *Dis donc, Maurice!—prête-moi ton Ivanhoé !*" — "Say now, Maurice !—lend me your *Ivanhoe !*"

47, 20. " *Rapaud, comment dit-on 'pouvoir' en anglais ?*"—" Rapaud, how do they say 'to be able' in English ?"

47, 21. " *Sais pas, m'sieur !*"—" Don't know, sir !"

47, 22. " *Comment, petit crétin, tu ne sais pas !*"—" What, little idiot, you don't know !"

47, 26. " *Je n' sais pas!*"—" I don't know !"

47, 27. " *Et toi, Maurice ?*"—" And you, Maurice ?"

47, 28. " *Ça se dit 'to be able,' m'sieur !*" —" They would say 'to be able,' sir !"

47, 29. "*Mais non, mon ami . . . 'je voudrais pouvoir'?*" — " Why no, my friend—you forget your native language—they would say 'to can' ! Now, how would you say, ' I would like to be able ' in English ?"

47, 32. *Je dirais*—I would say.

47, 33. " *Comment, encore ! petit cancre ! allons—tu es Anglais—tu sais*

bien que tu dirais !"—" What, again ! little dunce—come, you are English —you know very well that you would say, . . ."

48, 1. *A ton tour*—Your turn.

48, 4. " *Oui, toi—comment dirais-tu, 'je pourrais vouloir'?*"—" Yes, you —how would you say ' I would be able to will '?"

48, 7. "*À la bonne heure! au moins tu sais ta langue, toi !*"—" Well and good! you at least know your language !"

48, 17. *Île des Cygnes*—Isle of Swans.

48, 18. *École de Natation*—Swimming-school.

48, 26. *Jardin des Plantes*—The Paris Zoological Gardens.

49, 1.
" *Laissons les regrets et les pleurs
 A la vieillesse ;
Jeunes, il faut cueillir les fleurs
 De la jeunesse !*"—Baïf.

" Let us leave regrets and tears
 To age ;
Young, we must gather the flowers
 Of youth."

49, 13. *demi-tasse*—small cup of coffee.

49, 14. *chasse-café*—drink taken after coffee.

49, 19. *consommateur*—consumer.

49, 21. *Le petit mousse noir*—The little black cabin boy.

49, 24. " *Allons, Josselin, chante-nous ça !*"—" Come, Josselin, sing that to us !"

50, 7. "*Écoute-moi bien, ma Fleurette*"—" Listen well to me, my Fleurette."

"*Amis, la matinée est belle*"—" Friends, the morning is fine."

50, 12.
" *Conduis ta barque avec prudence,*" etc.
" Steer thy bark with prudence,
 Fisherman ! speak low !
Throw thy nets in silence,
 Fisherman ! speak low !
And through our toils the king
 Of the seas can never go."

52, 21. *Boulevard Bonne-Nouvelle*—Boulevard of Good News.

52, 24. *galette du gymnase*—flat cake.

464

sold in booths near the Theatre du Gymnase.

52, 26. *yashmak*—a double veil worn by Turkish women.

52, 34. *queue*—in a line.

53, 5. *chiffonniers*—rag-pickers.

53, 33. *Accélérées (en correspondance avec les Constantines)* — Express omnibuses (connecting with the Constantine line).

54. 3 *comme on ne l'est plus*—as one is no longer.

54, 6. *distribution de prix*—prize distribution.

54, 19. *"Au clair de la lune!"*—"By the light of the moon!" (A French nursery rhyme. Readers of "Trilby" will remember her rendering of this song at her Paris concert.)

54, 20.

"Vivent les vacances— . . . *Gaudio nostrò."*

" Hurrah for the vacations—
Come at length ;
And the punishments
Will have ended !
The ushers uncivil,
With barbarous countenance,
Will go to the devil,
To our joy."

56, 20. *Musée de Marine* — Marine Museum.

56, 28. *ennui*—tedium.

57, 7. *en rhétorique et en philosophie*—in the rhetoric and philosophy classes.

57, 9. *cerf - dix - cors* — ten - branched stags.

57, 13. *ventre à terre*—at full speed.

57, 17. *Toujours au clair de la lune*—Always by moonlight. ·

58, 2. *hommes du monde*—men of the world (in society).

58, 4. *Splendide mendax*—Nobly false.

58, 18. *salle d'études*—school-room.

58, 22. *en cinquième* — in the fifth class.

59, 16. *de service*—on duty.

59, 17. *la suite au prochain numéro*—to be continued in our next.

59, 19. *Le Tueur de Daims*—The Deer-slayer.

59, 20 *Le Lac Ontario*—The Lake Ontario.

Le Dernier des Mohicans—The Last of the Mohicans.

Les Pionniers—The Pioneers.

59, 31. *Bas - de - cuir* — Leather - stocking.

60, 10. *la flotte de Passy*—the Passy crowd.

voyous—blackguards.

60, 13. *Liberté — égalité — fraternité ! ou la mort! Vive la république*—Liberty — equality — fraternity ! or death ! Hurrah for the republic !

60, 22. *le rappel*—to arms.

la générale—the fire drum.

61, 11. *Brigand de la Loire*—Brigand of the Loire.

62, 3. *en pleine révolution* — in the midst of the revolution.

62, 5. *piou-piou*—the French equivalent of Tommy Atkins. A private soldier.

62, 17. *Sentinelles, prenez-garde à vous*—Sentinels, keep on the alert.

62, 22. *feu de peloton*—platoon fire.

63, 6. *" Ce sacré Josselin—il avait tous les talents !"* — "That confounded Josselin—he had all the talents!"

64, 10. *lebewohl*—farewell.

64, 11. *bonsoir, le bon Mozart*—good-night, good Mozart.

64, 13. *Château des Fleurs*—Castle of Flowers.

65, 5. *Tout vient à qui ne sait pas attendre*—Everything comes to him who does not know how to wait.

65, 13. *revenons*—let us go back.

65, 24. *impériale*—outside seat.

65, 26. *saucisson de Lyon à l'ail*—a Lyons sausage flavored with garlic.

65, 27. *petits pains*—rolls of bread.

65, 28. *bière de Mars*—Mars beer.

66, 12. *entre les deux âges*—between the two ages.

66, 18. *Le Gué des Aulnes* — Alders Ford.

67, 1. *Si vis pacem, para bellum*—If you wish peace, prepare for war.

67, 13. *tutoyées*—addressed as "thee " and " thou," usual only among familiars.

465

67, 16. *bonnets de coton* — cotton caps.

68, 19. *à l'affût*—on the watch.

68, 28. *"Caïn! Caïn! qu'as-tu fait de ton frère?"* — "Cain! Cain! what hast thou done with thy brother?"

69, 8. *le saut périlleux*—the perilous leap.

69, 20. *que j' n'ai jamais vu*—whom I've never seen.

69, 29. *"Dis-moi qué'q' chose en anglais."* — "Tell me something in English."

69, 32. *"Qué'q' çà veut dire?"* — "What's that mean?"

69, 33. *"Il s'agit d'une église et d'un cimetière!"*—"It's about a church and a cemetery!"

70, 5. *"Démontre-moi un problème de géométrie"*—"Demonstrate to me a problem of geometry."

70, 13. *"Démontre-moi que $A + B$ est plus grand que $C + D$"*—"Demonstrate to me that $A + B$ is greater than $C + D$."

70, 17. *"C'est joliment beau, la géométrie!"*—"It's mighty fine, this geometry!"

70, 24. *brûle-gueule* — jaw-burner (a short pipe).

70, 31. *"Mange-moi ça—ça t' fera du bien!"*—"Eat that for me; it 'll do you good!"

72, 1. *Sais pas*—Don't know.

72, 4. *Père Polyphème*—Father Polyphemus.

72, 12. *ces messieurs* — those gentlemen.

72, 22. *"Hé! ma femme!"* — "Hey! my wife!"

72, 23. *"Voilà, voilà, mon ami!"*— "Here, here, my friend!"

72, 24. *"Viens vite panser mon cautère!"*—"Come quick and dress my cautery!"

72, 27. *café*—coffee.

72, 32. *"Oui, M'sieur Laferté"*—"Yes, M'sieur Laferté."

72, 33. *"Tire moi une gamme"*—"Fire off a scale for me."

73, 3. *"Ah! q' ça fait du bien!"*— "Ah! that does one good!"

73, 20. *'"Colin,' disait Lisette,"* etc.— "'Colin,' said Lisette,
'I want to cross the water!
But I am too poor
To pay for the boat!'
'Get in, get in, my beauty!
Get in, get in, nevertheless!
And off with the wherry
That carries my love!'"

75, 18. *le droit du seigneur*—the right of the lord of the manor.

75, 27. *Âmes en peine*—Souls in pain.

75, 28. *Sous la berge hantée*, etc.
Under the haunted bank
The stagnant water lies—
Under the sombre woods
The dog-fox cries,
And the ten-branched stag bells, and the deer come to drink at the Pond of Respite.
"Let me go, Were-wolf!"
How dark is the pool
When falls the night—
The owl is scared,
And the badger takes flight!
And one feels that the dead are awake
—that a nameless shadow pursues.
"Let me go, Were-wolf!"

76, 29.
*"Prom'nons-nous dans les bois
Pendant que le loup n'y est pas."*
"Let us walk in the woods
While the wolf is not there."

77, 7. *pas aut' chose*—nothing else.

77, 10. *C'est plus fort que moi*—It is stronger than I.

77, 20. *"Il est très méchant!"*—"He is very malicious!"

77, 26. *"venez donc! il est très mauvais, le taureau!"*—"come now! the bull is very mischievous!"

78, 1. *Bon voyage! au plaisir*—Pleasant journey! to the pleasure (of seeing you again).

78, 8. *"le sang-froid du diable! nom d'un Vellington!"*—"the devil's own coolness, by Wellington!"

78, 15. *diable*—devil.

78, 17. *"ces Anglais! je n'en reviens pas! à quatorze ans! hein, ma femme?"*—"those English! I can't get over it! at fourteen! eh, my wife?"

80, 10. *en famille*—at home.

80, 18. *charabancs*—wagonettes.

80, 32. *des chiens anglais*—English dogs.

81, 1. *charmilles*—hedges.
pelouses—lawns.
quinconces—quincunxes.

81, 13. *Figaro quà, Figaro là*—Figaro here, Figaro there.

81, 17. *charbonniers*—charcoal burners.

81, 25. *dépaysé*—away from home.
désorienté—out of his bearings.

81, 26. *perdu*—lost.

81, 27. "*Ayez pitié d'un pauvre orphelin !*"—" Pity a poor orphan !"

82, 19. "*Pioche bien ta géométrie, mon bon petit Josselin! c'est la plus belle science au monde, crois-moi !*" —" Dig away at your geometry, my good little Josselin ! It's the finest science in the world, believe me !"

82, 26. *bourru bienfaisant*—a gruff but good-natured man.

82, 34. "*Enfin ! Ça y est ! quelle chance !*" — " At last ! I've got it ! what luck !"

83, 1. *quoi*—what.

83, 2. "*Le nord—c'est revenu !*"—"The north—it's come back !"

83, 7. *une bonne fortune* — a love adventure.

83, 10. *Les Laiteries*—The Dairies.
Les Poteries—The Potteries.
Les Crucheries — The Pitcheries (also The Stupidities).

83, 26. *toi*—thou.

83, 27. *vous*—you.

83, 28. *Notre Père*, etc.—See note to page 16, line 21

83, 30. *Ainsi soit-il*—So be it.

84, 4. *au nom du Père*—in the name of the Father.

84, 31. *pavillon des petits* — building occupied by the younger boys.

86, 4. *cancre*—dunce.

86, 5. *crétin*—idiot.

86, 6. *troisième*—third class.

86, 7. *Rhétorique (seconde)* — Rhetoric (second class).

86, 8. *Philosophie (première)*—Philosophy (first class).

86, 10. *Baccalauréat-ès-lettres*—Bachelor of letters.

87, 27. *m'amour (mon amour)* — my love.

87, 33. *en beauté*—at his best.

88, 8. "*Le Chant du Départ*"—"The Song of Departure."

88, 10
"*La victoire en chantant nous ouvre la carrière !*
La liberté-é gui-i-de nos pas" . . .
" Victory shows us our course with song !
Liberty guides our steps" . . .

88, 25. "*Quel dommage . . . c'est toujours ça !*"—" What a pity that we can't have crumpets ! Barty likes them so much. Don't you like crumpets, my dear ? Here comes some buttered toast—it's always that !"

88, 29. "*Mon Dieu, comme il a bonne mine . . . dans la glace*"—" Good heavens, how well he looks, the dear Barty !—don't you think so, my love, that you look well ? Look at yourself in the glass."

88, 32. "*Si nous allions à l'Hippodrôme . . . aussi les jolies femmes ?*"—" If we went to the Hippodrome this afternoon, to see the lovely equestrian Madame Richard ? Barty adores pretty women, like his uncle ! Don't you adore pretty women, you naughty little Barty ? and you have never seen Madame Richard. You'll tell me what you think of her; and you, my friend, do you also adore pretty women ?"

89, 5. "*Ô oui, allons voir Madame Richard*"—" Oh yes! let us go and see Madame Richard."

89, 9. *la haute école*—the high-school (of horsemanship).

89, 14. *Café des Aveugles*—Café of the Blind.

90, 4. "*Qu'est-ce que vous avez donc, tous ?*"—" What's the matter with you all?"

90, 5. "*Le Père Brossard est mort !*" —" Father Brossard is dead !"

90, 10. "*Il est tombé du haut mal*"— " He died of the falling sickness."

90, 13. *désœuvrement*—idleness.

467

91, 8. *de service* as *maître d'études*—on duty as study-master.

93, 27. "*Dites donc, vous autres*"—"Say now, you others."

93, 29. *panem et circenses*—bread and games.

94, 19. "*Allez donc . . . à La Salle Valentino*"—"Go it, godems—this is not a quadrille! We're not at Valentino Hall!"

95, 1. "*Messieurs . . . est sauf*"—"Gentlemen, blood has flown; Britannic honor is safe."

95, 3. "*J'ai joliment faim!*"—"I'm mighty hungry!"

96, 1. "*Que ne puis-je aller*," etc.
"Why can I not go where the roses go,
And not await
The heartbreaking regrets which the end of things
Keeps for us here?"

96, 8. "*Le Manuel du Baccalauréat*"—"The Baccalaureat's Manual."

96, 24. *un prévôt*—a fencing-master's assistant.

97, 5. *rez-de-chaussée*—ground floor.

97, 9. "*La pluie de Perles*"—"The Shower of Pearls."

97, 12. *quart d'heure*—quarter of an hour.

97, 17. *au petit bonheur*—come what may.

97, 26. *vieux loup de mer*—old sea-wolf.

98, 2. *Mon Colonel*—My Colonel.

98, 6. *endimanché*—Sundayfied (dressed up).

99, 11. *chefs-d'œuvre*—masterpieces.

99, 24. *chanson*—song.

99, 27. "*C'était un Capucin*," etc.
"It was a Capuchin, oh yes, a Capuchin father,
Who confessed three girls—
Itou, itou, itou, là là là!
Who confessed three girls
At the bottom of his garden—
Oh yes—
At the bottom of his garden!
He said to the youngest—
Itou, itou, itou, là là là!
He said to the youngest
. . . 'You will come back to-morrow.'"

100, 7. *un écho du temps passé*—an echo of the olden times.

100, 11. *esprit Gaulois*—old French wit.

100, 20. "*Sur votre parole d'honneur, avez-vous chanté?*"—"On your word of honor, have you sung?"

100, 22. "*Non, m'sieur!*"—"No, sir!"

100, 32. "*Oui, m'sieur!*"—"Yes, sir."

101, 5. "*Vous êtes tous consignés!*"—"You are all kept in!"

101, 10. *de service*—on duty.

101, 19. "*Au moins vous avez du cœur . . . sale histoire de Capucin!*"—"You at least have spirit. Promise me that you will not again sing that dirty story about the Capuchin!"

102, 24.
"*Stabat mater*," etc.
"By the cross, sad vigil keeping,
Stood the mournful mother weeping,
While on it the Saviour hung" . . .

102, 30. "*Ah! ma chère Mamzelle Marceline! . . . Et une boussole dans l'estomac!*"—"Ah! my dear Miss Marceline, if they were only all like that little Josselin! things would go as if they were on wheels! That English youngster is as innocent as a young calf! He has God in his heart." "And a compass in his stomach!"

104, 29. "*Ah! mon cher! . . . Chantez-moi ça encore une fois!*"—"Ah! my dear! what wouldn't I give to see the return of a whaler at Whitby! What a 'marine' that would make! eh? with the high cliff and the nice little church on top, near the old abbey—and the red smoking roofs, and the three stone piers, and the old drawbridge—and all that swarm of watermen with their wives and children—and those fine girls who are waiting for the return of the loved one! by Jove! to think that you have seen all that, you who are not yet sixteen . . . what luck! . . . say—what does that really mean?—that
'Weel may the keel row!'
Sing that to me once again!"

105, 21. *"Ah! vous verrez ... vous y êtes, en plein!"*—"Ah! you will see, during the Easter holidays I will make such a fine picture of all that! with the evening mist that gathers, you know—and the setting sun, and the rising tide, and the moon coming up on the horizon, and the seamews and the gulls, and the far-off heaths, and your grandfather's lordly old manor; that's it, isn't it?" "Yes, yes, Mr. Bonzig—you are right in it."

106, 29. *"C'etait dans la nuit brune,"* etc.
"'Twas in the dusky night
On the yellowed steeple,
The moon,
Like a dot on an i!"

108, 17 *en flagrant délit*—in the very act

109, 4 *la perfide Albion*—perfidious Albion.

109, 8 *"A bas Dumollard!"*—"Down with Dumollard!"

109, 17. *l'étude entière*—the whole school.

109, 19. *"Est-ce toi?"*—"Is it thou?"

109, 23. *"Non, m'sieur, ce n'est pas moi!"*—"No, sir, it isn't me!"

110, 17. *"Parce qu'il aime les Anglais, ma foi — affaire de goût!"* — "Because he likes the English, in faith—a matter of taste!"

110, 19. *"Ma foi, il n'a pas tort!"*—"In faith, he's not wrong!"

110, 24. *"Non! jamais en France, Jamais Anglais ne règnera!"*
"No! never in France,
Never shall Englishman reign!"

111, 5. *au piquet pour une heure*—in the corner for an hour.
a la retenue—kept in.

111, 6. *privé de bain*—not to go swimming.
consigné dimanche prochain—kept in next Sunday

111, 9. *de mortibus nil desperandum*—an incorrect version of *de mortuis nil nisi bonum:* of the dead nothing but good.

111, 27. *avec des gens du monde*—with people in society.

111, 34. *et, ma foi, le sort a favorisé M. le Marquis*—and, in faith, fortune favored M. le Marquis.

112, 9. *vous êtes un paltoquet et un rustre*—you are a clown and a boor.

112. 18. *classe de géographie ancienne*—class of ancient geography.

112, 25 *"Timeo Danaos et dona ferentes!"*—"I fear the Greeks even when they bear gifts!"

114, 3. *"Le troisième coup fait feu, vous savez"*—"The third blow strikes fire, you know."

114, 23. *tisanes*—infusions.

114, 31. *"C'est moi qui voudrais . . . comme il est poli"* — "It's myself that would like to have the mumps here. I should delay my convalescence as much as possible!"
"How well your uncle knows French, and how polite he is!"

116, 13. *Nous avons tous passé par là*—We have all been through it.

116, 33 *"Te rappelles-tu . . . du père Jaurion?"*—"Do you recall Berquin's new coat and his high-hat?"
"Do you remember father Jaurion's old angora cat?"

118, 7. *"Paille à Dine,"* etc , is literally:
"Straw for Dine—straw for Chine—
Straw for Suzette and Martine—
Good bed for the Dumaine!"

119, 1. *"Pourquoi, m'sieur?"*
"Parce que ça me plait!"
"What for, sir?"
"Because it pleases me!"

119, 18. *un point*, etc. — a period — semi - colon — colon — exclamation— inverted commas—begin a parenthesis.

119, 31 *"Te rappelles-tu cette omelette?"*—"Do you remember that omelette?"

120, 1. *version écrite*—written version.

120, 15. *qué malheur!*—what a misfortune!

120, 19. *"Ça pue l'injustice, ici!"*—"It stinks of injustice, here!"

120, 25. *"Mille francs par an! ç'est le Pactole!"*—"A thousand francs a year! it is a Pactolus!"

122, 7. *"Je t'en prie, mon garçon!"*— "I pray you, my boy!"

123, 24. *La chasse aux souvenirs d'enfance!* —Hunting remembrances of childhood!

124, 3. *"Je marcherai les yeux fixés sur mes pensées,"* etc. "I will walk with my eyes fixed on my thoughts, Seeing notling outside, without hearing a sound— By myself, unknown, with bowed back and hands crossed: Sad—and the day will for me be as night."

125, 4. *beau comme le jour*—beautiful as day.

125, 6. *la rossignolle* — the nightingale (feminine.)

125, 15. *"A Saint - Blaize, à la Zuecca,"* etc. "At St. Blaize, and at Zuecca... You were, you were very well! At St. Blaize, and at Zuecca... We were, we were happy there! But to think of it again Will you ever care? Will you think of it again? Will you come once more? At St. Blaize, and at Zuecca ... To live there and to die!"

125, 32. *fête de St.-Cloud*—festival of St. Cloud.

125, 33. *blanchisseuse*—laundress.

133, 30. *"Roy ne puis, prince ne daigne, Rohan je suis!"*—"King I cannot be, prince I would not be, Rohan I am!"

133, 34. *"Rohan ne puis, roi ne daigne. Rien je suis!"*—"Rohan I cannot be, king I would not be. Nothing I am!"

135, 10. *grandes dames de par le monde*—great ladies of the world.

137, 6. *"O lachrymarum fons!"*—"O font of tears!"

140, 28. Jewess is in French, *juive*.

141, 10. *"Esker voo ker jer dwaw lah vee? Ah! kel Bonnure!"* Anglo-French for *"Est ce que vous que je dois laver. Ah! quel bonheur!"*— "Is it that you that I must wash? Ah! what happiness!"

142, 12. *Pazienza*—Patience.

143, 8. *"Ne sutor ultra crepidam!"*— "A cobbler should stick to his last!"

145, 1. *"La cigale ayant chanté,"* etc. "The grasshopper, having sung The summer through, Found herself destitute When the north wind came." ...

146, 20. *"Spretæ injuria formæ"*— "The insult to her despised beauty."

146, 31. *billets doux*—love letters.

152, 8. *"La plus forte des forces est un cœur innocent"*—"The strongest of strengths is an innocent heart."

154, 3. *"Tiens, tiens! . . . écoute!"*— "There, there! it's deucedly pretty that—listen!"

154, 8. *"Mais, nom d'une pipe — elle est divine, cette musique - là!"* — "But, by jingo, it's divine, that music!"

155, 26. *bourgeois*—the middle class.

155, 34. *nouveaux riches* — newly rich people.

158, 2. *"La mia letizia!"*—"My Joy!"

160, 17. *"Beau chevalier qui partez pour la guerre,"* etc. "Brave cavalier, off to the war, What will you do So far from here? Do you not see that the night is dark, And that the world Is only care?"

160, 23. *"La Chanson de Barberine"*— "The Song of Barberine."

160, 28. *cascamèche*—nightcap tassel. *moutardier du pape* — pope's mustardman. *tromblon - bolivard* — broad-brimmed blunderbuss.

160, 29. *vieux coquelicot*—old poppy.

160, 31. *"Voos ayt oon ôter!"* Angio-French for *"Vous êtes un autre!"*— "You are another!"

162, 10. *C'est toujours comme ça*—It's always like that.

163, 17. *à bon chat, bon rat*—a Roland for an Oliver.

166, 14. *poudre insecticide* — insect-powder. *mort aux punaises*—death to the bugs.

470

166, 22 *pensionnat de demoiselles*—young ladies' boarding-school.

166, 28. *Je connais ça*—I know that.

168, 8. *eau sucrée*—sweetened water.

168, 18 *Cœur de Lion*—Lion Heart.
le Pré aux Clercs—Parson's Green.

169, 17. *rapins*—art students.

170, 14. " *Bonjour, Monsieur Bonzig! comment allez-vous ?*" — "Good-day, Mr. Bonzig! how do you do?"

170, 17. " *Pardonnez - moi, monsieur—mais je n'ai pas l'honneur de vous remettre !*"—" Pardon me, sir—but I have not the honor to remember your face !"

170, 19. " *Je m'appelle Josselin* — *de chez Brossard !*" — "My name is Josselin—from Brossard's !"

170, 20. " *Ah !   Mon Dieu, mon cher, mon très-cher !*"—" Ah !   My God, my dear, my very dear !"

170, 23. " *Mais quel bonheur. . . . Je n'en reviens pas !*"—" But what good luck it is to see you again. I think of you so often, and of Whitby ! how you have altered ! and what a fine-looking fellow you are ! who would have recognized you ! Lord of Lords —it's a dream ! I can't get over it !"

170, 34. " *Non, mon cher Josselin*."— " No, my dear Josselin."

172, 4. *un peintre de marines*—a painter of marines.

172, 16. *garde champêtre*—park-keeper.

172, 27. *ministère*—public office

172, 31. "*l'heure où le jaune de Naples rentre dans la nature*"—" the hour when Naples yellow comes again into nature."

173, 31. *bonne friture*—good fried fish.

173, 32. *fricassée de lapin* — rabbit fricasee.
pommes sautées—French fried potatoes.
soupe aux choux — cabbage soup.

174, 1. *café chantant*—music-hall.
bal de barrière—ball held in the outer districts of Paris, usually composed of the rougher element.

174, 3 *bonsoir la compagnie* — good-night to the company.

174. 26 *prix-fixe*—fixed price.

175, 6 *aile de poulet*—chicken's wing.
pêche au vin—peach preserved in wine

175, 9. *entre la poire et le fromage*—between pear and cheese.

175, 15 *flâning* — from *flâner*, to lounge.

175, 28 " *Ma foi, mon cher !*"—" My word, my dear !"

176, 3. *ma mangeaille*—my victuals.

176, 18. *Mont de Piété*—pawnshop

176, 24. *moult tristement, à l'anglaise*—with much sadness, after the English fashion.

177, 12. *un jour de séparation, vous comprenez*—a day of separation, you understand.

177, 14 *à la vinaigrette*—with vinegar sauce

177, 16. *nous en ferons l'expérience*—we will try it.

177, 19. *maillot*—bathing-suit.
peignoir—wrapper.

177, 21. " *Oh !   la mer ! . . . chez Babet !*"—" Oh ! the sea, the sea ! At last I am going to take my header into it—*and not later than to-morrow evening.* . . . Till to-morrow, my dear comrade—six o'clock —at Babet's !"

177, 27. *piquant sa tête* — taking his header.

178, 1. *sergent de ville*—policeman.

178, 4. " *un jour de séparation . . . nagerons de conserve* "—" a day of separation ! but come also, Josselin —we will take our headers together, and swim in each other's company."

178, 13. " *en signe de mon deuil* "—" as a token of my mourning."

178, 23. *plage*—beach.

178, 30. *dame de comptoir*—the lady at the counter.

178, 33. *demi-tasse* — small cup of coffee.
petit-verre — small glass of brandy.

180, 13. *avec tant d'esprit*— so wittily.

180, 14. *rancune*—grudge.

471

181, 14. *bon raconteur* — good story-teller.

181, 16. *"La plus belle fille . . . ce qu'elle a !"* — " The fairest girl in the world can give only what she has !"

182, 5. *comme tout un chacun sait* — as each and every one knows.

182, 24. *Tout ça, c'est de l'histoire ancienne* — that's all ancient history.

183, 8. *"très bel homme . . . que joli garçon hein ?"* — "fine man, Bob; more of the fine man than the handsome fellow, eh ?"

183, 12. *Mes compliments* — My compliments.

183, 19. *"Ça y est, alors ! . . . à ton bonheur !"* — " So it's settled, then! I congratulate you beforehand, and I keep my tears for when you have gone. Let us go and dine at Babet's : I long to drink to your welfare !"

184, 1. *atelier* — art studio.

184, 6. *le Beau Josselin* — the handsome Josselin.

184, 33. *serrement de cœur* — heart burning.

185, 22. *Marché aux Œufs* — Egg Market.

186, 4. *" Malines "* or *" Louvain "* — Belgian beers.

186, 25. *" Oui ; un nommé Valtères "* — "Yes ; one called Valtères " (French pronunciation of Walters).

186, 28. *" Parbleu, ce bon Valtères — je l'connais bien !"* — " Zounds, good old Walters — I know him well !"

188, 26. *primo tenore* — first tenor.

188, 29. *Guides* — a Belgian cavalry regiment.

188, 32. *Cercle Artistique* — Art Club.

191, 1. *" Ô céleste haine,"* etc.

" O celestial hate,
  How canst thou be appeased ?
O human suffering,
  Who can cure thee ?
My pain is so heavy
  I wish it would kill me—
Such is my desire.

" Heart-broken by thought,
  Weary of compassion,

To hear no more,
  Nor see, nor feel,
I am ready to give
  My parting breath—
And this is my desire.

" To know nothing more,
  Nor remember myself—
Never again to rise,
  Nor go to sleep—
No longer to be,
  But to have done—
That is my desire !"

191, 23. *Fleur de Blé* — Corn-flower.

192, 31. *" Vous allez à Blankenberghe, mossié ?"* — " You go to Blankenberghe, sah ?"

193, 1. *"Jé souis bienn content — nous férons route ensiemblé !"* (*je suis bien content — nous ferons route ensemble*) — " I am fery glad — ve will make ze journey togezzar !"

193, 5. *ragazza* — girl.

193, 7. *" un' prodige, mossié — un' fenomeno !"* — " a prodigy, sah — a phenomenon !"

193, 24. *Robert, toi que j'aime* — Robert, thou whom I love.

193, 29. *" Ma vous aussi, vous êtes mousicien — jé vois ça par la votre figoure !"* (*Mais vous aussi etes musicien — je vois ça par votre figure !*) — " But you also, you are a moosician — I see zat by your face !"

194, 4. *elle et moi* — she and I.

194, 5. *bon marché* — cheap.

194, 34. *en famille* — at home.

195, 7. *" Jé vais vous canter couelqué-cose* (*Je vais vous chanter quelquechose*) *— una piccola cosa da niente ! — vous comprenez l'Italien ?"* — " I vill sing to you somezing — a leetle zing of nozzing ! — you understand ze Italian ?"

195, 12. *je les adore* — I adore them.

195, 16. *" Il vero amore "* — " True Love."

195, 17.

*" E la mio amor è andato a soggiornare
A Lucca bella — e diventar signore. . . ."*

472

" And my love has gone to dwell In beautiful Lucca — and become a gentleman. . . ."

195, 29. " *O mon Fernand!*"—" O my Fernand !"

196, 13. " *Et vous ne cantez pas . . . comme je pourrai.*"

" And you do not sing at all, at all ?" " Oh yes, sometimes !"

"Sing somezing—I vill accompany you on ze guitar !—do not be afraid— ve vill not be hard on you, she and *I*—"

" Oh—I'll do my best to accompany myself."

196, 21. "*Fleur des Alpes*" — " Flower of the Alps."

199, 23. *médaille de sauvetage*—medal for saving life.

200, 2. *Je leur veux du bien*—I wish them well.

200. 17. *Largo al factotum* — Make way for the factotum.

201, 24. *bis! ter!*—a second time! a third time!

201, 26. " *Het Roosje uit de Dorne*"— " The Rose without the Thorn."

202, 15. *sans tambour ni trompette*— without drum or trumpet (French leave).

202, 29. *Hôtel de Ville*—Town-hall.

203, 4. " *Una sera d' amore*"—" An Evening of Love."

203, 16. " *Guarda che bianca luna*"— " Behold the silver moon."

204, 15. *boute-en-train*—life and soul.

205, 10. " *À vous, monsieur de la garde . . . tirer les premiers!*"

" Your turn, gentleman of the guard."

" The gentlemen of the guard should always fire the first !"

205, 20. " *Je ne tire plus . . . main malheureuse un jour!*" — " I will fire no more—I am too much afraid that some day my hand may be unfortunate !"

205, 33. " *Le cachet . . . je lui avais demandé!*" — " Mr. Josselin's seal, which I had asked him for !"

206, 4. *Salle d'Armes* — Fencing-school.

206, 10. *des enfantillages*—child's play.

206, 15. " *Je vous en prie, monsieur de la garde!*"—" I pray you, gentleman of the guard !"

206, 17 " *Cette fois, alors, nous allons tirer ensemble!*"—" This time, then, we will draw together!"

206, 23. *maître d'armes*—fencing-master.

206, 29. " *Vous êtes impayable . . . pour la vie*" — " You are extraordinary, you know, my dear fellow ; you have every talent, and a million in your throat into the bargain ! If ever I can do anything for you, you know, always count upon me."

208, 1. " *Et plus jamais . . . quand vous m'écrirez!*" —" And no more empty envelopes when you write to me !"

208, 10. *la peau de chagrin*—the sha-green skin. (The hero of this story, by Balzac, is given a piece of sha-green, on the condition that all his wishes will be gratified, but that every wish will cause the leather to shrink, and that when it disappears his life will come to an end. *Chagrin* also means sorrow, so that Barty's retina was indeed " a skin of sorrow," continually shrinking.)

208, 29. " *Les miséres du jour font le bonheur du lendemain!*" — " The misery of to day is the happiness of to-morrow !"

210, 23. *dune*—a low sand-hill. (They are to be found all along the Belgian coast.)

214, 22. *par*—by.

214, 32. *dit-on*—they say.

216, 22. *bien d'accord* — of the same mind.

217, 1. *née*—by birth.

217, 29 *moi qui vous parle*—I who speak to you.

219, 3. *Kermesse*—fair.

219, 6. *estaminet* — a drinking and smoking resort.

219. 10. *à la Teniers*—after the manner of Teniers, the painter.

219, 34. *in secula seculorum!*—for ages of ages !

473

220, 3. *Rue des Ursulines Blanches*— Street of the White Ursulines.

220, 5. *des Sœurs Rédemptoristines*— Sisters of the Redemption.

220, 11. *Frau*—Mrs. (This is German; the Flemish is *Juffrow*.)

220, 26. "*La Cigogne*"—"The Stork Inn."

221, 9. *salade aux fines herbes*—salad made of a mixture of herbs.

222, 28. *à fleur de tête*—on a level with their heads.

223, 6. *savez vous?*—do you know?

223, 26. *chaussées*—roads.

224, 26. *Les Maîtres Sonneurs* — The Master Ringers. *La Mare au Diable* — The Devil's Pool.

225, 21. *séminaire*—clerical seminary.

225, 29. "*Mio caro Paolo di Kocco!*" —"My dear Paul de Kock!"

225, 32. "*Un malheureux,*" etc.

"An unfortunate dressed in black, Who resembled me like a brother." (Du Maurier himself.)

228, 14. *mein armer*—my poor.

228, 17. *Lieber*—dear.

229, 5. *Bel Mazetto* — Beautiful Mazetto.

229, 7. "*Ich bin ein lustiger Student, mein Pardy*"—"I am a jolly Student, my Barty."

229, 15. *Katzenjammer*—sore head.

229, 18. *Liebe*—love.

230, 2. *tout le monde*—everybody.

231, 18. *autrefois*—the times of yore.

231, 21. "*Oh, non, mon ami*"—"Oh, no, my friend."

231, 29. "*Petit bonhomme vit encore*" —"Good little fellow still alive."

232, 1.

"*Hé quoi! pour des peccadilles,*" etc.

"Eh, what! for peccadilloes To scold those little loves? Women are so pretty, And one does not love forever! Good fellow They call me . . . My gayety is my treasure! And the good fellow is still alive— And the good fellow is still alive!"

233, 10. *Soupe-au-lait*—Milk porridge.

234, 2. *muscæ volitantes* — (literally) hovering flies.

242, 1. "*Mettez-vous au régime des viandes saignantes!*"—"Put yourself on a diet of rare meat!"

242, 4. "*Mettez - vous au lait!*" — "Take to milk!"

242, 9. *désœuvrement*—idleness.

242, 16. "*Amour, Amour,*" etc.

"Love, love, when you hold us, Well may we say ' Prudence, good-bye!'"

244, 1. "*Il s'est conduit en homme de cœur!*"—"He has behaved like a man of spirit!"

244, 3. "*Il s'est conduit en bon gentil-homme!*"—"He has behaved like a thorough gentleman!"

247, 9. *Les Noces de Jeannette*—Jeannette's Wedding.

247, 13.

"*Cours, mon aiguille . . de notre peine!*"

"Run, my needle, through the wool! Do not break off in my hand; For to-morrow with good kisses Jean will pay us for our trouble!"

249, 3. "*Hélas! mon jeune ami!*"— "Alas! my young friend!"

252, 1. *Sursum cor! sursum corda!*— Lift up your heart! Lift up your hearts!

252, 11. *coupe-choux*—cabbage-cutter.

252, 13. "*Ça ne vous regarde pas, . . . ou je vous . . .*"—"It's none of your business, you know! take yourselves off at once, or I'll . . ."

252, 19. "*Non—c'est moi qui regarde, savez-vous!*" — "No—it is I who am looking, you know!"

252, 20. "*Qu'est-ce que vous regardez? . . . Vous ne voulez pas vous en aller?*"

"What are you looking at?"

"I am looking at the moon and the stars. I am looking at the comet!"

"Will you take yourself off at once?"

"Some other time!"

"Take yourself off, I tell you!"

"The day after to-morrow!"

"You . . . will . . . not . . . take . . . yourself . . . off?"

252, 32. "*Non, sacré petit . . . restez où vous êtes!*"
"No, you confounded little devil's gravel-pusher!"
"All right, stay where you are!"

254, 16. "*. . . du sommeil au songe—Du songe à la mort.*"
". . . from sleep to dream—From dream to death."

254, 21. "*Il est dix heures . . . dans votre chambre?*"—"It's ten o'clock, you know? Will you have your coffee in your room?"

255, 14 *ça date de loin, mon pauvre ami*—it goes a long way back, my poor friend.

256, 8. *punctum cœcum*—blind spot.

257, 27. *mon beau somnambule*—my handsome somnambulist.

257, 33. *On ne sait pas ce qui peut arriver*—One never knows what may happen.

258, 17. *tiens*—look.

262, 10. *sans peur et sans reproche*—without fear and without reproach.

262, 15. "*Ça s'appelle le point caché—c'est une portion de la rétine avec laquelle on ne peut pas voir. . . .*"—"It is called the blind spot—it is a part of the retina with which we cannot see. . . ."

263, 13. *c'est toujours ça*—that's always the way.

263, 23. *plus que coquette*—more than coquettish.

269, 8. *père et mère*—father and mother.

271, 31. *more Latino*—in the Latin manner.

272, 12. *pictor ignotus*—the unknown painter.

273, 6. "*Que me voilà . . . Ôte ton chapeau!*"
"How happy I am, my little Barty—and you? what a pretty town, eh?"
"It's heaven, pure and simple—and you are going to teach me German, aren't you, my dear?"
"Yes, and we will read Heine together; by the way, look! do you see the name of the street at the corner? Bolker Strasse! that's where he was born, poor Heine! Take off your hat!'

273, 19. *Maitrank*—May drink. (An infusion of woodruff in light white wine.)

273, 34. "*Johanna, mein Frühstück, bitte!*"—"Johanna, my breakfast, please!"

276, 27. *la barre de bâtardise*—the bar of bastardy.

279, 15. *der schöne*—the handsome.

280, 24. *Speiserei*—eating-house.

283, 5. "*ni l'or ni la grandeur ne nous rendent heureux*" — "neither gold nor greatness makes us happy."

285, 22. *mes premières amours*—my first loves.

286, 3. "*Petit chagrin . . . un soupir!*"
"Little sorrow of childhood Costing a sigh!"

286, 9. *Il avait bien raison*—He was quite right.

289, 15. *rien que ça*—nothing but that.

290, 29. "*Il a les qualités . . . sont ses meilleures qualités.*"
"The handsome Josselin has the qualities of his faults."
"My dear, his faults are his best qualities."

297, 4. *Art et liberté*—Art and liberty.

299, 11. "*Du bist die Ruh', der Friede mild!*" — "Thou art rest, sweet peace!"

300, 19. *c'est plus fort que moi*—it is stronger than I.

304, 2. *dans le blanc des yeux*—straight in the eyes.

306, 20. *damigella*—maiden.

308, 27. "*Die Ruhe kehret mir zurück*"—"Peace comes back to me."

308, 30. *prosit omen*—may the omen be propitious.

309, 5. *prima donna assoluta*—the absolute first lady. (Grand Opera, the "leading lady.")

310, 32. *gringalet-jocrisse* — an effeminate fellow.

312, 3. *faire la popotte ensemble au coin du feu; c'est le ciel*—to potter round the fire together; that is heaven.

475

312, 29. *Ausstellung*—exhibition.

314, 8. *loch*—a medicine of the consistence of honey, taken by licking or sucking.

318, 10. " *Et voilà comment ça s'est passé* "—" And that's how it happened."

320, 14. *et plus royaliste que le Roi*—and more of a royalist than the King.

321, 13. *cru*—growth.

323, 32. *L'amitié est l'amour sans ailes*—Friendship is love without wings.

325, 9. *En veux-tu? en voilà!* — Do you want some? here it is!

327, 10. *kudos*—glory.

328, 9. *Dis-moi qui tu hantes, je te dirai ce que tu es*—Tell me who are your friends, and I will tell you what you are.

331, 20. *si le cœur t'en dit* — if your heart prompts you.

335, 5. *esprit de corps*—brotherhood.

335, 8. *Noblesse oblige*—Nobility imposes the obligation of nobleness.

336, 15. *bêtise pure et simple*—downright folly.

337, 15. *Je suis au-dessus de mes affaires*—I am above my business.

338, 11. *Maman-belle-mère* — Mamamother-in-law.

338, 30. *vous plaisantez, mon ami; un amateur comme moi*—you are joking, my friend; an amateur like myself.

338, 31. *Quis custodiet (ipsos custodes)?*—Who shall guard the guards themselves?

339, 2. *monsieur anglais, qui avait mal aux yeux*—English gentleman, who had something the matter with his eyes.

340, 5. *La belle dame sans merci*—The fair lady merciless.

342, 4. *de par le monde*—in society.

242, 18. *je tâcherai de ne pas en abuser trop!*—I will try not to take too much of it!

344, 15. *le dernier des Abencerrages*—the last of the Abencerrages. (The title of a story by Châteaubriand.)

347, 24. *à mon insu*—unknown to me.

354, 11. *On a les défauts de ses qualités* — One has the faults of one's virtues.

354, 15. *joliment dégourdie* — finely sharpened.

358, 10. *La quatrième Dimension*—The Fourth Dimension.

360, 25. *nous avons eu la main heureuse*—we have been fortunate.

360, 28. *smalah* — encampment of an Arab chieftain.

363, 19. *Je suis homme d'affaires* — I am a man of business.

373, 28. *un conte à dormir debout*—a story to bore one to sleep.

374, 23. *Où avions-nous donc la tête et les yeux?* — What were we doing with our minds and eyes?

377, 1. " *Cara deûm soboles, magnum Jovis incrementum* " — " The dear offspring of God, the increase of Jove."

378, 22. *Tous les genres sont bons, hormis le genre ennuyeux*—All kinds are good, except the boring kind.

380, 3. *C'était un naïf, le beau Josselin* —He was ingenuous, the handsome Josselin.

381, 9. *Arma virumque cano* — Arms and the man I sing.—The first words of Virgil's *Æneid.*

Tityre tu patulæ (recubans sub tegmine fagi)—Thou, Tityrus, reclining beneath the shade of a spreading beech. —The first line of the first *Eclogue* of Virgil.

Mæcenas atavis (edite regibus) —Mæcenas descended from royal ancestors. — Horace, *Odes,* 1, 1, 1.

381, 10. Μῆνιν ἀείδε—Sing the wrath. —The first words of Homer's *Iliad.*

381, 21. *Débats*—*Le Journal des Débats,* a Parisian literary newspaper.

386, 3. *sommité littéraire*—literary pinnacle.

386, 16. *Bouillon Duval* — a class of cheap restaurants in Paris.

386, 30. *Étoiles Mortes*—Dead Stars.

388, 5. *la coupe*—the cutwater.

476

388, 11. *à la hussarde*—head first.

389, 2. *la très-sage Héloïse*—the most learned Heloise. (Another of the ladies mentioned in Villon's " Ballade of the Ladies of Olden Time." See note to page 24, line 30.)

389, 5. *nous allons arranger tout ça*—we'll arrange all that.

389, 20. *C'est la chasteté même, mais ce n'est pas Déjanire*—It is chastity itself, but it is not Déjanire.

390, 20. *très élégante*—very elegant.

390, 22. *d'un noir de jais, d'une blancheur de lis*—jet black, lily white.

391, 1. *ah, mon Dieu, la Diane chasseresse, la Sapho de Pradier !*—ah, My God, Diana the huntress, Pradier's Sappho!

391, 8. *un vrai type de colosse bon enfant, d'une tenue irréprochable*—a perfect image of a good-natured colossus, of irreproachable bearing.

391, 15. *tartines*—slices of bread and butter.

391, 17. *une vraie ménagerie*—a perfect menagerie.

392, 7. *belle châtelaine*—beautiful chatelaine.

393, 1. *gazebo*—summer-house.

393, 18. *le que retranché*—name given in some French-Latin grammars to the Latin form which expresses by the infinitive verb and the accusative noun what in French is expressed by " que " between two verbs.

394, 32. *alma mater dolorosa* — the tender and sorrowful mother.

394, 33. *marâtre au cœur de pierre*—stony-hearted mother.

396, 19. *Tendenz novels* — novels with a purpose.

396, 28. *nouvelle-riche*—newly rich.

404, 11. *on y est très bien*—one is very well there.

406, 26. *" Il est dix heures,"* etc.—See note to page 254, line 21.

406, 30. *vilain mangeur de cœurs que vous êtes*—wretched eater of hearts that you are.

407, 30. *Un vrai petit St. Jean! il nous portera bonheur, bien sûr*—A

perfect little St. John! he will bring us good luck, for sure.

408, 27. *nous savons notre orthographie en musique là bas*—we know our musical a b c's over there.

412, 8. *in-medio-tutissimus (ibis)*—You will go safest in the middle.

412, 20. *diablement bien conservé* — deucedly well preserved.

413, 11. *O me fortunatum, mea si bona nôrim !*—O happy me, had I known my own blessings!

414, 23. *un malheureux raté*—an unfortunate failure

415, 9. *abrutissant*—stupefying.

416, 15. *affaire d'estomac*—a matter of stomach.

418, 1. *" Je suis allé de bon matin,"* etc.

" I went at early morn
To pick the violet,
And hawthorne, and jasmine,
To celebrate thy birthday.
With my own hands I bound
The rosebuds and the rosemary
To crown thy golden head.

" But for thy royal beauty
Be humble, I pray thee.
Here all things die, flower, summer,
Youth and life :
Soon, soon the day will be,
My fair one, when they'll carry thee
Faded and pale in a winding-sheet."

418, 19. *périssoires*—paddle-boats.
pique-têtes—diving-boards.

418, 21. *station balnéaire* — bathing resort.

419, 25. *utile dulci* — the useful with the pleasant.

420, 9. *la chasse aux souvenirs* — the hunt after remembrances.

420, 25. *s'est encanaillé* — keeps low company.

422, 25. *porte-cochère* — carriage entrance.

423, 1. *" Ah, ma foi ! . . . la balle au camp "*—"Ah, my word, I understand that, gentlemen—I, too, was a school-boy once, and was fond of rounders."

477

423, 11. *Le Fils de la Vierge* — The Virgin's Son.

423, 12. *mutatis mutandis*—the necessary changes being made.

423, 34. " *Moi aussi, je fumais . . . n'est ce pas ?*" — " I too smoked when it was forbidden ; what do you expect ? Youth must have its day, musn't it ?"

424, 3. *dame*—indeed.

425, 30. *cour des miracles*—the court of miracles. (A meeting-place of beggars described in Hugo's " Notre Dame de Paris." So called on account of the sudden change in the appearance of the pretended cripples who came there.)

426, 16. " *Ô dis-donc, Hórtense,*" etc.— " Oh say, Hortense, how cold it is ! whenever will it be eleven o'clock, so that we can go to bed ?"

428, 5. *nous autres*—we others.

428, 22. *Numero Deus impare gaudet* —The god delights in uneven numbers.

430, 22.

" *Aus meinen Thränen spriessen,*" etc.
" Out of my tear-drops springeth
    A harvest of beautiful flowers;
And my sighing turneth
    To a choir of nightingales."
                Heine.

435, 24. *Ah, mon Dieu !* — Ah, my God !

437, 34. *Établissement* — establishment.

439, 31. *Pandore et sa Boîte* — Pandore and her Box.

441, 12. " *C'est papa qui paie et maman qui régale* " — " Papa pays and mamma treats."

445, 8. *au grande trot*—at a full trot.

447, 12. *Nous étions bien, là* — We were well, there.

447, 21. *l'homme propose* — man proposes.

448, 1. " *O tempo passato, perchè non ritorni ?*"—"O bygone days, why do you not return ?"

448, 7. " *Et je m'en vais,*" etc.
    " And off I go
      On the evil wind
        Which carries me
      Here and there
        Like the
          Leaf that is dead."

448, 13. *rossignolet de mon âme*—little nightingale of my soul.

448, 23. *Da capo, e da capo*—Over and over again.

449, 4. *medio de fonte leporum (surgit amari aliquid)*—from the midst of the fountain of delights something bitter arises.

LaVergne, TN USA
01 April 2011
222564LV00001B/5/A